AN UNSUITABLE MATCH

A Regency Historical Romance

THE DUKE OF STRATHMORE
BOOK II

SASHA COTTMAN

Copyright © 2017 by Sasha Cottman

Cottman Data Services Pty Ltd

All rights reserved.

No part of this book may be reproduced in any form or by any electronic or mechanical means, including information storage and retrieval systems, without written permission from the author, except for the use of brief quotations in a book review.

Chapter One

LONDON, MIDSUMMER, 1817

I dream of the hours when you and I can finally be alone.
Softly sharing whispered words of love.

As the carriage slowly snaked its way up Park Lane, Clarice picked at a loose piece of thread on her gown. No matter how hard she pulled, it refused to come free.

She sighed, dreading that this was a sign of things to come. Tonight was going to be a trial, no matter what.

And I have no-one to blame but myself. You could have done it all in private, but no, you had to go and make a huge public scene. Well done, Clarice. Well done.

'At this rate we shall have to get out and walk if we are to arrive at the dinner on time,' Lord Langham grumbled.

Stirred from her thoughts, she looked across the carriage to her father. Everyone, it would appear, was headed to Strathmore House for the wedding celebrations of the Marquess and Marchioness of Brooke. It had taken them nearly an hour to get this far in the slow-crawling line of carriages.

'We could turn the horses around and go home,' she offered.

He shook his head. Reaching out, he took hold of her hand and gave it a gentle squeeze.

'We have to do this, my dear. We must show the rest of society that you are not crushed by the unfortunate event of your failed betrothal to the groom,' he replied.

She mustered a hopeful smile for him. Her father was right, of course. If she stayed away from the wedding celebrations it would only confirm what the rest of the *ton* no doubt thought of her. She was Lord Langham's poor little broken bird. An object of pity.

'Yes, of course, Papa,' she replied.

The truth was, she didn't particularly mind what the rest of London thought of her. In fact, she rather preferred they didn't think of her at all. Being unremarkable was at times a blessing.

She shifted in her seat and forced herself to sit upright. As she straightened her back, the tight garments under her gown shifted and eased. She took in a shallow breath. The discomfort meant little. For her father's sake she would endure far worse.

Tonight she would stoically bear all the whispers and sly looks that came her way. This evening was for her father. London's elite would know Henry Langham was a man capable of forgiveness. But Clarice knew there was a limit to her father's magnanimity.

She knew she could never confess her terrible crime against him. To have him know that she had stolen from him the thing he had held most dear. Earl Langham might forgive others for their sins against him, but Clarice knew there could be no forgiveness for what she had done.

Her wish to remain invisible for the evening was not to be granted. Within minutes of their arrival at Strathmore House, she had been discovered.

'Clarice!'

A mass of hair and a smiling face filled her field of vision and she was caught up in a warm embrace.

Lucy Radley.

'We were so worried you would cry off,' Lucy exclaimed, when she finally released Clarice from the heartfelt hug. She stepped back and Clarice could see the smile which stretched across Lucy's face.

'Yes, Papa and I were delighted to accept your parents' invitation; it just took a little longer than expected to get here,' she replied.

Lucy looked at the earl.

'Lord Langham, I'm so pleased you came,' she said, dipping into an elegant curtsy.

'Lady Lucy,' he replied, with a formal bow.

Lucy looked at the other guests mingling around them in the enormous entrance to Strathmore House. She wrinkled her nose and leaned in close.

'Lord Langham, would it be acceptable for me to take Clarice away at this moment? I am sure there are plenty of your friends and business partners here tonight whom you would like to greet. I promise to take good care of her.'

Clarice looked at her father, and breathed an audible sigh of relief when he nodded his head.

'Thank you,' she whispered as Lucy took hold of her hand and quickly spirited her away. Lucy made a beeline for the nearest footman bearing a drinks tray and returned to Clarice's side with a glass of champagne in either hand.

'I hope it didn't take too long for you to travel here tonight. From what I hear all streets west of Grosvenor Square are at a standstill,' Lucy remarked.

Clarice gave a gentle shake of her head. She was going to be anything but disagreeable this evening. Besides, it wasn't every day that the heir to one of the most important titles in England got married. A crush of carriages was to be expected.

'Tonight is a night for champagne. Here's to a wonderful dinner and a magnificent ball,' Lucy said, raising her glass.

Clarice took a sip of her champagne, holding the bubbles in her mouth for a moment as she savoured the excellent French wine.

'Good evening, Lady Clarice,' a deep male voice murmured.

She turned and her gaze fell upon him.

David Radley.

Tall. Dark. When had he become so handsome?

Author of a passionate love letter which had recently gone astray and accidentally fallen into Clarice's hands. Hour after hour she had spent poring over the words of his letter. Words she knew had been written with her in mind. Words which meant she could never marry his brother. His declaration of love burned deeply within her soul.

'Mr Radley,' she replied, willing herself to remain calm.

He stepped forward and as he did, the light from the chandelier hanging overhead reflected in his eyes. The blue and green hues turned momentarily to a dazzling emerald, forcing her to blink.

He bowed deeply.

For the first time in the many years she had known him, Clarice was at a loss as to what she should do or say. At such proximity, she found herself decidedly uncomfortable.

How does one react to a long-time friend who has unexpectedly and most passionately declared that he loves you?

You have me at sixes and sevens.

Lucy cleared her throat. 'So how are the dinner preparations, David; did you spend the last hour polishing silver? I hear the downstairs servants were beginning to complain.'

He shot his sister a sideways glance and growled. Clarice spied the edge of a grin on his lips.

Lucy chuckled. 'Such an easy target, it's almost unsportsmanlike.'

'Ignore my darling sister, would you please Clarice; she is determined to make me a laughing stock this evening,' David replied.

A gasp escaped Lucy's lips and she placed a hand on his arm.

'Oh no, I would never do that to you. Especially not in present company.'

Clarice smiled, suppressing the familiar twinge of envy which came from being an only child. A gong sounded and dinner was announced.

'Saved by the bell,' David replied. He shot a forgiving smile in Lucy's direction.

How she managed it, Clarice was not entirely sure, but Lucy suddenly vanished into the crowd of other dinner guests, leaving her and David standing facing one another. As the other guests found partners for the procession into the dining room, the reason for her friend's disappearance soon became apparent.

'Since I suspect your father may have been waylaid by my sister in order for you and I to spend a brief moment together, Lady Clarice, would you do me the honour of allowing me to escort you into dinner?' David said.

She hesitated briefly before taking his arm. Lucy's less than subtle attempt at playing Cupid was the last thing she needed this evening.

Strathmore House, home of the Radley family, was one of the largest private residences in the whole of London. Over fifty people were seated on either side of the two tables which lined the length of the dining room. The head table seated another dozen guests as well as the hosts.

Enormous chandeliers hung overhead from the ornate ceiling. At intervals along the long, elegantly carved oak tables, towering three-armed silver candelabra were set, giving enough light for the guests to see each other clearly.

Clarice's gaze followed the seemingly never-ending line of

huge, food-laden platters and dishes which covered the tables. All manner of delicacies beckoned to her.

'How many are coming for the wedding ball?' she asked, as David escorted her through the room.

'I understand it's somewhere in the vicinity of a thousand. Mama sealed the guest list at eight hundred, but my father kept inviting more. You should have seen her face when he told her he had invited another thirty guests only yesterday'.

As they reached her chair, he stopped.

'Since it is unlikely that I will get an opportunity to speak with you privately later, Clarice, may I say now how delighted I am that you are here tonight.'

She gave him a non-committal nod of the head. With her father present, it seemed unwise to offer him any further sign of encouragement. Earl Langham did not approve of David Radley.

At dinner, she was seated across from David. While he remained standing, she could see him clearly, but as soon as he took his seat, only the top of his black hair remained in view. He picked up the silver candelabra which sat in the middle of the table and moved it to one side.

He raised a single eyebrow and a titter escaped Clarice's lips. She briefly closed her eyes. 'You are incorrigible.'

'True, but now I have an uninterrupted view,' he replied. A wolfish smile appeared on his face.

Clarice was pleased to see that whoever had devised the seating plan had managed to put most of the younger members of the gathering at one end of the table. They were far enough away from the senior members to be able to relax and share the latest *on dit*.

Lucy, having slipped away from Lord Langham, took a seat to the left of Clarice. Close by, Millie and Alex, the newly-weds, sat across the table from one another. Every so often they would share a love-struck glance.

'You should have heard the row Mama and Alex had when

he said he wasn't going to sit at the head table. I tell you she was fit to be tied,' Lucy said.

'Yes, I did think it rather odd that they did not sit in the place of honour,' Clarice replied, picking up her wine glass and taking a sip. She leaned forward in her chair and peered down the long table, smiling with pride when she saw her father was many seats further down the line of guests, almost at the head of the table.

She sat back in her seat, sensing that his presence tonight was more than just a last-minute change of heart. He had flatly refused to attend the wedding. Now it would appear that the rift caused between the two families over Clarice and Alex's failed betrothal was being publicly smoothed over.

Thank you, Papa.

The dinner was far more enjoyable than she had expected. It was full of laughter and friendly banter. Her earlier concerns that she would feel awkward in the presence of the Marquess and Marchioness of Brooke were quickly swept from her mind. At one point she and Alex shared a knowing smile. All was right between them once more.

She made a point not to stare long at the still-healing scars which dotted Alex's face. They were reputedly from a pre-wedding horse riding accident, but Clarice had her doubts. Her father had sworn retribution against the Marquess and she could only pray he had not followed through with his threat.

She picked at several of the early courses when they were served, eating little. When a large platter containing a sliced piece of roast beef surrounded by roast potatoes was placed in the centre of the table, she knew her patience was about to be rewarded. While David regaled the gathering with a slightly risqué story, the guests all hanging on his every word, Clarice took the time to savour her favourite meal.

She cut a piece of roast potato in half and put it into her mouth. Cooked long in goose fat, it was delicious. She sat chewing, savouring the caramelised crust while listening to the buzzing conversation which continued unabated around her. Was there anything better than a well-cooked potato?

'How are you enjoying this evening, Lady Clarice?' David asked from across the table.

With a mouth full of roasted vegetable she was unable to respond politely. She picked up her glass of wine and took a sip, hoping to quickly wash down the potato and reply.

The instant the potato and the wine met in her throat, she began to choke.

Doing her best not to make a scene, she pulled her napkin from her lap and tried to hide her face. Shudders wracked her body as she coughed and struggled to breathe. No matter how hard she tried to dislodge it, the potato remained firmly lodged in the back of her throat.

On her fourth attempt to take a breath of air, a hard thump landed between her shoulder blades. The offending potato dislodged from her throat and she spat it into her napkin.

Sitting back in her chair, she sucked in air, relieved when she felt the colour go back into her face. Lucy handed her a handkerchief and Clarice wiped away the tears in her eyes.

'Clarice, are you all right?'

The hand which had helped to dislodge the potato now began to gently rub her back. She looked up over her shoulder and saw David standing behind her.

In the blink of an eye, he had leapt up from his chair, dashed around the end of the table and gallantly rescued her.

'Yes, yes I am fine. I was in too much of a hurry to speak, and failed to chew my food properly. Please forgive my dreadful lack of manners.'

David knelt down next to her chair, and she looked at him. His worried gaze searched her face. She placed a reassuring hand on his arm. 'I am fine; thank you so much for coming to my aid.'

He smiled. 'Think nothing of it, Clarice.'

As David stood and walked back to his chair, she brushed a stray lock of hair back behind her ear. She tried not to stare at him.

You are rather lovely. Not only did you just save my life, but you called me Clarice. In public.

A footman quickly replaced her soiled napkin and she calmly reassured the other concerned guests that she was fine.

She politely excused herself from the table and sought refuge in the ladies' retiring room. Needing a moment alone, she asked the maid to fetch some fresh warm water.

Slipping into one of the small private stalls, she stood with her back against the wall.

'Breathe slowly and remain calm,' she whispered to herself.

She had managed to get through dinner mostly intact, now she just had to find a way to endure the wedding ball. To make her father proud.

'I must stay away from David Radley,' she vowed.

Chapter Two

An hour or so later, David Radley found himself, whisky glass in hand, watching some of the other guests dancing.

The enormous summer ballroom was awash with the finest members of London society, all come to celebrate the newly wed Marquess and Marchioness of Brooke.

He looked up and smiled at the ornate gilded ceiling. It had always been with a sense of pride that he watched new visitors to Strathmore House commenting on the series of paintings depicting Aesop's fables which adorned the ceiling. He knew every one of the tales by heart, silently correcting the newcomer who guessed wrong and smiling with satisfaction when they conceded defeat.

In addition to the usual decorations in the two huge ballrooms, a series of imposing gold banners had been hung along the walls. On each of the banners was displayed the Strathmore coat of arms: a large black shield upon which was emblazoned a gold horse rearing up on its hind legs. Above the horse was a crown, while the horse stood over a series of three four-pointed stars.

He had to credit his father: this night was not just a celebration of Alex's marriage, but a chance to make a statement about the power and wealth of the Radley family. He raised a silent toast to the Strathmore coat of arms.

Standing to one side of the dance floor, he observed the various couples as they danced a quadrille. He was only half-watching the proceedings, as any form of dancing which did not involve him holding a woman in his arms, he found to be rather pointless.

He would dearly love to shake the hand of the genius who had invented the waltz, a dance in which a man could actually touch a woman of his social acquaintance and not be in danger of being bound in matrimony to her by the end of it. A dance which allowed time for a couple to exchange words in private, which no-one else could hear. Little wonder it was frowned upon by the stricter mothers of the *ton*'s unwed misses.

David, along with his brother Alex, had become an accomplished master of the waltz as soon as it was deemed socially acceptable. At every ball and party they attended, they made a point of finding a partner for it. Quadrilles and minuets were only undertaken under sufferance, or if the lady in question was a suitable and willing partner for other nocturnal activities.

Young, unmarried and with the taint of illegitimacy, David Radley was a magnet few *ton* matrons could resist. Across the room, his gaze fell upon his most recent conquest. He swore before quickly averting his gaze. Tonight of all nights he was keen not to catch *that* lady's eye. A three-night encounter in Soho Square earlier in the year with the hard, cold wife of a politician had finally revealed to him the futility of his rakish ways.

With Lady Clarice Langham now aware of his love for her, he was resisting the temptation to find a new mistress. He was playing for higher stakes now.

'What was her bloody name?' he muttered, before forcing

the memory from his mind. The days of allowing bored wives and merry widows to use him for their sexual gratification were over. He drained the last of his glass of whisky and handed it to a passing footman. He harrumphed quietly to himself. Who was he fooling; he had used them as much as they had used him.

Now, having watched his younger brother leap joyfully into the arms of wedded bliss, he found his thoughts constantly returning to his own unwed predicament.

As the acknowledged son of the Duke of Strathmore, he was granted a certain degree of licence within society. However, when it came to marriage, matters were more complicated. The younger daughter of a good family would likely be an acceptable match in the eyes of London society, but the young lady whom David had his heart set on was an entirely different matter.

At dinner, he had spent a pleasant two hours in Clarice's company. His sister Lucy, playing at matchmaker, had seated them as close to one another as social strictures permitted.

He smiled. Truth be told, dinner had been wonderful. Clarice had laughed at all his outrageous stories. It had not failed his notice that she'd declined at least two courses because she was so intent on listening to him.

She hung on my every word.

The music stopped and David's thoughts returned to the present. He looked around and saw Lucy making her way toward him.

'Where have you been?' she asked, as she stopped at his side and took hold of his arm.

'What?'

'I have been looking for you for ages; there is a waltz coming up shortly.'

He shrugged. There was no-one in the room he had in mind to ask to dance. He gave a resigned nod. As a member of the host's family, he should be making more of an effort to ensure all the ladies had a dance partner.

'All right; which miss does Mama wish me to dance with?'

Lucy gave him a hard thump on the arm. 'Not Mama, me, you dolt. I didn't spend the whole week rearranging the seating at dinner just so you could abandon her at the ball.'

'Mama?' David replied, utterly confused.

'Not Mama. Clarice,' Lucy snapped. She gave him another thump on the arm for good measure. 'You have to dance with Clarice!'

David looked down at his aching arm. For a gently bred woman, Lucy had a particularly mean punch.

'Are you mad? You know I cannot dance with her. The earl would have my guts for garters.'

Lucy growled. 'Lord Langham and Papa are busy burying the hatchet in front of everyone tonight, so Langham is hardly going to cause a scene in the middle of the ball, now is he?'

David shook his head. Clarice's father had made it very clear that he did not consider David suitable company for his daughter. The Marquess of Brooke had been an entirely different proposition as far as the earl was concerned.

Alex was legitimate and the heir to the Duchy of Strathmore; David was a bastard with nothing but an annual allowance to his name. Only his father's good graces kept him from having to take up a military career or the clergy.

'I can't, Lucy; he has forbidden me to dance with her and I cannot go against Clarice's father,' he replied.

'Oh, you are impossible!' Lucy cried. She threw up her arms and stormed off.

'Daaavvvviiid, where have you been, you naughty boy?'

At the sound of his name being drawled out in such a manner, he suddenly remembered his former lover's name. With his social mask firmly in place, he straightened his shoulders and turned.

'Mrs Chaplin, how pleasant to see you again,' he replied, with a formal bow.

Fiona Chaplin, wife of a cabinet under-secretary, gave him her best impression of a young girl's laugh and batted her eyelids.

'That's not what you said to me last time we met.' She leaned in close and rubbed her hip provocatively up against his thigh.

'In fact, I don't recall a great deal of what was said; you do tend to let your hands do the talking for you. What I do know is that you have been avoiding me.'

David swallowed. It had been several months since he'd parted with Mrs Chaplin. Any hope that she had moved on to a new bed mate was fast slipping away.

'I was in Scotland for quite some time, and I have been busy since I returned to London,' he replied.

I also made it very clear when we last saw one another that our affair was over.

A very unpleasant discussion with his father about meddling with other men's wives had put an end to matters. The roar of his father's blistering tirade still rang in his ears.

'Well, not to worry; I forgive you for neglecting me so badly. Fortunately, my husband is out of town all next week. He is accompanying the Spanish ambassador and his wife on a trip to Lanercost Priory in Cumbria. How thoroughly tiresome. I shall be home all alone and in need of company. You can make everything up to me then,' Fiona smugly replied.

David shook his head.

'I am sorry, Mrs Chaplin, but when we parted earlier in the year I was certain I made my position clear.'

She gave a mew of disappointment. Then she hit him hard on the arm with her folded fan. He winced. It appeared to be his evening for being attacked by displeased women.

'You've got yourself someone new, haven't you?' she said a little too loudly for his comfort. Discretion had been the key to his success with his previous lovers, but Mrs Chaplin had never been one to heed the rules.

He was cornered. If he said no, she would not leave him alone. If he said yes, she would want to know who it was, and whether the woman was at the gathering. After which she would no doubt spend the rest of the evening spying on his new paramour.

'I am no longer in pursuit of that to which I am not entitled,' he replied.

His pride in himself for such an honest, eloquent response was tempered by the cold sweat he felt trickling down his back.

Fiona Chaplin stepped in closer. Close enough that her breasts pressed into the front of his evening jacket. Looking up, she gave him the enticing smile which had successfully lured him to her bed more than once.

'All right, David darling. You have my permission to play hard to get; I enjoy a little sport before bed.'

Over Mrs Chaplin's shoulder he saw Lucy rapidly returning. His sister turned her nose up at the sight of the woman plastered to David's front.

'Mrs Chaplin, how lovely to see you,' Lucy said, as she reached her brother's side.

He grimaced. His sister knew the identity of the woman without having actually seen her face.

So much for discreet dalliances.

The politician's wife removed herself from David's jacket and gave Lucy a deep curtsy. His eyebrows raised. He had to give Fiona her due. She hadn't flinched when Lucy spoke to her; rather she had casually stepped away from him and made certain she gave full respect to the eldest daughter of a duke.

'Mama said to tell you that the orchestra will be commencing shortly and that Mr Chaplin is over by the French doors,' Lucy said, staring hard at her brother.

'Oh, thank you,' Mrs Chaplin replied. She made her

hurried goodbyes and headed off in the direction opposite to the doors.

Lucy smiled.

'I thought you were done with her?'

He frowned; how on earth did his sister know about Fiona Chaplin?

'I don't know what you mean,' he lied.

Lucy harrumphed with frustration. 'You don't think for a minute that Papa tears strips off you without the whole of Strathmore House hearing about it? Granted, it did cost me a few coins to find out the reason why, but I consider it money well spent.'

As he had done too many times to recall, David had made the fatal mistake of underestimating his younger sister.

'You shouldn't be bribing the servants; it's not the done thing,' he replied.

'Considering I learnt the practice from you and Alex, I think it's all a little too late to be lecturing me on the morality of paying for information. Anyway, I didn't return here to discuss your wicked ways; I came back so you could thank me for salvaging your evening.'

David bent down and placed a kiss on his sister's cheek.

'Thank you; I didn't know how I was going to rid myself of Mrs Chaplin,' he murmured.

She swatted him away. 'Not for rescuing you from that horrid woman, for finding a way for you to dance with Clarice!'

He sighed. Lucy never gave up. 'It's impossible,' he replied.

She wagged a finger in his direction and David knew she would not accept his answer.

'I have come upon a solution. You shall dance with me for the waltz,' she announced with satisfaction.

'How is that a solution?' he replied.

Lucy leaned in close.

'Trust me, dear brother; it shall all turn out for the good. Now come along, we need to find Papa.'

※

The latter part of Clarice's evening was becoming as boring as she'd hoped it would be. She prayed her presence at the wedding festivities would go unnoticed by all but the keenest of observers. Her father had fortunately not borne witness to the moment David saved her life, and she intended to keep it that way. She couldn't bear the prospect of the dozen or so razor-sharp questions her father would ask if he knew.

Once the private dinner had ended, all the guests assembled in the two huge adjoining ballrooms. She had intended to find a nice quiet spot in which she could sit and hide in plain sight, but her father had decided a further show of Langham family unity was required. Standing alongside him, watching couples glide around the huge summer ballroom, she resorted to counting the number of times her father made a comment about the size of Strathmore House. A coin for each time he made mention of money.

'I dread to think what Strathmore pays to heat this place in winter; I've counted ten fireplaces in this room alone,' Earl Langham said.

She mentally put another penny in her pocket.

Her father looked at her and then back to the dance floor. A furrow appeared in the middle of his brow, which Clarice knew was never a good sign.

'You should be dancing, my dear. I am sure I could scout around and find a partner or two for you if you so desired.'

Clarice's already glum mood darkened. The last thing she needed was to have her father's business partners lining up to do their duty and take her for a turn around the floor.

She looked down at her drab, ill-fitting evening gown. She had forgotten to wear her favourite strand of pearls, so the line of her gown fell to her slippers as an unbroken grey shroud. Her black slippers peeked out from under the bottom edge of her gown.

Little wonder the men of the younger set did not ask for her dance card. Long after her father and grandmother had come out of mourning for the late Countess Langham, Clarice had remained in her blacks.

The dance ended and she got her first glimpse of David since dinner. From where she stood, she could see he was having a rather animated discussion with Lucy, at the end of which Lucy threw up her arms and walked away.

Curious.

Of even greater interest to her was the next person to whom David spoke at the edge of the dance floor. An older matron sidled up to him and began making a less than discreet display of her interest in him.

Clarice blinked. While she didn't know the older woman's name, from the way she attacked David with her hand fan, it was obvious he and the lady were more than mere acquaintances. She had seen enough in the years she had been out in society to know something of the ways of the world. Strangers did not behave in such a manner toward one another.

'Mrs Chaplin; her husband is rather senior in the Foreign Ministry,' her father said. She noted the decided tone of disapproval in his voice before nodding her head briefly in reply.

'Just remember what I said: the likes of him are not for a lady of quality such as you. You deserve better,' he continued.

'Yes, Papa,' she replied.

When Mrs Chaplin departed, Clarice felt an unaccustomed sense of relief. David had certainly shown no interest in the woman. To her mind, he had looked very uncomfortable. For herself, she was left struggling to understand her unexpected emotional response to another female attempting to lay claim to David.

Had she just felt the first pangs of jealousy?

The earl tapped her on the arm and pointed toward Lord Strathmore, who was now striding toward them.

'Langham, enjoying the evening?' the duke asked. The two men shook hands and exchanged a smile in yet another display of friendship for anyone who happened to be watching.

Clarice smiled at Lord Strathmore. Grateful that peace had been made between the two old friends, she was happy to play her part.

'And Clarice, why aren't you dancing? I am sure there are many young men who would love to dance with you this evening,' the duke said.

She blushed, embarrassed by the attention.

'I forgot to get a dance card,' she replied, failing to mention she had done it deliberately.

'Well, that simply will not do,' he replied. The duke bowed and offered Clarice his hand.

'May I?'

She gave her father a quick glance and met his approving nod.

'Thank you, your grace; I would be delighted,' she replied.

Taking the duke's arm, she accompanied him out on to the dance floor. The strains of a waltz soon began.

'Are you a devotee of the waltz, Lady Clarice?' the duke asked with a smile.

'Yes, but I wouldn't say that it loved me,' she replied.

He laughed. 'Trust me, I shall not let you fail at that which you love so dearly.'

※

It didn't take long, or a brilliant mind, to deduce Lucy's scheme once she and David began the waltz. As they completed the first turn, he spied Clarice across the dance floor. She was in the arms of his father, who was chatting amiably with her. Clarice smiled up at Ewan and gave a gentle laugh in response to his words.

At that exact moment, Lucy let out a whimper and David looked down to see a pained look appear on her face. She slowed her steps and he found himself having to shuffle his feet to avoid standing on her toes.

'What's wrong?' he whispered.

'Oh, my back. I have a terrible twinge,' Lucy replied. She let go of his arm and placed a hand in the small of her back.

'Should we stop? I could escort you to one of the chairs along the wall if you like and you may take a rest there,' he replied.

Lucy gasped and quickly taking hold of his hand once more, resumed the dance.

'No, no, I shall be fine. One must soldier on at these sorts of events. Family expectations and all that.'

David looked down once more at his sister. Her sudden ailment did not seem to be having a detrimental effect on her movements; in fact if he was not mistaken, Lucy was leading him in the dance.

Slowly they edged closer toward Clarice and their father. As Lucy skilfully sidestepped a couple of other guests, David began to smell a rat.

'So you have recovered now, and the pain is gone?' he ventured.

She sighed mournfully and wearily replied. 'No.'

He stifled a snort.

They drew alongside the duke and Clarice, at which point Lucy stumbled and her father quickly released his hold of Clarice and caught his daughter.

'Oh Papa, thank you, you saved me!' she exclaimed, fiercely clutching his arm.

From the many plays to which he had been forced to escort Lucy over the years, David knew exactly where she had learnt her sense of melodrama.

The duke helped Lucy to regain her footing. 'My poor girl, what on earth is wrong?'

She blinked her eyelids rapidly and fanned her face with her fingers. 'I have no idea; I suddenly came over all faint.'

'I thought you had hurt your back,' David replied. Lucy shot him a bullet-like glare.

'My back probably brought on the dizzy spell,' she said.

David rolled his eyes and admitted defeat.

'Well, whatever the cause of your ailment, you shall come with me. We shall seek out your mother. I am certain she will know what to do,' Lord Strathmore said, and put a comforting arm around his daughter.

'Please excuse us, Clarice. David, would you please take my place for the rest of the dance?'

As his father led Lucy away, David stood silently chuckling. He turned to Clarice and smiled.

'She is good, my sister. I have to credit her that.'

Clarice turned her gaze from the retreating back of her former dance partner and looked at him.

'So, here we are, Mr Radley. How do you propose we should continue?'

'You know your father's edict, he will not permit us to dance together,' he replied as his smile disappeared.

She murmured softly; and true to form, his body hardened in response, as it did whenever he was close to her.

'Yes, and he is watching. He and your father appear to have made amends, but I would not like to test his good humour by disobeying him. He was in a stinking mood earlier, and I think his veneer of congeniality is stretched thin.'

They walked over to the far side of the ballroom, away from the dancers and her father. David felt like the wolf who had separated a sheep from the flock. A sheep who swiftly turned into a lion.

'I saw you talking to Mrs Chaplin earlier; is she a family friend?' Clarice asked, releasing her hand from his grasp.

An icy finger of premonition touched him on the shoulder. If Clarice had seen his exchange with Fiona Chaplin, how long would it take for her to discover the true nature of his relationship with the politician's wife?

He ground his teeth in frustration. He had been a fool to allow his former lover to throw herself at him so openly. Now that Clarice, and probably her father, had seen the exchange there was little he could do except lie.

He hated himself for it.

'Yes, she is an old family friend. Unfortunately, she had partaken of the wine at dinner excessively and found the floor a touch slippery. I had to steady her on her feet.'

Even as he said the words, he could picture the shovel digging into the ground, making the hole he was standing in grow ever deeper.

'Oh, poor thing. It was fortunate you were on hand to come to her aid. Twice this evening you have been a hero.'

Their gazes met and they silently stared at one another. There was nothing he could think of to say which would improve the situation.

'Would you please take me back to my father?' Clarice said, when she finally blinked.

She took hold of David's arm and they began the long walk back around the room to where Lord Langham waited.

David's evening was beginning a slow slide downward into failure. Clarice's face had shown only the merest flicker of emotion as he'd brazenly lied to her, but it was enough to know she didn't believe his tale. He sensed she could have stood and stared him down for a great deal longer than she had.

'Will you take supper with me?' he asked. Lucy had always told him food was a good, safe way to salvage a poorly handled conversation with a young lady.

He glanced over at Clarice as she walked beside him and saw her shake her head.

'Thank you, no; I see my friend Lady Susan Kirk has arrived and I must spend some time with her. I thank you for returning me from the dance floor, but I'm afraid I cannot keep you from mingling with the other guests any longer.'

Lord and Lady Kirk and their daughter were engaged in a pleasant exchange with Lord Langham when David finally brought Clarice around to the other side of the ballroom. He gave the required bow of respect to the earl and viscount, to which Lord Langham and Lord Kirk gave him a curt nod of the head. In normal circumstances, both men barely acknowledged his existence.

To the devil with the pair of you.

David knew full well they had only acknowledged him because they were standing in the ballroom of Strathmore House.

As Clarice let go of his arm and took hold of Susan's hands in greeting, he saw Lady Susan give him her customary glare of disapproval.

'You didn't dance with him?' Susan whispered to Clarice, but loudly enough for David to hear.

He smiled back at Susan, silently congratulating himself for not having taken the bait.

You think you are the first to snub me in public? I shall remember this moment when the best you can manage on the marriage mart is the sixth son of a penniless baron. Lord knows no man with any means would want to bind himself to such a shrew.

'My sister hurt her back on the dance floor; I was simply ensuring Lady Clarice was returned safely to her father,' he replied, dampening down the anger which welled up inside him.

'Ladies,' he said. He gave a deep bow to the women and left.

Sucking hard breaths into his lungs, he sought out the nearest footman he could find bearing a tray of drinks. He reached for a glass of whisky, but stopped when he saw his fist was still tightly clenched.

He waved the footman away. While his own evening had reached an unsatisfactory point, he was determined not to fall into the trap of throwing liquor down his throat. This was Alex and Millie's celebration; he would not spoil it for them by getting blind drunk.

His personal creed dictated that while drink was for merriment, a sober mind was required to control a burning rage. Taking one long look around the ballroom, full of the cream of London society, he quietly scolded himself. As a member of the host family, he was being remiss in his duties. There were stories to tell and laughs to be had. If Lord Langham and his friends were not interested in sharing his company, there were plenty of others present who were more than willing.

He spied his cousin Bartholomew, close by among a group of guests and with a bawdy jest ready on his lips, he headed for his prey.

'I cannot believe you actually let him hold your hand,' Lady Susan sneered a little while later. The look of disgust on her face made Clarice's stomach turn.

'If it were me, I would have left him standing on the dance floor. His kind deserves no better.'

Why Susan held David in such low regard, Clarice had never truly understood. At first she thought it was because he showed not the slightest bit of interest in her, but eventually she had concluded that being able to look down upon anyone made Susan feel superior.

She had hoped Lady Susan Kirk, the friend her father had foisted upon her, would not be in attendance this evening, but her luck had not held. With Lord Kirk rumoured to have lost a fortune in a recent bad investment, it was clear his daughter was set on securing the hand of the first suitable man who offered her marriage. Large society gatherings were the perfect hunting ground for prospective spouses.

'Mr Radley was simply being a gentleman; he stepped in when Lady Lucy came over all faint,' Clarice replied.

Susan raised an eyebrow.

From where she stood in the heated crush of the enormous summer ballroom, Clarice could just make out the familiar form of David as he worked his way around the room. At every group of guests, he would stop and make small talk, always leaving the other guests smiling.

The current cluster of guests, she observed, were standing with their eyes wide open as David held court. They all fell silent for an instant, before a loud whoop of laughter rose from the group, followed by an appreciative round of applause. David gave them a bow worthy of a stage performer.

'Charmer,' she whispered.

'Pardon?' Susan replied.

'Nothing.'

Susan let out a loud tsk. 'You really are a bit of a wet blanket this evening, Clarice dear. Anyone would think you had other matters on your mind. I do worry sometimes as to what goes on in your head. Personally, I think it's because you read too many books.'

'Hmmm,' Clarice murmured, her gaze still firmly fixed on a certain dark-haired gentleman.

The beads of Susan's oversized reticule brushed against Clarice's arm. She turned in surprise, but found Susan had suddenly and rather conveniently turned her head away.

Did she just hit me?

Clarice looked down at the ugly, heavily beaded bag, but decided against making any comment. Susan was never one for subtlety, whether in her dress sense or her manners.

'Will you partake of supper with me?' she ventured. The

last thing she needed was to put Susan in a bad mood. In keeping with the spirit of the evening, she would endeavour to keep the peace.

Susan looked back to Clarice and acknowledged her assent.

'I still don't understand why you didn't press Lord Brooke into marrying you; he would have had little choice if you did. This evening could have been your wedding celebration, Clarice, and one day you would have been mistress of this house. You could have had all this,' Susan said with an expansive wave of her hand.

'Instead you let him marry that foreign-born girl. For heaven's sake, Clarice, she has a ring in her nose!'

Clarice chanced one last look across the room to where David stood, before falling in step beside Susan as they headed to the supper room.

'You know full well why I didn't force him. Alex sent a love letter to the wrong girl; he shouldn't have to spend the rest of his life being be punished for making such a mistake. He loves Millie and they are happy. I for one am more than content with the outcome,' Clarice replied.

At no point was she going to mention the fact that she now knew it had been David who wrote the letter for his prose challenged brother. Nor that David had used Clarice as his muse.

Susan harrumphed in obvious disgust.

While Clarice was relieved that the situation with Alex was now resolved, matters with David had become far more complicated. He had lied to her this evening, and she didn't understand why he felt the need to do so.

Or why it had caused her such pain.

The supper room was a cornucopia of edible delicacies. The tables were laden with all manner of pies, cakes and sweet ices. Clarice's eyes grew wide at the sight. With all the courses she had sat through at dinner, she doubted there was room in her stomach for more than the merest of bites.

She picked up a small chicken pie, and stood nibbling on it while Susan piled her own plate high with food.

'Mama has put me on this strict diet at home. I get soup for supper and very little for the rest of the day,' Susan complained. She took a seat next to Clarice in the far corner of the room.

Clarice vacantly nodded her head. She hadn't actually heard a word Susan had said since they left the main ballroom, but the occasional nod was always safe when she pretended to pay attention to her friend.

He can't actually think anything can come of this, can he? Only a very brave man or a fool would take on my father.

'He wouldn't, would he?' she muttered.

Susan stood, turned and shoved her plate of half-eaten supper into Clarice's hands.

'I don't know what has got into you this evening, Clarice, but you are being exceptionally rude. I suppose you think yourself better than me because you received an invitation to the private dinner, but...' she leaned in close to Clarice, her face red with anger.

'Don't think for a moment that your presence at the dinner was anything more than an act of penance. Lord and Lady Strathmore know Alex made a fool of you *and* your father. They are simply trying to smooth things over and hope that everyone forgets that ugly scene at the Bishop's ball. Though I doubt anyone will ever forget the exhibition you made of yourself. Your poor father was so embarrassed.'

'You don't understand,' Clarice stammered. She knew her friend's short temper well, having witnessed it on a regular basis. But this was the first time she had been on the receiving end of Susan's sharp tongue and it was far more unpleasant than she had anticipated.

Susan angrily wagged a finger at her.

'No, you are the one who does not understand how ridiculous you are at times. It wouldn't surprise me in the least if the Radley family were not all laughing at your expense. Who knows what they say about you behind your back. I hope that next time we meet, you will have the good sense to remember who your real friends are, as opposed to those who are only using you to achieve their own ends. Good night, Clarice.'

She stormed off, leaving Clarice sitting alone, still holding the plate. She studied an untouched smoked salmon sandwich for a moment, before picking it up and stuffing it into her mouth.

She yawned and lay her head back against the wall, praying that her father would not stay too long at the ball.

What a mess.

❦

Early the following morning, David climbed into his carriage and made the short journey to his new rooms in George Street.

It had been a long night of speeches and toasts. Watching the smiles on Millie and Alex's faces as they waltzed for the first time as a married couple had filled him with a mixture of both joy and jealousy.

'Good to see you safely returned, sir; I hope the celebrations went well,' his valet, Bailey, remarked as David stepped inside the front entrance of his new home. It was odd to have servants all to himself.

He and Alex had only shared their house in Bird Street for less than a year, but in the days since his move, David had found himself mourning the loss of his old home.

The Duke of Strathmore had thrown his two eldest sons out of Strathmore House the previous summer.

'You two have taken the term *drunk as a lord* to its fullest extent and it is time you both grew up and found something else to do with your time. You may even consider taking on a wife,' their father said. At the time he gave this lecture, he was standing over David and Alex as they both lay in an inebriated state on the cold tiles inside the front entrance to Strathmore House.

Within hours the duke had both David and Alex and their possessions packed and their abode adjusted to a tall, elegant townhouse in Bird Street. After the initial complaints over such mistreatment, the Radley brothers soon discovered the delights of having their own house. They could come and go as they pleased and do whatever they wanted without being under their father's watchful eye.

For the first few weeks it was all a great lark. Wild parties, drunken orgies and uninterrupted sleep on the tiles of their *own* front hallway. But boredom and their father's threats to cut them off soon put paid to the level of frivolity which the brothers enjoyed.

'Yes, thank you; it was a wonderful evening. Though there is something nice about coming home to your own place, however late it might be,' he replied, as Bailey took his coat and gloves.

A short time later he was standing, leaning on the back of a chair, staring at the gilded mirror which hung on the wall between the windows of his bedroom. He gave a dejected sigh.

Tonight he had held Clarice's hand within his own. In the years since she had become an adult, it was the closest he had been. Though cotton gloves still kept skin from heated skin, to him it had been nothing less than divine.

The reflection which stared back at him reminded him that he shared the same father as his siblings, but not the same mother. He rubbed his fingers across the dark stubble on his chin. All his brothers and sisters had the fair looks of Lady Caroline Radley, while David had the dark colouring of his long-dead mother.

He closed his eyes, recalling the sheer terror he had felt

when he saw Clarice choking on her food. The seconds it took for him to race around the end of the table and come to her aid had passed in a blur. All he could think of at that moment was how much he truly cared for her. That she was about to die and he had never had the chance to tell her to her face that he loved her.

He might have saved her life, but she was still unwilling to defy her father. By the time he'd escorted Clarice back to her father's side, he was back to his usual status with Lord Langham's only daughter.

Nowhere.

He slowly began to unbutton his shirt. He considered using a valet to assist him in undressing to be unmanly and odd. The only people he was comfortable with touching his naked form were himself and his lovers.

In the months since he'd penned his letter of devotion, there had been no-one else in his bed. Clarice now knew how he felt about her, and he was determined to make her his wife. The prospect of taking on a new lover no longer held any appeal. Until he could secure Clarice's hand he would simply have to endure long, lonely nights of sexual frustration.

'Bollocks,' he muttered.

What would it take for Clarice to be the one touching him with her light, feminine fingers?

'A bloody miracle is what it would take,' he muttered to himself as he settled beneath the sheets. As he slid slowly into sleep, one thought continued to echo in his mind.

There had to be a way.

Chapter Three

❦

It was well past midnight before Clarice also made it home. Her father had spent the evening smoothing over so many cracks with the rest of London society that they ended up staying far later than intended.

Clarice managed to hide for several of those hours in the ladies' retiring room and then the Strathmore family library before her father sent a maid to find his elusive daughter.

Only when the Duchess of Strathmore yawned a third time did Clarice manage to persuade her father to take his leave.

'I do hope you are not too tired from such a late night out, my dear; I know your nerves can become frayed if you over-exert yourself,' her father said as he escorted her up the stairs and into the front entrance of Langham House.

'No, I am fine, thank you; the evening was a delight. I had a most enjoyable time. Dinner was wonderful,' she replied.

Her father didn't need to be told anything else of her evening, or of the falling-out with Lady Susan; his spies no doubt would have apprised him of every detail of Clarice's movements before they had left the ball.

'Clarice?'

'Yes, Papa?'

'I saw how closely David Radley watched you during the evening. But I am pleased to see you did as I instructed. For a moment I thought he was going to take his father's place with you during the waltz.'

Clarice shook her head.

'Good. It would have made the rest of the evening rather difficult if I had been forced to intervene.'

'May I please retire to bed now? I feel a headache coming on,' she replied.

'Of course my dear, good night,' her father replied, and brushed a kiss on her cheek.

As soon as she reached her bedroom, Clarice woke her maid, who was dozing in a fireside chair.

'Go to bed, Bella, I shall deal with my hair myself. You shouldn't have waited up for me, especially with such a terrible cold as you have. Go and get some rest. Good night.'

She quickly ushered the bleary-eyed maid out of her bedroom and locked the door behind her. Leaning back against the door, she closed her eyes.

The sound of the orchestra flooded back into her mind, but this time she was held safely within David's strong arms as he spun her around the dance floor. Other guests observed how smart a couple they made, how well they were suited.

The words of his letter crept back into her mind

Your hand held in mine, willingly given up in trust and love.

'Oh David, all these years and I never saw it,' she whispered.

Throughout the evening he had shadowed her every step. More than once she had sought him out across the crowded room, only to find him standing staring at her, a hopeful smile on his face.

'Oh, what am I to do?' she said, toeing off her slippers.

While this evening had removed all doubt that David had written the letter, in its place now stood confusion and concern. If he truly loved her, then why had he allowed Mrs

Chaplin to flirt so openly with him? There had been more than a hint of possessiveness about the way she'd touched his body. Clarice was certain he had lied to her when she asked him about the under-secretary's wife.

She rubbed her tired eyes and tried to forget about the evening's events. Nothing could come of it, and David was a fool if he thought otherwise.

Taking a seat at her dressing table, she began to methodically pull the pins out from her chignon. Each pin was placed neatly in a small box on her dressing table. As her pale golden hair fell to her shoulders, she sat and stared at herself in the mirror. Her hair was not cut in the latest of fashions, and neither for that matter were her clothes.

In the three years since her mother's death, Clarice had slowly progressed from wearing high-necked black mourning gowns to dark lavender ones. The last time she had worn white was the morning her mother died. When she was finished with removing the pins and brushing out her hair, she stood.

The over-sized gown fell back into place.

It was so large on her slender frame that no visible outline of her figure was discernible. No breasts and no hips. Under her clothes Clarice was completely invisible. She gave her reflection a nod. Things were exactly as they should be.

With such a dowdy wardrobe she was never asked by any society matrons as to when she was going to be married. The few men who asked her to dance at balls were usually business partners of her father's or those who owed him money.

She smiled, thinking of how close she had come to dancing with David. The scent of his cologne when he stood close to her had filled her senses with heady delight.

His imaginary presence stole into her room, took hold of her hand and spun her into the dance. She hummed the music of the invisible orchestra to keep in time as she moved with him around the room. Memories of his witty dinner remarks came readily to mind and she laughed out loud.

'Oh David, what a naughty man you are,' she murmured to her imaginary dance partner. She batted her eyelids. Mrs Chaplin was not the only one who could capture a man's eye. The only thing missing was the powerful but gentle grip of his hand holding hers.

She turned one last time and caught a glimpse of her own reflection in the mirror. She stopped. The laughter died on her lips and she was alone again.

A chill rippled through the room.

She closed her eyes, fighting another, more painful memory as it surfaced once more. Laughter and love had no place in her life; they were only given to those deserving of such wonderful gifts.

She slipped the oversized gown over her head and draped it over a chair. Returning to the mirror, she considered her reflection. Looking back at her from within the glass was a shy young woman, with muslin bindings wrapped tightly around her body. Beneath the bindings her curves and breasts were kept hidden.

Kept secret.

Under her dowdy, dull over-sized clothing Clarice wore her armour. Her body cocooned within, she remained hidden from the rest of the world. Safe and protected.

She looked down and found the pin which held the bindings together at her cleavage. She opened the pin, removed it, and then slowly, meticulously, began to unwrap the bindings.

No-one who attempted to see past the limp, featureless gowns she wore could tell that she possessed feminine curves. No man could be attracted to her; even David's words of desire were for a woman who lived only in his imagination. He did not see the real her. Clarice Langham did not exist.

Long ago she had accepted that being a nobody with few

friends was a suitable punishment. David's declaration of devotion now threatened her cloistered, safe world.

She pursed her lips, remembering his life-saving thump on her back. Even her hero of the evening had not felt the thick wad of bindings under her dress. Or if he had, David had masked his surprise well.

As her naked skin began to appear from under the bindings, she saw the red marks which criss-crossed her body. She traced a gentle finger over the angry lines and bit back tears. Would she ever be free of the shame and the guilt?

Unlocking the top drawer of her dresser, she slipped the bundle of bindings inside a small calico bag. Next to the bag sat several other bundles of new muslin strips. She had donned a fresh coat of armour for every day since her mother's death.

Tomorrow, as with every other day, Clarice would hide the small bag in her reticule and once she was far from the house, she would remove the bindings and throw them away. Her secret was her own, too shameful to share.

She locked the drawer once more and removed the key.

David had written a powerful and passionate love letter to her, or so she had foolishly allowed herself to think. After seeing him with Mrs Chaplin, she wondered if the truth was somewhat less pure.

She opened the second drawer of her chest of drawers and took out a nightgown. Long and unadorned with any kind of ribbon or pattern, it continued the shroud-like manner in which she dressed herself. She turned and started for the bed, but stopped and went back to the chest of drawers.

Unlocking the top drawer once more, she took out a small box. She frowned at it, briefly pondering the fact that her life was like a series of locked boxes. All of which contained her most precious secrets.

She unlocked the box and withdrew two letters.

The first was from a firm of solicitors; she glanced at her

name written on the outside of it, before putting it aside. She had read it only once and constantly asked herself why she still kept it.

The second letter was a copy of the love letter which David had penned. Before giving the original back to Alex, she had made her own copy. As with the first letter, she questioned her judgement in keeping it. She could recite it by heart.

She opened the love letter and stared at it.

She now understood that David had written the letter on behalf of Alex, using his own love for Clarice as his muse. Alex had intended to send it to Millie, but it had gone to the wrong address and Clarice had received it instead.

Knowing Alex to be of an impetuous nature, it had come as no surprise that he had not bothered to check the details on the front of the sealed letter before posting it.

All of London society had then waited for the announcement of Alex Radley and Clarice Langham's betrothal, only to watch as a very public jilting ended all hope of their future union.

How much more upheaval would those words of devotion create? Alex, having mistakenly sent the letter to Clarice, had nearly lost Millie forever over them; and now they threatened to fracture her own fragile existence. To expose her to the world.

She had known David as the older brother of her childhood friend, Lucy. The few times she had seen him while she was growing up had been during his visits home from school. While Alex had always been the first one to ruffle Lucy's hair and give Clarice a cheery greeting, David had remained distant and aloof.

When Clarice was twelve, Lucy confided in her that David wasn't her full brother. Later she had questioned her mother about it and the countess had quietly explained the circumstances of David's birth and what being a bastard actually meant. Elizabeth Langham's hands were shaking as she made Clarice promise never to speak of such matters again.

At the time she couldn't see the reason for her mother's emotional response, but years later when she unexpectedly received the solicitor's letter, the truth of her own birth finally made her understand.

A burning log split in half and fell in the bedroom fireplace. Clarice stirred from her thoughts and scowled at David's letter.

'Why now? Why suddenly declare that you love me?'

Her dowry was significant and would enable a natural-born son like David to establish himself in the world. Was his sudden display of charm and interest in her just a ploy to find himself a wealthy wife? If she had been prepared to accept that Alex had chosen her as a wife of convenience, why could she not accept the same for his brother?

She wiped away a tear, but a second one soon followed. Disappointment was a bitter pill to swallow.

Everything made perfect sense. No man in his right mind would find her attractive, no-one would want Clarice for herself. The gods were determined to continue their punishment of her. She looked down at her hands and clasped them tightly together.

'Tis no wonder he would continue with a mistress even if he did marry me. My dowry and an heir is all that he could truly want from me. How could anyone possibly love me, when I killed my own mother?'

Chapter Four

Clarice came downstairs late the following morning, not so much due to the hour at which she had finally fallen asleep, but rather as a ploy to avoid her father.

As soon as she entered the breakfast room, she knew her plans had been for nought.

Seated at the head of the breakfast room table sat her father, Henry, Sixth Earl of Langham. He was a man renowned within the *ton* for his uncanny ability to make vast sums of money out of nothing. Those foolish enough to cross Lord Langham quickly discovered he also possessed a fearsome temper.

The one person who seemed able to avoid the full wrath of Lord Langham was his only child, Clarice.

'Good morning Clarice,' the earl said as he snapped the spine of his newspaper and turned the page over.

'You are breakfasting late,' she replied.

'I went for an early ride in Hyde Park and then decided to wait for you,' he replied, continuing to look at the paper.

She sat down and watched silently as a footman poured her a cup of coffee. Unlike many of her social peers, Clarice couldn't stand the taste of tea. The footman brought over a plate laden with eggs, bacon and roast potato. With the memory of her near-death experience the previous night still fresh in her mind, she left the potato well alone.

Silence reigned for several minutes, broken by her father dismissing the servants from the room.

She swallowed a piece of well-chewed bacon and waited.

'So what are your plans for today? Will you be walking in the park with Lady Susan and her cousins this afternoon?' he asked.

She looked at her father. Was there any doubt as to what she would be doing today? The same as every other day during the season. Hiding at home until late afternoon and then going out with Susan and the Winchester sisters for their daily ramble in Hyde Park.

She began to count slowly from one to ten. Was today the day she got past three?

'You should go out and do a spot of shopping with them this morning. I'm sure you could find some new things to buy,' her father added.

Two.

She gave her father a smile as she stabbed another piece of bacon with her fork. Every morning came with the same list of questions. And every morning she gave him the same answer.

'Yes Papa, I shall see if I feel up to it.'

He held her gaze for a moment. And as with every other day, Clarice thought her father was going to say something more. That he was going to plead with her to come out of mourning for her mother. But every day, he would simply look at her, and then give a resigned nod of his head.

Once, only a few weeks ago, when rumours of a possible betrothal between Clarice and the Marquess of Brooke had been circulating, her father had risen from his chair and come to her side. With a hand placed gently on her shoulder, he had mentioned that Wilding and Kent was having a sale and that he had arranged a new account with them.

She'd agreed to visit the shop, but had not actually managed to set foot inside it yet.

'I might go and spend some time at the drapers; I understand they have some lovely new fabrics,' she said.

Clarice picked up a piece of toast and crushed some orange marmalade on to it. With any luck, that would placate her father. The earl stood and walked over to her chair. He handed her a note, which she briefly read.

It was from Lady Alice, her paternal grandmother. When she got to the part where the dowager Countess Langham announced her intention to arrive in London within a matter of days, Clarice gritted her teeth. Her life was complicated enough at present; the prospect of Lady Alice joining them for the rest of the season only added to her list of woes.

'Perhaps you could wait a day or two before you go shopping and take your grandmother with you. I am sure she will have an opinion on the type of cloth you should purchase.'

She folded up the paper and handed it back to him.

'Yes, of course.'

Lady Alice Langham had an opinion on every subject.

'Good,' he replied before placing a fatherly kiss on her forehead.

As he turned and headed toward the door, Clarice let out the breath she had been holding. Her father stopped just before his hand reached the door handle.

'My diary is rather full over the next few weeks, and since your grandmother is due to arrive sometime within the next few days I shall ask her to chaperone you to most social events for the rest of the season. I hope that meets with your approval. She will keep a careful watch over you.'

'Yes, Papa.'

He closed the door behind him.

She picked up the rapidly cooling piece of toast and licked the marmalade off the top before putting it back on the plate. The mixture of sweet and tangy citrus sat in the middle of her tongue as she sucked it to the roof of her mouth.

With no-one to correct her manners, she leaned forward and placed her elbows on the table, cupping her chin in her hands.

'Sleep, I just need sleep,' she murmured.

Tired from the late night, she had hoped to fall asleep as soon as she went to bed. But last night, as with most others, she lay awake in the dark. When sleep finally arrived, it gave her little rest.

Somewhere in the hour just after dawn, she had woken, chilled by the damp sweat on her skin. Sitting up in bed, she wiped away the dream-induced tears.

It was always the same dream. Her mother falling and Clarice racing to catch her before she hit the ground. Every time, she would get her fingertips to her mother's outstretched hand and every time she failed to save her. The punishment for her crime, it would seem, was for her to relive that moment over and over again each night.

She yawned and, putting her fingers to her face, felt the puffy bags under her eyes.

'Another good reason to stay indoors today.'

She sat back in the chair and surveyed the table. Since it was now only the two of them at home, she and her father used the breakfast room for all their meals at Langham House.

The earl had not held a dinner party in the house since his wife's death. With his mother resident in the country for most of the year and Clarice still effectively in half-mourning, he lacked the services of a society hostess.

'And no-one in their right mind would think me a suitable alternative,' she muttered to the empty room. Susan's unkind words of the previous evening still echoed in her mind.

She winced, recalling the single time her grandmother had dared suggest her son remarry. The blistering row had continued unabated for hours, at the end of which Lady Alice summoned her travel coach and left for the family estate in Norfolk. Mother and son had spent the best part of a year barely speaking to one another. Christmas 1816 was not a happy one for the Langham family.

'Perhaps this year will be different; who knows?' she said and rose from her chair.

She opened the door and her heart gave a start when she discovered someone was on the other side.

'What are you doing here?'

Lady Susan Kirk gave Clarice her customary tired, put-upon look and sighed. She waved her hand, languidly pointing further down the hallway. Clarice stepped into the hallway and saw the reason for her friend's expression. Susan's two cousins were there, staring at a large oil painting of a horse.

The Winchester sisters. To say they were a little dim would be kind. Nature had fortunately blessed Heather Winchester with startling beauty, but the contents of her brain consisted mainly of lace and frippery. Having been promised since birth to a much older but titled man didn't seem to faze her the least. She would be married by the end of the season, and her intended husband would simply be a new source of spending money.

The other Winchester sister, or 'Screech' as Susan called her behind her back, was the most untalented of budding violin players in the whole of London.

'I didn't realise we had arranged to go out this morning,' Clarice said.

Susan shook her head. 'We didn't, but if I had to stay and listen to Daisy strangle one more cat, I would have committed murder. Sorry, Clarice, but you were the only person I could count on being out of bed at this hour of the day. Besides it gives you an opportunity to make things up to me after last night.'

Clarice was in two minds. Should she take offence at being

used as an excuse to escape Daisy's violin practice, or be glad that Susan had thought to repair their friendship?

Heather Winchester pointed toward the painting and whispered hurriedly in her sister's ear. They both put a hand over their mouths and giggled.

'Oh lord; they have seen the male part of the horse's anatomy, we shall never get out of here now,' Susan moaned.

Clarice stifled a chuckle.

'So do you have plans for the four of us to go somewhere today, or are we just going to leave the two of them to their own devices and slip out through the rear mews?' she asked.

Susan clicked her fingers and when the Winchester sisters turned their heads, she pointed to a spot on the hall carpet a foot or so in front of her. Heather and Daisy exchanged one last insipid giggle before making their way towards her.

'It really is like having two small children with me at times. We don't need a footman to chaperone us, we need a nursemaid,' Susan said.

She turned and looked at Clarice, her gaze taking in her pallid complexion.

'Another bad night?'

Clarice nodded. 'Over-tired again and then couldn't get to sleep. Papa decided to stay to the bitter end.'

The surface reasons for her insomnia were simple enough. Since her mother's death, Clarice's nerves had been on edge and she found it difficult to sleep. Knowing that whatever confidences she shared with Susan would find their way back to her father, she kept to this socially acceptable story. The truth of her constant, guilt-ridden nightmares was hers alone.

'So where are we off to?' the Winchester sisters asked in unison. They looked at one another before dissolving into another fit of giggles.

'Tattersall's! We can go and see the horses!' Heather exclaimed. She clapped her hands together in appreciation of her own cleverness.

'Would you please go and get your things, Clarice?' Susan said through gritted teeth.

Clarice groaned.

It was going to be a long day.

❦

After a whole day spent with Susan and the Winchester sisters, Clarice decided they would test the patience of all the saints.

Endless hours in the gloves section of several different shops in Cranbourn Alley, during which Daisy tried on no fewer than twenty pairs of almost identical white gloves, and Clarice was ready to help Susan murder them and hide the bodies. In the last shop, Daisy and Heather finally both chose matching pairs of kidskin leather gloves and headed to the counter to pay for their purchases.

'You do realise that apart from the tiny blue button on the wrist they are *exactly* the same gloves as they are both already wearing,' she murmured to Susan.

'Don't mention it; otherwise I think I shall scream,' Susan replied.

Clarice bought a pair of plain white gloves. With several weeks still left in the season, she was bound to lose a pair at some point. Susan, for her part, kept her reticule tightly closed.

The thought of offering to buy her a new pair as a peace offering crossed Clarice's mind, but knowing Susan, there was every chance the gesture would be misconstrued and only cause another tiff. By the time the party returned to Langham House, after spending nearly two hours in Hyde Park, Clarice was nursing a dull headache which throbbed behind her left eye. Susan finally lost her temper with the Winchester sisters as they headed back up Park Lane, and both Heather and Daisy departed from Langham House in floods of tears.

A note from her father informing her of his expected late arrival home was the perfect excuse for her to take supper in her room and retire early. Bella prepared a strong tonic for Clarice's headache and laid out a clean nightgown behind the dressing screen.

'Are you all right, Milady? Did you wish me to draw you a hot bath?' Bella asked.

Clarice attempted to shake her head, but quickly thought better of it.

'Thank you Bella, but no. I shall try and get some sleep, or at least lie down so that my head stops spinning.'

Bella opened the small paper and string package from the shopping trip and put the new gloves inside the drawer along with the others. Clarice pretended not to hear her maid's disappointed sigh when she took out the single pair of plain white gloves. Shopping had never been one of Clarice's favourite pastimes. The endless hours spent going from shop to shop, tagging behind her mother while Lady Elizabeth searched for the perfect pearl button, had left a lasting impression on her.

'Did you go near Wilding and Kent's today? One of the housemaids told me they have a sign in their window announcing a brand-new shipment of fabric just arrived from Paris. The latest exotic prints,' Bella said, quietly closing the drawer.

'No,' Clarice replied, knowing that her father would be disappointed. Behind the dressing screen she removed her bindings and hid them under a cushion. She slipped the nightgown over her head.

She crossed the floor and slowly climbed the bed steps. Bella pulled back the bedclothes and removed the warming pan. Clarice slid under the blankets and lay down. She loved feeling the heat on the sheets just after the pan had been taken away.

'Warm enough for you, Milady?' Bella said as she pulled the covers up.

'Yes, thank you,' she murmured. The tonic began to work its wonder; and before she had a chance to fight it, sleep over came her and she slipped into a deep, drug-induced slumber.

❧

Clarice hid in her room for most of the following day, only coming down for luncheon. If Lady Alice had stuck to her usual travel route and overnighted at Harlow, then she would likely be in London within a day. Then the questions would begin.

It was not that she disliked her grandmother, but rather that in the years since her mother's death, Lady Alice had made it her personal mission to take Lady Elizabeth's place as Clarice's mother figure.

With guilt her constant companion, her bright and jovial grandmother made Clarice decidedly uncomfortable.

'Ah, there you are my dear; I was beginning to think you had run off to the Outer Hebrides. Come and give me a hug, child.'

Caught in the middle of descending the stairs, later that afternoon, Clarice had little option other than to greet her grandmother, who was standing surrounded by travel trunks in the front entrance of Langham House. She continued down the stairs, albeit reluctantly.

'I thought you wouldn't be arriving until at least tomorrow,' she said.

As she reached Lady Alice's side, she gave a quick glance down at the trunks.

Lady Alice's laugh echoed in the cavernous space. 'Never one to travel light, my darling. You never know when you may suddenly be summoned to appear at His Majesty's court, or to meet a foreign prince.'

Clarice smiled. The dowager Countess Langham was truly a larger-than-life woman. Warm, friendly and full of energy, she was the sort of woman kings fell in love with and whom armies marched behind.

Her grandmother reached out and pulled Clarice into her embrace. Clarice's leg came up against something solid and she stepped back. In Lady Alice's right hand she held a hickory walking stick.

Their gazes met.

'You have a walking stick,' she said, her voice edged with concern. While Lady Alice had seen many summers, to consider her as anything other than invincible was unthinkable.

Lady Alice smiled. 'It's all right, child; nothing to be alarmed about. I slipped on some loose stones in the front garden at the Hall and fell rather heavily. This used to be your grandfather's walking stick, so I decided to make use of it while I was travelling. Damn nuisance of a twisted knee, I don't expect I shall be partaking of much dancing while I am in town. That's why I arrived a little earlier than expected. Sitting in a coach all day having my leg bounced all over the place is not my idea of a pleasant trip. I ordered the driver to push on this morning so I could get here and stretch it out properly.'

Clarice tried to look away, but her grandmother held her with an all-knowing gaze.

'Something is different about you, my dear,' she said, taking Clarice's hand. 'Or perhaps something troubles you? I must confess I find you rather difficult to read these days; you hide yourself so well from the world.'

'Just tired, that is all,' she replied, knowing that lying to her grandmother would be childish and imprudent.

Lady Alice raised an eyebrow. 'Still having nightmares?'

She blushed. She had forgotten Lady Alice knew something of her restless nights. She averted her eyes.

Her grandmother brushed a thumb across Clarice's cheek.

'You forget that my room is next to yours upstairs. Many times when I have been sitting up late, I have heard you cry out in your sleep. Since you keep your bedroom door locked I haven't been able to come to your aid on any of those occasions.'

'They are just silly dreams,' Clarice replied.

'Ones which leave you looking as if you haven't slept in weeks. I wish you would let me help you, my dear. But since you are a young woman now, I cannot force you to confide in me. Just remember, if you need me I am here to do whatever I can for you.'

A smile found its way to Clarice's lips.

'That's better. Now come, my dear; once I have rested this devilishly annoying leg, you shall have to tell me all the wicked things you have done since last we met.'

Chapter Five

David gave a quick rap on the half-opened door of his father's study. The Duke of Strathmore did not like closing himself away from the rest of the house, even when he was at work. The only door he ever closed was that to the ducal suite, which he shared with his wife.

'Good morning,' David said, as his father raised his head and gave him a welcoming smile.

'And a good morning to you too, my boy,' Ewan replied. He came out from behind his desk and father and son exchanged a hug.

'You are looking very bright for such an early hour; I half expected you to arrive in your evening clothes.'

David ignored his father's half-hearted jest. One because he was in a very bright mood, and two because more often than he cared to admit, he *had* arrived for his weekly meeting with Ewan still in his evening attire.

'Actually, I didn't venture out last night. I had a quiet evening at home reading a book. I had a couple of glasses of wine at dinner, and a whisky during the evening, and turned in early,' he replied.

His father's eyebrows lifted. It was most unlike David to stay at home while the season was still in full swing.

'Not coming down with something, are you?' Ewan replied.

David chuckled. 'I suppose it is a little out of character for me to hold back on the usual evening entertainment, but no I am fine, I just didn't feel the need to imbibe or make merry. I have other matters on my mind.'

Father and son walked over to where a pair of leather couches faced one another. David threw himself on to his favourite couch by the window, while Ewan took a seat on the couch opposite.

'It wouldn't happen to have anything to do with Lady Clarice Langham, would it now?

David gave his father a sly grin, but said nothing.

'Or your sister's sudden delicate head at the ball the other night?'

'I have told Lucy not to bother with trying to play matchmaker, but she has a tendency to ignore me when it suits her. Not that her clumsy attempt to get Clarice and me together at the ball met with much success.'

Ewan sighed and then fell silent. He looked at David and held his gaze.

'Langham came to see me a few days before Alex and Millie's wedding ball. Rumours of an incident at a garden party out at Richmond had reached my ears and I wanted to give him the opportunity to deny them. I tell you this, David, if he had not come at my summons, I fully intended to track Langham down and give him the thrashing of his life. Old family friend or not.'

David felt the blood drain from his face.

Oh God.

'What happened?' he replied.

'He was surprisingly calm about the whole thing. He told me that he sent some of his lads to rough Alex up because of what had happened with Clarice. That poor girl was led to believe that Alex wanted to marry her, before suffering the indignity of being told it was all a terrible misunderstanding. To tell you the truth, by the time he left here I was ready to go over and give your brother a clip behind the ear myself. It was a sobering experience to realise that I would have done exactly the same thing if it had been one of your sisters who had suffered such an outrage.'

'So it wasn't because of his pride?' David asked. Both he and Alex had assumed Lord Langham had taken personal offence.

Ewan shook his head. 'Clarice suffered a public humiliation because of your brother. Mind you, I don't think Langham intended your brother to collect the scars he has on his face; his lads got a touch carried away.'

David closed his eyes and lowering his head, rubbed a finger over the fine lines of his furrowed brow. If it took him all night, he would scour this evening's social events and find Clarice. He too had caused her pain and now he must explain himself. He had to make amends. Securing her heart was now the highest priority in his life.

He cleared his throat.

'I didn't know you had become aware of the circumstances surrounding Alex's injuries,' he replied. He looked up at his father, and met Ewan's disapproving gaze.

The duke shook his head. 'I forced myself to believe that Alex had fallen heavily from his horse, but in the back of my mind I knew something was wrong. I cannot begin to tell you how disappointed I was when I discovered the truth of the matter. To think that my two eldest sons would tell a barefaced lie to me caused me to question my skills as a father.'

David nodded. 'Alex was desperate not to cause any further pain to Millie or Clarice. He feels personally responsible for the whole mess.'

'Because he is, though you must also share a large part of the blame,' Ewan snorted.

If his father knew about the incident then, David was certain, so did his mother. He puffed out his cheeks and ventured to ask.

'What did Mama say when you told her?'

Ewan puffed out his cheeks.

'Suffice to say she was not pleased. Langham owes the fact that he still has the skin on his back to me keeping your mother in the dark until after the ball.'

David winced. He dreaded to think what his father had suffered in order to keep the peace.

He stood and cast his gaze downward. 'I am deeply sorry, Father, for having lied to you. It was not meant with any malice or disrespect on my part. It was an error of judgement.'

He felt the weight of his father's hand on his shoulder as Ewan rose and stood beside him.

'I know why you and your brother did it. And while it was with the best of intentions, may I remind you that this is not a schoolyard brawl we are discussing here? This is a serious assault on a member of the Radley family. The family of which I am the head. I shall be having words with Alex over this matter in the very near future, but for the time being I shall let it rest. Besides, I did not summon you here this morning to tell you what a pair of bloody fools you and your brother have been. Sit down, son.'

Feeling rather sheepish, David did as his father instructed and took his seat on the couch once more.

A smile appeared on Ewan's face and he clapped his hands. David blinked twice, unsure of what to make of the sudden change in his father's mood.

'I have news for you; wonderful news,' Ewan said.

He retrieved a large pile of papers from his desk and placed them on a low table. Picking up the table, he positioned it in the space between the two couches, before finally taking a seat on the same couch as David.

'Move up, lad, make some room for me.'

David frowned. He had made plans to catch up with friends this morning at his club. Now it would appear his day was going to be spent going over ducal estate matters.

He sighed. 'I was hoping now that Alex is married, you might instruct Millie on some of the duties of the estate. It will eventually fall to her to handle most of the paperwork. Speaking of which, where is Alex?' said David.

'Your sister-in-law knows exactly what tasks she will be assigned once this season is over. I have had several meetings with her already. Fortunately for us, Alex has decided upon a rather clever young lady as his future duchess, so both your and your mother's workload will soon lessen. Alex isn't here today because today is a moment for just you and me. Father and firstborn.'

David looked at the papers once more. They didn't look like the usual letters and accounts he and his father worked through together. Alex, having suffered all his life from an inability to read the written word, usually sat and listened to proceedings.

Ewan sifted through the pile and pulled out a folded document. He handed it to David.

It was marked *Contract of Sale*.

'Open it and read the first page or so,' he said.

David untied the string which bound the document and began to read. After the fourth sentence he let out a loud yell and shot to his feet.

'No! You haven't?' he shouted, brandishing the paper toward his father.

Smiling, Ewan stood. 'Yes I have, and it's all yours. Signed, sealed and settled.'

'But how? I know how much they were asking for this;

how can you possibly carve that sort of money out of the estate? Alex will be livid,' David stammered.

He looked down at the contract, and shook his head. What his father had given him was beyond anything he had ever dreamt possible.

Ewan handed him another document. It was clearly marked as a deed of title.

'Alex and Millie were thrilled beyond words when I told them what I planned to do with Millie's dowry money. They both agreed it was time you forged your own future. Alex even stole away for two days before his wedding and made a secret visit to the estate with me.'

Hot tears pricked in the back of David's eyes. He blinked them away as he stared once more at the papers he held in his trembling hand.

He was now the proud owner of Sharnbrook Grange. His own estate.

His father put an arm around David's shoulder. 'And one of the nicest aspects of this estate is its proximity to London. You will be able to travel up and back with ease.'

David chuckled. 'I had often wondered if you were going to bequeath me some far-flung piece of Scotland – not that I would have been ungrateful. But the prospect of being based so far from London was not one I can honestly say I relished.'

'No, your brother can be the one who undertakes the long journey to Strathmore Castle several times a year. If he is going to be the duke someday, he knows there are sacrifices to be made.'

Ewan took the title deed from him and opened it up. Inside was a surveyor's map of Sharnbrook.

'This is the village; you can see it is only a stone's throw away. And here is the manor house,' he said, pointing to a large rectangle shape drawn on the map. To the right of the house was a shaded area marked, *Temple Wood*.

David gave a nod. He had seen Sharnbrook Grange once

before, when he and Alex had journeyed to visit a friend who lived on the other side of Bedford.

'When can I visit?' he replied.

His father folded the title paper, and handed it to him.

'It's yours; you can do with it whatever you please.'

David looked down at the bundle of papers in his hand and made an instant decision. He knew the task of securing Clarice's hand would be long and perilous. Until today, apart from his charm and good looks, he possessed little to offer her. Owning a working estate which generated an ongoing income could only serve to strengthen his case.

'I shall leave tomorrow morning. There is only one urgent matter which I need to attend to this evening, so the timing of this magnificent gift could not have been better. Besides, the sooner I make my presence known to the staff there the better we shall all be.'

His father put a hand in his jacket pocket and withdrew a folded piece of paper. Another surprise?

'You may wish to delay until later in the week. Your mother and I are attending the opera tomorrow evening with Alex and Millie. We were hoping you would join us,' he said, unfolding the playbill and showing it to him.

David grimaced. He hated opera.

'Really? Do I have to sit through an entire evening of opera? Couldn't you just flay me with a cat o'nine tails?'

Ewan laughed. 'Did I mention that I had invited Langham and his daughter and that he sent his apologies late yesterday? Fortunately, Lady Alice Langham has just arrived in town so the dowager countess will be escorting Clarice in his stead.'

A wave of relief washed warmly over David and he gladly took the playbill.

'I thought that might get your attention. So we shall see you here on Thursday for dinner at seven, ready for the opera at nine?' Ewan said.

David nodded. An opportunity to steal a private moment with Clarice without her father being present was too good to pass up. Perhaps his fortunes were finally beginning to turn for the better.

After a quick hello to his mother and younger siblings, David left Strathmore House. He was halfway to Bird Street to give Alex the good news, when he changed his mind and decided to head home instead.

Calling on Alex and his new bride early on any morning would have been foolish, to say the least.

'And good luck to the pair of you,' he chuckled, thinking of how happy Millie had made his brother.

He made a mental note to find a way to thank Millie's father for having amassed enough of a fortune in India to give his daughter such a sizeable dowry. There were few other girls in the whole of England whose dowry could have bought Sharnbrook Grange.

'I take it from the wide smile on David's face that your gift met with his approval,' Lady Caroline Radley said as she stepped into her husband's study shortly after David had left.

The duke, who held a letter in his hand, looked up and smiled. 'A tad overwhelmed, I would say. I thought he was going to expire on the spot when I handed him the title papers.'

Caroline came to her husband's side and Ewan pulled her into his arms.

'I'm just so pleased we were able to do this for him. With Alex now married, I feared he would be at a loss. This at least will give him a sense of direction,' he said.

The duchess looked up at her husband and offered him her lips. He placed a long and tender kiss on them.

'What's that you have?' she asked as they finally drew apart.

The duke looked down at the letter and scowled.

'The letter your sister wrote,' he replied and handed it to her.

Caroline opened the letter and quickly read it, before angrily screwing it up in her hand. She shook her head.

'How could she ever write such hateful words about an unborn child? It wasn't David's fault that she chose to run off with that naval officer when she should have stayed and gone through with marrying you. And it certainly wasn't his fault that she found herself abandoned by that cad. When I think that she took a dose of poison to rid herself of your babe, I want to rain all of heaven down on her grave. Thank god she didn't take enough of it.'

Ewan sighed. The pain of discovering that his fiancée had hidden her pregnancy from him and condemned their son to a life of illegitimacy still burned fiercely in his heart. No matter it had been long years since Beatrice had died in childbirth, he still found it impossible to forgive her.

'Please tell me you do not plan to show this to my son? He does not need to know that she tried to kill him before birth,' Caroline said.

Ewan could see the fierce determination in her countenance. She might not have given birth to David, but having raised him from a babe, she considered him her flesh and blood. Caroline was David's mother and the good Lord have mercy on those who questioned it.

'No, I would never do that to him. I have kept the existence of that letter a secret for nearly twenty-six years, and I intend to take its contents to the grave.'

'As do I,' Caroline replied.

'Today is a watershed in his life. A major step forward for him. It pains me to think this could reach out and hurt him.' He glanced at the fireplace and the golden flames which licked at the logs in the grate. 'I don't know why I keep it.'

Caroline looked up at her husband. 'Neither do I.' and with one deft flick of her wrist, the crumpled letter flew from her hand and landed in the fire. It burst into a bright ball of flame.

The Duke and Duchess of Strathmore stood and watched as the inferno ate the bitter words of regret and recrimination, before turning them to ash.

Ewan put his arms around his wife once more and placed a tender kiss on Caroline's forehead.

'Thank you. I should have done that years ago. I know she was your sister, but I will not have her destroy my son from beyond the grave,' he said.

'Our son,' Caroline replied.

Chapter Six

Clarice stood in front of her bedroom mirror and pursed her lips.

The high neckline of her midnight-blue gown rose almost to her throat. Laying a tentative hand to the bodice of her dress, she felt the slight bulge of the freshly wrapped bindings underneath.

Her maid was humming a happy tune as she knelt and busied herself with ensuring Clarice's hem was straight.

'Did you like the gown Lady Lucy wore to the wedding ball, Milady? The maid who accompanies Lady Susan said that she was the prettiest of all the unmarried ladies there that night. Such a pity I didn't get to see it,' Bella said, coming to her feet.

When she caught Clarice's reflection staring at her from within the mirror she blushed.

'Well, of course Lady Lucy has not been in mourning. I am sure when the time comes you will look as fetching as she does. Begging your pardon, Lady Clarice,' she stammered.

Clarice smiled and reached out her hand. Taking hold of Bella's wrist she gave it a gentle squeeze.

'No need for apologies, Bella. I did like Lady Lucy's gown;

it was the softest pale blue I think I have ever seen and the lace edging on the cuff was exquisite. It was a shame you were not well enough to come. I know you love to see the ladies' fashions.'

Bella sucked in a breath and Clarice waited for her to speak. The expectant silence was broken by a small sob. Clarice looked in the mirror and saw her maid blinking back tears.

'Would you fetch my pearl earrings, Bella? We must not keep Lady Alice waiting?' Clarice said, managing a smile.

For such a dedicated student of fashion, she knew it was particularly cruel for Bella to serve a mistress who dressed as she did.

A short time later she met Lady Alice downstairs.

'Is that gown black or blue?' the dowager asked, squinting through her glasses, as she inspected Clarice's gown. She pinched her lips together in obvious disappointment at the way her granddaughter was dressed.

'So what performance are we attending this evening?' Clarice asked, once she and Lady Alice were inside the carriage and on their way. Clarice loved the opera.

The dowager shifted in her seat and after rummaging around in her reticule, pulled out a piece of paper. She unfolded it and held it up to the coach light.

'Some chap named Lee,' she said.

'That's not very Italian-sounding,' Clarice replied.

Lady Alice snorted. 'Well, that would be because he is English. We are going to see the English Opera perform a production of *Artaxerxes* at the Theatre Royal. Thankfully Lord and Lady Strathmore chose an opera in English. I am prepared to endure a night at the opera, so long as I can understand what they are singing.'

She handed the playbill to Clarice.

'I well remember when your mother dragged your father and me to see that Italian virago Catalani at the King's

Theatre. Mid-way through the whole mess I was ready to throw myself over the balcony of the box. There can be no doubt, Clarice that you didn't inherit your love of opera from your father's side of the family.'

Clarice nodded. Tonight was the first full opera she had attended in a long time and no matter what language it was performed in, she was excited.

She also knew how important this evening was to her father. He had been offered another olive branch by the Radley family and she was determined to do him proud.

She was still waiting for the right moment to raise the matter of Lord Brooke and his so-called riding accident.

Inside the main entrance of the Theatre Royal in Drury Lane there was a stifling crush of people. Obviously there were many other opera lovers with the same disinclination as her grandmother to sit through an evening of Italian arias.

They soon met up with the Duke and Duchess of Strathmore and were escorted to their private box. Lady Alice hobbled to her seat and ordered champagne from the attendant.

The curtain of the box opened and Alex and Millie appeared. Clarice rose from her seat and greeted them.

Millie wore a scarlet cape over her matching silk gown, a ruby nose ring completing the ensemble. Her evening attire was breathtaking, but it was her eyes which caught Clarice's attention. They shone brilliantly with happiness.

'I'm so glad you were able to come tonight, Clarice,' Millie said. She gave her a friendly hug. Clarice laughed when she heard Millie gasp.

'Look how big this theatre is, and look at those gas lamps near the stage! I'm so excited to be here tonight. This is the very first time I have been to a real opera. We had nothing like this in Calcutta,' Millie exclaimed.

'Well then, Lady Brooke, I think you are in for a treat,' Clarice replied with a grin.

From what she knew of the new Marchioness of Brooke, she sensed a kindred spirit. Millie was an intelligent and passionate woman. The perfect candidate to convert into an opera-lover.

The box curtains opened once more and Lucy stepped inside. Behind her, handing their tickets to the attendant, was David. Millie gave them a wave.

Clarice's breath caught in her throat at this unexpected turn of events.

What is he doing here?

If there was one thing she knew David and her father did have in common, it was a vehement dislike of opera.

'Sorry we are late; Emma asked me to read her another chapter of her story book,' David said.

Lucy laughed. 'Emma so loves it when her big handsome brother reads to her. You are her hero because she now knows the princess escaped the fiery dragon.'

He smiled. 'One can never leave a damsel in distress.' His gaze fell on Clarice and his easy smile disappeared.

He stepped forward and gave her a solemn bow.

'Lady Clarice, what a pleasure it is to see you this evening.'

She forced a social smile to her lips and offered him her gloved hand.

'Mr Radley, I'm surprised to see you here. I was certain that the opera was not to your liking. What could be so compelling as to draw you here tonight? Don't tell me you have a secret love for ancient Greek history.'

'I knew you would be here, Lady Clarice, and that was all the reason I needed,' he replied, placing a kiss on her fingertips.

Rattled by his response, and his forward manner, she quickly withdrew her hand.

The string section of the orchestra began to tune their instruments and the gathered guests took their seats. Whether by design or not, the only empty seat remaining after Lucy sat next to Lady Alice was the one next to Clarice. She shot a quizzical look at Lucy, who in turn grinned back as David took the unoccupied seat. She gritted her teeth, annoyed that her plans for an enjoyable evening at the opera had been press-ganged into Cupid's service.

'I hear this Lee chap is rather good. At least I will be able to understand him when he is bellowing his lungs out on the stage,' David said.

Lady Alice, seated on the other side of Clarice, chuckled.

'Quite right, Mr Radley, though I do find a couple of glasses of champagne does help to take the edge off the sopranos when they assault one's ears.'

Inside her slippers Clarice curled up her toes and prayed for the stage curtains to open. Once the opera began, all would be quiet within the box.

By the end of the first aria, she was beginning to feel less than charitable toward her grandmother. When Lady Alice wasn't picking at her fingernails, she was complaining of being too cold. Finally, the dowager countess rose from her seat snatched up her walking stick and disappeared from the box.

To his credit, David remained silent throughout the performance. At one point, late in the first act, Clarice ventured a look across to him. His gaze was fixed firmly on the stage and his lips were silently moving. She stared at him. Was he actually singing the words? He turned and met her gaze.

'He is rather good,' he whispered, pointing to the lead tenor.

She nodded. When David turned his head back in the direction of the stage, she scowled. Straightening her back, Clarice sat high in her chair and focused her attention once more on the music. After he had lied to her at the ball, she was convinced he was simply saying all the things he thought she would wish to hear. If David thought he could manipulate her in such a cavalier fashion, she intended to set him straight.

At the end of the first act, the singers left the stage and the majority of the patrons filed out of the box to find the rest rooms and socialise. Having politely declined Lucy's invitation to accompany her and Millie to the ladies' retiring rooms, Clarice remained behind. She stood staring at the empty stage. Aside from the annoying and inexplicable behaviour of some of her fellow patrons, she was having a wonderful time.

'Aren't you joining the other ladies?' a deep male voice murmured behind her.

She shook her head and continued to make a thorough study of the scenery at the edge of the stage. If she ignored David, perhaps he would have the good sense to leave her alone.

'Refreshments should be here shortly. Would you like me to fetch you something?' he added.

'Thank you, I shall wait until your parents return. His Grace said he would seek out my grandmother and ensure she is back in time for the second act,' she replied.

When he reached out his hand and touched her elbow, she flinched. A frisson of heat sparked in her brain and Clarice felt her breasts tighten in the bindings. She shuddered as David spoke and the slightest of warm breaths blew on to her neck.

'Clarice, may I speak with you?'

He came and stood beside her, looking out over the edge of the box. Groups of other opera guests were clustered all around the stalls, laughing and sharing supper boxes.

'Yes,' she replied, knowing that to say otherwise would be socially unacceptable. She was a guest of his family.

'I think you might have witnessed some unpleasantness at my brother's wedding ball, for which I must give a truthful explanation.'

'Go on,' she replied.

He fell silent beside her, leading Clarice to look at him.

'In the past, I have not always behaved in an appropriate manner when it comes to the fairer sex. The outcome of that poor behaviour was the rather unfortunate exchange you witnessed between Mrs Chaplin and myself. For that I apologise.'

The curtain of the box opened, and two attendants brought in trays laden with all manner of supper delights. They set them down on a nearby table. David motioned toward the food.

'Shall we?' he said.

Clarice shook her head.

'I don't think you are anywhere near finished in your explanation, do you Mr Radley?' she replied.

Explaining away matters to her as one would to a child had her blood at the edge of boiling. He was going to get one chance to explain himself, and one chance only.

'I see,' he said.

David Radley was blessed with an intelligent mind, and she was certain he didn't require further clarification from her as to how far from accord they currently stood. She steeled herself for the truth, knowing he would not dare to furnish her with another lie.

'As a gentleman I will not go into the details of my relationship with Mrs Chaplin, suffice to say what I did was wrong and I deeply regret it. I also regret any pain which I may have inadvertently caused you. It was never my intent to hurt you, Clarice.'

'And what of your other lady friends?' she replied, pressing the advantage.

He frowned.

'There are no others and nor will there be in the future. Since I wrote that letter, I have pledged myself to you. Only you.'

She closed her eyes and put a finger to her lips. To hear him actually speak the words was heartbreaking.

'Papa will never allow us to be together,' she whispered.

More guests had begun to wander back into the box and

gather at the supper table. Their moment of privacy was quickly coming to an end.

'I know the road ahead will be difficult, but if we are united in our purpose we shall succeed,' he replied. She felt the heat from his gaze burn into her as he searched her face for a sign that she agreed with him.

'I don't know, David, I really don't know. I am unsure of so many things.'

'Do you believe me?' he replied.

She pulled in a sudden breath. 'Yes, I do.'

'Then we have made progress.'

He took hold of her hand.

'Pity about the gloves,' he whispered sotto voce. He placed a delicate kiss on the end of each of Clarice's fingers. One by one, he gave every digit intimate attention.

Unlike their earlier greeting, she now stood enraptured by his display of unashamed affection. Heat began to pulse through her body, finally appearing as a blush on her cheeks.

Oh my good Lord, what was that?

'David,' she whispered.

'Hmmm,' he replied.

'Your family.'

She withdrew her hand and he straightened as the rest of the Radley family and Lady Alice returned to the box.

'They had better have some decent Scotch eggs,' Lady Alice gruffly remarked.

The Duke of Strathmore had hold of her arm and gently aided the dowager countess to her chair.

'Let me see what the supper table has and bring it to you, Alice,' the Duchess of Strathmore offered.

Clarice smiled as the duke and duchess shared a conspiratorial grin. Lady Alice was playing the invalid guest role to the hilt and they all appeared to be enjoying the game.

Alex, Millie and Lucy joined Clarice and David at the front of the box.

'May I get you an orgeat, lemonade or champagne, Clarice?' Alex asked.

Lucy huffed and answered for her. 'Champagne of course; we are at the opera. And thank you dear brother, Millie and I shall also have a glass.'

Alex hurried over to the supper table and after a quick conversation, returned leading the attendant, who carried a tray laden with champagne glasses. David took two glasses and handed one to Clarice.

As she took a sip of the delicious bubbles, Clarice could see Lucy and Millie exchange a hopeful look with David. He in turn screwed up his nose. Was there anyone in his family he was not prepared to enlist to further his cause?

'Clarice my dear, do come and sit with your poor old grandmamma,' Lady Alice announced.

'Excuse me,' she said and hurried to take her seat.

When the second act began, David took the seat next to her once more. He continued as before, paying close attention to the singers on the stage. Clarice for her part found herself unable to concentrate on the performance.

The champagne began to make her feel drowsy and she struggled to stay awake. Feeling cold, she unfolded her evening wrap and placed it round her shoulders. Slowly she slid down in the chair and finally her eyes closed.

As the final act reached its crescendo, the attention of everyone in the Duke of Strathmore's opera box was riveted to the stage. All except Lady Clarice Langham. She was fast asleep in the second row, her head resting gently on David's shoulder.

Chapter Seven

David left London early the following morning, politely refusing his father's late offer to accompany him for his first visit. With the contract of sale, including a list of household goods and chattels, in his possession, he had a firm idea of what to expect at Sharnbrook Grange.

'Thank you but no; much as it may make me seem ungrateful, I must do this on my own. If you come with me, then it looks as if I am a spoilt child whose parent has indulged him with a new plaything. I need the people of the estate to understand I am true in my purpose to manage it properly.'

After leaving London, he headed northwest toward Bedford, staying overnight with friends en route.

Late in the afternoon of the third day out from London, he crossed the river Ouse and reached the small village of Sharnbrook. A mile and a half east of the village, he turned off the dusty road and passed through the gates of Sharnbrook Grange.

The long driveway, edged with silver birch trees at either side, created an entrance fit for a more opulent house. As the manor house came into view, he smiled. Many of his friends had their own grand estates; some owned castles, but at that moment he would not have traded his new home for any of them.

As he drew on the reins of his pair of bays and brought them to a halt out the front of the main house, he sat for a moment in the curricle surveying what was now his.

The house, of surprisingly recent origin, was a pale grey wash in colour, almost white. Its roof was well-kept dark grey slate. Along the front of the house, either side of the main front door, ran a series of large double-hung windows.

He smiled again; his father had chosen exactly the right house for him. David saw himself as a modern man of the world. While he loved the Radley ancestral home at Strathmore Castle in Scotland, he was always looking for ways to modernise Strathmore House in London.

When he had seen the first gas lamps in a theatre earlier in the year, he spent hours extolling their virtues to his father. Finally, Ewan relented and allowed a gas lamp to be installed out the front of the stables in the rear mews of Strathmore House. The duke had, however, drawn the line at any form of dangerous gas within the house itself.

He jumped down from the curricle and dusted off his clothes. A bubble of excitement bounced around in his stomach. Beneath his greatcoat the ownership papers crunched. Since his father had handed him the papers, David had slept with them under his pillow. He dreamt of striding up to the front door of his new house, rapping on the wood and with the papers held high in his hand demanding his right of entrance.

He gave a sheepish chuckle.

He would knock on the door and politely introduce himself.

After tying the horses' reins to a nearby tree, he took off his hat and strode toward the house.

The front door opened and a middle-aged man stepped

out. Upon seeing David, and the tethered horses, a broad smile lit up the man's face. He hastened his step and reached David's side, a hand held out in greeting.

'Mr Radley?'

David nodded, a smile finding its way easily to his face.

'Yes, are you Bannister?' he replied taking the man's hand.

'That I am, Sir, and most honoured to make your acquaintance. Welcome to Sharnbrook Grange,' Bannister replied.

'How did you know I was Mr Radley?' David asked.

'I met Lord Strathmore and Lord Brooke when they came to inspect the property. The familial likeness is obvious, if you don't mind me saying so, Sir. I saw you from the upstairs window as you arrived.'

David glanced over Bannister's shoulder and looked at the house once more. From the state of the grounds as he had observed them coming up the drive and the well-maintained gardens around the side of the house, it was obvious Bannister ran a tight ship. He nodded his approval.

'So how many staff do you currently employ here?' David asked. His father had made mention that the previous owner, having lost interest in the estate, had run the household staff down to a small number. If David was to make a success of the estate, he would need to have it running as efficiently as possible, and that meant ensuring he had the right people.

'Only a handful at the moment, Mr Radley, but on your father's recommendation I have put together a list of local people who have either worked at Sharnbrook in the past or who would make an excellent addition to the staff.'

David liked Bannister immediately. He made a mental note to ensure his new steward employed a needy family or two. The Duke of Strathmore had instilled in his sons the concept that aid came in many forms, and allowing a man to keep his honour as well as feed his family was far better than charity.

'Wonderful; I would like to review that list as soon as possible,' David replied.

Bannister took David's hat and followed him inside the front door. David stopped and looked around. The entrance area was simple, but elegant. The red, grey and white diamond-patterned encaustic tiles created a warm and inviting ambience.

A thrill ran up his spine. He was going to be happy in this house. Now he just needed someone with whom to share it.

He looked at the staircase, frowning when he saw the state of the carpet. His father had set aside funds to bring the estate up to scratch, money which David had thought to use for livestock. The torn and in parts balding fabric of the carpet told him otherwise.

The faded green curtains which hung in the front windows reflected the tired state of the house's interior. He swore silently. All his personal savings would have to be spent getting the house into suitable condition for a future wife.

Much as Sharnbrook Grange had potential, he would be ashamed to show it to Clarice in its current state.

Clarice.

Their private discussion at the opera had been all too brief, but his instincts told him he was making progress. The moment she had fallen asleep, her head coming to rest on his shoulder, the longing had stirred once more within him. He had lain awake late into the night thinking of the little catches her breath made while she slept.

He smiled, remembering when the opera ended and Clarice woke to discover she was all but sleeping in his arms. The blush which raced to her face when she looked down and saw her hand was merely an inch from his lap had been beyond price.

Some day you will sleep exhausted and sated in my arms, and it won't be the bloody opera that got your pulse racing.

'Cook has gone to the village to get some provisions, so I am afraid you will have to make do with me making the coffee if you require sustenance, Mr Radley,' Bannister offered.

Roused from his private thoughts, David put his hands behind his back, and sagely nodded. 'Very good, Bannister,' he replied. He was not in need of refreshment, but the temptation to play lord of the manor was too strong to resist.

Half an hour later and with a cup of lukewarm, bitter brew in his hand, David vowed never to ask Bannister to make him a cup of anything ever again. He was sitting at the long wooden table in the kitchen, legs stretched out in front of him. Bannister had offered to serve him his drink in one of the sitting rooms upstairs, but true to family form, David had preferred to sit downstairs in the warmth of the kitchen.

'So, has the cook been with the estate long?' he asked. If she was anything like Bannister when it came to matters in the kitchen, he would have to find a new one. The coffee was liquid mud.

A sly smile appeared on the corner of Bannister's mouth. 'You mean can she make a palatable cup of coffee?' he replied.

David laughed and put the unfinished cup of coffee down.

'Rest assured Mr Radley, cook knows her way around the kitchen. She used to work in one of the big houses in London, but her sister got sick and she had to return to Sharnbrook to help her family. I am sure, with a sensible kitchen allowance, she can bring things back up to a suitable standard. Bedford has an excellent town market at which to procure supplies. We travel down river and back every week.'

David pushed the bench back from the table and got to his feet. He buttoned his greatcoat and picked up his hat and gloves.

'Thank you Bannister; the finances are something you and I need to attend to at our earliest convenience. Now, I would like to take a tour of the grounds if that is convenient.'

'Very good, Mr Radley.'

He followed his steward outside and into the rear yard. His carriage and horses had been brought around to the stables and a large middle-aged man was busy unhitching the horses from the curricle.

As soon as he saw David following Bannister, the man stopped. His gaze ran down from the top of David's hat and stopped at his highly-polished hessian boots. The merest shift in the man's eyebrows signalled his disapproval.

While it was not the first time a stranger had sized him up in such a way, David felt an unexpected twinge of discomfort. If he was to be accepted as master of this estate he needed to gain the workers' respect.

Judge me at your peril.

'Mr Radley, this is Mitchell, the estate stable master,' Bannister said.

David offered Mitchell his hand. Mitchell stared at it, and then blinked. A flush of red appeared on his already ruddy cheeks.

You weren't expecting that now, were you?

Mitchell raised his hand to his head and pulled on the edge of his cap. Then he took hold of David's still-proffered hand and gave it a solid shake.

'Mr Radley, welcome to Sharnbrook Grange,' he replied. He turned and stroked the head of the nearest horse. 'If you don't mind me saying so, Sir, this is a fine pair of animals. Beautiful legs and very strong necks.'

David smiled, recalling that his father had been less than impressed to discover David had bought the horses with winnings from the cards table. He stepped forward and gave the closest horse a friendly pat on the rump.

'Thank you, Mitchell; they were a prudent purchase if I do say so myself. Cost me a pretty penny, but you can never underestimate the value of good bloodlines.'

He gestured toward a large stone barn nearby.

'What other livestock do you have in the stables?'

Mitchell screwed up his nose.

'Nothing in the stables here, Mr Radley; there is a milking

cow in the barn over yonder and some chickens, but that is all Sharnbrook has at the moment. The previous owner sold off all the other horses last winter.'

David slowly nodded his head and tried to think.

'What about sheep? I know the area around here is famous for breeding Southdowns. Last time I passed the estate it had quite a sizeable head of sheep.'

Mitchell and Bannister both shook their heads.

'The last of the sheep were sold off in the spring after the ram died,' Bannister replied.

Without breeding livestock, David's plans for making Sharnbrook pay its way were merely a dream. He dragged his boot across the loose stones in the yard and pondered his predicament.

'I see. Thank you, gentlemen. Bannister, how long have you worked at Sharnbrook?'

The steward scowled. 'Fifteen years, Mr Radley, the last five as steward,' he replied.

'Good, then you should know how many head of sheep this farm can run. First order of business will be for you to locate me some breeding Southdowns. The price and the quality of the flock you put together will have a major bearing on whether you make it to sixteen years at Sharnbrook.'

The steward's face turned pale, but to his credit his back remained straight.

'Very good Mr Radley, I shall see to it right away.'

In his boots, David quietly wriggled his toes as he forced himself to hide his bitter disappointment at this unexpected development. He had hoped that at least some animals had come with the estate when it was sold.

Fool! How did I miss that in the contract?

He had been too concerned with enjoying the view of the countryside as he drove down the long entrance that he had missed the absence of sheep in the nearby fields. He dampened down his anger with himself, forcing himself to contemplate a solution.

If he was going to be real gentleman farmer, he needed a viable flock of sheep. This coming year would be the first real test as to how well he could run his own estate.

A list of matters to attend to once he returned to London began to form in his head. First order of business would be to give up the monthly lease on his rooms in George Street. Every spare coin he could save would have to go into the estate. He pursed his lips together, not relishing the prospect of having to ask his father's permission to move back to Strathmore House. At least he had a month to get used to the idea.

Needs must.

The horrid brew of coffee was not the only sour taste currently in his mouth.

'Let us review the rest of the estate, Bannister, and with any luck by the time we return to the house, cook will have something prepared. Good day to you, Mitchell,' he said.

He turned and followed Bannister out of the yard and down the narrow path which ran between the stables and the barn. A wry smile slowly found its way to his lips. True to Ewan Radley's nature, he had not simply handed his eldest son a fully working estate. If Sharnbrook was going to be a success under David's ownership, he was going to have to work for it.

Once clear of the buildings, he got his first glimpse of the open fields and his dark mood immediately lifted. He clapped his hands together with delight.

Huzzah!

His father and Alex could not have chosen a better place. While there was a complete dearth of animals in the fields, he could see that the fences were all in good repair. The grass, lush and green, was ready-made for a new influx of sheep. What Bannister lacked in coffee-making skills, he made up for in his management of the most precious commodity of all. Land. His estimation of his steward's value rose quickly in his mind.

'Bannister, I think you and I shall do well together,' he said. The steward gave him a respectful nod of the head.

After another hour walking the boundary line of the estate, David was convinced he could make Sharnbrook a success. He returned to the manor house, his head full of plans.

By evening's end he and Bannister had put together a list of matters which required urgent attention, coupled with an estimate of costs.

As he lay awake in the master bedroom later that night, he pondered how quickly things had moved in his life during the past weeks. He had seen his brother happily married and now he, the bastard son, had his own estate.

Marvellous though these developments were, they only served to make him more acutely aware of what he lacked in his life. He reached over and pulled a pillow into his arms, holding it tightly to himself. His last thoughts before he slipped into a deep sleep were of Clarice and how she would feel when he held her in his arms in this bed.

He dreamt a deeply satisfying dream in which he took a pair of scissors and slowly cut away her long, dark, shapeless gown. Finally, when she stood before him in all her naked glory, she offered him her hand and begged him to make love to her.

David slept late the following morning.

On the afternoon of his third day at Sharnbrook Grange, and following a hearty midday meal, David and Bannister rode into Sharnbrook village and set themselves up at a table in the village inn. One after another of the former staff from Sharnbrook Grange sat in front of them and made their case for employment. As the new master of Sharnbrook, David was at pains to be seen as a fair and good employer.

By afternoon's end, they had a full household complement and enough farm workers to get things moving again at the estate.

After a visit to the local vicar at the old Norman-era church, David had a list of families who were in desperate need and who could take up residence in the many empty estate cottages.

Back in the yard at the manor house, David climbed down from his horse. Satisfaction at a job well done warmed his veins. He was kicking the mud from his boots against a tethering post when he spied a small girl, aged about ten, out the corner of his eye.

She was standing several yards away, hands on hips, studying him. Loosening the last of the mud from the bottom of his boots, he raised his head and gave her a friendly wave. With her long golden hair tied in up in a pretty blue ribbon, she reminded him of Emma, his youngest sister.

Her hands slipped from her hips and she took a few hesitant steps toward him. Then she stopped and dipped deep into a curtsy.

'My Lord,' she said solemnly.

David, frowned and then, seeing how much effort the young girl had put into her greeting, he smiled.

He pushed away from the wooden post and walked over to her. Then giving her a deep bow, he replied.

'My Lady.'

Her bended knee wobbled and the young girl looked up at him with serious intent.

'I ain't no lady, I'm Tunia,' she replied.

At the stable door, Mitchell coughed. David gave him a sideways glance and saw the stable master stifling a grin.

'Petunia,' her father corrected her.

Petunia screwed up her nose in disgust. 'No one but me ma calls me that, and only when she's cross.'

A gasp of mock indignation escaped David's lips. 'No. I cannot believe that such a graceful and beautiful young lady as yourself would ever be in trouble with her mama.'

The stable master turned away, his shoulders shaking with mirth.

David knelt down on his haunches and took hold of Tunia's hand.

'Lady Tunia, I think you are the loveliest lady I have seen since last week.' He kissed her sun-freckled hand and watched as a tear came to Tunia's eye.

'A whole week?' she stammered. 'Including church at St Peters on Sunday?'

'Yes, Lady Tunia, including church,' he replied, with the sudden realisation he had not seen Clarice in nearly a week.

Mitchell returned and took hold of his daughter's hand. 'Come now Petunia, we must not take up any more of Mr Radley's time. He is a very busy and important man.' David appreciated the respectful nod which accompanied Mitchell's words.

Father and daughter began to walk away, heading in the direction of the house at the other end of the barn.

The feisty imp shook her hand free from her father's hold and ran back to David. 'Pa says you are a mister, but I think you dress and look just like a lord. I know because I saw the big lord when he came a few weeks ago and you look just like him.'

David smiled. It was comforting to know that even a young country lass could see he was his father's son.

'Thank you, Lady Tunia. I will be your lord, if you will be my special lady. We shall bow and curtsy to one another, and to no one else. Good day to you, Milady,' he said, and bade her farewell with a bow.

Petunia blushed a deep red, but held his gaze. 'Thank you, my lord,' she replied.

He stood, hands on hips, and watched as Mitchell finally extricated his young daughter from the yard and took her home.

'Enchanting,' he whispered, as he turned and headed back into the house.

※

'Ah, ladies, perfect timing,' Earl Langham said as Clarice and her grandmother arrived home from an afternoon visit with one of Lady Alice's friends.

'Come and join us,' he said and ushered them into the main drawing room. The earl assisted his mother to a nearby chair and slipped a small leather footstool under her injured leg.

'Such a dutiful son,' a male voice spoke.

Clarice turned and as she did she felt her skin crawl.

Seated comfortably on a deep burgundy leather couch was her father's new heir, Thaxter Fox.

New, because the old heir had suffered the misfortune of catching a virulent case of croup and dying the previous summer. Clarice had liked her second cousin Rupert, and thought he would have made an excellent earl, not to mention a potential husband. As for Mr Fox, there was something about him which she found unsettling. Having only met him on a handful of occasions, she was yet to put a finger on exactly what it was.

She blinked as she took in all his physical features. It certainly wasn't his looks which put her on edge. If she was honest, he was a handsome, well-built specimen of the male sex. His hair was dark brown, bordering on black, though not as dark as David's mane. His new, well-cut clothing hugged his muscles in all the right places. Even his highly-polished boots gave him the air of a sophisticated, well-bred gentleman. He looked every inch the future earl.

He rose and strode with great purpose to Lady Alice and gave her a deep, elegant bow. 'Lady Alice, what a great pleasure to see you once more. Lord Langham was just telling me of your terrible accident.'

Lady Alice coughed. 'Thank you Mr Fox, but I merely slipped on some wet stones and injured my knee.'

He gave her another bow and turned to Clarice.

'Lady Clarice, my dear,' he said as he walked toward her. Though he moved normally, she had a sudden vision of an alley cat as it stalked a mouse. A cold shiver slid down her spine.

He took hold of her of hand and placed a kiss on her gloved fingers.

'You grow lovelier by the day,' he murmured.

He straightened and from under the wisp of his fringe, he looked at her with a sad, almost mournful face.

'May I offer my sincere condolences on your recent misfortune? I must say your father has exhibited his usual steady hand and good nature during this most trying of times.'

At this point Clarice was in two minds as to which of the two men in the room she distrusted the most. Her father, who had obviously given his own well-edited version of recent events, or Mr Fox.

'Thank you, Mr Fox. Fortunately matters have been resolved and we are all good friends once more,' she replied. She removed her hand from his grasp.

'Would you ladies care to join us for a spot of afternoon tea?' her father asked.

She gripped the frame of her reticule and tried not to look too disappointed. She had hoped to steal some time for herself before supper. In the days since her grandmother had arrived at the house, Clarice had barely managed a moment alone.

'We actually came home early from visiting because I felt a headache coming on,' Lady Alice noted from her chair.

Clarice gave a silent prayer of thanks to her grandmother. This was the first time she had heard mention of the headache, but she instantly decided to play along.

'Yes, poor Grandmamma is not yet fully recovered from her long journey. She travelled all the way from Norfolk with that painful knee.'

'Oh dear, how unfortunate,' Thaxter replied.

He motioned toward the couch. 'My physician says headaches are often the result of dehydration. Perhaps a cup of tea would lessen your ills, Lady Alice?'

Lady Alice muttered something, but Clarice couldn't quite make out the words. She doubted that they were fit to be repeated. A quick glance in her father's direction gave her no joy; he just smiled back at her.

Heel.

The women were cornered and there was nothing else for them to do but sit and listen to Mr Fox boast of his minor achievements, while constantly reminding everyone that he was a simple and unassuming man.

As she counted the leaves on the rose-patterned floor rug, Clarice mused over the fate of her family title and estate. Her father, for all his enemies, was not an evil man. She comforted herself with the hope that if he had indeed been the cause of Alex's injuries he had taken no pleasure in meting out the punishment.

The only reasonable conclusion she had been able to draw was that the earl, having seen his daughter publicly humiliated, had refused to accept the insult to his family name. Seated beside her father on the couch, she looked at him and nodded. In his defence of her honour, she could find no fault.

The man seated on the couch opposite posed an entirely different set of problems. He was a very distant relative, one who had only been discovered after many months of searching. The thought that if anything should happen to her father, Thaxter Fox would take over as her guardian filled Clarice with a cold dread.

If only her father would consider marrying again. A new, young wife could possibly give the earl his own heir. One who would move Mr Fox one step further down the line of succession.

'I am barely out of mourning for my wife,' had been her father's terse response the one time she had dared to broach the subject.

She nursed a cup of tea, allowing it to go cold and undrinkable. Finally, Lady Alice let out a loud sigh and announced it was time for her to ascend the stairs and take a long pre-dinner nap. The assistance of her granddaughter was of course expected. The gentlemen stood and bade them both farewell. Clarice stifled a grin as Lady Alice made a point of holding stiffly on to her granddaughter's arm and wincing as they started for the door.

As they entered the hallway, they exchanged looks. 'Thank the dear Lord that is over,' Lady Alice whispered.

Chapter Eight

'David is here tonight, did you know?' Lucy said.

Millie turned and raised her eyebrows. 'No, I thought he was still in Bedfordshire. I don't think Alex knows either,' she replied.

'He arrived back in London earlier today. He did call in at home, but only paid Papa a short visit before he left. Papa didn't make mention of it at dinner, so I am assuming that it was a private matter. I only found out because my maid saw David leaving.'

Millie raised her head and began to scan the ballroom, looking for her brother-in-law.

'Alex should be back shortly; once he returns we should be able to run David to ground.'

She raised a hand and pointed across the room. 'There he is; I would know that mop of black hair anywhere.'

Lucy grinned. David was a good two inches taller than most other men of the *ton*, so it was never a difficult task to find him in a crowded ballroom.

Arm in arm, the two women crossed the floor. Once they reached where David stood talking to some friends, they took a place either side of him.

'And were you planning to pay your respects to us this evening, Mr Radley, or are we no longer acceptable company?' Millie said. Lucy laughed.

David turned and faced them, looking from his sister-in-law to his sister.

'Ah, my dear sisters, I was not aware that you had arrived.'

'Well, you can see that we have,' Lucy replied, and swiped his arm with her fan.

'Indeed. And where is your blond-haired buffoon of a husband?' David replied with a nod in Millie's direction.

'Right here, you deaf fool,' Alex replied.

The other guests around them laughed. Bearing witness to the banter between the Radley siblings was considered a particular highlight of any social gathering.

The brothers exchanged a mutual slap on the back. 'So how was Sharnbrook? Did we not choose well?' Alex asked.

'It was a first-class choice. With some work I think Sharnbrook will make an excellent estate,' David replied.

'And one which will support a wife and family,' Lucy added. As the words left her mouth, she groaned. A patch of red appeared on her cheeks.

'Yes indeed, Lucy. It will be the perfect place in which to raise a brood,' Alex replied, with a chuckle. Her brothers fortunately understood Lucy's habit of making public *faux pas*.

The family group quickly joined up with David and his friends, forming a large circle to one side of the room.

'He is rather a handsome chap; I can see the attraction,' Lady Alice murmured, from where she and Clarice stood on the opposite side of the expansive ballroom. Clarice gave her grandmother a shy smile.

'Yes, but not suitable enough for Papa,' she replied.

Lady Alice took hold of Clarice's arm. 'Let us sit for a moment, my dear. I am certain you will still be able to see Mr Radley from this side of the ballroom.'

The two women found some chairs; and after gaining the attention of a footman to bring them refreshments sat drinking punch and watching the other guests as they mingled.

'It's so good to take the weight off this blasted leg,' Lady Alice said with a sigh. Clarice reached out and took hold of her grandmother's hand.

'You seem to be able to walk a little further on it each day, so it must be starting to heal.'

Lady Alice sipped her drink and nodded.

'Yes, but I don't expect to be walking in Hyde Park any time soon, more's the pity. But that is not why I wanted to come and sit here with you. It's about that young man and what we are going to do to capture him.'

Clarice snorted as a sudden vision of David, bound and gagged, appeared in her mind.

She stared at the cup of punch in her hand and sighed inwardly. Matters with David had not progressed any further since the night at the opera. She had not seen him for over a week.

'What do you suggest I do?' she replied.

Lady Alice clicked her tongue. 'Well, for a start you should go over and talk to his sisters. Those Radley girls seem to have your best interests at heart and I suspect they have plans to help bring the two of you together at some point this evening. This is a ball, so there will be plenty of opportunities for you to get his name on your dance card.'

Clarice shook her head. 'You know Papa would never allow it.'

Lady Alice's solid walking stick rapped sharply on the floor.

'Now listen here, my girl, I don't want to hear you say that again. Your father is a stubborn man who gets silly notions into his head at times. As a boy, he was convinced he could fly from the rooftop of Langham Hall if he flapped his arms hard enough. I am telling you to go and dance with David Radley and if your father has a problem with my edict then he can take it up with me in the morning.'

Clarice looked from Lady Alice back across the room to where David stood deep in conversation with his brother. Almost as if he had heard Lady Alice's words, he stole a sudden glance in Clarice's direction.

'Go on girl, get yourself over to his sisters and I guarantee you will be dancing with him in no time.'

She nudged Clarice's leg with her stick. 'Go on.'

With her empty dance card swinging from the satin ribbon around her wrist, Clarice made her way across the floor. Twice she looked back over her shoulder only to see Lady Alice wave her on. As she drew close to the Radley family members, Lucy saw her and rushed eagerly to her side.

'I was wondering if you were going to come and see me this evening,' Lucy said. She gave Lady Alice a furtive glance before turning back to Clarice.

'Is your grandmother making you play lady's companion?'

Clarice shook her head. 'Actually, she bade me come and see you.'

Lucy's eyes grew wide with delight. 'And?'

'And she said I should dance with David,' Clarice said, unconvinced of the notion.

The words had barely left her lips before Lucy let out a squeal of delight.

'Oh, oh, that's marvellous news! Quick, where's Millie?'

They both looked around, but Millie had somehow disappeared. Lucy tapped Alex impatiently on the shoulder.

'Where is your wife?' she demanded.

He looked down beside him, and frowned. In the short time since they had married, it was clear the Marquess and Marchioness of Brooke had become accustomed to being in very close proximity to one another.

'Ah, there she is,' he replied, pointing across the other side of the room.

In the time it had taken Clarice and Lucy to exchange greetings, Millie had whisked across the ballroom and made herself known to Lady Alice. As they watched, Lady Alice motioned for Millie to take the seat beside her, which she did.

'What is my little turtledove scheming?' Alex said.

Lucy took hold of Clarice's hand and swung her back toward the group.

'It does not matter; what is important is that Lady Alice has given Clarice permission to dance with our brother.'

A huge smile appeared on Alex's face.

'Really? That is good news. David!'

David looked over his shoulder and was startled to see Clarice standing so close. He quickly excused himself from the other guests and re-joined his siblings. When he got to Clarice, he sank into a deep bow.

'Lady Clarice, such a pleasure to see you tonight. It has been too long since last we met. I trust that you are well. How is your grandmother?'

Lucy rubbed her hands together with glee and then pointed at Clarice's dance card.

'Don't worry about her grandmother's knee. You have to mark her card!'

'Lady Alice has given leave for me to dance with you this evening. If, of course, that is agreeable to you. If not, I fully understand,' Clarice explained, feeling just a little bit sheepish.

What if he says no?

With his gaze fixed firmly upon her, he stepped forward. The wicked glint in his eye sent butterflies fluttering through her stomach.

A sudden warmth coursed through her body. The bindings tightened across her breasts. She had been a little too heavy-handed with them earlier that evening and as a result was only able to take short breaths.

I should never bind myself when I am in a hurry.

He took hold of the end of the ribbon which was wrapped around her wrist and slowly, enticingly, pulled on the length of it, until he held her dance card in his hand.

'May I have the next waltz, Lady Clarice?' he asked.

She swallowed.

Somewhere on a distant plain she heard herself reply. 'Yes.'

Lucy handed David a small pencil and, spellbound, Clarice watched as he wrote his name on her card. One of the final lines of his love letter came to mind as she struggled for air.

Never far from my thoughts, always in my heart.

Lucy gave her a kiss on the cheek and Clarice turned to see David's sister with tears in her eyes.

'Don't mind me, I'm just a watering pot,' Lucy whispered.

David laughed a deep and gentle laugh.

'Well, that is sorted out,' Millie said, coming back to the group and breaking the spell.

The opening notes of a waltz began to fill the room. David offered Clarice his hand, and she took it before she had time to ask Millie the purpose of her visit to Lady Alice. He gave one last look at his sisters as he led her toward the dance floor.

'Fear not. Whatever Millie is planning I am sure it is all for the good. I don't think she has an evil bone in her body,' he said.

As Lucy stood and watched Clarice and David walk away, Millie came to her side.

'So, dearest sister, for what purpose did you impose yourself so suddenly upon the dowager countess?' Lucy asked.

Millie placed a gloved hand gently on Lucy's arm.

'I have been thinking about how we can move matters along. Tonight is a very good start and now that we know Lady Alice is on our side, I plan to utilise her as much as possible.'

David and Clarice completed a turn and passed close by them.

'Millie, do you really think they may have a chance? I

know David would marry Clarice tomorrow if he could, but as for her, I am not so certain.' Lucy said.

Millie screwed up her nose.

'Who knows, sister dearest, but there is one thing of which I am certain: something has to be done about her wardrobe. I know David thinks she is beautiful, but I don't believe Clarice sees herself in the same light. If she did, then perhaps she might feel more confident and take some risks.'

Lucy let out a deep sigh. The plain lilac gown Clarice was wearing that evening did little to show her figure in a favourable light. The shade was dull and dowdy, and it drained the natural colour from her face. She wore no necklace, only a tiny pair of plain gold earrings.

'Agreed. I don't think any of her clothes actually touch her body except at the shoulders. She didn't always dress this way. I recall when she and I were girls, she was quite the kick,' Lucy replied.

Millie turned to face her. 'So what happened? What changed to make her look like someone who has just crawled out of the Dark Ages? I swear every time I look at her gowns, all I can think of is the Spanish Inquisition.'

A sense of overwhelming sadness touched Lucy's heart as she remembered how shattered Clarice had been at the sudden death of her mother.

'Clarice's mother died in an accident three years ago. Poor girl; she was so overcome with shock and grief, she has been in mourning ever since,' she replied.

Millie gasped and brought a hand to her chest.

'How terrible, poor Clarice. What happened to her mother?'

'The countess fell down a flight of stairs and broke her neck,' Lucy replied, blinking away a tear. 'Clarice and I were quite close when we were younger, but since her mother's death she has restricted herself to only a handful of friends. All of whom I suspect were chosen by her father.'

Millie frowned. Included in that small group was Lady Susan Kirk. The spiteful young woman had taken particular delight in Millie's heartache over the misplaced letter earlier in the season.

Lucy watched as her sister's gaze followed David and Clarice. She heard Millie suck in a deep breath, before uttering 'Yes, a perfect solution.'

Lucy harrumphed. 'Are you going to let me in on your big secret, or am I going to have to listen to you muttering incoherently under your breath for the rest of the evening?'

Millie looked back over her shoulder, in the direction of Lady Alice. Clarice's grandmother was talking to the Duchess of Strathmore. She smiled once at the two ladies, and then again at Lucy.

'I think it's time Clarice had some help. Her wardrobe is abysmal. If I had to wear those clothes every day, I too would be a timid wallflower. Under all that mess of lavender, I suspect there is a butterfly just waiting to spread her wings.

'While we cannot bring back her beloved mother, we can do something about ensuring her future happiness. David would do anything for her. I think if she starts to believe in herself, then perhaps she may begin to believe in him. Fortunately, we have an appointment with the modiste later this week. An invitation from the Duchess of Strathmore and her daughters to go shopping is unlikely to be refused.'

Lucy stepped forward and squeezed Millie's hand. 'I knew Alex had chosen right when he fell in love with you. I take it that is why Mama has suddenly found the need to enquire as to Lady Alice's health. I did think she and Papa were overplaying the attentive hosts at the opera last week. Don't tell me Mama has also decided to enlist in David's campaign to win Clarice over?'

'I think she may have, I know she has a tender spot for him,' Millie replied.

Millie took hold of Lucy's arm and pulled her in close.

'Much as we both would love to see our brother happily married, we have to bear Clarice's wishes in mind,' she said.

Lucy scowled. 'What do you mean?'

'I mean, we should not assume that she holds him in the same regard. Of course she now knows that he wrote that love letter, but to be honest, have you seen her exhibit any sign that she reciprocates his affections? We need to tread very carefully. We cannot make the mistake of assuming that just because we wish them to be together, it will be so.'

'Oh,' Lucy replied. In all her excited haste to see two brothers wed in quick succession, the possibility that Clarice did not love David had never entered her mind. She bit her bottom lip, feeling rather foolish.

Millie smiled. 'Cheer up, Lucy; that does not mean that we cannot help Cupid's arrow to remain true in its aim. We may just need to hold the bow for a while. As soon as we can get Clarice out of those widow's weeds, we shall begin our campaign in earnest.'

'Excellent. Now, can we please go and get some champagne? All this plotting and intrigue is making me thirsty,' Lucy replied.

Millie nodded her agreement.

'This is a pleasant experience to which I could become addicted,' David said as he spun Clarice into the next turn of their dance.

She smiled in return.

With the warmth of his hand permeating through her cotton evening gloves, she felt the first unexpected stirring of passion. When he laughed, her breathing faltered again and she knew it was not just the tight bindings.

His dancing skills were on par with his father's; she felt safe, confident in his sure step as they moved around the floor. As the dance progressed, he pulled her ever closer to him.

He gave her a smile. He was skirting the boundaries of socially acceptable behaviour but she doubted he cared. His hold on her remained strong.

'Forgive me for taking all the liberties I can while your father is not present,' he said.

Clarice shook her head.

'Let's not talk of my father, and just enjoy the dance,' she replied.

Her father would hear soon enough that she had defied him and danced with David; until then she simply wished to savour the moment. Burn every heated memory of their embrace forever into her brain.

His hardened body pressed up against her as they completed the next turn and he let out a groan. She looked up and saw his jaw was set firm, the smile gone.

'Clarice,' David whispered, blinking a second too long. He faltered in his step, only saving them both at the last possible moment. He regained his composure and they made one last turn of the dance floor before the waltz ended.

As the music slowed and finally came to a halt, he tightened his grip on her waist and pulled her close.

'Thank you, Lady Clarice, I shall remember this special evening always,' he murmured into her ear.

The faintest kiss of his lips brushed her neck, before he pulled away and sank into a bow.

'Shall I escort you back to your grandmother, or would you care to join my family for supper?' he asked.

Clarice looked across the ballroom to where Lady Alice and the Duchess of Strathmore were seated together. She put a hand to her chest. Beneath the bindings, her heart was drumming a strong military beat, begging for her to say yes.

The words were close to her lips, when out of the corner of her eye she spied Thaxter Fox making his way purposefully towards her grandmother. After she'd indulged Clarice with permission to dance with David, it would not be fair to abandon her grandmother to yet another session of making polite conversation with the self-centred Mr Fox.

She turned back to David, noting that his gaze had followed hers.

'Who is that?' he asked.

She sighed. 'Thaxter Fox, my father's heir.'

David nodded. 'Yes, a terrible pity for poor Rupert to die so suddenly; he was a decent chap. I liked him.'

She closed her eyes and swallowed, forcing back the tears. The pain of loss still too recent and raw.

He squeezed her hand. She lowered her head, acknowledging his regard.

'Anyway, it took a surprisingly long time to sort through the rest of the family tree and Mr Fox was found to be next in line for the title. Since he was not a member of London society, it was only quite recently that Papa's solicitor managed to finally find him. Papa suggested he join us in Norfolk later in the year, so he could become acquainted with Langham Hall, but for reasons known only to himself, he has decided to join the social set at the earliest opportunity,' she replied.

'I expect, as the future earl, he would have to make his social debut some time,' David replied.

'Yes, and unfortunately he has decided it is to be at my father's expense. He has already had several large advances given to him, and it would not surprise me if he runs out of blunt before the end of the season. For someone who was until recently just a country-bred man, he has quickly acquired expensive tastes. And from the way he has allowed all the match-making mamas to fawn all over him, I expect he will shortly be in the market for a wife.'

A cold touch of realisation gripped David as he looked from Mr Fox, who was now being introduced to Lady Caroline, back to Clarice.

A wife.

Preferably one with a substantial dowry. He tried to dismiss the notion that Thaxter Fox would attempt to access estate funds through a marriage to Clarice, but to his consternation he failed.

Watching Clarice, he was relieved to see that the only emotion she appeared to display towards that gentleman was one of slight annoyance. The thought that Mr Fox might have more than Lord Langham's purse on his mind, took a deep hold in his brain. He had been so preoccupied with smoothing the waters with Clarice that the existence of a possible rival had never entered his consideration.

Even at a distance he could see that Thaxter Fox was a threat. The way he stood, looming over the seated women, made David's blood boil. He was sorely tempted to stroll over to Mr Fox and teach the future earl a lesson in good manners.

Across the room, Thaxter Fox gave Clarice a friendly wave. When David saw a tentative smile appear at the edge of her mouth, his fists clenched into tight balls.

'I must join them,' she said and took a step forward.

He swallowed and inwardly cursing the gods who had so recently bestowed him with their favour, reached out and placed a hand on her arm.

Not without me.

She stopped and looked up at him.

'*We* should join them. It would be remiss of you not to introduce me to your father's heir,' he stated firmly.

She nodded. 'Yes, of course.'

With Clarice's arm in his, David made a pointed show of possession by gently patting her hand before they set off across the ballroom.

'Clarice, my dear girl, I was beginning to think you had forgotten your manners,' Thaxter said, greeting them before they had reached the gathering. Without the slightest sign of acknowledging David, he thrust out a hand and pulled her toward him. Seeing there was no other option without Clarice becoming the centre of an unpleasant tug-of-war, David released his grip.

She staggered forward and nearly fell into Thaxter's arms.

'Steady on, young thing, no need to be throwing yourself at me in public,' he said loudly with a laugh.

David saw the hurried, disapproving looks from some of the other guests. A gentleman did not address a young lady in such a common fashion, nor manhandle her.

Then he saw Clarice's face. Fear was in her eyes.

He stepped forward, ready to take issue with Mr Fox, when Lady Caroline suddenly cleared her throat. His mother's social signal was loud and clear. David stopped himself.

'Mr Fox, this is my son David. David, this is Lord Langham's heir, Mr Thaxter Fox,' she said, opening her silver evening fan and fanning herself.

With proper introductions now made, David gave a formal bow of the head. Thaxter Fox responded with a half nod.

The two men exchanged a silent glare.

After a lifetime of dealing with others who judged him to be socially inferior, David had developed a thick skin. He gave Thaxter Fox a languid smile.

Enjoy it, Mr Fox, you will soon discover it will be one of the few times you get to best me in this city.

He turned to the dowager countess and asked with genuine concern, 'Lady Alice, how is your knee? I haven't seen you since we attended the opera together; I do hope it has improved. And may I say it was a particularly enjoyable evening, with both you and Lady Clarice present as our guests.'

He took great pleasure in the snort of disgust which came from Thaxter. The future earl was no doubt receiving invitations to the major society events courtesy of his connection to Lord Langham, but private parties for the moment at least would be out of his reach.

David's enjoyment was tempered by the knowledge that Thaxter Fox's bachelor status was the key to his social acceptance. Once he put himself openly on to the marriage market, every family with an unmarried daughter would be scrambling to send him an invitation to dine with them privately.

Lady Alice held out a hand. He took it and placed a kiss on her glove.

'David, always a pleasure to see you, young man. Thank you so much for the opera; it was a delightful evening. I know Clarice had a most enjoyable time in your company.'

He caught her gaze and the very edge of a wink. She had addressed him by his first name. He breathed a sigh of relief: the dowager was in his camp.

'Your mother was just regaling me with the wonderful news that you have been visiting your new estate. How marvellous. You must accompany your mother when next she comes to visit me at Langham House and tell me all about it. I do so love the Bedfordshire countryside.'

'Grandmamma?'

'Yes, Clarice?' Lady Alice replied.

'Would you like me to bring you something from the supper table? Mr Radley has offered to escort me if you would like a seed cake or two. Or I could bring you back a flavoured ice.'

'I could accompany you, Lady Clarice,' Thaxter interjected.

David saw a glint in Lady Alice's eye and smothered a smile.

'No, no, Clarice and David can bring me back a cup of tea,' she replied with a dismissive wave of her hand. 'Why, Mr Fox, you and I have only just begun to get acquainted this evening. Come, stand over me once again and tell me more about your new boots. There is something absolutely fascinating about the cut of a man's boot.'

'Thank you, we won't be long,' Clarice said.

As he and Clarice began to walk away, David risked one

look over his shoulder. Thaxter Fox was standing stony-faced while Lady Alice prattled on about her preference for jewelled tassels. Lady Caroline sat beside her, a sly smile on her lips.

He didn't need to read her mind to know what had his mother wearing such a contented look. The smile of the victor. Mr Fox might have enjoyed giving her son an intended slight, but it was David who was accompanying Clarice to supper.

'Make sure we bring your grandmother back a double helping of the best cakes,' he murmured.

Chapter Nine

'This will be such fun,' Lucy said, as she led a reluctant Clarice up the stairs and into Madame de Feuillide's salon.

All morning Clarice had been trying to come up with a plausible excuse to cry off the trip with the Radley women to one of London's most exclusive modistes.

As she lay in her bed in the early hours of the morning, she prayed her grandmother would wake with a sore knee and have to cancel.

Lady Luck had, however, decided upon other plans.

The only thing she could find of benefit about the shopping trip was that she was out of the house and able to avoid her father. When he'd finally confronted her about accepting a dance with David, Lady Alice had stepped in and given him a piece of her mind. By the end of her grandmother's tirade, she was beginning to feel sorry for her father.

But since Clarice refused to apologise for her actions, the earl had sent her to her room for the rest of the day. In the days since then, both parties had remained stubborn. Clarice would not speak to her father and he had continued to ignore both his mother and daughter, taking his meals at his club.

'I expect he will speak to one of us once he sees the size of the bill for our shopping,' Lady Alice observed as they alighted from the Duke of Strathmore's town carriage out the front of an elegant shop in Coventry Street.

Climbing the stairs, Clarice stopped repeatedly and asked if Lady Alice wished to go home, but the Duke of Strathmore's footman, who was assisting the dowager countess, was more than up to the task. At one point he offered to carry her up the stairs, at which she roared with laughter.

'You poor boy; His Grace would never forgive me if I took such liberties with his staff. No, I am quite all right to make it to the top, just keep a firm grip on my arm.'

Clarice forced a smile to her dry lips and continued up the stairs.

Her heart thumped hard in her chest, knowing that very soon someone was about to take her measurements.

Someone would see the marks from her bindings.

Someone would know.

Once she began binding her body, she'd started taking her own measurements and ordering her oversized clothes from a catalogue. After countless arguments, her grandmother had finally given up on trying to get Clarice into the hands of a society dressmaker and left her to her own devices.

'There is no need to be shy, my dear; this dressmaker has seen it all before,' Lady Alice noted before they left the house earlier that morning.

As they reached the top of the stairs and entered Madame de Feuillide's elegant salon, Clarice temporarily forgot about her fears.

She stood open-mouthed in awe at the sight which met her eyes.

Pale pink wallpaper with a Grecian-patterned gold border graced the walls. Long lace fabric panels covered the windows, framed by deep gold curtains.

Three richly stuffed pink and gold striped couches formed

a semi-circle in the centre of the room. Set on a low table between the couches was a crystal tray laden with champagne glasses, each filled with soft yellow bubbles. Lucy let go of Clarice's arm, raced over to the table and picked up two glasses. She handed one each to Millie and Clarice, before going back and collecting one for herself.

She raised her glass and said, 'A perfect pair of sisters,' before taking a sip of her champagne.

Millie raised her glass and gave Clarice a warm smile. 'I certainly hope so.'

'Ah, my best clients have arrived,' Madame de Feuillide announced as she entered the room. She curtsied deeply to Caroline and Lucy. Then after paying her respects to Lady Alice, she turned to Millie.

'Lady Brooke, how wonderful of you to grace us with your presence today,' she said, and began to curtsy. Millie put down her glass and threw her arms around Madame.

'It is so wonderful to see you again, Madame, I have not had the chance to personally thank you for my magnificent wedding gown,' Millie replied.

Clarice raised an eyebrow; she had never seen a member of London society be so friendly with a shopkeeper. Lady Brooke, it would appear, was determined to live by her own rules.

The small French woman gave Millie a warm kiss on the hand, before stepping back and making a close study of the new bride.

'The flowers you sent were a delightful surprise and so unexpected; you truly are a duchess in the making,' she replied as she fixed her all-knowing gaze on Millie's waistline.

'The line of the skirt still fits, excellent. But I expect I shall be making some more comfortable gowns for you by Christmas. I see the sparkle of love in your eye and your new husband loves you very much. You will be giving him an heir very soon, n'est-ce pas?'

Millie smiled and put a finger to her lips.

Clarice studied her gloves intently. She had heard enough talk in the ladies' rooms at parties and balls to have a fair inkling as to how babies were made, but to hear someone speak of such a thing in public was out of her limited experience.

'And whom do we have here? A new young lady, whom I have not seen before.'

A finger placed under Clarice's chin gently lifted her head and she found herself gazing into a pair of warm brown eyes. 'Mon Chéri, you look terribly uncomfortable. May I enquire as to your name?' Madame asked.

'Clarice,' she whispered.

Lady Alice stepped forward and took hold of Clarice's hand. She gave it a reassuring pat and turned proudly to the seamstress.

'Madame, this is my granddaughter Lady Clarice Langham. It is my heartfelt wish that you will accept her as a new client.'

A single eyebrow was raised at the sound of her family name and Clarice frowned at the not-uncommon response. A small, secretive smile came to Madame's lips.

'So, you are the young lady whom Lady Alice has never been able to get to the top of my stairs? I am most pleased that you have finally come.'

She softly clapped her hands. 'C'est bon! I have waited years to be able to serve you, my dear. Your beautiful mother was one of my best customers. It would be an honour to dress her lovely daughter. If you will have me, then I am yours.'

Clarice watched as Madame de Feuillide looked closely at her gown. The expression on the modiste's face was not one of disdain, but rather curiosity. She looked to Lady Alice in alarm. What was this woman about to do to her?

'Trust me, I would not have brought you here today if I did not think Madame was exactly what you needed. Today is the beginning of a lifelong relationship. Apart from your husband, your modiste will be your closest confidante. And for many women she is even closer,' her grandmother reassured her.

'Ladies, if you would like to take a seat, my assistants will bring out some new fabric samples which arrived this week from Paris. I am sure you will find something which will catch your eye. In the meantime, Lady Clarice and I shall get better acquainted,' Madame announced.

Taking Clarice by the hand, she guided her through a doorway and into a small dressing room. Clarice removed her dark blue kerseymere spencer, revealing the plain coal-grey muslin dress she wore underneath, and waited.

She flinched as the modiste laid her hands ever so lightly upon her shoulders. 'Your dress as well, my dear, I need to be able to take accurate measurements.'

A spear of panic coursed through her body. Her breath caught tight in her throat. She whipped her head around, searching for the door.

She closed her eyes as hot tears began to run down her cheeks. Having managed to avoid anyone seeing her undressed for so long, she was ill-prepared for the modiste's request.

'Could you just take note of my measurements? I know them by heart,' she pleaded.

'I promise you, my dear, that whatever minor imperfections you have, I shall make you shine. You can trust me,' Madame murmured softly. She handed Clarice a clean handkerchief.

'Thank you,' she replied, drying her face.
She summoned her courage and nodded her head.
'Bon.'

With her back to Madame, she removed her dress and stood clad only in her chemise. When she turned back to face

Madame, her arms were crossed over her chest. Her last line of defence.

Madame offered her a hand. Clarice looked at it and reluctantly released one arm.

'And now the other, *ma bichette*,' Madame said, as she reached out and took Clarice's other hand. She smiled as she slowly pulled Clarice's arms open.

'Trust me,' she whispered.

She stepped forward and with a quick motion, slipped the chemise over Clarice's head.

Clarice closed her eyes, too afraid to look.

The merest of sighs whispered in the room before she felt a warm hand on her cheek. A thumb brushed away a tear as it rolled down her face.

'Fear not, my child. It is not wrong to be unsure of your womanly figure. Many young ladies are just the same as you.'

Clarice opened her eyes and stared at Madame de Feuillide. Her face was a study of warmth and honesty. The woman had not sought to judge her, only to reassure.

'Please,' Clarice whispered.

Madame hummed knowingly. 'Of course no-one will ever know. The secrets of my clients are something I shall take to the grave. I take it, from your reluctance to visit me before today, that your grandmother does not know you bind your body?'

A shake of the head was all Clarice could muster.

Lady Alice had always been kind to her. For her grandmother to know she hid herself from the world in such a way would only cause her pain.

'And that is how it shall stay,' Madame replied. She pointed to the pin at the top of the bindings and softly said, 'They must come off.'

Clarice raised a hand to her chest, her fingers touching the cold, hard pin.

'Please,' she pleaded.

Madame stepped forward and removed the pin. When she nodded, the unspoken message was clear. Clarice would have to remove the rest of the bindings herself.

She fumbled with the muslin, eventually locating the end. Slowly she unwrapped the topmost layer of the bindings. Madame gave her another encouraging nod and Clarice continued to unveil her body.

When finally she was finished, Madame took the bindings and placed them on a nearby chair.

'Tell me, Lady Clarice, do you like how your friends dress?'

'Yes.'

'Would you like to bloom into a beautiful flower? Now that I can see your figure, it is obvious you are perfectly proportioned,' Madame said.

She stepped back and held up a hand before disappearing into an adjoining room. Within a minute she returned with a large armful of fabric samples.

When Clarice looked at the modiste, she could see the glint of excitement in her eyes.

Madame de Feuillide dropped the bundles of fabric on to a nearby chair and then stood over them for a moment, muttering to herself in her native tongue. Finally she clicked her fingers and pulled out a pale blue piece of silk. She turned and with a most uncharacteristic giggle, raced back to Clarice.

Holding the fabric up against Clarice's skin, she continued to mutter to herself.

Finally she stepped away and stood nodding. Whatever discussion Madame had been conducting with herself, she had obviously reached an accord. She took hold of Clarice's hand and gave it a squeeze.

'Do you wish to be loved?'

Clarice felt her ears burn as she uttered, 'Yes.'

'Good girl. Beautiful girls like you deserve to be loved, but it is the brave ones who find it. I think it is time you decided to be brave, Lady Clarice.'

'What should I do?' Clarice replied. She had no idea how to be brave in love.

Madame picked up a second piece of fabric. It was a deep gold satin, which Clarice barely felt as the modiste draped it over her shoulders. Madame hummed with satisfaction.

'I understand your father is very wealthy, which is good, because you are going to need a whole new wardrobe, my dear. Everything from your undergarments to your slippers. I will make you the most wonderful and exquisite gowns, but you have to promise me something.'

It didn't require a fortune-teller to predict what came next. But the vehemence with which the words were delivered took Clarice by surprise.

'I want you to deliver to me, without delay, every piece of binding that you own. All of them! *And* along with them, I want your promise that you will never bind your beautiful body ever again,' Madame de Feuillide demanded.

She crossed her arms and stood with her back ramrod-straight, her gaze fixed firmly on Clarice.

A nervous titter escaped Clarice's lips. It had been a long time since another woman had spoken so strongly to her.

She nodded.

'Say it.'

She swallowed deeply. 'I will be brave. I will send all my bindings to you today and from this day forward I will no longer bind my body.'

'Bon. Now let us spend lots of your papa's money,' Madame replied with a clap of her hands.

'Within reason,' Clarice replied, not wishing to be a burden on her father's purse.

Over the next half hour Madame de Feuillide measured every inch of Clarice's body, constantly reassuring her that she was neither the first nor the last girl the Madame would see who hid her charms from the world.

By the end of her private session with the warm French widow, Clarice understood why Millie and Lucy had insisted she accompany them to their appointment.

Stepping out into the main salon, her bindings carefully reapplied for the last time, she gave her friends a confident smile. Millie raised her eyebrows in expectation, to which Clarice nodded.

'Wonderful; now we can choose fabrics. Millie and I have already decided on several we think would be perfect,' Lucy said.

As she walked over to a display panel laden with silks and satins, Clarice heard the modiste and her grandmother share an exchange. Madame de Feuillide rattled off a quick but extensive list of all the things Clarice would require for her new wardrobe.

Lady Alice nodded her head as she listened, and then finally announced:

'Excellent, Madame; we shall take a dozen day dresses, a dozen walking dresses and six new evening gowns. It is past the mid-point of the season, so we won't need a full complement of ball gowns. Oh yes, and we shall need slippers and matching shawls.'

Millie, Clarice and Lucy stared at one another wide-eyed with delight, before they took to the fabric samples with unbridled enthusiasm.

'Oh, and ladies?' Lady Alice said.

'Yes?'

'No black, grey or lavender.'

Millie and Lucy replied in unison. 'Yes, Lady Alice!'

Chapter Ten

❦

'We have missed you over the past few weeks, Mr Radley; it's good to have you back, Sir.'

'Thank you,' David replied.

Gentleman Jackson's saloon, which was situated in Bond Street, was almost a second home to him. Every Thursday afternoon for as long as he could remember, he had indulged in an hour of hard, muscle-building boxing. While others viewed the sport as an often painful test of their manliness, David found it the best way he knew to relax.

'Are they tight enough, Sir?' the room master, Mr Smith asked.

David looked down at the mufflers which all members of the *ton* were expected to wear on their hands when they boxed at the academy.

'Thank you, yes', he replied.

In other parts of London, bare-knuckle boxing still had its place, but when a gentleman planned to dine in mixed company, he could ill afford to be sporting facial injuries. Black eyes and stitches did not make for polite dinner conversation.

Not that anyone had recently landed a punch within two

feet of David's head. He was the master of the one-punch fight if the mood so took him. His record of six wins in one afternoon was the current house record.

'Are there any other gentlemen here today who would be interested in a session of gentle sparring?' he asked, knowing few men would willingly take him on in a real bout.

'I shall check for you, Sir, but if no one is available, I am certain one of the saloon lads will agree.'

As the man closed the door behind him, David flexed his fingers within the soft wool padding. The work he had undertaken chopping wood at Sharnbrook Grange was reflected in his tender cracked knuckles. He chuckled softly, recalling the look on the farmyard workers' faces when they saw their new master pick up an axe and wield it with an experienced hand.

Little did they know of the countless hours the Duke of Strathmore had made his sons chop wood at Strathmore Castle in the middle of the Scottish winter. Character-building he called it. Hard work was the reality for all three of his sons. Even bookish young Lord Stephen had not been spared.

The man soon returned, wearing a pensive look on his face.

'There is one gentleman who has offered to give you a three-round match, Sir,' the man said.

'But?' David replied.

The man shuffled uneasily on his feet. 'The gentleman is a potential new member; he has some experience from boxing in the country, but does not yet know the rules of the club.'

David snorted. What the man really meant was for David to go easy on the poor chap; otherwise he might not pay his membership dues. He nodded.

'Of course.'

He rose from the wooden bench and followed Mr Smith out into the main boxing room.

As soon as he saw his opponent, his blood turned to ice.

Shadow boxing in the corner, fully kitted out in brand-new boxing gloves and boots, was Thaxter Fox.

David stood and sized up his opponent. Tall, but well built across the shoulders, he likely possessed a decent punch. David's fists clenched as he recalled the ungentlemanly way Thaxter had manhandled Clarice at the ball earlier that week. The fear he had seen in her eyes still haunted him.

He made a silent promise to himself. He would not give Mr Fox any cause to call his own gentlemanly status into question. He did, however, draw the line at letting the blackguard lay a gloved hand on him.

Let's see how much of a real man you are. There are no women here, so you will have to contend with me.

Thaxter Fox strode confidently over to where David stood and stopped. Rolling his head from side to side and doing a small jig on the spot, he gave the air of one who had seen more than his share of fights.

Neither of them bothered with the social niceties of a formal greeting.

'Damn nuisance, these muffler things; what happened to being able to fight a man with your bare fists? I didn't realise how many fops there were in London. I should not be surprised if they allowed girls to join this club,' he sneered.

'House rules, Fox,' David replied, refusing to take the bait. A quick nod to his second and David was ready.

He punched his gloves together, mentally rehearsing for the moment he intended to land a solid whack to Thaxter's head.

Lord knows you need a good thrashing.

'Mr Smith, will you do us the honour of refereeing the bout?' David asked. He stepped back and assumed the standard opening stance for a bout.

Thaxter stood and looked him slowly up and down, contempt burning in his eyes.

David took a deep breath and cleared his mind. He was no

wet-behind-the-ears pup; it would take more than that for Thaxter to get a rise from him. The playing fields of Eton had taught him how to control his temper in a fight. This newly arrived heir to a title would have to learn the ways a true gentleman conducted himself within the *ton*.

Mr Smith stepped between the two men and held out his hands. 'Broughton rules apply, so I must remind you that there is to be no kicking, biting, eye-gouging or hitting below the waist. Any breaking of these rules will result in the immediate loss of the bout and possible expulsion from the club. Are we clear, sirs?'

David gave the requisite bow of his head.

'Get on with it, man,' Thaxter snapped, clearly itching to get at his opponent.

They danced around one another for several minutes, each man sizing the other up. Thaxter made several feint moves, but David simply stepped out of the way. He was looking for the usual tell-tale signs of a poor boxing master.

Mr Smith rang a small bell signally the end of the first round. David casually walked over to a chair and allowed his second to serve him a warm cup of tea. He had an unbreakable rule never to imbibe when he was boxing, a clear head being of crucial importance. David smiled, hearing Thaxter's disgusted snort at his opponent's choice of drink.

Thaxter took an opened flask from his own second and clenching it between his gloves, threw a long swig down his throat.

Round two was almost a repeat of round one. They danced around one another at the beginning, only finally managing to lock gloves towards the end.

By the sound of the second bell David could see Thaxter was getting more than a little frustrated. It took a great deal of fortitude not to smile at his opponent. He was toying with him and Thaxter knew it. While Thaxter had lines of perspiration pouring down his neck, soaking his shirt, David was yet to break a sweat.

He had just taken another sip of his tea when he felt a dull thump on his shoulder.

'Next round I want a proper fight, Radley; no more of this namby-pamby prancing around the room. If you think you can hit me, then bloody well try.'

David turned to see his irate opponent storming back to his position, arms pumping out to the sides in a clear display of aggression.

He looked down at his gloves and calmly checked the laces before dismissing his second with a nod.

It was time to move in for the kill.

As soon as the bell rang for the start of the final round, Thaxter came at him in a mighty rush. He swung his arms wildly at David, brushing the outside of his shirt, but otherwise missing his intended target. He quickly retreated back to his mark.

David felt a twinge in his side and remembered the hours he had spent wielding an axe. He was obviously not in as good condition as he had thought.

He turned to the referee. 'Mr Smith, are you satisfied, that I have conducted myself in a proper manner?' he asked.

The boxing master nodded his head. 'Yes you have, Sir; you may finish the bout. Mr Fox, please resume the fight.'

Thaxter made a second wild attempt to land a punch on David. He opened his mouth and began to complain that the bout was becoming a farce, when David landed a powerful blow to the side of his head.

It stopped Thaxter in his tracks.

For a moment he stood and stared at David, clearly unable to register the fact that his brains were rattling inside his head. He blinked hard several times, before his legs crossed beneath him and he crashed to the floor.

Mr Smith and the other staff quickly came to his aid, and lifting him to his feet, helped him to a nearby chair.

'Mr Radley has been awarded the bout, by means of a knock-out. If you wish for a rematch, Mr Fox, you will need to pay your full membership,' Mr Smith said. He put a small bottle of smelling salts under Thaxter's nose.

He flinched and swore violently.

As soon as he was freed from his padded gloves, David came over to the chair where Thaxter was sitting awkwardly. He offered his hand, as was customary, but it was refused.

'I might box with bastards, but I don't shake hands with them,' came the bitter reply. He waved his hands at the saloon staff and demanded they remove his gloves.

David shrugged his shoulders. 'Please yourself, Fox. Oh and Mr Smith, make sure you put a pint of good ale on my monthly chit for each of the lads who assisted with the bout today. They did a fine job.'

He turned on his heel and quickly headed back to the change rooms to grab his jacket and coat. If he hurried, once he left Gentleman Jackson's saloon, he had just on an hour to change clothes and make it to Hyde Park. A promise to Alex and Millie that he would join them for a walk this afternoon was a commitment he intended to keep. Considering how little he had seen of them outside of parties and balls since their wedding, he found himself looking forward to joining the crush of London's elite for their daily promenade.

'Next time I shall finish you off in the first round,' he muttered as he stepped out into Bond Street and saw Thaxter Fox being assisted into a nearby hack.

He flexed his fingers. 'I didn't think I hit him that hard,' he muttered.

His own carriage arrived as arranged and he climbed inside.

Disappointed in himself for not having stayed the power

of his punch, David threw himself back on to the leather padded seat.

'Bloody hell!' he bellowed, and sat forward, holding his left side. Searing pain took his breath away as it speared through his body.

When finally he was able to calm his breathing and see straight, he pulled open the side of his jacket. There he saw a slit about two inches long had been cut in the fabric of his shirt. Under the shirt was a small wound in the top of his hip.

He had been stabbed.

It took a moment for the reality of what had happened to sink in. He dug his hand into the pocket of his coat and found his purse still intact. No street urchin had tried to knife him for his money as he left the saloon.

'No, he couldn't have,' he whispered.

He looked down once more at the wound in his side. Whatever had stabbed him was short and thin. Just enough to have been kept hidden within a boxing glove. He had not felt the knife penetrate his skin and very little blood had seeped from the puncture wound. Thaxter Fox was a man who knew how to wield a sly blade.

Sitting forward on the bench seat as the carriage made its way the short distance to George Street, David pondered the reason for Thaxter Fox's vicious assault on him.

By the time he reached his rooms, he was on the verge of committing murder.

The way Thaxter Fox had spoken so freely toward Clarice, and the obvious attention he had lavished on Lady Alice, all pointed to him having designs on Lord Langham's daughter. And her dowry.

He swore for a second time. Much as he had tried to deny it, Mr Fox as the future earl presented a far more suitable candidate for Clarice's hand than he did. And by marrying his daughter off to his heir, Henry Langham ensured his own bloodline would continue to be bound to the family title.

David's situation was worse than ever before. Thaxter obviously viewed him as a threat. Someone who stood in the way of his plans to secure Clarice's hand. Someone who had to be eliminated.

Arriving back at George Street, he made the uncomfortable climb up the stairs to his suite of rooms. Once inside, he stripped off his jacket and shirt and examined the wound closely. Fortunately it had only cut through skin and muscle; the stroke had gone wide of any vital organs.

He slowly ground his teeth together as he pondered the growing fear that permeated his mind. If Thaxter Fox was prepared to draw a knife on a member of the Duke of Strathmore's family, what else was he capable of?

Clarice was a vulnerable young woman. In the hands of someone like Thaxter, she might not survive.

His valet Bailey, a man of many talents, was able to lightly stitch and then bind the wound. He offered to repair the shirt, but David refused. He hung it over a chair in his bedroom. It would be the first thing he saw when he woke in the morning and the last thing at night when he snuffed out the bedside candle.

After Bailey left the room, David stood with his eyes closed, slowly opening and then tightly clenching his fists. He was is no mood to be exchanging pleasantries with Millie and Alex in Hyde Park. When he opened his eyes once more and looked at the shirt, his mind was set.

War had been declared for the hand of Lady Clarice Langham and there could only be one victor.

Chapter Eleven

❧

Clarice did as she had promised.
As soon as she and Lady Alice returned home from their visit to Madame de Feuillide's salon, she went upstairs to her bedroom and emptied the drawer of binding strips on to the floor.

She stood for a moment, staring at the tightly bundled rolls. It had taken a level of self-control she did not realise she possessed to agree to give up the bindings. As she uttered the word *yes* to Madame de Feuillide, the little voice inside her head had been screaming *no!*

Taking a deep breath, she bent down and scooped up the muslin bindings, quickly stuffing them into a calico bag before going in search of a footman. After handing the bag over and giving him instructions for their delivery, she went back upstairs to her room.

She closed the door behind her and locked it.

'I will remain forever in this half-life if I don't free myself from them,' she reassured herself.

Placing a hand to her chest, she could feel her heart beating. Under her gown she wore the very last piece of muslin binding she would ever own. Tonight she would burn it and from tomorrow, she would be stripped of her armour.

She clasped her hands together and putting them to her lips, tried to stem the rising tide of panic which welled within.

'I can do this, I can,' she promised herself.

A knock at the bedroom door distracted her from her anxiety. She unlocked the door and Lady Alice stepped inside. Immediately taking Clarice's hand, she gave her granddaughter a warm smile.

'I cannot begin to tell you how proud I am that you have finally decided to put your grief aside and re-join society,' Lady Alice said.

Clarice blushed.

'Did you enjoy our outing with the duchess and the girls? They certainly seemed to have a wonderful time. I like them all immensely, especially Lady Brooke. I hope that there are no remaining difficulties between the two of you.'

'Millie and I are friends,' Clarice reassured her.

The afternoon at the modiste salon had been the most fun Clarice had had in a very long time. She certainly couldn't remember the last time she had laughed so much.

The truth was, she was more than happy that Alex had chosen the feisty, India-born Millie as his bride. While they had been lifelong friends, Clarice had never considered the Marquess of Brooke as a serious prospect for marriage and was secretly relieved to have escaped marrying him. Alex Radley was a bright and shining star; whomever he married was guaranteed to be the centre of attention along with him. From the time she had spent with Millie, it was obvious to Clarice that Alex's new bride was gifted with enough backbone to keep her husband in line.

'Oh, and I have a surprise,' Lady Alice said.

'Yes?'

Her grandmother smiled. 'Madame promised to have at least one of your new gowns ready and delivered in time for

Lady Brearley's garden party. She had her seamstress cutting the fabric before we left. You will only have to wear your old gowns for a few days more; isn't that wonderful?'

Clarice nodded her agreement, because whether she wished it or not, once her new gowns arrived there would be no going back.

※

'Oh, Lady Clarice, I cannot begin to tell you how beautiful you look in your new gown,' Bella exclaimed.

She stood back and with hands clasped, stared lovingly at the dress.

The day gown had a simple rose-coloured bodice, edged with French lace at the top of the fitted bust line. While the cut of the bust line was modest by current standards, it still displayed a great deal more flesh than Clarice had ever shown before.

The striped skirt was a rose, white and green pattern finished off at the bottom with the same French lace as the bodice. The matching half-boots were a deep rose with white laces, which Clarice took a moment to examine appreciatively before looking up to the mirror.

She stared hard at the young woman who looked back at her.

Who are you?

Gone were the dull grey and lilac mourning dresses; in their place was a joy in colour.

'I'm so pleased you have put your greys away; not that you won't always miss Her Ladyship,' Bella said.

'Thank you, Bella,' Clarice replied.

The cut of the gown would permit the lightest binding of her breasts. She toyed with the tempting proposition momentarily before remembering the promise she had made to the modiste. Madame de Feuillide had thrown all the efforts of her salon into completing Clarice's full order within a matter of days. Her side of the bargain had to be kept.

She swallowed deeply. No longer with the protection of the muslin bindings, the world would finally begin to see the real Clarice Langham.

At least it's only my outer shell; the rest is still safe.

She held a hand up to her décolletage and pressed her fingertips into the tops of her breasts. The only time she normally saw this much of her own flesh was in the bath.

'You don't think it shows too much?'

Bella giggled.

'I think it shows just enough, if you wish to be noticed.'

'No!' she cried.

Bella stepped forward and took hold of Clarice's hand. 'Yes,' she whispered.

The relationship between the earl's daughter and her maid was a close one. In the months following her mother's death, it had been Bella who held Clarice through the long nights of tears.

'Rest assured, Lady Clarice, Madame de Feuillide has a reputation for the best-cut cloth in London. She always dresses her clients on the respectable side of propriety; she would never send you out in a day gown which would bring your honour into question.'

Clarice looked down. 'It is only a garden party, perhaps I should save it for a more special occasion,' she replied.

A shiver of fear and excitement coursed down her spine.

'What if he doesn't like my new clothes? What if...oh,' she muttered in frustration. She wriggled her fingers in an effort to calm herself down.

Millie and Lucy had been very persuasive in their efforts to help her choose her new wardrobe. A second glass of champagne had weakened her already-faltering resolve and before she knew what she had done, she'd placed an extra order for five new day gowns. Her eager request to Lady Alice was met with immediate acquiescence.

'Everyone will love your new gown, don't worry,' Bella replied.

A knock at the door interrupted their discussion and Lady Alice entered Clarice's bedroom. Bella sighed with relief.

'Oh my darling, that gown is perfect. You look so beautiful. So radiant,' Lady Alice said, as a huge smile spread across her face.

Bella raised her eyebrows and nodded at Clarice. Bella had spent the whole afternoon in a rapture of delight as she opened one after the other of the boxes of new gowns. As her maid hung the last of the gowns in the wardrobe, Clarice had caught Bella wiping away tears.

A pile of her drab old gowns sat neatly in the corner of her room.

'Doesn't my granddaughter look divine?' the dowager announced to the world in general. With a nod of her head, she dismissed the maid who made a discreet exit from the room, her arms full of Clarice's old gowns.

Lady Alice walked across to where Clarice stood and kissed her cheek.

'I am so happy you have given up your widow's weeds, my dear. I was beginning to think you had resigned yourself to a life of drabness. The Madame does wonders, does she not? Come, show me how you twirl; I want to see how well the skirt is cut.'

Clarice twirled and found herself laughing. Joy filled her heart. The day was full of possibilities.

'I cannot wait to see the look on a certain young man's face when he first sets eyes upon you today,' Lady Alice said.

Clarice looked pensively at the closed bedroom door. 'You mean David?' she whispered.

Lady Alice continued to smile. 'Of course. Though you may need to be discreet at the garden party; your father has suddenly decided to accompany us. Why is beyond me, as it's not exactly the sort of function he normally attends. But since he is actually speaking to me once more I was hardly in a position to argue the point.'

The warmth in Clarice's heart rapidly cooled.

With her father in attendance, she would have to stay near her grandmother and be on her utmost best behaviour. It was at times like this she wished she had not been raised to be quite such a lady. That perhaps a small rude word of disappointment could find its way to her lips.

'Bother,' she replied.

Lady Alice patted her gently on the arm. 'Not to worry, my dear; I shall do my best to distract your father so you can spend time with your friends. Though you may wish to consider this as being the perfect opportunity to get back into your father's good books. Word has reached his ears that you have been spending time with the Radley girls in preference to your other friends. If he adds that piece of news to the fact that you danced with David, then you can see how things might look to him.'

Clarice sighed.

She had managed to avoid Susan Kirk and the Winchester sisters for the better part of a week, the pressing need to attend to her feeble grandmother being the best excuse she had had at her disposal for a long time. At some point she would have to resume her afternoon walks with them.

'I shall be the perfect daughter this afternoon; Papa will have no reason to be displeased with me.'

Lady Alice hugged her. 'Just be very careful when it comes to your heart, Clarice. You have suffered enough pain for one so young, and believe me a broken heart never fully mends.'

For the first time in years Clarice was going out in public not dressed in mourning garb. With her breasts no longer bound, she felt naked and vulnerable. Before they left she spent several minutes in the front entrance of Langham House fussing with the skirts of her new dress. Then her bonnet became unpinned from her hair and Bella had to find more pins.

She was about to give up and go back to her room when her father appeared.

'Clarice?' the earl said.

She spun and faced him as he reached the bottom of the grand staircase.

'Yes?' she replied.

He stood for a moment, silently staring at her, entranced. Then he pulled a small cream object from his pocket and held it up to her gaze. It was her mother's favourite cameo brooch. As he pinned it to her gown, she heard the tremor in his breath.

'You look so much like her,' he said.

She searched his gaze. Gone was the hard countenance, the mask which he always wore. In its place, she saw the lines of pain and grief etched into his skin. Her father aged before her eyes.

The tears came quickly to her as she whispered 'Papa.'

He reached into his jacket and, pulling out a white handkerchief, proceeded to wipe away her tears. He kissed her tenderly on the forehead.

'I am so pleased you have taken Lady Alice's advice and come fully out of mourning. Just remember to proceed slowly; you are still delicate.'

She nodded. She was not going to argue with her father's judgement of her state of mind. Today she would do exactly what her grandmother had said; she would be a perfect, dutiful daughter.

With luck he would still feel the same happiness for her when he received the enormous bill from Madame de Feuillide.

She handed the cloth back to her father.

'Oh, and did I tell you Mr Fox will also be in attendance

this afternoon? I managed to secure him a late invitation,' her father said.

'I see,' she replied. The fact that her father had even bothered to mention Thaxter Fox did not bode well, but she was loath to spoil this special moment.

'I was hoping you would spend some time with him this afternoon. Perhaps share a spot of luncheon with him. He is new to upper society and knows few people. As he is the future of the Langham title, I am counting on you to assist him in gaining a foothold.'

Keeping to the promise she had made, Clarice respectfully replied 'Yes Papa.'

A short time later, with her bonnet and hair arranged, Clarice took her father's arm and walked out into the warmth of a summer's afternoon.

The earl made his excuses not long after they arrived at Lady Brearley's party. A select group of older gentlemen were slowly making their way upstairs to the private rooms of the host. Clarice waved her father farewell.

'Cigars, whisky and billiards,' Lady Alice remarked as they both watched the earl ascend the stairs. 'Your luck must have changed; I expect we won't see him again until shortly before the party ends.'

Clarice smiled. With her father otherwise occupied, her hopes of spending time with Lucy and perhaps one or two other members of the Radley family rose.

'Clarice?' said a voice to her right.

She turned and was met with the sight of Lady Susan Kirk and her cousins. While Susan had at times a modicum of decorum, her two cousins were as socially inept as could be. Daisy and Heather, true to form, were giggling and whispering behind their hands.

Do those two ever stop?

'So you have finally stopped dressing like something out

of a graveyard,' Susan sniffed, as she looked Clarice up and down.

Clarice's heart sank. She had not been in Susan's company for a number of days, and it was clear her absence had been taken as a personal slight. A twinge of guilt reminded her that she had abandoned Susan to days alone with the giggling misses. She looked from her friends to her grandmother and back again.

'Susan, I am so pleased to see you. I told Papa how eager I was to show you my new clothes; he said he knew you would approve. With any luck you will be able to say hello to him before we leave. He headed upstairs with your father not long ago.'

She dared not look at Lady Alice, fervently hoping that her grandmother would say nothing untoward.

'That he did,' Lady Alice added.

The other girls dipped into a curtsy to the dowager countess, who acknowledged them with a small nod.

'So when did you grow some apples?' Heather asked, staring at Clarice's bust line. Susan rolled her eyes.

'She didn't. She had them made by a dressmaker. Anyone can see that the bodice of her dress has been specially cut. I hear you have been seen about town with the Radley women; pray tell, Clarice; when did we become superfluous to your needs?'

A flash of heat raced up Clarice's neck and her cheeks turned bright red. She had abandoned Susan and was now getting her just reward.

'Now now, young lady. As it so happens I am a good friend of the Duchess of Strathmore and Clarice, being the doting granddaughter that she is, has spent most of the week assisting me. No-one is casting anyone off as old goods,' said Lady Alice.

She lifted the wooden walking stick an inch up off the floor and pointed the end toward Susan. The warning was clear.

'I do beg your pardon, Lady Alice,' Susan replied.

Clarice looked at the walking stick. How odd it was that earlier in the day her grandmother had been moving freely about the house without the need for it. Yet as soon as they were out in public, it suddenly reappeared. She looked up and met her grandmother's innocent gaze.

One good lie deserved another.

'Be a sweet dear, Clarice, and help me to find a comfortable chair in the shade. You can spend time with your friends later.'

Clarice frowned. Her plans had included spending time with Susan to please her father, but it was clear Lady Alice had other ideas. Her grandmother began to hobble away toward a pair of open French doors which led out on to the huge green lawn.

Susan's eyebrows rose and fell. 'Well, I am certain you and your grandmother have lots to talk about. I hope you have a pleasant afternoon keeping her company.'

'Clarice!'

'Coming, Grandmother,' she said and hurried after Lady Alice.

'Over there,' Lady Alice said, pointing to a pair of garden chairs with large well-stuffed cushions on them. She made a great show of the effort it took for her to sit down, eliciting sympathetic glances from other guests.

For the next hour Clarice sat beside her grandmother and listened as Lady Alice told her stories of garden parties from her youth.

'...it was absolutely scandalous and of course they had to marry,' Lady Alice said with a wicked laugh. Clarice shook her head. Her grandmother had seen and heard a great deal of gossip over the years.

'And you were there?'

Lady Alice sat back in her garden chair and surveyed the guests around them; no-one was within earshot.

'Who do you think told her brother where to find them?'

Clarice's eyes grew wide. 'No!'

A wicked grin was all the answer she got.

'Lady Alice, Lady Clarice, how wonderful to see you. We were beginning to worry you were not in attendance.'

From the door closest to them, Lucy and Millie Radley appeared. Clarice smiled; from the looks on their faces they were pleased to have finally run their quarry to ground.

Lady Alice motioned for a nearby footman to bring them more chairs and soon a merry gathering had formed.

They were in the middle of a lively discussion regarding where Alex and Millie were planning on taking their honeymoon, when Lucy put down her cup of tea and suddenly clasped her hands together. 'Speaking of exciting news, isn't it marvellous that David has been given his own estate. It's absolutely wonderful; don't you think so, Clarice?'

She cast a non-too subtle look in Millie's direction, and Clarice stifled a snort. Lucy had spent the better part of the past five minutes casting furtive glances at her new sister-in-law, clearly waiting for the moment when she could change the subject.

'Yes, well, it is high time that he had his own place. And now that Alex has married, I expect David's thoughts will soon turn to finding himself a bride. With a well-run estate to his name, his chances in the marriage market should be somewhat elevated,' Millie replied. The sly smile which formed on her lips betrayed her otherwise cool demeanour.

Clarice gave the expected smile in response, but failed to muster any hope. Knowing her father, it would not matter if the Duke of Strathmore had given his son the island of Java. Her father had made his opinion clear on the subject of who was and was not good enough to marry his daughter. David Radley was not for his beloved Clarice.

How can you define a person by someone else's actions? It's not as if he made the conscious decision to be born out of wedlock.

'You should see how he has been since he returned to London; it is like a hundred birthdays and Christmases have come all at once. And he is forever making lists and asking questions of Papa,' Lucy exclaimed.

Millie wore a self-satisfied grin. It was her dowry money which had enabled the Duke of Strathmore to buy his eldest son an estate.

'Where did you say it was?' replied Clarice. David had made mention of his new estate at the ball, but her mind had been elsewhere. Her memories of that night consisted mainly of the strong grip of his hands and the intoxicating scent of his cologne. That, and the powerful way he had spun her so effortlessly around the dance floor.

'Sharnbrook, a few miles north of Bedford. Which Alex informs me is somewhere over there,' Millie replied and pointed her gloved hand in a north-westerly direction.

Lady Alice nodded her agreement. 'Lovely place, Bedford and so close to London. Nothing worse than those long trips up and down the country from far-flung estates. Poor Clarice is a terrible traveller; the rolling motion of the carriage plays havoc with her stomach.'

She gave her grandmother a weary look.

'Which reminds me, I need to go and lie down if I am going to make it through the rest of the day. A huge breakfast is never a good idea. One would think that by my age I would have learnt that lesson,' continued the dowager, ignoring Clarice's discomfort.

Clarice stood and offered her grandmother a supporting arm, but Lady Alice waved her away. 'No, I'm fine. I shall get one of the footmen to escort me upstairs; you stay here and spend time with your friends.'

The girls rose and farewelled the dowager.

As soon as she was gone, they pulled their chairs closer together and ordered more refreshments.

'I do so love your new gown, Clarice; you look wonderful.

And that cameo is so beautiful, is it a family piece?' Millie said. The grin that both she and Lucy wore on their faces was an obvious reflection of their happiness in having got Clarice out of her drab clothing.

'Thank you. Yes, the brooch was my mother's,' she replied.

She looked down at the pretty pattern on her dress. Lifting her feet, she looked at the delicate white ribbons which criss-crossed her half-boots.

She looked *and* felt wonderful.

'Oh, so you did order a pair of those, aren't they the kick?' Lucy asked. She lifted her feet and showed her half-boots to be of exactly the same design, only in a different colour to Clarice's.

Millie laughed. 'Lucky for me that I didn't wear either of the two pairs *I* ordered.' She lifted her skirt to show a pair of dark blue slippers with little bells on the end of the tassels.

'I didn't see those!' Lucy exclaimed.

Millie raised her eyebrows and wagged a finger in Lucy's direction. 'You need to ask to see Madame's special orders, including her wedding night pieces,' she replied.

Lucy's eyes grew wide before she dissolved into a fit of giggles. Millie was deliciously wicked. Millie and Clarice joined in the mirth and soon all three were wiping tears from their eyes.

A shadow passed over them and darkened the space between Clarice and Lucy. Clarice ceased laughing and quickly looked up. Standing there, blocking out the sun, was Thaxter Fox. Clarice's happy mood evaporated.

He was attired in a smart black redingote, pale grey trousers and a sage-green waistcoat. She frowned as she thought of her father's money being spent on Mr Fox just to enable him to *look* the part of a future earl. Then, remembering her own substantial wardrobe outlay, she forced a smile to her lips.

Don't be a hypocrite.

He bowed to her.

'I must apologise for my tardiness; the tailor only finished my new jacket this morning. What do you think, Lady Clarice; does it meet with your approval? And how clever of you to choose a dress with the same colour green in it as my waistcoat. I am touched that you went to such an effort in order for us to be a matching pair.'

She gave an embarrassed nod.

Out of the corner of her eye, she saw Lucy's eyebrows lift. At the same time, Millie coughed.

Thaxter turned and paid his overdue respects to the others.

'Lady Lucy, a pleasure to once again make your acquaintance. If you recall we were seated four chairs away from each other at a recent party. You asked me to pass the salt.'

Lucy looked down at her hands, and Clarice held her breath. They had met before and social custom dictated she offer him her hand.

'Why yes; Mr Fox, is it not? How observant of you to remember such an auspicious occasion,' she replied, and offered him her gloved hand.

He placed the merest of kisses on her fingertips before she withdrew her hand. He turned to Millie and Clarice saw him make a quick study of her friend's face. The diamond and pearl in Lady Brooke's nose ring matched the cream underskirt of her dress. A hint of disapproval was reflected in his half-blink.

'Lady Brooke, may I offer my sincere congratulations on your recent nuptials. To marry into such an elevated station must truly warm your mother's heart.'

Millie's sapphire-blue eyes flashed wide open in obvious shock, but to her credit, Clarice noted, she maintained her composure. With both her grandsires being titled men, Millie had married well within her social level.

'I'm sorry, but have we been introduced? I don't recall having ever set eyes upon you before, Sir, because I am certain that if I had I would not forget such an *interesting* face,' she bit back.

Before Thaxter had a chance to speak, Millie leaned forward and picked up her cup of tea. She sipped it slowly as silence reigned among the group.

Thaxter cleared his throat and Clarice felt his gaze fix upon her. There was no escape; social niceties must be observed.

'Lady Brooke, may I present Mr Thaxter Fox of Whitby, Yorkshire. Mr Fox is a distant relative of mine, but by chance of his birth he has recently become heir to my father's title and estate,' she said. A wary look formed on Millie's countenance as she looked him up and down. It was obvious his handsome looks and well-cut clothing had not escaped her notice. She sucked in a breath.

'Well then, Mr Fox, we both have fortune to thank for our future successes,' she said.

Clarice looked to Lucy, who looked utterly enthralled at the exchange. Thaxter sniffed the air and gave a nod of his head. 'As you say, Lady Brooke, a fortunate life.'

He turned and offered Clarice his hand. 'I came to collect you, Lady Clarice. I believe you and I have an arrangement to eat a spot of luncheon together. Your father would be most displeased if we did not keep to our promise. I understand Lady Alice is indisposed, but since your father approved of our appointment, it should not present a problem for you and I to fulfil our social obligations.'

She looked at his brown leather glove. When she didn't immediately accept his hand, he pushed it closer to her face.

'Lady Brooke, Lady Lucy, would you please excuse us?' he said as Clarice took his hand with great reluctance.

He pulled her gently to her feet and gave a self-satisfied nod of his head. Thaxter Fox had won the first round.

Lucy and Millie sat and watched as Clarice and Thaxter walked away toward the garden, where a series of long tables held all manner of cakes and sandwiches.

'What an odious, self-righteous prig of a man,' Lucy muttered as she watched them leave.

'Don't forget dangerous,' Millie replied.

Lucy scowled. 'What do you mean?'

Millie shook her head. 'I saw the look he gave Clarice when she told us that he was her father's heir. I've seen that proprietary look before in men's eyes; my own husband gets it every time another man offers to dance with me. I would be less concerned if Mr Fox were not so devilishly handsome. If he begins to work his charms on poor Clarice, David's cause may be in vain. Gather up your things, dear sister; we need to go and find our brother. Because if I am not mistaken, David has a serious rival on his hands and time may be of the essence.'

She rose up from the chair and fixed her gaze on the back of Thaxter Fox's head.

'I think it is time we put our plan in motion. Because if we don't make haste, Clarice may be pressured into giving her hand in marriage to that man. Pleasant looks and all, I don't like the way he deals with her.'

※

There was only one thing which David disliked more than opera, and that was garden parties. At least at evening events he could steal away into the garden or terrace to smoke. At a ball he could get a drink of something more alcoholic than tea. At Lady Brearley's party, only the older gentleman were permitted to hide themselves away from the guests and partake of whisky and cigars.

The younger set, which included him and his siblings, were expected to play outdoor games or sit in comfortable chairs and make polite conversation. While he and Alex were both accomplished players of pall-mall, David never played unless he was compelled.

'How long do you think we will have to stand here like fools until Millie and Lucy locate Clarice?' he said.

Alex shrugged his shoulders. 'I am not about to try to anticipate the actions of my wife or our sister; they are the masters of the garden party domain. We should just take our time to mingle with the other guests, have a spot of something to eat and wait. Unless, of course you fancy being beaten yet again at pall-mall.'

David kicked away a loose stone on the garden path which led down to the ornamental lake and summer house. With so much time spent on paperwork for his new estate, his patience for proceeding slowly with Clarice was being sorely tested.

'Oh all right, but no cheating this time, otherwise you may find yourself going for a swim in that lake.'

Alex gave a friendly wave in David's direction and laughed. 'I don't need to cheat to best you, dear brother.'

It was almost an hour later by the time Lucy and Millie sought them out.

'About time,' David snapped. He had lost three games to Alex and his mood was beginning to darken. The stab wound in his side bit painfully every time he wielded the mallet.

Millie and Lucy both ignored his display of temper.

'Yes, well, time is something which you may not have. Thaxter Fox is here and Clarice is sharing a picnic with him on the west lawn,' Lucy replied.

'What?' the men replied.

Millie nodded. 'Apparently Lord Langham wants Clarice to help Mr Fox navigate his way through the rocky shoals of London society. I wouldn't be so concerned about that if I hadn't heard rumours that he is in the market for a wife. If you list all of Clarice's attributes, including her dowry and family ties, she is likely to be at the top of his list. And after seeing the way she let him drag her away from us this afternoon, I am concerned she will take the path of least resistance and agree to marry him.'

'You have to do something, David!' Lucy cried.

He held up a hand and the look he gave his sister was enough cause for her to fall silent.

'Calm down. I would have thought you had more faith in me than that. You didn't think I came here unprepared, did you?'

In the boxing saloon, Thaxter Fox had already shown his hand. He was prepared to be underhanded to win Clarice. David looked at his siblings and smiled. Mr Fox might have his sly ways, but he didn't have the resources of the Radley family at his disposal.

'I have a plan and you all need to play your parts exactly as I say.'

※

'This looks like as good a spot as any; shall we sit?' Thaxter asked.

He pointed the laden plate he held in his hands in the direction of a vacant rug spread out on the garden lawn.

'Yes, though if it gets too hot we may need to move back towards the terrace,' Clarice replied. She had hoped that Lady Alice would have returned by now and joined them. Her grandmother's forthright manner was just what the situation needed.

Thaxter took hold of her gloved hand and helped her to sit. After setting the plate down, he took a seat next to her. She shuffled further away from him.

'Bother,' he said, clearly unused to using such timid language when frustrated.

'Pardon?'

'We should have got tea.'

She shook her head. 'I am not that partial to tea myself, but if you like I shall wait here with the food until you get some.'

He gave her a friendly smile. 'Back shortly,' he said and got to his feet.

While she waited for Thaxter to reappear, Clarice rearranged her skirts and tilted the tip of her bonnet down to shade her face from the sun. She had been so preoccupied with her new attire that she had left her parasol under the garden chair. Getting up from the rug unassisted presented some difficulty, so she decided to stay put. If, at some point, she needed a break from Thaxter, she would ask him to retrieve her parasol.

'Would you mind taking this from me?' he asked upon his return with a hot cup of tea. She took the cup and saucer from him.

'Thank you,' he said as she handed it back to him, once he had resumed his seat.

'A lot of messing about just to have a drink and a sandwich,' Clarice replied.

A sigh of annoyance escaped Thaxter's lips. 'I forgot to get you a drink. I really am a country bumpkin.'

She laughed and gave him a reassuring pat on the shoulder.

Why on earth did I just do that? And in public. Don't fall for his feeble charms, Clarice.

'Forgive me for being overly familiar,' she said, her face turning red.

He reached out and took hold of her hand. 'That is perfectly all right, Lady Clarice. In fact, I appreciate your concern. As you can see I struggle with the nuances of polite society. Which reminds me, I must beg your humble pardon for the cack-handed way I took hold of your hand at the ball the other night. It was most impolite of me to address you in such a way. I seem to find myself constantly tripping up and making mistakes at present.'

She nodded. He did seem to find a way to easily offend most people.

'Which is why, if I may be so bold to discuss such a matter with you, I am in search of a wife.'

Oh.

Clarice sat silent on the rug, staring vacantly out over a nearby bed of brightly coloured peonies. Her mind had gone completely blank and she was incapable of speech.

Please no, please no.

She blinked and looked down at her hands, only then realising she had somehow picked up the plate of sandwiches and small cakes. Taking a salmon and thinly sliced cucumber sandwich in her hand, she took a bite. She offered him the plate and he took it from her, placing it on the ground behind him.

'A wife who would be able to guide me in the ways of high society. Someone born into the *ton*. Someone who possessed the requisite skills in running a country estate as well as a town house.'

'Yes, well, I am sure that there are many suitable young ladies here today. As a future earl you have quite a lot to offer,' she stammered, before taking another bite of the sandwich.

He shifted closer to her and she felt the sandwich stick in her throat. She watched with growing trepidation as he reached out and took hold of her hand. He leaned in close. So close she could smell his overpowering cologne. So close she could hear him breathing. Her heart began to race.

No! No! No!

Her mind's protest cried out in ever-increasing fervour.

His lips pressed against her outer ear and he murmured. 'I know you and I have not known one another very long and I am yet to find your good favour. But I am certain that if we were to spend more time together, you would find I am a man with hidden talents and delights. Lady Clarice, if you would at least consider my…'

'Susan!' she cried.

Lady Susan and her cousins had fortuitously chosen that exact moment to make an appearance at the edge of the pathway. Clarice shot up her hand and in a most unladylike manner waved furiously at them. The girls looked towards her and the Winchester cousins gave a cheery wave in reply.

The three girls made a direct line for them. Thaxter withdrew his hand and made a show of picking up the plate.

As they drew near, Clarice could see the look of thunder on Susan's face.

'How lovely to see you again; do come and join us,' Clarice said. She patted the empty space on the other side of the blanket and motioned for Susan to sit down. Thaxter let out a barely disguised sigh of frustration and got to his feet. After assisting Susan and the Winchester sisters to take a place on the rug, it quickly became apparent that there was not enough room for the five of them.

'And you have food, how thoughtful of you, Mr Fox,' Susan said. She held out her hands and Thaxter reluctantly handed her the plate. Out of the corner of her eye, Clarice saw the two of them exchange an odd look.

'So where is Lady Alice?' Daisy Winchester asked.

'She went to lie down a little while ago,' replied Clarice.

As soon as the words left her lips, she knew she had been saved. Being a dutiful granddaughter, she should really go and check on the health of her beloved grandmother. An unexpected means of escape had suddenly presented itself and she quickly took it.

'Speaking of which, I must go and make sure she is resting comfortably. Her injured leg causes her great pain,' she added.

Hurrying away from the group back to the house, she gave a quick glance over her shoulder. Thaxter Fox had taken her place next to Lady Susan and was seated with his back to the house.

She stopped by the chair where she had been sitting

earlier, and retrieved her parasol. Stepping inside the house, she thought it wise to at least make the appearance of checking on Lady Alice. She had one foot on the staircase, when a hand reached out and took hold of her arm.

'We thought you would never escape that wretched man,' Lucy said.

Millie and Lucy stood shoulder to shoulder with their backs to the garden, effectively blocking any view of Clarice which might be had from the west lawn.

'What?'

'We have been watching and waiting for the right moment to come and rescue you. We were halfway out the door when Macbeth's three witches appeared,' Lucy added.

Clarice couldn't help but laugh at Lucy's less than kind remark.

'Sorry, I shouldn't say that about your friends; they probably think the same of us,' Lucy said.

'Speak for yourself,' Millie replied.

I didn't actually need rescuing; I'm on my way upstairs to see my grandmother,' Clarice replied.

Her friends looked at one another and nodded. 'We have already been upstairs and spoken to Lady Alice. She says she will rest for a little while longer and that when you have finished in the garden you may go and sit with her,' Millie said.

Lucy and Millie positioned themselves either side of Clarice and guided her across the room and out through the other door. Opposite the door was a small path which meandered down one side of the garden and headed in the direction of the lake.

Seeing that the sun was still high in the sky, Clarice began to open her parasol.

'No!' Millie whispered. She quickly took hold of Clarice's parasol and swapped it with her own. She then dashed off down the path and out of sight. A minute or two later she reappeared further down the path with Alex, Clarice's opened parasol in her hand. They waved, and Lucy waved back.

'Good, now we can begin,' Lucy said. She took Millie's parasol out of Clarice's hand and opened it fully before handing it back. She raised her hand and adjusted Clarice's grip.

'You must keep it close to your head; that way no-one will be able to tell it is you. People know it belongs to Millie.' The parasol was painted with dark blue birds, giving it a distinctive character.

They followed the path down to where Alex and Millie waited. They had barely reached them when the newlyweds gave a quick hello and headed back up the path.

They walked on for a few more yards, before Lucy stopped and looked back toward the house. At this part of the garden, they were below the line of sight of anyone sitting on the lawn.

Already at a loss as to what was going on, Clarice's confusion further increased when Lucy took hold of her arm and began to lead her toward the small summerhouse at the edge of the lake.

As they neared the house, Lucy looked furtively from left to right. At a point in the path where it split into two, she stopped. The path before them continued around the garden and back up to the house. The second branch of the path led down to the edge of the lake.

'Good; I think we are alone. Now listen carefully. Alex and Millie will hold a position at the top of the stone steps and intercept anyone who wanders down this way. Millie's brother, Charles Ashton, is over the other side of the garden keeping watch on Mr Fox and his harem. All you have to do is go around to the front door of the summerhouse and go inside.'

Clarice sighed with frustrated confusion. 'What on earth are we doing?'

Lucy stepped in close.

'David is waiting for you in the summerhouse. This is your secret rendezvous. Just follow the path down,' she whispered.

She gave Clarice a quick farewell kiss on the cheek before shoving her gently in the direction of the summerhouse. Clarice took several tentative steps before stopping.

What secret rendezvous?

She turned and saw Lucy still standing in the middle of the path, her gaze fixed on the path which led back to the house. Clarice sighed. All routes to the summerhouse were being watched by David's friends and family.

Turning back to the path which led down to the lake, she began to walk.

With every footstep a growing sense of helpless panic rose within her. She had barely managed to escape Thaxter Fox's clutches and yet here she was, willingly going to meet with another potential suitor.

'This is madness,' she muttered. She passed under the shady trees, around to the front door of the summerhouse, and there she stopped.

With her gloved hands tightly gripping the handle of the parasol, she considered her situation. If she decided to walk away, if she refused to meet David, would he give up the fight for her?

By all rational thoughts, she shouldn't care what he did. If he went and found another woman to marry it should be none of her concern.

'I should just go back to the picnic, find Lady Alice and go home,' she muttered. David and his well-intentioned family would have to accept that her decision was no.

She could give a thousand plausible excuses for crying off at this very moment. Refusing to meet him was the eminently sensible thing to do. Her father would expect it. Lord Langham would be furious if he knew his daughter was making a secret assignation with a man he considered entirely unsuitable for her.

She chortled nervously. A secret meeting with David was far worse than a public dance.

'Yes, utter madness,' she said, closing her parasol.

She opened the door and stepped inside.

The cool sweet air of the summerhouse kissed her face and, closing her eyes, she took a deep breath.

'Welcome, Lady Clarice.'

She opened her eyes and her gaze fell upon him.

The summerhouse was a small room, obviously designed for Lord and Lady Brearley to relax in when they spent afternoons by the lake. David crossed the floor with three long strides and, stepping past her, closed the door. He turned and faced her.

If she had been asked to describe the room, other than the striking oriental pattern border on the curtains, she would have been at a loss for words. All her attention was taken by David.

He was clad in an expertly cut deep blue jacket, which displayed his strong, broad shoulders to brilliant effect. Beneath the jacket was a gold, silver and pale blue striped waistcoat, complemented by his pure white linen shirt. She was powerless to stop her gaze from drifting lower. His pale suede buckskins clung to his muscular thighs. Her breathing faltered.

Her newly rediscovered love of fashion appreciated the way the gold tassels on his highly-polished hessian boots matched perfectly with the gold thread of his waistcoat.

His immaculately cut hair was as black as a moonless night.

Other men of the *ton* might dress themselves as well as he did, but few carried themselves with such command. If she had not known him all her life, she might have feared the man who stood before her. Every blink of his eye held the promise of unleashed power.

She swallowed.

David Radley truly was a magnificent male specimen, the pinnacle of English nobility. He stepped forward and took hold of her hand. An easy, reassuring smile came to his lips.

'I am so glad you came. I know your father is here, so I promise not to keep you too long. I would not wish for you to suffer his wrath on account of me,' he said.

She shook her head. For all her father's failings, he only wanted what was best for her.

'He is just trying to protect me. He thinks I suffer from a deep melancholy because of my mother's death.'

David raised an eyebrow.

'And do you?'

'No. As you can see from my new attire, I am now fully out of mourning. And as for my nerves, they are perfectly fine. I just have the occasional bout of insomnia, nothing more.'

This was not the time nor the place to mention the guilt she still carried. Or why she knew he would never fully love her.

He nodded. 'I must compliment you, Clarice, on your beautiful new gown. If I am not mistaken that cameo was once your mother's. I remember her wearing it.'

She watched his eyes as they took in all that stood before him. A secret warmth rippled through her body when his gaze lingered appreciatively at her bust line. Bella had been right to say that Madame de Feuillide knew what she was doing when it came to the cut of a young woman's gown.

He took a deep breath before lifting his head and meeting her gaze.

'It warms my heart greatly to see you coming back into society. I hope it is a sign that you are thinking and planning with your future in mind.'

He motioned toward a low, floral-patterned couch.

'Would you like to sit for a moment; there are matters which I would like to discuss if you are amenable?'

Clarice looked at the couch and thought better of the idea. She was already in a very compromising situation. If anyone happened upon them, she would be left with no choice but to marry him.

'Thank you, no; I cannot stay long. My father has many pairs of eyes in his service.'

He nodded.

'Very well.'

He straightened his back and gave her a small bow.

'Lady Clarice, as you no doubt have come to realise, the love letter which was accidentally sent to you by my brother was in fact written by me. While the letter itself came to you by way of a series of unfortunate events, it does not change the fact that the sentiments within it are true.'

He stopped, cleared his throat and frowned. It was obvious his eloquent speech had been rehearsed and somehow he had forgotten the rest of the words. Clarice smiled, humbled by the thought that he had gone to such effort on her behalf.

'Just say what is in your heart,' she replied.

She saw her wishful smile reflected back at her in his gentle laugh.

'Clarice, I love you. I have loved you for as long as I can remember. I want you as my wife; it is really that simple.'

She nodded. It really *was* that simple. David was not a man who played games with others' feelings. He spoke his mind. Now that he had been honest with her, she trusted his words to be true.

'Thank you. I know it took a great deal of bravery for you to say that to me,' she replied.

'But?'

She curled up her bottom lip and sucked it under her top

teeth. Over the proceeding weeks, alone in her bedroom, she too had rehearsed this encounter, her response constantly changing and evolving.

'But I am uncertain as to how I should respond,' she replied.

'Because of your father, or because of who I am?'

She clenched her parasol tightly. Men were such stubborn creatures; why did they always think themselves at the centre of everything?

'Neither. It is because of me.'

He scowled. She could see this was not the answer he had been expecting, nor seeking. She slowly loosened her grip.

'My life, as you can see,' she said, looking down at the figure she cut in her new clothes, 'is undergoing a period of transformation. At this moment I am unsure of a lot of things, including how I truly feel about you.'

His shoulders stiffened in disappointment as his arms fell to his sides. She held up a hand.

'I am not saying that I don't love you. I am just saying I need time. Time to decide what *I* want from my life. Not what you want, nor what my father wants.'

The bewildered look on his face said it all. He had been expecting her to accept or decline him, and had prepared suitable responses for both, but this left him floundering. David was a man of decision and action, and now he was rudderless. The battle was neither won nor lost.

'I'm sorry if this encounter has not been as productive as you had hoped for, but if you are still serious in your intentions then there are some things which you can do to further your cause,' she said.

'Name them,' came the immediate response.

She allowed herself a moment to let her gaze take in all his manly form once more. To indulge with pleasure in the secret knowledge that he wanted her for his own.

Stepping bravely forward, she laid a hand on his chest and looked up into his eyes.

'I need you to remain steadfast. To accept that I have to take time to make up my mind, and for you to be sure enough of yourself to allow it. Because if I do agree to marry you, we are going to have to fight forces other than my father to make our union a success. There will always be ignorance and intolerance from others.'

He sighed. He was not happy with her demands, but at that moment she knew she held all the cards. He was strong, powerful and oh-so-handsome a man – and he was at *her* command.

'I have lived my entire life dealing with others who do not accept me as a full member of society; I am well equipped to deal with them,' he replied.

She nodded. During the past three years she too had felt an outsider, but that had been through circumstances beyond her control. Willingly marrying a duke's bastard was an entirely different matter.

'Yes, I expect you are, but there are other matters which I am not in a position to discuss with you at this time. These may have a greater bearing on your desire to marry me than I can currently predict. What I am asking for is time; if you cannot give me that then this conversation is at an end.'

He reached out and ran the back of his hand down the side of her cheek. He closed his eyes for an instant, and she watched him savour the moment.

If only she could say yes to this man, knowing that her heart was full of love and conviction. The strength and willpower to defy her father could only come from such a steadfast place.

He opened his eyes once more. 'If I agree to your demands, I expect to be able to add a few of my own conditions. It is only fair.'

Knowing David as she did, it would kill him to let a

woman dictate all the terms of an agreement. But if she did eventually decide to marry him, establishing some rules for their ongoing relationship was crucial. Give an English gentleman an inch and he would take the proverbial mile.

A wry grin appeared on his lips.

'Three conditions, to be precise, starting with this.'

His fingers tugged gently on the ribbons of her bonnet and the bow came undone. He pulled on the bonnet, catching several hairpins. He slipped a hand to her hair and with a flick of his wrist, pulled the pins out. Once he had the bonnet free, he took both bonnet and pins and tossed them on to the nearby couch. Several pins clattered to the floor. He took hold of her parasol and set it down next to her bonnet.

He laughed a deep and sensual laugh as he took hold of her hands and removed her gloves.

'It's a good thing Lucy is keeping watch close by, she may need to help you find the rest of the pins when we are done.'

'Done with what?' Clarice replied.

'This,' he replied, his voice confident. He slid a hand under the nape of her neck and bending his head, set his hot lips to hers. The warm of his lips and the heady scent of his cologne enveloped her in a world where she was held powerless.

'Open your mouth,' he murmured. A moment later his tongue swept past her lips and into her mouth.

They both moaned.

His mouth worked over her soft and pliant lips. She grasped the lapels on the front of his jacket and pulled him closer. The passionate words of the love letter, permanently seared into her brain, roared to life. His other hand slid down her back and when it reached her bottom, he gripped tightly and pulled her against him in an open display of possession.

Immediately she felt the hardness of his body. His strong muscles held her imprinted against his length. On the side of her hip, the tell-tale sign of his sexual arousal pushed against her. She gasped and tightened her grip on his clothes.

At twenty-three, she knew enough to understand the powerful effect she was having on him. Her heart thumped loudly in her chest. To know he wanted her, that he lusted after her was intoxicating. No champagne had ever made her feel this heady.

She kissed him back with every ounce of passion and desire she could muster. Temptation and instinct now overruled her previous resolve. Their hungry lips moved in furious agreement with one another. Danger and risk meant nothing compared to the flames his passion had ignited. Her whole body screamed for her to succumb to this moment, to give in to his masterful command.

'David,' she whispered as she released his lips and began to trail small butterfly kisses across his cheek and down to his jawline.

'Don't stop,' he moaned, and gripped her more tightly to him.

A shrill whistle broke the moment. He froze and growled with disappointment. He released his grip and stepped back.

'That was the warning signal. Someone is coming.'

Clarice hurried over to the couch and picked up her bonnet. A moment later Lucy's face appeared at the window and she tapped on the glass. David opened the door and Lucy poked her head inside.

'Some other guests are heading down to the lake, Alex and Millie are delaying them as best they can,' she said. Her gaze drifted from Clarice's bonnet to her ruffled hair. She smiled. The matchmaker's plans were moving along nicely.

'Give us a minute or two more and then come back,' he replied. Lucy nodded and quickly closed the door.

He walked over to where Clarice was picking up the scattered pins. She turned as he reached her side. Putting a hand into his jacket pocket, he withdrew a small box.

'It would soothe my wounded male pride if you would please accept this gift, Clarice,' he said.

He opened the box and took out a long gold chain. On the end of the chain was a black onyx orb held in place by a gold bail. He offered it to her.

She shook her head.

'Please understand I am serious when I say I need time to consider my future. If I take that necklace, you will expect me to wear it. You will think it confirms something which has not yet come to pass. Something which may not.'

She held a finger to her swollen lips. Allowing him to kiss her senseless had only further complicated the situation.

'I do not seek to tease you, David; you know I would never do that.'

He held out the necklace once more. 'Then take it. Take it as a symbol of our agreement. If you decide you do not want me, then you may give it back at some future point.'

Lucy rapped on the door once more and Clarice knew it was now or never.

'Very well then,' she sighed and, taking the necklace from him, held it in her hand. It was clear David was not happy, but she was adamant in her resolve.

She studied the black and gold pendant. While the gold was cold to her touch, the onyx was warm, quickly absorbing the heat from her hand. She hesitated, now unsure as to whether she should keep it. David placed a warm, tender kiss on the back of her neck, and she shivered. David whispered into her ear, his hot breath further threatening to muddle her mind.

'Do you like it? The onyx is the symbol of powerful love, which is why we have black on our family coat of arms. We Radleys love deeply those whom we take to our hearts.'

She turned and faced him. 'David, it's beautiful. Are those the Strathmore stars on the bail?'

He nodded. 'How perceptive of you. Yes they are; it's a family heirloom. I may not be my father's heir, but I am still his firstborn and I claimed this necklace especially for you. I hope to see you wearing it very soon.'

She nodded. He would continue to promote his cause for as long as it took to gain her acceptance. She slipped the necklace into her reticule.

'We have an agreement and I expect you to keep to your side of it,' she said.

As the necklace dropped to the bottom of the rose-coloured satin bag, David took hold of her hand.

'The final condition of our agreement, and this is probably the most important,' he said.

'Yes?' she replied, looking at her bare hand held within his.

'You have to do whatever is required to avoid Thaxter Fox. If he offers for you, you must refuse him. If your father starts to make arrangements for you to marry him, you must fight. Can you do that for me? For us?'

She rose up on her toes and placed a kiss on his cheek.

'I may not be certain of a lot of things at present, but rest assured I will *never* marry Thaxter Fox,' she vowed.

He gave her one last kiss on the lips, as Lucy knocked once more on the door, and whispered, 'Thank you.'

By the time Alex and Millie arrived at the summerhouse, Lucy had fixed Clarice's hair. Her gloves and bonnet were back in place. The two girls were seated serenely side by side on the couch chatting, while David stood a respectable distance away from them on the other side of the room.

Alex and David exchanged a furtive glance, but Clarice caught it. In response to Alex's raised eyebrow, David shrugged his shoulders.

'If you ladies would please make your way back up to the main garden party, David and I shall follow behind. It is getting late and no doubt Clarice's father will be looking for her shortly,' Alex said.

Clarice followed Lucy and Millie back to the garden party.

In her reticule lay the necklace David had given her. In her heart a tiny spark of something new had begun to burn.

Was it possible that she was falling in love with him?

Chapter Twelve

David was in no mood to haunt the parties and balls of London later that day, settling instead for an evening at his club. His private rendezvous with Clarice had left him in the oddest of tempers.

She had not refused his suit, but neither had she accepted him. 'Maybe' and 'perhaps' were such foreign concepts to a man who lived his life making unequivocal decisions that he didn't know what to think.

'At least she didn't say no,' he'd muttered to himself as he followed the rest of their group back to the garden party.

Now, hours later, he sat cards in hand trying to get his mind to focus on a game of whist. He looked across the table at his playing partner before making a slow study of the other players sitting on either side of him. All were several glasses of whisky and brandy further into the evening than him.

He smiled to himself. How ironic it was that Alex's marriage had been the spur for David's recent run of sobriety. Without his drinking partner beside him each evening, he had lost the taste for long evenings of drunken debauchery.

'Come on Radley, play,' said the man to his right.

David gave his cards a cursory glance. He always knew

exactly what he held in his hand at any time. He pulled a card out and threw it down on the table, confident that he had remembered the cards already played. The opposing pair of players put their cards down and reached for their drinks. He yawned.

When did gambling become so boring?

The final trick played itself out, at the end of which he drained his glass and got to his feet. He picked up his gloves and left the table.

While waiting for his hat and coat to be retrieved by a club servant, he checked his money. He had arrived at White's with fifty pounds in his pocket and he was leaving with exactly the same.

'It appears to be my day for not making any headway,' he said and headed out into the night.

He hailed a hack, but once inside could not decide where he wanted to go. Finally, he instructed the driver to head to Strathmore House. Even at this point in the season, someone from his family would be at home.

He chuckled at the thought of what his youngest sister Emma would say if he suddenly decided he wanted to continue reading to her at this late hour.

Sitting back in the seat, carefully avoiding putting any pressure on his slowly healing wound, he looked out into the London night.

Usually, when faced with a problem, the decisive David Radley met it head-on. If it had been a man causing him such grief, he would have tracked him down and sorted out matters like gentlemen. Occasionally a disagreement had resulted in a dark laneway brawl, but he never left a fight without having resolved matters.

Clarice Langham was an entirely different matter. Only the most dishonourable blackguard would coerce a woman into marrying him. She presented a problem to which he was forced to admit he had no skills or experience to overcome.

A sly grin formed on his lips. He might not know how to soften her resolve, but he knew someone who did. He rapped on the roof of the carriage and bellowed to the driver.

'Change of plans. Take me to George Street.'

Making a mental note to find a small gift for his youngest sibling when next he ventured out, he headed home.

Late the following morning, he travelled to Park Lane. After calling upstairs and saying a quick hello to his youngest sibling, he knocked on the door of Lady Caroline's sitting room. At this hour of the day he could count on his stepmother being busy with her needlework.

As he entered the room, the duchess put down her fabric and needle. She rose from the couch and greeted him with open arms. She brushed a kiss on the side of his cheek and gave him one of her special smiles.

'My beautiful boy,' she said.

He chuckled. For as long as he could remember, she had always called him her beautiful boy. Whatever terms of endearment she used for his brothers, she always reserved this one just for him.

'Your Grace,' he replied.

Her eyebrows rose in disapproval.

'Mama,' he corrected himself.

'Better. It's lovely to see you today; I was wondering when you would come and visit me. Lucy told me you were at the Brearleys' garden party yesterday, but you didn't attend the Archers' evening ball. Are you well?'

He nodded. 'Yes, I just didn't feel I could spend the evening at yet another gala ball. I think I may be suffering from mid-season fatigue.'

Caroline laughed.

'Have you put your head into your father's study yet? I think he will be back by now. How was the trip to your new estate? We have not had a moment to catch up on all your news. I can't wait to hear how things went.'

David smiled.

'Sharnbrook Grange is exactly what I would have chosen. Of course it needs work, and the bloodlines of the livestock will need to be re-established, but yes, I think I can make it a viable estate once more.' He nodded. 'And yes, I shall make sure I see Papa before I go. But the truth is, I came especially to see you.'

Caroline's brow furrowed as David began to rub the smallest finger on his right hand. Since childhood, it had been the tell-tale sign that he was decidedly uncomfortable about something.

She motioned toward the couch and he took a seat beside her.

'So?' she said, taking his hand before he could do further damage to his now-reddened finger.

He took a deep breath. 'It's about my mother.'

Caroline nodded.

'I need to understand why she left. Why she ran away.'

Caroline closed her eyes and fell silent. When she opened them, she blinked away tears.

'What can I tell you that you do not already know? My sister decided that she did not wish to marry your father and she left.'

'I need to know it all. I am certain that, being her sister, you know more about this than either Papa or I do,' he replied.

She looked away. 'Your father knows everything that I know regarding what happened then. I have no secrets from my husband. But you are correct in thinking that *you* do not know the whole story. Before I tell you, can I ask why? Why would you now want to drag out painful old memories? They cannot serve any purpose but to cause you distress.'

'I have decided to marry, and have made my feelings plain to Clarice in both letter and, as of yesterday, also in person.'

Caroline let go of his hand. 'Go on.'

He scratched his cheek, remembering the long hours he had lain awake the previous night. It was only in the early hours of the morning that it occurred to him he might have to put his own shadowed past behind him in order to move matters forward with Clarice.

'Clarice did not say yes, but fortunately she did not say no to my proposal either. I have thought long and hard about this, and while a major impediment in my suit is her father, the fact that I do not know the whole story of my birth also plays a part. I cannot fight a battle when I do not know how the war began.'

Caroline sat silent for a moment before she gave him a smile that filled him with hope. His beloved stepmother, whom he thought of as his true mother, could always be counted upon to bolster him in his occasional bouts of self-doubt.

'At five and twenty I suppose it is time. But wouldn't you rather hear it from your father?' she replied.

'No. I need to understand matters from a woman's perspective,' he replied.

'Yes, of course.'

※

David did not call in to see his father before he left Strathmore House, he was too numb with shock. He hailed a hack from out in the street and once inside, pulled the window blind down.

As he sat listening to Caroline explain how an earl's daughter had jilted the Duke of Strathmore for a penniless naval officer, he felt an icy hand take hold of his heart. Lady Beatrice Hastings had made a terrible error of judgement in assuming her paramour would accept her once he knew she carried another man's child.

Abandoned and alone, she had given birth to her son. And died.

Eyes closed and with his head resting against the thick leather squab of the carriage, the cruelty of fate's hand burned in his heart.

If his mother had come back to his father, gone through with the marriage and given birth to him as the Duchess of Strathmore, *he* would be the Marquess of Brooke, not Alex.

'Your father begged her not to call off their betrothal, but she refused. Even after she jilted him, he would have taken her back, forgiven her. No-one knew where she was; our families searched the length and breadth of the country. We only discovered your existence because the maid she took with her felt honour-bound to write to your father,' Caroline noted sadly.

At that moment she looked away, and would not meet his eyes. He suspected there was more to the tale, but seeing his beloved mama in such pain, he decided he had heard enough for the time being and took his leave.

'Bloody hell, he would have taken her back,' he muttered. No wonder his parents had kept the truth of the circumstances of his birth quiet for over a quarter of a century. He had lived his entire life believing his mother had been too scared to return to his father. That she had died of shame.

He was a bastard because she'd refused to put her own bitter disappointment aside and return to marry his father. Instead of giving her son all that by rights should be his, she had deliberately condemned him to a lifetime wearing the stain of illegitimacy.

'I am sorry you are dead, but I can never forgive you for what you did. How could you do that to your own child?'

Chapter Thirteen

In the early afternoon Clarice received a note from Susan asking her to walk in Hyde Park with her cousins at five o'clock. Considering how things had been between them of late, she decided it was prudent to agree.

At half-past three Bella knocked on the bedroom door and admitted Lady Susan Kirk.

She was alone.

Susan stood just inside the doorway and waited until Clarice had dismissed her maid.

'You are early; I thought we were going to the park at five?' Clarice said. She put down the book she had been reading and rose from the window seat.

Susan nodded. 'Yes, well, I wished to speak to you in private before my cousins arrive. There are important matters which we need to discuss and I don't think having them present will serve any useful purpose.'

In all the time she had known Susan, they had never shared more than the mere semblance of a friendship. They walked in the park regularly, they shopped together very rarely, but never did they share anything akin to a secret. She ushered Susan to the small drawing room across the hallway and after ordering some refreshments took a seat on the couch next to her.

Susan cleared her throat. Her hands were held tightly together in her lap.

'Firstly, I must apologise for my behaviour yesterday. I was rude to you in front of your grandmother and that was unacceptable. I offer my unreserved apology.'

Clarice watched as Susan slowly wrung her hands.

'Accepted. But only if you will accept my apology,' she replied.

Susan stared at her, her brow knitted in confusion.

'I spent time with the Radley girls during the past week at the cost of spending time with you. I treated you poorly and for that I am sorry. I know things are difficult for you at the moment, and it was wrong of me to abandon you.'

She took hold of one of Susan's hands and held it in hers.

'Now, let's have something to eat and we can go to the park as soon as the others arrive,' she said.

A small, terse smile formed on Susan's lips. 'Thank you; that was very kind of you, but it was not the main reason why I came here today. It's Mr Fox.'

An image of the small exchange between Susan and Thaxter Fox at the garden party leapt into Clarice's mind.

'Yes?'

Susan shifted uncomfortably on the couch and turned to Clarice.

'Do you intend to marry him?' she asked. Susan was never one to soften her words if she needed to know something.

Clarice was stunned. She sat for a moment feeling the overwhelming sense of nausea as it slammed through her body. What had Thaxter Fox told Susan?

'Because if you do, I don't want you to,' Susan continued. A single tear snaked slowly down her cheek.

A key in Clarice's mind turned and she suddenly understood.

'Has he proposed to you?' Clarice replied.

Susan shook her head. 'No. Not yet.'

She managed to stifle a sigh of relief. The prospect of Susan as the future Countess of Langham filled her with dread. There were a hundred other girls in London society better suited to the role. The Langham women down the years had maintained a reputation for being of the finest cut. Social, amiable and of good temper.

Susan was none of that. In all the time Clarice had known her, Susan had taken particular delight in causing discomfort and embarrassment to others. She had been the one at pains to ensure Millie knew of Clarice receiving the love letter from Alex. Susan had positively gloated over the look of shock on Millie's face.

Susan's confession of her feelings was an unexpected turn of events.

A footman knocked at the drawing room door and a maid carried a tray with teacups and some small oatcakes in. After setting the items down on a low table, they withdrew.

'I didn't think you liked tea,' Susan said, as Clarice picked up the pot and poured a cup.

Clarice nodded. 'I don't, but from the look on your face when you arrived, it was apparent you were in need of some.'

She handed the cup to Susan, content herself to break off a piece of oatcake. How was she going to handle this mess? If Susan thought Thaxter was planning to offer for Clarice instead of her, heaven knew what sort of mischief she would create.

'If I tell you a secret will you promise to keep it?' Clarice said. Susan put her cup down on the table.

'Go on.'

Until she could find a way to ensure Susan didn't become the next Countess of Langham, Clarice knew she would have to take her friend into her confidence.

If she knows I am not interested in Mr Fox, she will spend her time in pursuit of him while I think what to do about David.

Considering that rumours of Lord Kirk's financial straits were rife within the *ton*, she was prepared to wager her future on Thaxter Fox being aware of them.

'I don't intend to marry Mr Fox; I have another suitor,' she said.

As soon as the words left her lips, she began to regret them.

'You cannot mean David Radley? Tell me you are not seriously considering asking your father to allow you to marry him? Did you really go and check on your grandmother at the party, or were you meeting David?' Susan exclaimed.

Clarice took a bite of the oatcake and pondered her precarious situation. She had seriously underestimated Susan. There was nothing to stop her friend pounding on her father's study door and informing him that his daughter had had a secret rendezvous with David Radley.

The only solution was to lie and pray that Susan thought her incapable of such deception.

'I did go into the house to check on my grandmother, but I got waylaid by Millie and Lucy. Apparently the newlyweds had just had their first row and Millie needed somewhere private to go and cry. I went with them down to the lake, but I didn't see Alex or David. They must have been somewhere else in the garden.'

Susan nodded her head, picked up her cup and took a sip of tea.

'So you are not the least bit interested in Mr Fox?' she replied.

'No.'

'And what about Mr Radley?'

At that point Clarice remembered she was terrible at telling lies, but she was already too committed to change her mind. The irony of her confronting David over his attempt to lie to her about Mrs Chaplin was not lost on her, but she was quickly running out of options.

'It's not David Radley on whom I have my heart set, its Lady Brooke's brother, Charles Ashton,' she replied.

'Oh, I had no idea. I don't think I have ever seen you in his company,' Susan said.

Seeing the surprised look on Susan's face gave Clarice immediate hope. She leaned in and smirked at Susan.

'That is because we have made every effort to be discreet. He is likely to be the next Viscount Ashton *and* his father made an enormous fortune in India. You must know his sister had a king's ransom for a dowry. He is the perfect catch for a girl like me.'

She put a finger to her lips and gave a small 'Ssh' for added effect.

A sly grin appeared on Susan's face. The idea of Clarice outwitting the Radley girls and their obvious attempts to match-make with David would certainly appeal to her sense of spite.

'You sneaky little minx. Here was me thinking you were playing coy with those two potential suitors, when in fact you have been going behind everyone's back and making doe eyes at Charles Ashton. I can't wait to see Lucy Radley's face when she finds out.'

As she watched Susan clap her hands with uncustomary joy, Clarice felt her skin crawl.

'Of course, I am telling you all of this in strictest confidence. Only yesterday morning my father mentioned that he wants me to help Mr Fox find his feet in society. It was his idea for me to spend time with Mr Fox at the garden party.'

She gasped and took hold of Susan's hand.

'What if Papa has decided he wants me to marry Mr Fox! Oh Susan, what shall we do?'

Susan gently removed her hand from Clarice's grasp.

'Have no fear, Clarice, your secret is safe with me. Whatever I can do to facilitate your continuing romantic involvement with Mr Ashton, you only have to ask. In return all I ask is that you help me to secure Mr Fox's hand.'

Clarice nodded her agreement. If she did have to make a deal with the devil, at least this was one she thought she knew.

Chapter Fourteen

The following morning, David was woken by a resounding knock on his bedroom door.

'Go the hell away!' he bellowed. He had barely slept and was in no mood for early visitors. Bailey had slipped the newspaper under the door earlier in the morning, but otherwise stayed well away.

'No,' came the firm reply.

He opened one eye to see Alex standing over him, riding hat and gloves in hand.

Before he had the chance to grab the blankets and drag them back over his head, they were forcibly pulled from the bed and dumped on to the floor.

'Get up. You and I are going riding in the park this morning,' Alex said.

'Sod off, you bastard,' David replied.

'I shall do no such thing, and I can prove my parents were married when I was born,' Alex replied.

Others might have found such an exchange more than a little harsh, but the Radley brothers were steadfastly loyal to one another. Anyone who tried to tell them that they were not full blood brothers was met with firm resistance. And as brothers, they felt perfectly entitled to insult one another.

David sat up and scowled at Alex. It was obvious that his family had noted his failure to appear in polite society the previous evening. There was a price to pay for being part of such a close-knit family.

'Did Mama send you?' David asked.

Alex shook his head. 'Millie.'

David raised a quizzical eyebrow. 'Don't tell me your new bride has tired of your bedroom skills already?'

Alex laughed heartily.

David snorted and threw a leg over the side of the bed. Alex was not going to take the bait.

'My wife says I need to get out and expend some energy first thing in the morning. She muttered something about needing more sleep when I left her in our bed an hour ago. I plan to call in at the apothecary on Bond Street later today.'

'To get her a sleeping draught?'

Alex rolled his eyes. 'No, to get something to give her more stamina.'

David scratched the stubble on his chin, and chuckled.

'Why would Mama send me here?' Alex replied.

David sighed. 'Because I spoke to her yesterday and found out some rather unsettling news about my real mother. I always knew she ran off to avoid marrying Papa, but what I didn't know was she deliberately condemned me to a life of being a bastard. Did you know he would have taken her back, even if she had not been pregnant with me?'

Alex screwed up his face. 'Forgive me if this sounds a little callous. I cannot imagine what it must be like to know that everything I shall inherit would have been yours but for an act of unforgivable selfishness. But there is nothing any of us can do to change the past.'

David looked at his brother and nodded. He could never

begrudge Alex his luck in being born as their father's legal heir.

'My audience with Clarice went well enough. She took the necklace, but said if she were to wear it, it would be in her own good time. I'm suddenly and very acutely aware of how precariously balanced my situation is with her. For all these years my longing for her has been private. Only you, and more recently other family members, knew I was in love with Clarice. Now she knows.'

Even as he shared his concerns with his brother, David dared not voice his greatest fear. He had spoken to Clarice and confessed his love, but she had not responded in kind. Unrequited love would be the bitterest of pills to swallow after so many years of silent worship.

'I spoke to Mama yesterday, because I need to be certain of exactly who I am. At times I feel as if I am in a stranger's body.'

Alex tapped his fingers on the top of his hat. 'You have at times been a drunkard, a womaniser and a gambler, but *ton* society does not appear to condemn you for that. Only the fact that you were born on the wrong side of the blankets seems to be the problem for some. Of course once you have made a success of Sharnbrook and have plenty of your own money, you should see a few people change their minds.'

'I don't know about the womanising part; I am renowned for my gentlemanly discretion when it comes to matters of the fairer sex,' David replied.

A feigned cough was Alex's response.

Bailey knocked tentatively on the opened door, interrupting the discussion. At David's nod he began to assemble his master's riding clothes. Alex marched over to the window and threw back the curtains, flooding the room with the morning's light.

David covered his eyes against the sudden brightness.

'Come on; I shall be downstairs waiting. Those new horses

Father purchased last week have arrived at the Strathmore stables. He wants us to take them out for a morning run. There is little purpose to staying in your bed railing against life's unbearable misfortunes.'

With tired reluctance, David climbed off the bed and went about his toilette.

Half an hour later, he and Alex were racing each other down the Rotten Row in Hyde Park at breakneck speed. With his wound still not fully healed, he dared not risk stretching out on the horse. He spurred his mount on as best he could, but it was impossible to catch his brother. He roared with frustration as Alex left him behind easily. At the end of the run, Alex brought his horse about and trotted back to David.

'Still asleep, are we?'

David ignored the jibe. He and Alex shared a great deal of secrets, but he had not mentioned the incident with Thaxter Fox at the boxing saloon. He would deal with Mr Fox in his own way and in his own good time.

'They are good. Father is an excellent judge of horseflesh,' David remarked as he slowed his horse and drew alongside his brother.

Alex leapt down from his horse and gave it a congratulatory pat on the neck.

'Good boy.'

David sat back on his mount and surveyed the early-morning scene. The park was a hive of activity. Anyone who considered themselves an accomplished rider was out enjoying the crisp London air. He touched his hat to acknowledge a passing group of riders.

'Are you staying up there or coming down to walk with me?' Alex said.

'Sorry,' David replied and climbed down from his horse.

They began to walk, but only got a few short yards before David swore and stopped.

'What?' Alex asked.

David took off his hat. 'I've been going about this wooing of Clarice all the wrong way. I need a sound slap to the head.'

Alex laughed and swung a lazy arm toward David, who quickly sidestepped the poorly aimed blow.

'Ever the pugilist,' he said, through gritted teeth. He managed a smile, but the sharp pain of his injury had him struggling for air. Reaching a hand to where the bandages had stuck to his skin, he swore once more. Alex stood and looked him up and down, concern clearly etched on his face.

'What have you done?' he said.

David sucked in another painful breath. 'Fox,' he replied.

His brother moved quickly to his side, pulled up his shirt tail and revealed the fresh bandages.

'What did he do?'

'I fought him at Gentleman Jackson's; it was only after I left that I realised he had stabbed me,' David replied, surprised by how calm he felt.

'What! Why haven't you had the blackguard arrested?' Alex shouted, his face contorted with rage.

David held up his hands.

'The same reason you didn't tell Father about Lord Langham: there are innocent parties involved. How do you think it would look if I accused Langham's heir of trying to kill me? I can't get within ten feet of Clarice when her father is around; he is not likely to thank me for having his heir placed in irons.'

Alex opened his arms and looked to the heavens.

'So what are we going do? Fox has to be dealt with, you can't let him get away with this outrage,' he said.

'As I said I have been a fool up to now; allowing Langham to deny us a possible future. But no more. And as it suddenly occurred to me, what I need to do is protect Clarice at all costs. Fox can only have attacked me because he sees me as a threat to his chances of getting hold of her dowry.

'I have spent my whole life trying not to make the circumstances of my birth a matter of much import. Never taken offence when others have sought to judge me. And where has it got me? When it comes to the woman I love, most certainly nowhere. If Langham knew I had kissed Clarice, he would have my guts for garters.'

A knowing smile crept across Alex's lips. David groaned. Of course Lucy would have shared with Millie what she saw in the summer house. And once Millie knew, she would have told Alex.

David shook his head before fixing a hard stare at his brother.

'I am sick and tired of behaving correctly, of always being the one who has to make way for propriety's sake. From this moment on, I am going to do everything I can to win Clarice's heart and hand. And if her father doesn't like it he can go to the devil. I will protect what is mine.'

'So does this suicidal folly of yours actually involve a plan?' said Alex.

David nodded.

'Yes, though what Clarice will think of it is a matter for conjecture. She asked for time to consider her future, but I'm afraid I'm going to have to break my promise. I have to increase my efforts.'

With Thaxter Fox now using dirty guerrilla tactics, David knew he had no choice. As he walked slowly back along the track with Alex, he drew comfort from the knowledge that if he succeeded in his plans, he would have the rest of his life to make it up to Clarice.

'Millie told me Clarice will be at the Tates' rout this evening,' Alex replied.

'Good, then it begins tonight.'

※

Clarice sucked in another deep breath.

'I hope he likes this one,' she whispered to herself.

Behind her Bella was fixing the last hairpins into place. The simple coronet of small red roses was designed to complement her new evening gown. While her recent purchases had included several stunning creations designed to display her figure to its utmost, she had also erred on the side of caution and had one or two simpler muslin gowns made up.

With her father expected as a late arrival at this evening's function, Clarice and Lady Alice had chosen a modest white gown with a bodice ringed by red roses. A trail of roses then ran down the skirt to finish in a small bunch gathered at the hem.

Simple and elegant, it was very much suited to a young unmarried lady. Her father would no doubt approve, but in the depths of her heart she knew it was David she was dressing for this evening.

'You look so beautiful, Lady Clarice,' Bella remarked. Her maid had been in a happy mood all afternoon since Clarice had finally relented and given her permission to dispose of her old gowns. At her age and plump figure Bella would not be able to wear them, but Clarice knew a thriving trade in old gowns existed between the maids of the great houses. Bella would be able to make a tidy sum selling off Clarice's mourning gowns.

Clarice gave her reflection in the mirror one last look and rose from the chair.

David's confession in the summerhouse and his gift weighed heavily on her mind. Refusing his suit was the most practical and obvious response. It was what her father would demand.

But what about me?

To accept would change her whole world. She would gain a husband, but at what cost? Bella wrapped the warm cream cashmere shawl about Clarice's shoulders, but she hardly noticed. Lost deep in thought, she barely recalled leaving the house and arriving at the latest of the season parties.

'Clarice my dear, you are wool-gathering,' Lady Alice said, a few minutes after their arrival at Lord and Lady Tate's elegant home. Clarice turned and scowled, before realising she was standing in the middle of a crowded room.

'I do beg your pardon,' she replied.

Her grandmother smiled before leaning in close. 'David is here tonight. I saw him with his family when we arrived.'

Clarice shook her head. 'Papa will be here shortly. We cannot meet.'

'So that is your answer. You will spend the rest of your life avoiding the man you love just because you might displease your father?'

The man I love?

She stared at Lady Alice. 'Who said I was in love with him?'

The dowager harrumphed. 'Don't tell me I cannot see love when it is written all over a young woman's face. What other possible reason could there be for the change in your whole demeanour whenever David Radley's name is mentioned?'

A shiver fluttered between Clarice's shoulder blades and her mouth formed a small 'o' as she absorbed her grandmother's words. She put a hand to her lips, but a chortle escaped.

'Am I wrong?' Lady Alice continued.

'I don't know, truly I don't,' Clarice replied.

'Well, only you can decide, my dear. Just remember if you do come to the obvious and inevitable conclusion that you are in love with him, you need to take your father's opinion into account.'

Clarice nodded. 'Meaning that he would oppose any union.'

'Meaning you may have to elope,' Lady Alice muttered, as she turned from Clarice and greeted a friend who had just arrived.

She watched Lady Alice exchange small talk with her friend, her outward manner displaying no obvious sign that she had only a minute ago suggested her granddaughter elope with a duke's illegitimate son.

Clarice smiled. Her grandmother had a solution to every problem.

Could she do it? If she was indeed falling in love with David, was she prepared to defy her father? One single waltz in public, without her father being present, and a private meeting was as far as her bravery had thus far extended.

Looking down at her evening reticule, she remembered the onyx necklace she had slipped inside it before leaving Langham House for the ball. Perhaps Lady Alice was right. Why else would she have brought the necklace with her?

She followed her grandmother through the crowd, ever grateful that her father had a business meeting to attend before he joined them. The crowd parted as they neared the dance floor and she caught her first glimpse of David.

He was, as always, deep in conversation. The light from a nearby chandelier made his black hair shine. His elegantly cut evening jacket hugged his broad, muscled shoulders.

She swallowed.

Lady Alice's attention returned to her. 'See,' she whispered.

Clarice nodded as she beheld him in all his magnificence. He turned his head in her direction and started to smile, then something seemed to catch his eye and he stopped. He turned back to his companion.

Disappointment clutched at her heart. He had barely acknowledged her.

The reason for his supposed indifference was soon made apparent when beside her Lady Alice hissed, 'Lord save us.'

Clarice looked in the direction she was pointing her walking stick and her mouth went dry. Striding across the room, with Lady Susan Kirk following closely behind, was Thaxter Fox. As they approached, Clarice saw that they both wore the same supercilious expression on their faces. She wished she could be anywhere else.

'Good evening, Lady Alice. Good evening, Lady Clarice; what a comfort to see you both in possession of such good health that you could venture out to attend such a sophisticated occasion,' Thaxter said and dipped into one of his overdone bows.

Lady Susan gave a deep curtsy to Lady Alice, before stepping up and taking Clarice by the hand. She looked Clarice's clothing up and down and gave an approving nod.

'I am so pleased to see you here this evening, my dearest Clarice. And such a pretty gown. So much more suited to an unmarried miss than, dare I say it, the revealing one you wore to the garden party.'

Lady Alice snorted her displeasure. Clarice bit her tongue. Her grandmother had chosen the dress for the garden party.

'I am happy to see you and Mr Fox have become such fast friends,' she replied, remembering her side of the bargain.

Susan blushed. 'Well yes, we...'

'Your father introduced us a few weeks ago; Lord Langham looks to those who understand proper behaviour to help guide you. Lady Susan has given me a wealth of considered advice. Though I must say it was a pity you were unable to stay with us for very long at Lady Brearley's garden party. I found your sudden disappearance rather disappointing,' Thaxter replied, his voice turning to ice.

Clarice looked at Thaxter and Susan and quickly came to the conclusion that they had formed some sort of unholy alliance. She gritted her teeth in disgust.

That was not part of our bargain.

Clarice spied a footman bearing a tray of champagne glasses.

Ladies and gentlemen, actions speak louder than words.

She reached out and took two glasses. With a glance at her avowed teetotaller friend, she quickly downed the first and handed the footman the empty glass. A tsk of displeasure escaped Susan's lips, but Thaxter remained silent.

'Clarice!' Susan hissed, as she lifted the second glass to her lips.

Clarice gave her a wicked smile, which quickly disappeared as Lady Alice stretched out a hand and silently took the glass from her. As the effects of the first glass rapidly began to dull her senses, she was more than grateful for her grandmother's timely intervention.

'I believe you may have other priorities, Clarice,' Lady Alice said, and motioned toward David, who was making his way across the ballroom toward them.

'Mr Radley, a pleasure to see you as always,' Lady Alice gushed as he drew close. She held out a gloved hand to him and gave him the sweetest of smiles. Clarice looked at her grandmother and wondered just who this woman was standing beside her.

'Lady Alice,' David replied and placed a kiss on her hand.

The look of disgust on both Susan and Thaxter's faces had Clarice wishing she could break into a round of applause.

Oh, well played.

David gave Lady Susan the greeting which her status required, but ignored Thaxter. Clarice curled her toes up in her slippers. It was not every day that you actually witnessed someone being given the full cut. Silently she chastised herself for enjoying the uncomfortable atmosphere. Her late mother would never have approved of such behaviour.

David's gaze now fell upon her.

'Lady Clarice,' he said.

She wondered if only she heard the warmth and longing in his voice. She smiled. In the presence of the man who had declared his love for her, she was unable to find the requisite social mask.

'Mr Radley,' she replied, fighting to maintain her composure.

'Lady Alice, I would like to request your permission to dance with your granddaughter,' he said.

Thaxter stepped forward, and attempted to come between Clarice and David.

'Out of the question, Radley! You know Lord Langham's decree. His daughter does not dance with the likes of you.'

'You forget your place, Mr Fox. You might one day be an earl, but at this particular moment you are just a rude usurper. While my son is otherwise occupied, I shall be the arbiter of whether a gentleman is suitable or not to dance with my granddaughter. Mr Radley, you have my approval,' Lady Alice said, in a tone which brooked no argument.

A flash of anger crossed Thaxter's face. Twice in the space of five minutes, Clarice suspected he had revealed his true self.

'My sincerest apologises, Lady Alice, I meant no disrespect to you,' Thaxter replied.

Clarice took a deep breath. David was not just flouting the rules of their private agreement, he was tearing it to pieces. By rights she should be furious with him and refuse his request. But knowing how much satisfaction that would give Thaxter and Susan, she knew she couldn't deny him. Something told her that after tonight, she would never be able to deny him anything again.

If he could be brave enough to publicly invite her father's wrath, then the least she could do would be to stand alongside him. She held out her hand to him.

'I would love to waltz with you, Mr Radley, and who knows; if you are skilled enough, perhaps I may grant you a second dance this evening.'

His eyebrows rose just enough to show he agreed with this change in plans. They were in this together.

'I shall bring her back in time for supper,' he said. Lady Alice waved them away.

'You do know my father is expected here tonight?' she muttered as David led her toward the dance floor.

'Yes,' he replied.

The orchestra struck up the opening strains of a waltz.

'Are you ready to cross the Rubicon with me, Clarice?'

She looked at him and nodded, lamenting the fact that it was her father they would have to deal with, rather than a whole invading army. An army could be made to see reason.

He took hold of her hand and, placing the other hand on her waist, pulled her close. 'Come, let us enjoy the moment. I expect your father would not wish to see you at the centre of another scandalous public scene this season.'

She looked up and into his eyes. 'It's the aftermath that worries me. After what he did to your brother, are you really prepared to risk it?'

A look of shock appeared fleetingly on his face.

'I am not a fool, David,' she added.

He looked deep into her eyes.

'I know. And yes: for you, Clarice, I would risk your father's wrath.'

In that moment something shifted within her soul. Whether it was love or the realisation that David truly meant to fight for her, she could not discern. But she would do as he asked and join him in living in the moment.

The dance floor was crowded, but Clarice saw only David. Holding her tightly in his arms, he whirled her effortlessly around the floor. At every turn he took the opportunity to whisper terms of endearment to her. At first they were heartfelt and she found a tear in her eye, but as the dance progressed they became wittier, bordering on the ridiculous. When he whispered she was his warm cup of bedtime milk, she laughed with delight.

'Mr Radley, you are utterly outrageous,' she exclaimed.

His wide-eyed look of mock surprise made her miss the next step. A strong arm pulled her close, lifted her off the floor, and set her back down at exactly the spot where she should be standing. She had never danced with anyone who was so at one with the music. Skills could be learnt, but the way he moved was pure instinct.

If only this moment could last a little longer. A lifetime, perhaps?

She was no fool, though; nor was she one to hope for things to last forever. The music finally came to a close and David pulled her through the last turn. They stood hand in hand, staring at their entwined fingers, ever reluctant to let go.

'Thank you,' she said, when she finally withdrew her hands.

He lifted his head and she saw his Adam's apple move as he swallowed.

'I will not fail you and I shall never give up hope for us,' he said.

She looked at his face and saw his gaze was focused on something behind her. She frowned.

'My father?'

'Yes.'

'Angry?'

He nodded.

She paused for a moment, before bobbing a short curtsy to him and turning to face her father. David caught her by the arm and pulled her back to him.

'You are mine, no matter what he says or does,' he said, his voice resolute.

Clarice said nothing. Her heart was thumping loudly in her chest. She was unable to think. Slowly she walked away from him and toward her stony-faced father. Alongside Lord Langham stood Mr Thaxter Fox and Lady Susan Kirk.

She ignored her father's heir, reserving her gaze for Susan, her supposed friend. Tears welled in her eyes when she saw Thaxter and Susan exchange self-satisfied nods of the head. No-one needed to explain to Clarice how her father came to be standing at the edge of the dance floor, wearing a face like thunder.

As she reached the small gathering, she heard Susan whisper, 'Clarice, it takes a skilled liar to know when someone else is not telling the truth. You didn't really think I fell for your cock and bull story about Charles Ashton, did you?'

The other guests wandered away, chatting and laughing. Anyone else observing the small group gathered around Lord Langham would see nothing of any particular note. A kindly father come to take his socially awkward daughter home; some friends to bid her farewell.

A single tear slid down Clarice's cheek as her father silently took her by the arm and led her away from the dance floor. Lady Alice rose from her chair, gathered Clarice's things and followed them out into the night.

David stood, hands fisted by his side for as long as it took for the earl's party to leave. Lucy came to his side and after some convincing, he accepted her point that beating Thaxter Fox in the middle of a public gathering would not further his cause.

'Time for a tactical retreat; causing a scene will get you nowhere,' she said.

She took him by the arm and they walked together through the open garden doors and out on to the moonlit terrace.

Once outside and away from other guests, David released his pent-up fury.

'Bloody fool!' he swore.

'He only thinks he is doing what is right for his daughter,' Lucy replied, ignoring her brother's uncouth tongue.

He shook his head.

'Not Langham. Me. I'm the fool. I went too far. I should have stolen Clarice away and brought her out here, but no, I had to go and make a grand gesture in public. Once that filthy blackguard Fox showed Langham he was being challenged, he had no other option but to drag his daughter away.'

He leaned back against the wall of the house and in the darkness rested his head against the cold Portland stone.

'So what will you do now?' Lucy asked.

David sighed. His sister had removed her evening gloves and was nervously chewing on one of her fingernails. He might have been the one in love, but he knew Lucy was desperate for him to be successfully united with Clarice.

He pushed away from the wall, taking care not to strain his left side. Taking hold of Lucy's hand, he pulled it gently away from her lips.

'Don't do that, you know how much it annoys Mama,' he chided.

'Oh, what does a nail matter when your future is at stake?' she replied.

Lucy was always the one for melodrama when it came to matters of the heart, but he had to agree: this time she was right. The life he had planned was predicated on Clarice becoming his wife. No-one else would do.

He brushed a kiss on Lucy's forehead.

'Don't fret, dear sister, when did you ever know me to back away from a fight? I'm only just getting warmed up. There is still plenty of time left in the season – time to convince Langham that Clarice belongs with me.'

'Yes of course,' Lucy replied, clearly unconvinced.

'Come on Lucy, let's go back inside. The last thing I want is for either Thaxter Fox or bloody Susan Kirk to think they have ruined my evening.'

Chapter Fifteen

Clarice dressed early the following morning, fully intent on escaping Langham House and seeing Lucy. After last night's humiliation, she needed to formulate a new plan.

Reaching the bottom of the staircase, she heard raised voices coming from behind the door of the downstairs sitting room. Her father and Lady Alice were having a heated row.

She sighed. It didn't take much guessing as to the reason for their discord.

'I cannot believe you took her in hand in such a public way! You verily dragged your daughter from the ballroom and out into the night. How on earth do you expect her to show her face in society after that?' Lady Alice shouted.

'I don't!' the earl bellowed.

Clarice opened the door and was met by the sight of her father and grandmother facing off against each other like gladiators. Her father, hands fisted by his sides, faced his mother, while Lady Alice leaned on her walking stick and glared at him.

She stepped into the room and closed the door behind her, praying that the household servants had made themselves scarce.

'What do you mean, I won't be out in society?' she asked.

The earl shook his head, and let out a loud huff of frustration. He came to Clarice and took hold of her hand.

'I'm sorry about last night, Clarice; I should have handled matters in a more delicate fashion, but as you and your grandmother had openly defied me I had little other option,' he said.

Lady Alice harrumphed loudly. The earl shot her a look which could have frozen the River Thames before turning back to Clarice.

'My lack of social decorum aside, removing you from the party was for your own good. I am concerned that matters are developing in your life and you are not in control of your faculties,' he said, patting her gently on the shoulder. With Lady Alice armed and ready to go to war with him, it was apparent her father had decided that gentle tactics were in order, if peace was to be restored.

'Papa, there is nothing wrong with me,' she said.

He gave her one of his kind smiles. The ones that really meant *my poor, dear, mixed-up little girl.* He took her in his arms and wrapped her up in a fatherly hug.

Once his embrace meant comfort and protection; now it only made her angry. She pulled away and took a step back, glaring at him.

'You humiliated me last night; you had no right!'

Lord Langham closed his eyes and took a deep breath. At that moment Clarice would have given anything for her father to lose his temper with her. If he did, she could release the rage which simmered just below her calm exterior, consuming him in its wake.

He held out a hand. Dejected, she took it.

'Good girl. Now, I have spoken with Mr Fox and he has apprised me of various matters, which concern me greatly. I know you think me harsh, but I have decided that the best thing under the current circumstances is to send you home to the country.'

'No,' Clarice whimpered. 'Please, Papa don't send me away.'

'Henry no, that's not fair!' Lady Alice cried.

He looked from disappointed daughter to outraged mother.

'I will not have my decisions, nor my motives, challenged by either of you. Common sense must prevail. Clarice, your grandmother will take you home to Norfolk. While you await my arrival at Langham Hall I hope you will spend time contemplating your future. You leave today. *That* is my final word.'

Clarice looked at Lady Alice, who closed her eyes in silent resignation. There was no point in arguing with the earl when he was in this kind of mood.

'But it's still the season! What about my friends? What will they think?' she asked.

What about David?

'I don't care for the good opinion of your so-called friends, Clarice; you are my only concern. Please realise that you are not being punished. I am simply doing what I think is right for you. Trust me, someday you will thank me for this,' her father replied flatly.

'Why does everyone think they need to live my life for me? I might as well go back to Norfolk and stay there. You won't let me choose my friends; you won't even let me decide whom I should love. You won't let me live,' she said. Her lungs seized and she began to gasp for air.

The room began to spin slowly and Clarice reached out a desperate hand to steady herself. The room spun faster and faster as she clutched at thin air. Then her eyes rolled back and blackness overtook her.

Her last recollection was that of her father's strong arms wrapped tightly around her as she sank into his embrace.

'Nooo.'

※

David arrived at Langham House at the stroke of one o'clock the following afternoon. If ever he were to gain an audience with Clarice's father, he knew he had to adhere to the strict rules of society. A true gentleman would not dare to call at a private residence any earlier in the day, especially in the middle of the season.

A footman showed him to a small reception room just off the front entrance and after taking David's calling card, asked him to wait. Within a minute or so, the door of the room opened and he found himself in the presence of Lord Langham.

'Lord Langham, I would...' David said before the earl cut him off with a raised hand.

'Young man, I will not allow you to court my daughter. You may think poorly of me, as others no doubt do, but I will protect Clarice, no matter what the cost. If you truly hold any kind of affection for my daughter, I would ask that you do the right thing by her and cease your attentions.'

He offered David back his calling card, to which David shook his head.

'Please, I would like Clarice to have it; for her to know that I have called.'

The earl looked at him for a moment then put the card on the mantelpiece.

'Clarice is not here to accept your card. I have sent her home to my estate in Norfolk. It was foolish of her to offer your suit any encouragement. With luck, by the time she returns to London, she will have seen the error of her ways. My daughter is not for the likes of you. Good day to you, Mr Radley.'

And with that curt dismissal of his visitor, he turned on his heel and left the room. The footman quickly returned and silently ushered David out the front door.

As the door closed firmly behind him, David pulled out his pocket watch and looked at the time. He had been inside Langham House for less than five minutes, and his hopes lay in tatters.

As he put the watch back into his pocket, he was suddenly possessed by an almost overwhelming urge to climb back into his carriage, head to White's and quickly find his way to the bottom of a whisky bottle. His driver climbed down and opened the door of his carriage.

David took two steps before he stopped and checked himself.

He waved his driver away.

'Thank you, but I feel the need to walk; I shall hail a hack if I decide otherwise,' he said.

※

Henry Langham went back upstairs to his study, which overlooked the street. At the window nearest to his desk he watched as David made his way along Mill Street, crossing over at John Street. He pressed a single finger against the glass of the window, covering David's ever-retreating figure. When he removed his hand, David was a tiny speck in the distance. He stepped back from the window and lightly clasped his hands behind his back.

'Now then, Mr Radley, let me see what you are truly made of, because only the tested and bloodied hero can lay claim to the greatest prize.'

He turned from the window and went back to his work.

※

The midsummer rain fell steadily down, soaking David's black formal breeches and chilling his skin. If he had cared, he would have taken shelter out of the wet, but with his attention focused on the tight anger in his chest, rational thought eluded him.

A door opened and closed behind him. A scuff of boots on the stone steps preceded a familiar shape as it entered into his peripheral vision.

Alex took a seat on the step next to David.

'I could say something about you not living here anymore, but from the look on your face, I think this is the best place for you,' Alex said.

David sucked in a deep breath and looked away, his gaze focusing on a broken hinge on the stable door at the rear of the yard.

'You should get that fixed,' he replied, nodding toward the door.

'Yes, of course.'

If only everything else in the world were as easy to repair as a rusted hinge.

He turned to his brother. Alex had at least had the good sense to put on a coat before he came out into the rain. His blond hair was hidden beneath a top hat, giving him the look of a coachman. David scowled. He had taken his own hat off and it was sitting upturned beside him on the step, slowly gathering raindrops.

'Joining the four-in-hand club, are we? I didn't think your good lady wife would allow you that,' he said.

Alex looked down at his coat and chuckled. 'I grabbed the first thing I could find on the hook at the back door; this must belong to my new coachman.'

'How did you know I was here?' David replied.

After leaving Langham House, he had walked. Taking what little was left of his pride, he knew he needed a very long walk. Whether by subconscious design or sheer happenstance, his meandering journey had ended at the mews at the rear of the house he had until recently shared with Alex.

'Millie saw you from the sitting room upstairs and came to find me. I was going to wait until you knocked on the door, but since it started to rain and you didn't move an inch I thought it better that I come and collect you,' Alex replied.

David shifted uncomfortably on the hard stone step, noticing the rain for the first time. He frowned at the large muddy puddle which had formed to one side at the bottom of the steps. From the size of the dirty brown mess, it had been raining for quite some time. He looked up at the grey skies and snorted. The gloomy day matched his mood perfectly.

'She's gone,' he muttered.

'Where?' Alex replied.

'Norfolk. Langham sent Clarice to bloody Norfolk.'

Alex landed a heavy, consoling slap to David's thigh.

'Well, at least it's not Scotland. If you do decide to go after her, you will have only half the journey ahead of you that I had to make,' he replied.

'You conveniently seem to forget that I also made the mad dash back to London in order to save your heart after Millie rejected you Alex, so please grant me a boon and shut up.'

No amount of sympathy or attempted humour from his brother was going to lift him out of the dark depths in which he currently resided.

It began to rain even harder, ensuring that whatever part of him had managed to avoid the previous downpour was now thoroughly soaked.

'Can we please go inside? The way my luck is running today, I am likely to catch a cold and be dead by morn,' he said, getting to his feet. Alex nodded and stood. David bent down and picked up his hat, tipping it over and letting the water run out.

'A hatful of rain; could it get any worse?' he said.

Alex turned and opened the door, ushering David inside.

'Come on then; I think a couple of stiff whiskys and an afternoon in our old sitting room is in order. Lingering out here getting soaked to the skin won't do you or anyone else any good,' Alex replied.

David staggered to his bed somewhere around three the following morning. Alex and Millie had offered for him to sleep over at Bird Street, but he insisted he had to go home. The evening spent with his brother mulling over the earl's rejection of his suit and the sudden disappearance of Clarice, whilst downing several bottles of good French wine, was exactly the tonic his heart needed.

Alex, who had made such a mess of his pursuit of Millie, was the only person whom David felt truly understood his own situation. Knowing the pain Alex had gone through as he struggled to convince Millie he was serious about marrying her had brought the Radley brothers even closer together.

'You always knew there was a risk in pursuing Clarice,' Alex said, as he poured them both another glass of wine.

David took the wine and stared at his own glum face, reflected at him in the glass.

'Yes of course; I just thought that since I now have something to offer her, Langham would relent. I can see now I had allowed myself to become deluded. That for all my good intentions, I had stopped seeing the reality of the situation.'

'Which is?'

'He will never allow me to marry her. I have never been, nor will I ever be good enough for his daughter. Langham made his feelings clear, and just to ensure that I got the message, he sent her away.'

He swirled the glass and watched as his reflection blurred in the spinning wine.

The long evening of imbibing had taken the edge off his anger, but the humiliation still burned like acid in his mind. He had been illegitimate all his life, but today had been the first time he had truly felt he was less than a full member of the *ton*.

Alex sat forward in his chair. 'So what will you do now? You are not going to admit defeat, are you?'

'I don't know, which only goes to prove how poorly I had thought things through. What I do know is that I need to go home, get some sleep and pray that today was all a bad dream. Hopefully tomorrow I shall wake and none of this will have happened.'

He downed a large mouthful of the wine, and put the glass down. Getting to his feet, he suddenly felt the effect of the alcohol as a rush to the head. He swayed.

Alex offered a helping hand, but it was refused.

'Thank you, but as I am still capable of speech, I should be able to find my way out of this room without assistance.'

He stopped. 'The fact that you and I are sitting in this very room, as we did when your own life was such a mess, has not escaped me. My only regret is that you have had to return the favour.'

Alex shook his head. 'It's so bloody unfair.' He threw an arm around David's shoulder. 'Don't give up hope yet, dear brother; we Radleys have a knack of prevailing.'

David squinted as he struggled to focus his gaze on Alex's face.

'You won because you played by the rules, but since I am not considered by some to be a full member of the Radley family, I think it's time I changed tack. If I'm not good enough to be part of the team, then I shall just have to play outside of the rules. Bastard is as bastard does.'

'David, promise me one thing,' Alex replied.

'What?'

'You won't go running off after Clarice tonight. I don't want to have to come and haul you out of a ditch somewhere on the Great North Road.'

David buttoned up his jacket and managed his first real smile of the evening.

'Don't worry, brother, I shall return these borrowed clothes of yours in good order; I know your dear wife chose them. And no, I won't be giving anyone the satisfaction of thinking I rode off into the night while drunk and broke my bloody neck because Langham won't play fair.'

Chapter Sixteen

The Langham family coach pulled out of the coaching inn at Fakenham, Norfolk a few days later. The carriage jerked as the fresh horses took up the slack, causing Clarice to stir from her sleep.

'Where are we?'

'Fakenham, my dear,' Lady Alice replied from the seat opposite. She reached into the cloth bag next to her and pulled out a small bread roll. She offered it to Clarice.

Clarice turned her head away. 'Thank you but no. The movement of the coach has left my stomach unsettled. Food is the last thing I need.'

Lady Alice put the roll back into the bag. 'You need to eat something, Clarice. We have been on the road since Monday and apart from a piece of dry bread at supper last night you have not eaten anything. It cannot be good for your health. Would you at least try and have some barley water? You don't want to faint again.'

She offered a flask to Clarice, who waved it away before pulling her blanket up around her shoulders. 'Perhaps in a little while. In the meantime I think I shall just try to sleep.'

Lady Alice picked up her embroidery and continued to

work on the piece she had started not long after they set out from London.

'You do know your father is not doing this to punish you? He said so himself.'

Clarice closed her eyes and swallowed. If exile was not punishment then what was? And how could he possibly think she would thank him for sending her away?

'He thinks I am not right in my mind,' she replied sadly.

After she'd fainted in the sitting room, her father had carried her to her bedroom and sat with her until she regained consciousness. Tears and pleading had got her nowhere. Her dizzy spell had only further confirmed his decision to send her away.

Lady Alice leaned across and put a hand on Clarice's knee. 'He is only concerned for your wellbeing. You are in a delicate state of mind and he fears you are being influenced by others into doing what they want, rather than what is good for you.'

'There is nothing wrong with me; I simply hadn't eaten since the day before. You know what is really happening here. Thaxter Fox and Susan Kirk have poisoned Papa's mind. They don't want me to marry David, so they have conspired to ensure it doesn't happen. I have been sent away in the hope that David may change his mind and give up on me.'

'And what of you, Clarice; what do you want?' her grandmother said, sitting back in her seat.

The last cottage in the town disappeared from view and open fields now lay stretched for miles either side of the road. Clarice lay back in her seat and stared out the nearest window of the carriage.

'To be honest, I don't know,' she replied.

In her heart she knew she was in love with David. But love, even with all its complications, was unfortunately the easy part. It was better she kept the truth hidden from Lady Alice.

'Then perhaps you ought to trust your father's instincts.

This time away from London might be exactly what you need,' Lady Alice said.

Clarice massaged her temples with her thumb and forefinger. The past days had seen her emotions stretched to their limit. From the highest of highs when David had held her in a passionate embrace, to the utter despair of discovering Susan had betrayed her.

To know that Susan had put her jealousy ahead of their friendship burned deeply. She sighed and shifted on the seat. Who was she trying to fool? Theirs had been a friendship born of mutual need and nothing more; Susan had done exactly what she needed to secure her own future.

She had set her sights on Thaxter Fox and the promise of being the future Countess Langham. Clarice doubted the union of Thaxter Fox and Susan Kirk would be a happy one, but since she had already seriously misjudged Susan, who was to tell?

Outside the carriage the clouds overhead were grey and threatening. With luck the travellers would arrive at Langham Hall before the heavens opened. Nothing made her travel sickness worse than being on the road in the middle of a rainstorm. Heaving the contents of her stomach out on the side of the road in the rain had been the low point of her last journey back to Norfolk; one she did not wish to repeat.

She sat up in the seat and blinked hard, trying to clear her mind. The smell of the sea had awakened her senses and sleep would no longer come. Very soon she would be home.

Unless her father changed his mind and sent word from London that she could return, she was stuck at her family seat. Defying her father and leaving Langham Hall would be foolish to say the least. She could only pray that fate would intercede on her behalf.

At least while she was in Norfolk she would be away from Thaxter Fox, a small blessing for which she knew she should be grateful.

'Would you mind if I borrowed your writing desk?' she asked, pointing to the rosewood box stored under Lady Alice's seat. She had been sent to the country, but if Clarice remembered his words correctly, her father had not forbidden her to send letters.

She pushed the blanket off and bent down to pick up the handle of the box. Lady Alice raised an eyebrow.

'I shall have that drink now, if you don't mind,' Clarice said, depositing the box on the seat next to her. While she didn't know the exact address of David's rooms, a letter sent to Strathmore House would no doubt find its way to him.

Lady Alice handed over the small leather-covered canteen and Clarice took a sip of the lemon barley water. She shuddered as it went down her parched throat. Horrid and bitter though it was, it was better than nothing.

'Thank you,' she replied.

Clarice smiled. Who knew what possibilities could eventuate from this letter? As soon as David discovered where she had gone, she knew there was every likelihood he would follow.

She opened the writing box and set it on her knee. With pen dipped in ink, she sat and stared at the blank page. What was she to write?

Come, save me from my evil father, who has sent me away?

She pursed her lips. Unlike David, she was not certain that she could pen a love letter. Not only did the words fail her, but truth be told, she was still uncertain of how to proceed. Was she ready to share with him everything of her life, all of her secrets?

The look of pain which crossed his face when she refused to put on the necklace had haunted her dreams. A reciprocal declaration of love would have been the easy way out. It would have made him happy.

By telling him she was at Langham Hall, it would no

doubt create an expectation in his mind. An expectation she was not entirely sure she could meet.

Could she be that cruel?

The carriage hit a large hole in the road and swayed. A fresh wave of nausea hit her stomach and the decision was made for her. She put the pen back into it the holder and closed the writing desk.

'I shall think on things before I send any missives.'

※

David gave a short flick of the reins and urged his horses on. The more quickly he got to Sharnbrook, the sooner he could inspect his new livestock. Bannister's letter informing him of their arrival had been the much-needed catalyst for pulling him out of his dark mood.

With Clarice now resident in Norfolk, there seemed little point in making further overtures to Lord Langham. Instead David had spent the days since his ill-fated meeting with Clarice's father organising his financial affairs and settling his household purchases.

'So when does the ram arrive?' he asked his steward several hours later as he cast a studious gaze over the new flock. Bannister looked at him, and gave a nod.

'The lads will bring him up the river Ouse from Bedford to just south of the village, then cart him the rest of the way. He should be here later in the week,' he replied.

David saw the sly grin on his steward's face and chuckled. They were both excited at the prospect of breathing new life into the estate.

'Very good, Bannister,' he replied.

Once back inside the manor house, David pulled out his satchel of papers, ready to finish the last of his current pile of correspondence.

He sat back in the chair and looked out into the garden. As

was so often the case when he was alone, his mind drifted to Clarice. For more years than he could count, she had never been far from his thoughts.

It was a warm summer's day, not unlike the day when he had fallen in love with her. He had been sitting reading a book in the large rear garden at Strathmore House, pretending not to listen as Lucy and Clarice played at a game of 'guess your future husband's name'. Lucy, for her part, had settled on the safe option of Harold and was pressing Clarice to decide whom she would marry. When she refused to reveal his name, Lucy threw a small cushion at her.

The ensuing squeals and giggles caught David's attention and he looked up.

At that moment a ray of afternoon sunshine filtered through the ornamental English holly bush which stood nearby and bathed the garden in a surreal golden light. The air surrounding Clarice was full of tiny specks of pollen and dust, made visible by the sun.

She lifted her head and, staring straight at him, softly said, 'David'.

The roar of Lucy's laughter momentarily broke the spell. 'You're going to marry David!' she squealed with obvious delight.

Blushing, Clarice had turned away, but not before her gaze had irrevocably pierced his heart.

Yes.

A small voice in the recess of his mind had spoken, and from that day on he was smitten. He closed his eyes, recalling her laughter when they'd last danced together. Hope had flared once again in his heart. More telling, however, was the look of despair on her face when Lord Langham took Clarice from the dance floor.

At that instant his desire for her had roared into flame. She hadn't attempted to disguise her anguish at being parted from him. The pained look on her face, which he knew from bitter experience could only come from the deepest place in her heart, confirmed once and for all that she loved him. He knew it in the depths of his soul.

Picking up his pen, he dipped it in the inkwell. For the time being he would focus his energy on urgent estate matters, ensuring that every other aspect of his life's sphere of control was in order.

Considering he had broken the terms of their agreement, he found himself oddly pleased that Clarice for the moment was at a distance. At least she would now have the time she had asked for in which to consider her future. When next they met he would press her for the answer he so desperately needed.

With Clarice at her father's estate, she was away from London and, more importantly, away from Thaxter Fox. As long as she remained at Langham Hall he could draw comfort in the knowledge that she was safe.

Chapter Seventeen

As the late afternoon sun sank to the west, the Langham family coach passed between the ancient stone pillars which stood either side of the long drive leading to Langham Hall.

Climbing down from the carriage, Clarice felt the first chill of the North Sea wind on her face. She shivered. Coming home should be a happy occasion, but as she looked up and took in the view of the house she felt little joy. The towering grey stone walls, with their haphazard patchwork of soft green ivy, mirrored her own confused state.

In her childhood she had loved the Hall, as it was known to all in the local district, imagining how her ancestors had fought battles to defend their precious home. The many happy hours she'd spent roaming the estate with children of her father's tenants, coming home at all hours grubby and hungry, were some of her fondest memories.

But when she turned twelve, her parents had appointed a new governess and all childish games were brought to an end. She was to be a lady, and only ladylike behaviour was now acceptable. Her former friends became strangers, made to bow and call her Lady Clarice.

The housekeeper greeted them, interrupting her reverie.

'I am so sorry for the manner of your reception, my lady; we had no idea you were coming. If we had known, the household staff would have assembled to greet you. I shall send immediate word to the village and have the rest of the servants here as soon as possible,' she said.

Lady Alice gave her a forgiving smile.

'Our journey home was a spur-of-the-moment decision and we had no time to send word. Whatever accommodations you have for us tonight will suffice. It is too late to call the staff back from the village; they may return tomorrow.'

Clarice followed Lady Alice into the house and heard the housekeeper close the front door behind her. The only thing missing was the sound of a key being turned. The Hall was to be her prison until her father decided on her future.

'Do you think you could keep a spot of supper down?' her grandmother asked.

Clarice nodded. 'But first I need to attend to my hair and face.'

Lady Alice gave her a kiss on the cheek. 'I know the journey was difficult for you, my dear. I hope that within an hour or two your stomach will settle. Go and lie down and I will send word when supper is ready.'

After the long, draining journey, Clarice had little interest in doing much else. The lure of her soft, warm bed beckoned.

With her maid following hard on her heels, she made her way to her bedroom. As soon as she opened the door, she encountered a sharp reminder of how many months it had been since she and her father had left for London.

Her bed and all the bedroom furniture were hidden under large Holland covers.

'I suppose that is to be expected; we weren't due to arrive back here for another month or so. I shall go downstairs and see what can be done to set your room to rights,' Bella said and left the room.

Clarice walked to the window, slowly unbuttoning her coat. Her room overlooked the garden and the thick woods beyond the stone garden wall.

Her first smile in many days found its way to her lips. Without her father in residence, she would be free to roam the woods and sit at the water's edge of the nearby lake. Deep and well stocked with wily tench, it presented the perfect place to hide away from her troubles.

Her mind was still in turmoil; and she knew that even once her bed was set to right, sleep would not come.

'I shall find my brushes and paints,' she said.

❧

Silence hung in the room.

Lady Alice picked at a small bunch of grapes hanging over the side of the ornate gold fruit bowl, pulling one small grape free and rolling it slowly between her thumb and her forefinger.

'It is going to be a long, tiresome evening if I am the only one making any attempt at conversation,' she said, arching an eyebrow.

'Sorry,' Clarice replied, as she continued to push her spoon around her bowl of soup.

Out of the corner of her eye she could see the worried look on her grandmother's face.

'You should try and eat something, my dear.'

She nodded. Her travel-weary head and stomach had finally settled, but the food held little appeal. In the hours since their arrival, she had moped about the house, only agreeing to come to supper in order to remain in Lady Alice's good graces.

Without her father at home, she was adrift. She was still angry with him, but she also missed him.

'Much as I resent being packed off to the country in the middle of the season, I think we should take a happier view of the situation,' Lady Alice continued.

'What do you mean?' Clarice replied.

'I don't think you are certain as to what you actually want. You have dallied with both Mr Fox and David Radley. Neither gentleman, I expect, would be happy to know you had been trifling with them.'

She examined the grape she'd spent the better part of a minute rolling in her hand, and put it down on the table. Sitting back in her chair, she fell silent.

Clarice put down her spoon and stared at her grandmother. Had she just been branded a flirt?

'I did not think I had given Mr Fox any sort of encouragement for him to form a *tendre* for me,' she replied.

'That is not what I had gathered from the afternoon you spent with him at Lady Brearley's garden party. In fact, several guests noted how well you and he seemed to suit. I expect there are those who would not be surprised to hear of a betrothal between you.'

Thaxter Fox? Thaxter Fox!

Clarice was adamant she felt nothing for Thaxter Fox. How could others have leapt to the preposterous conclusion that she would marry her father's heir?

She had assumed her father's *only* reason for sending her back to the country was to get her away from David. Had she underestimated her father?

Please Papa, not Thaxter Fox.

'I think David is going to offer for me; he had intended to speak to Papa this week,' Clarice replied bravely.

'Fool,' the dowager replied.

Clarice nodded her head. 'Out of respect, I would not dare to say that of my father, but yes, I don't believe he is fair in his conduct toward David.'

Lady Alice picked up her knife and fork.

'I refer not to your father, but Mr Radley. Though I must agree that your father could do with a cuff behind his ear every so often. What I meant was the folly of David considering to offer for you and expecting your father to accept him at the first.'

Clarice's hopes fell. Lady Alice no longer supported her cause.

'If I were him, I would have bundled you into a carriage and spirited you away to Scotland the second I thought *you* would accept me. His father does have a rather large castle in which he could hide you.'

'What?' Clarice stammered.

'Well, of course. Fine young man though he may be, the circumstances of his birth make it more difficult for him to utilise the prescribed ways of attaining such a prize as you. Stealth and a fast horse should be the means he uses to claim you. Once he has you alone in a carriage, that would be grounds enough for the rest of society to demand a wedding.'

Clarice sighed. She doubted David would find her grandmother's solution to his liking. To elope was unthinkable.

'He would never do such a thing. His honour means everything to him.'

'Even at the cost of losing the woman he professes to love? If that is the case, you may have been spared marriage to a man who does not know the value of what he has.'

'He is not like that; I know he truly loves me,' Clarice replied.

Her brow furrowed at her own remark. Defending David had become something of a habit of late.

One thing she did know for certain: her grandmother was right. Spending time away from London and all its distractions would give her time to think.

A knock at the door heralded the arrival of the main course. A small platter of roasted root vegetables and a rather small chicken with apple and walnut stuffing were the evening's meagre offering. The footman placed the platter in between the two women and then left.

Lady Alice chortled. 'I shall give cook a list of things to purchase in the village tomorrow morning so you can have some of your favourite things.'

'Thank you. And the chicken is fine; I have always been partial to a simple meal. Much of the extravagant fare in London does not agree with my constitution,' Clarice replied.

For the next hour they enjoyed a comfortable meal, exchanging small talk on the other happenings in London. At the end they both rose and adjourned to a nearby sitting room.

She took a seat in a comfortable chair by the fire, while her grandmother sat down in her own special chair opposite. Lady Alice picked up her embroidery. Clarice smiled. Her late mother had always had a gift for beautiful needlework, and had been even more skilled than the dowager countess. Sadly, she had not passed on her gift to Clarice.

Her grandmother raised her head and looked at Clarice's empty hands.

'Why don't you go and find a suitable book in the library, my dear, and bring it back here? I know there is no point in asking you if you have any needlework to go on with.'

Clarice rubbed her hands together in front of the fire. 'Yes, Grandmamma, you may rest assured in the certain knowledge that I shall never take to the needle with anything other than a healthy degree of reluctance. If ever I marry, my house shall be infamous for its lack of fancy table runners.'

Lady Alice snorted loudly.

'Oh my dear girl, it does me a power of good to see your old spark coming back,' she said. Her laughter settled to a soft chuckle and she took hold of Clarice's hand and held it.

'Something tells me that here at our family home, you will soon discover the answers that you seek.'

'Thank you for being so patient and understanding with

me; I know it isn't easy. And yes, it is good to be home,' Clarice replied.

Later, as she lay in her bed, she decided Lady Alice was right. She would accept this time away from David and her father as a blessing and put it to good use. With luck her heart would find the answer she sensed was just out of reach.

Chapter Eighteen

It was barely light when Clarice made the pilgrimage to her mother's grave.

The dell was to be found over a small rise on the far side of the front drive of Langham Hall. Within the sheltered dell was a stone chapel, used for generations by the family. Lady Elizabeth Langham had been laid to rest in the private graveyard next to the chapel.

Wrapping a warm scarf around her neck and pulling on her favourite pair of soft kid leather gloves, Clarice closed the front door of Langham Hall behind her and slipped quietly away. After the turmoil of her row with her father and her sudden exile to Norfolk, she needed solace.

A well-trodden path ran through the trees and ended at the door of the chapel. Stepping off the path, she crossed to the most recent headstone and stopped.

Three years, yet at times it felt like fifty since her mother had left her life.

Suddenly and so tragically.

'I'm sorry I have not been to visit since the funeral, Mama; I didn't think it was right.'

She closed her eyes and fought back tears.

'No, no that is not the truth. I haven't been here because I was afraid. Afraid of what you would say. I still am.'

Dropping to her knees before the gravestone, she placed her hands together. The time had come to ask for forgiveness.

'If I could do anything to change what happened that day, you know I would. If I could pay a thousand kings' ransoms in order to bring you back, I would. I should never have shown you that letter; I should have burned it. I am sorry I failed you, Mama.'

When the first of the tears fell, she welcomed it. She brushed her thumb against her face and looked down at the tear glistening in her hand.

'I miss you every day,' she whispered as the second tear fell.

Later, when there were no more tears left to cry, she felt a calm peace settle within her mind. She had taken the first tentative step in facing the black despair of her grief. Sitting back, she pulled her knees up to her chest. With arms wrapped around her knees, she sat staring at Elizabeth's headstone.

Beloved wife and mother.

A smile came unbidden to her lips. The words were true. Lady Elizabeth Langham had been well loved, by both her husband and her daughter.

'Papa is angry with me,' she addressed the headstone. 'He has banished me from London because I danced with David Radley.'

Countess Langham had always held a special place in her heart for David. More than once, Clarice had seen her mother single him out for special attention.

She chuckled softly.

'You should see him now, so handsome and serious. And in love. With me, of all people; how unexpected is that? Or perhaps you always knew.'

She picked at a nearby blade of grass until it came free in her hand.

Twirling the grass between her fingers, she opened her heart.

'He wrote me a beautiful love letter. Perhaps when next I visit you may permit me to read it to you. It is truly…'

She placed a hand over her heart as she fought for composure. David's words reflected so much of how she felt about the loss of her mother. Of the longing.

She swallowed deeply before attempting to continue.

'Papa is against our union. He says it is because David is not right for me, but I know that is not true. I've thought long and hard about it over the past few days and if David still wants to marry me, then I am his. I am stronger than Papa thinks. David has helped me to believe in myself once more. Mama, I love him.'

She put a hand to her chest, feeling the shape of the onyx orb hanging on the chain between her breasts. Unpacking her things the previous night, she had come across David's gift at the bottom of her reticule. She had taken it out, looked at it for a moment and then slipped the gold chain over her head.

The moment the cold orb touched her skin, she knew her heart was sealed with love. She would wear the necklace always. A full and rich life as David's wife now beckoned. Only her need to make peace with her mother could hold her back.

The Madame had been right, love was for those brave enough to claim it.

A bird in a nearby ash tree whistled its morning tune. London, for all its people and historic buildings, lacked the subtle beauty of the Norfolk countryside. She leaned back, arms outstretched on the grass behind her, and looked up.

On a low branch of the tree she saw the bird.

'Hello,' she said.

The bird hopped across the branch it was on and on to the next one. It turned its head and looked at her.

Clarice stared back. She could not recall having seen a bird with such grey and black plumage before. Its rippling whistle was certainly not one she had ever heard. She laughed uncertainly at the realisation that while she was studying the bird, it was studying her back.

'Odd,' she mused.

'What is odd?' Lady Alice said.

Clarice's head shot round and she saw her grandmother standing in the doorway of the small chapel.

The dowager walked slowly toward her.

'How long have you been here?' Clarice asked.

'Long enough. I come here early every morning during summer. I like to spend time praying in the chapel before talking to your grandfather.'

She nodded in the direction of a huge tombstone a yard or so away from Elizabeth's grave. The space between the two graves was reserved for Lady Alice and for her son. They would sleep next to their respective spouses in death.

Clarice got to her feet.

'What did you hear?' she asked.

Lady Alice came and took hold of her granddaughter's hand.

'Enough to have a greater understanding of what has troubled you since your mother's death. I know it was wrong of me to listen to your private conversation with Elizabeth, but I am not sorry that I did.'

Clarice looked into her grandmother's eyes. Lady Alice had been instrumental in helping her find the courage to finally face her grief and guilt. She owed her the truth.

'Just before Mama died, I received a letter from a firm of solicitors, they represented the estate of...'

'No!' Lady Alice roared. 'Do not say his name!

Her body shook as tears welled in her eyes.

'He caused so much heartache within this family; I never want to hear his name again. Especially not in this most sacred of places,' she said sadly.

Clarice stood dumbfounded. Lady Alice knew the truth of her real sire.

'Can you at least tell me how this came about? I thought my parents were devoted to one another. How could my mother betray Papa in such a way?'

Her grandmother looked down at the stone path.

'A year or so before you were born, your mother had a miscarriage. In his grief, your father blamed her for the loss of his heir. They separated for a time, during which your mother found comfort with someone else. She fell pregnant with you.'

'And my father was forced to take her back to avoid a shocking scandal?' Clarice replied, angry with her mother for such a callous deception.

Lady Alice's head shot up and she gripped Clarice's hand tightly.

'No, no. Your father begged her to come back to him. He promised that no matter what happened, he would claim you as his own. He never stopped loving your mother; it just took him some time to realise what a fool he had been. As far as your parents and the rest of your family are concerned, you are his daughter.'

'No wonder Mama was in such a state when I showed her the letter.'

'Do you wish to tell me about your mother's death?' Lady Alice asked.

It was time to share the awful truth of that day with someone she trusted.

'We had a frightful row. She was terrified someone would find out. I ran from the room. Mama followed me and she tripped on the stairs. I tried to catch her, but I was too late. It was my fault she died.'

Lady Alice's shook her head.

'Oh, Clarice no, it was an accident. Please don't tell me this has been what has kept you from confiding in your father and me all this time? You cannot blame yourself for your mother's death.'

'What it says in the letter about me; you know what that means, don't you?' Clarice replied.

Her grandmother pulled her into her arms and whispered in her ear.

'It means that you are a daughter of the House of Langham and no bloody missive from a solicitor can change that, especially if you believe it in your heart. It means that you are now and always will be *my* granddaughter. I shall take violent issue with anyone who tries to say otherwise.'

'Yes, Grandmother,' a relieved Clarice replied. She reached up and wiped away a tear from Lady Alice's cheek.

'All this happened such a long time ago, I had hoped never to hear of it again. Promise me that you will continue to keep this a secret. If anyone ever discovered the truth, you, your father and this family would be crushed. Society does not treat women well when it comes to this kind of situation. You would be ostracised.'

'I promise,' Clarice vowed.

'Good girl; now can we please go and have some breakfast? These early-morning starts make me rather hungry.'

They walked arm-in-arm from the dell.

After breakfast Clarice retrieved her paint box from a storage cupboard and sorted through her paintbrushes. She found a stack of clean linen canvases at the back of the cupboard and chose several small ones to use.

Painting was one accomplishment she knew she excelled in. Clarice's landscapes were good enough for her father to have several of them framed and displayed in both their Norfolk and London homes.

Her morning had been filled with revelation and it was good to spend time alone with familiar objects and tasks. It was well past midday before she made her way back downstairs and spoke to Lady Alice.

Luncheon was spent discussing every topic apart from the events of the morning in the dell. Supper and the rest of the evening ran to the same pattern.

By the time she retired to her bed, Clarice understood that as far as Lady Alice was concerned, the matter was closed.

On the following morning, she waited until after her grandmother had returned from the dell before venturing to visit her mother once more. She took with her a fresh bouquet of her mother's favourite apricot roses, gathered from the gardens. She tied them with one of her white satin ribbons and placed them in front of Elizabeth's headstone.

Taking a seat on the grass, she spent the next hour or so talking to her mother, telling her all the things that had happened in her life since they'd parted.

On the third morning, as soon as she reached the graveyard, she heard the now-familiar bird whistle. Looking up into the tree she saw the bird.

'Hello again,' she said.

The bird chirped once more and then flew from the tree, landing on top of her mother's headstone. In its beak it held a tiny twig.

Clarice stood still and for a moment, bird and young woman stared at one another.

'Mama, I know you always said that portents and visions were silly superstitious nonsense, but perhaps that was only in this life. If you are listening to me, and I am choosing to believe you are, then I want you know how sorry I am. That I understand you were only trying to protect me.'

The bird chirped.

'I ask for your forgiveness and your blessing.'

A gentle breeze moved in the dell and the tree-tops stirred. The bird flew away. She watched as it landed high in a distant tree, where it began to sing once more.

She walked the short distance to her mother's gravestone. There on the top lay the twig the bird had carried in its beak. She swung round and tried to catch a final glimpse of the bird, but it was gone.

She tentatively picked up the twig and examined it. Apart from a small notch part way along its length, it was a plain ash tree twig. To her it was priceless.

While ancient Greek gods had conspired to send their messages to earth in the form of lightning and great storms, Clarice felt she had been sent a simpler message of love and forgiveness. There, alone in a quiet English dell, she finally made peace with her mother and herself.

Taking the twig, she slipped it into her coat pocket.

'Thank you,' she said.

She turned and walked from the dell, certain in the knowledge that she was once again her mother's daughter.

Chapter Nineteen

❦

Lucy was having a thoroughly boring evening.
Millie and Alex had cried off from most social events in order to spend time alone together. David, having spent the better part of a week at his estate, had dropped out of circulation upon his return to London. To make matters worse, her fledging career as a social matchmaker was off to a terrible start, with the prospective bride being inconveniently banished to the country. The final, and possibly worst indignity, was that she was now having to attend parties and balls alone with her parents.

Her last line of defence against the simpering misses, Millie's brother Charles, had come down with a heavy cold and taken to his bed.

After dancing with several eligible gentlemen to please her mother, Lucy decided the ladies' retiring room was as good a place as any to while away the hours before the Duke and Duchess of Strathmore decided to go home.

'Why are there no interesting men this season?' she muttered as she turned the handle of the ladies' room door.

She was surprised to discover that apart from two ladies' maids, the room was empty. Waving away the maid who offered to attend to her perfectly set hair, she dropped down on to a well-padded couch and kicked off her dancing slippers. With her head against the cushions, she closed her eyes.

The door to the ladies' room opened and closed.

The maids whispered something inaudible between themselves and she heard them leave the room. A body plopped heavily down on the couch next to her. She half-opened one eye.

Lady Susan Kirk. Red-eyed and very distressed.

Lucy sat up and eyed her warily. Susan had been the cause of more trouble among the younger set than Lucy cared to remember. She made a move to rise from the couch, but stopped when Susan laid a shaking hand on her arm.

'I know you do not hold a very high opinion of me and for my own part, I have always found you to be too high in the step and a little odd, but I need to speak with you,' Susan said.

Lucy scowled.

'It's about Clarice.'

'Yes?' she replied, feeling a growing sense of unease.

'I know you don't agree with what I did at the Tates' rout, telling Lord Langham that your brother was dancing with Clarice. But I did it for her own good. Or so I thought.'

Susan pulled an already sodden ladies handkerchief from her reticule and dabbed at her tears. Lucy sighed. She pulled a clean handkerchief out of her own reticule and handed it to Susan.

'Thank you,' Susan replied.

'What do you mean, or so you thought?' Lucy asked.

Susan put her hand over her eyes and began to sob loudly. Her shoulders shook, such was her distress. Lucy reluctantly put a hand to Susan's back and gave her a comforting pat.

It was several minutes before Susan finally looked in control of her emotions and able to continue. When the maids reappeared, Lucy told them to go and find some supper.

Susan sniffed back her tears and sucked in a deep breath.

'Firstly, I would ask that you keep the matter of my involvement in this a secret. My marriage prospects have already suffered enough this season; if word of my involvement with Mr Fox became public I would likely be ruined.'

Mr Fox. Oh no.

'You didn't?' Lucy replied.

Susan shot her a look of utter outrage.

'No, I am not that foolish! A kiss was all that we shared. That, and what I thought was an understanding.'

'I don't understand,' Lucy replied.

Susan shook her head.

'Neither did I, until Clarice's father sent her away. She and I had agreed she would step aside and let me pursue Mr Fox.'

Lucy frowned. 'And you agreed to let my brother woo Clarice, except you lied?'

'Actually, no. Clarice lied to me. She told me she had some kind of understanding with Charles Ashton. I knew it was a lie, of course, but decided it suited my cause to pretend to believe her. It didn't really matter since I thought I was so close to success.'

'Really?'

A look of disdain appeared on Susan's face.

'You see, I thought Mr Fox was going to offer to marry me. We have spent some time together over the past few weeks and...'

'And what?'

'I thought we shared the belief that your brother is not suitable for Clarice. Mr Fox convinced me to aid him in scuttling their budding romance. I thought he was trying to curry favour with Lord Langham, but now I know he was just using me.'

Lucy decided to ignore the pointed insult about her brother. Susan Kirk evidently possessed information of great importance. She nodded her head and prayed that no-one else would need to use the ladies' retiring room at that exact moment. She took hold of one of Susan's hands and gave it a gentle, reassuring squeeze.

Susan looked away and sighed deeply, then looked back to Lucy.

'Mr Fox has left London. I believe he is headed for Norfolk. From the little that I was able to garner from him before he left, I understand he intends to seek out Clarice at Langham Hall and get her agreement to marry him.'

Lucy shot to her feet.

'Why? Why would he do such a thing?' she cried.

Still clutching Lucy's handkerchief, Susan rose from the couch. In the brittleness of her posture, Lucy saw a young woman struggling to come to terms with the repercussions of her self-serving nature. Her spiteful ways it would appear had finally caught up with her.

Even after all the horrid things Susan had done, Lucy pitied her.

'Because Mr Fox has spent all the money that Lord Langham gave him and then some. By getting Clarice to marry him, Mr Fox will gain access to her dowry.'

Lucy clasped her hands together and held them prayer-like to her lips.

'I cannot see Clarice readily agreeing to marry Mr Fox,' she said.

She and Susan exchanged a pained look of understanding. If Thaxter Fox compromised Clarice, there would be nothing anyone could do to save her. She would be compelled to marry him.

'Which is why I needed to find you. Much as it goes against everything I think is right, the only hope to save Clarice from Mr Fox is your brother. Now that I know the sort of man Mr Fox really is, I have come reluctantly to the conclusion that David may well be the lesser of two evils. Clarice does not deserve to be forced to marry a blackguard such as

Mr Fox; and for all his shortcomings, I know she loves your brother.

I have searched all the public *and* some private rooms at this party tonight, but have not been able to locate your brother. Whilst I am relieved to have found you, Lucy, it is far more imperative that *you* find David.'

For the first time in her life Lucy found herself in the unusual situation of being in complete agreement with Susan Kirk. She had to find David, and quickly.

'He isn't here tonight, but I know where I can find him,' Lucy replied.

She offered Susan her hand.

'Thank you. I know this must have been difficult for you, but I am glad that you sought me out. Let us shake hands and agree to keep this conversation a secret.'

Susan looked down at Lucy's hand and gave a small nod of her head. They shook hands.

'I must go and see if I can do anything to save our mutual friend,' Lucy said.

She picked up her slippers and hurriedly put them back on. Once back out in the main ballroom, she searched frantically for her father. Of all the people she knew, the Duke of Strathmore would know what to do. Across the crowded room, she set eyes upon her parents.

Under her breath she swore. Both the Duke and Duchess of Strathmore were with the Prince Regent. She clenched her fists and let out a frustrated 'Oh!'

She dared not risk trying to speak to her father. If she came within a few feet of the prince, she would be caught up in the social niceties of curtsying and paying her respects to him. And since her parents were close friends of the Prince of Wales, she knew they would remain in his company for quite some time.

The situation seemed hopeless. If only Alex and Millie

hadn't decided they needed to drop out of social circulation for a few days of privacy.

There was only one thing left to do.

Lady Lucy Radley was going to break the cardinal rule for all unmarried *ton* misses. She was going to head out into the London night without an approved chaperone.

True to form, once she had decided upon this rash and reckless course of action, her mind was set.

All in the course of Cupid's work.

She made her way through the ballroom, stopping once or twice for a brief chat to various friends, establishing her alibi. If her parents came in search of her while she was gone, there were several guests who could verify that they had only recently spoken with her.

A young couple she was good friends with, were leaving as she reached the front door. Lucy hurried and caught up with them.

Outside, she instructed the head footman to summon the driver of her parents' carriage. When her parents inevitably discovered what she had done, she could at least argue she had made every effort to mitigate the risk. She had travelled in her family's carriage, with several trusted servants on board.

She would deal with her father's wrath all in good time; David's heart was in deadly peril.

&

David yawned and pushed the pile of papers away from him.

He rubbed his tired eyes and checked the time. Squinting at his pocket watch, he saw it was only eleven o'clock. On any other evening he would barely be getting into the swing of things.

'It's all that fresh country air,' he muttered to himself.

The large pile of paperwork he had brought back from

Sharnbrook with him had been joined by several more bills which had arrived that morning.

He picked up the bill for the manor house's new curtains from the top of the pile and tried not to wince. Who would have known window fabric could cost that much?

With early starts the current order of his life, he contemplated turning in for the night. He yawned again.

'You are becoming an old man, Mr Radley,' he chided himself.

He stretched his arms above his head, but lowered them when he felt the twinge of his slowly healing stab wound.

'And tomorrow will be another battle,' he groaned.

Back in London; and now, having attended to business matters, he planned to confront Lord Langham in the morning and give him one final ultimatum before taking matters into his own hands.

A frown creased his brow when he saw the door to his study opening. The handful of staff who served him knew to knock before they entered into a room with a closed door.

Lucy's head appeared around the side of the door, giving him a start.

'I am so glad to see you are still up,' she said.

David rose quickly from his chair and hurried to her. He checked the doorway behind her and frowned a second time when he saw it was empty. Words of reproach were on the tip of his tongue. She held up a hand.

'Before you ask, yes, I came alone. And before you start to bellow, yes, I came in the Strathmore carriage, with three servants who are known to me.'

'But why?' he replied, surprised at his even temper. He was clearly more tired than he realised. Lucy gave him a look which reflected her own surprise at his response.

'Clarice,' she replied.

His ears pricked up at the name.

'I stole away from a ball in Curzon Street; Mama and Papa

are paying court to the Prince Regent so I couldn't get their attention. You know I would never do anything this foolish if the situation weren't so dire. I've just had a very disturbing conversation with Lady Susan Kirk.'

'Horrid Susan; why were you talking to her?'

'She had been labouring under the misconception that Thaxter Fox was going to marry her.'

David stifled a derisive snort.

'What has that got to do with me?'

'Everything, dear brother, because according to Susan, Mr Fox left London yesterday morning and is en route to Langham Hall to press his case with Clarice. Being the kind of charmer that we all suspect he is, she might not be able to say no to his offer of marriage.'

A whoosh of air exploded from his lungs.

'Oh god!' he said as he struggled to absorb the news.

Lucy placed a comforting hand on his arm. 'I don't know what it is about Mr Fox, but I don't trust him. David, I am afraid for Clarice.'

He fixed her with a steely gaze. 'And so you should be. Thaxter Fox is not the gentleman he pretends to be; rather he is a deceitful blackguard who will stop at nothing to get what he wants.'

'You don't suppose he would really try and force Clarice to marry him? Susan Kirk seemed to be of that opinion.'

'It's exactly what I expect he will try and do. If she refuses him, Lord knows what he will do to her. You know as well as I do that it only takes the merest smudge of a young woman's reputation for marriage to be the only possible solution.'

He walked back to his desk and began to pick up his papers and stuff them back into the leather satchel. He crossed to the doorway and called for Bailey.

He handed the valet his satchel. 'Find the stable master and tell him I want the horses and the coach ready to depart within the hour. Add my heaviest greatcoat to the travel trunk and get the footmen to bring it downstairs as soon as possible. I will be with you shortly.'

When Bailey hesitated, David pointed toward the door. 'Go!'

He returned to Lucy and took hold of her arm. 'We need to get you back to the ball before anyone notices you are missing. I will write a note and have it delivered to Strathmore House after I have departed. That, and the bribe I shall give to the servants who brought you here, should keep your secret for long enough.'

When they reached the bottom of the stairs, David grabbed his coat and gloves.

'You're not leaving now, are you? You won't get very far in the dark,' Lucy said.

'I am leaving this instant. Fox already has several days' head start on me. I fear I may arrive just in time to give the newly betrothed couple my best wishes, but if there is any chance of saving Clarice from that cur's grip I have to try.'

Two burly footmen brought down his travel trunk and deposited it at the front door. They both groaned as they set the heavy trunk down. Bailey laid David's woollen greatcoat on the top of the trunk. It was the one he always wore when he was in Scotland.

He nodded his head, pleased that he had had the foresight to be packed and ready for the journey to Norfolk. Anticipating that he would meet with another firm refusal from Clarice's father, David had been planning to leave London within the day. Earlier that afternoon, one of the smaller Strathmore coaches had been brought around into the rear mews.

Lucy cast an eye over the men and back to the trunk.

'I didn't think it was that cold in Norfolk at this time of the year,' she said.

David nodded. 'One must always plan for contingencies. If it comes to it, I might be compelled to make a sudden journey further north. And if I do, it will be to hole up at Strathmore Castle for the forthcoming winter with Langham's daughter as my bride.'

They made the quick journey back to Curzon Street, where David strolled nonchalantly into the ball with his sister on his arm. Not one guest gave them a second look.

'I had better go before Mama or Papa sees me,' he said. He let go of her arm and they exchanged a brief hug. Lucy rose up on her toes and gave him a quick kiss on the cheek.

'That is for Clarice. Good luck, David and god speed. I hope to see the two of you back in London soon. If not, I shall see you and your new wife when I get to Scotland. Depending on how things go with Papa, I too may be banished after tonight.'

David grimaced, before turning on his heel and hastening back out into the street. His own travel coach and valet were waiting for him further down the street. As he reached the top of the step, about to climb inside, he looked up and called out to the driver.

'Do what you can within reason, but we need to put as many miles as we can behind us tonight.'

The man tipped his hat and once David was safely on board, the driver turned the coach northward in the direction of the Great North Road.

Chapter Twenty

The one advantage the country did have over London was the freedom it afforded Clarice. In London she could not go anywhere without a maid or a footman as chaperone, but here at Langham Hall she could roam the estate and local area as she pleased.

After leaving the dell, she decided to walk into the nearby village of Langham. The baker's wife had a talent for pork pies and with her mind now clear, it was Clarice's stomach which required attention. It would have been easy enough to head back to the Hall and breakfast with Lady Alice, but after making peace with her mother, Clarice needed to walk.

And walk she did.

Langham village was only two miles from the Hall as the crow flies, but leaping over ditches and climbing stiles made the going slower for Clarice than taking the road. By the time she reached the village she was both hungry and thirsty.

After buying a pie, she sat on a small bench outside the baker's and sipped a warm cup of coffee. Then, refusing the baker's offer to give her a ride back to Langham Hall, she began the long trip home on foot. Today was a day to make plans, and for that she needed solitude and peace. Nothing was better than walking the quiet country roads for contemplating one's future.

However, her peaceful solitude was interrupted by a new boot, which rubbed the heel of her left foot. She was still a good half-mile from the Hall when she finally had to stop. She walked over to a nearby low stone wall and leaned against it while she unlaced her boot and took it off. Slowly pulling her stocking off her foot, she winced in pain as the blister on her ankle burst.

'Bugger,' she muttered, then quickly covered her mouth with her hand.

Clarice had actually managed a curse. Where had that ability suddenly appeared from? Then she remembered the choice words Millie had utilised at times from her extensive repertoire. The Marchioness of Brooke was a deliciously bad influence.

'Bollocks,' she said, and giggled.

What would David think if he could hear his beloved use such words? She raised an eyebrow at the thought that he might have to get used to the prospect if he intended to marry her.

She dropped the boot to the ground and balanced her injured foot on it. She looked up and down the road, hoping that someone would happen along and give her a ride home.

'Where is a bloody carriage when you need one?'

With only the occasional cart making its way back and forth from the village to the Hall, she knew she might sit on the side of the road for hours before anyone came along. She looked up at the sky. A few miles away a bank of dark grey clouds were slowly making their way toward her.

She groaned. A good solid downpour was the last thing she wished to be caught in. With a shrug of her shoulders, she picked up the empty boot and began the long, uncomfortable hobble back to Langham Hall.

Clarice was in sight of the Hall when she heard the rumble

of wheels on the road. She turned and saw a black travel coach approaching at speed. Her heart leapt. Word had somehow reached him of her plight: David had come to save her!

'Thank God,' she said, and waved madly at the driver.

He saw her and began to rein the horses in. The hatch next to him flipped open and he leaned down. Whoever was in the carriage was issuing instructions. He righted himself in the seat and shook his head at her. He urged the horses on toward the house, leaving Clarice standing on the side of the road covered in dust.

She looked down at her filthy coat, completely nonplussed. Why hadn't the coach stopped? Obviously the passenger did not know who she was, as no-one would intentionally leave Lord Langham's daughter stranded by the roadside.

'He must not have recognised me,' she said. Under her bonnet and long woollen coat, she looked just like any other country lass. With a resigned huff of disgust she hobbled on her way, following the coach.

'Just wait until I get my hands on you, Mr Radley; fancy not coming to the aid of a damsel in distress. What sort of gentleman are you?' she muttered.

With the pad of her blistered foot sore and her other boot beginning to rub, it was some time before she finally reached home. By the time she reached the house, the coach had gone around the back and in to the stables. She rushed inside the front door.

'Is he here?' she asked the first footman she met.

He nodded. 'The gentleman is with her Ladyship in the upstairs drawing room.'

Catching a glimpse of her reflection in the hall mirror, she stopped. Having taken her bonnet off toward the end of the return journey, her hair now bore testament to the strength of the Norfolk wind. Her face was red and dry.

'This will not do,' she said.

If David had come all the way from London for her, the last thing he needed to see at the end of his long journey was Clarice in such a bedraggled state. Especially when she planned to take him to task for his lack of gallantry in leaving her on the roadside.

She headed upstairs, found Bella and set to the task of making herself presentable for her future husband.

Half an hour later, shod in soft, comfortable slippers, she took a deep breath and knocked on the door of Lady Alice's drawing room. The necklace hung outside the bodice of her gown in plain view, a statement of intent.

As she opened the door, she saw her grandmother seated on a couch facing the door. The visitor had his back to her. Clarice stepped into the room and then stopped.

The look on Lady Alice's face was enough to dash Clarice's hopes.

'Come in, my dear, and join us,' her grandmother said, her hand patting the empty space on the couch next to her.

As Clarice walked toward her grandmother, the visitor rose from his seat. Out of the corner of her eye, she saw a familiar form.

Thaxter Fox.

She turned and quickly tucked the pendant back inside her gown.

'Good afternoon, Lady Clarice,' he said.

She turned to face him and watched with a fading heart as he took in her beautifully coiffured hair and newly pressed gown. His gaze stopped when it reached her bodice.

His eyes widened and he let out a low, lustful moan. In her haste, she had forgotten to bring her shawl and she realised to her horror that Thaxter had caught a greedy eyeful of her ample cleavage.

Behind Clarice, Lady Alice cleared her throat. Her action had the desired effect and he bent his head and bowed.

'Mr Fox, what are you doing here?' Clarice replied. The

last time she had seen him, he was standing to one side of the dance floor as her father dragged her away from the party.

He raised himself to his full height and gave her a hard smile. She felt a shiver run down her spine. Millie had once made mention of the cold-blooded snakes which inhabited the area around her home in India. Thaxter's smile and the way he held himself reminded her of a cobra. Coiled and ready to strike.

She forced herself to smile back at him.

Be polite. If anything ever happened to Papa, he would control my purse strings. And much of everything else.

'Why, my dear Clarice, I came to visit Langham Hall, and indulge in all it has to offer,' he replied.

She blinked. 'Why?'

His smile turned down at the edges. 'Someday all of this will be mine, so I decided it was time for me to survey my future home,' he replied. The patronising tone in which he spoke had Clarice digging her nails into the palm of her hand.

Pig of a man.

Lady Alice gathered her skirts, stood and came to Clarice's side.

'Mr Fox informs me that your father thought it a good idea for him to visit while you and I were in residence. Since your father will not return to the Hall for another week or two, it falls to us to be convivial hosts.'

'Oh,' Clarice replied. Instead of her knight in shining armour, she was going to have to endure long evenings in the company of Mr Fox. The polite smile she had painted on her face would be dry and peeling by the time her father arrived.

Thaxter Fox's arrival put in peril all her well-laid plans. By the time she had reached the village earlier that morning, Clarice had decided to return to London. A dozen good excuses were at the ready for the inevitable confrontation with Lady Alice. But now with her father's heir an unexpected and most assuredly unwelcome addition to their home, she was, for the time being, stuck in Norfolk.

Lady Alice, took hold of Clarice's hand and gave it a gentle pat.

'I am sure your father's decision is for the best. As Mr Fox is your father's heir, it is our duty to show him the Hall and its surrounds. Your father would expect us to make Mr Fox welcome in his future home.'

Thaxter placed a paternal hand on Clarice's shoulder. 'As always, your elders have seen the brightly lit path that is the future. I look forward to spending many hours with you, Lady Clarice taking in the pleasures of the estate. Of course we shall have to await your father's arrival before I can properly examine the records of account.'

As Lady Alice gave an agreeable nod of her head, Clarice caught the wry smile which appeared and quickly vanished from the dowager's face. Henry Langham was a man who kept his finances secret from all but a few trusted staff. And his mother.

The dowager countess knew every penny which was earned and spent on the estate. The chances of Mr Fox being given free rein to peruse the Langham family finances were less than nothing while the current earl lived. The estate records would be under lock and key before Mr Fox had his bags unpacked.

'Well, I expect you are tired from your long journey Mr Fox; I shall have one of the servants show you to your room. Did you bring a valet?' Lady Alice replied. Clarice silently applauded her grandmother's skill at changing the subject.

He yawned in a most ungentlemanly manner and added a roll of his shoulders.

'Yes, it was a most tiresome trip. I had no idea Norfolk was *this* far from London. Though I expect in the future I shall spend most of my time in town and only make the occasional trip here. My valet was unwell, so I didn't bother bringing him with me. I have my man of business to attend to my personal matters,' he replied.

Clarice scowled. 'If you are going to only make the occasional trip to the Hall, who is going to manage the estate?'

Thaxter blinked at what he must have considered a completely ludicrous question.

'Doesn't your father have a steward? All the titled chaps in London have one, I was led to believe.'

She was about to open her mouth and set him straight about the amount of work involved in running a large estate when Lady Alice stepped in.

'Now, now Clarice, you mustn't bother Mr Fox with such matters,' Lady Alice replied. She limped over to the bell pull and rang the bell. 'Go and rest, Mr Fox and we shall see you for dinner.'

As soon as he was gone, Clarice and her grandmother exchanged a look of dismay.

'I had no idea he was coming; if I had known I would have refused to come. You were there; you know he is the reason Papa discovered me dancing with David and made me leave the rout,' Clarice said.

The burning anger she felt at the way Thaxter and Susan had betrayed her continued unabated.

Lady Alice shook her head. They both knew Lord Langham had given them no choice. 'I am at a loss to explain why your father would send him, and it is odd that your father did not furnish Mr Fox with a letter of introduction for his visit. Though I have heard rumours Mr Fox was making a nuisance of himself at some of the London clubs.'

'Not to mention running up a small mountain of debts,' Clarice replied, staring at the closed sitting-room door.

Lady Alice raised an eyebrow. 'Really?'

Clarice nodded. On Thaxter's most recent visit to Langham House, she had inadvertently overheard her father refusing to give him any more funds. Her father's heir had stormed out of Langham House in a filthy temper shortly thereafter. Thinly veiled remarks by Millie a few days later confirmed her suspicions.

'Perhaps that is the real reason why our friend is visiting the countryside. He may be avoiding some creditors from town,' Lady Alice replied.

'Yes, well, he might take the opportunity to learn some manners while he is here. He drove past me on the road a little while back and refused to stop when I hailed his carriage.'

Clarice turned to leave. Her days of happily rambling about the estate on her own were, for the moment, over. Worry and disappointment now filled her mind. Where was David? He must know by now that she was no longer in London. She was not inclined to believe that he would have given up their cause so readily. She held a clenched hand over her heart, and forced herself to hope that her father had at least considered David's offer when David came to call on him.

'Clarice, a word of warning. Until we can fully understand Mr Fox's reasons for being here, especially without the presence of your father, I would suggest you make every endeavour to keep well away from him. It would not surprise me in the least if your father did not know Mr Fox was here. Lies seem to come readily from his mouth and there is something about that man I do not like. The hairs on the back of my neck stand on end every time I see him.'

Clarice recalled the way Thaxter had looked at her when she walked into the room. She had a sense of being sized up like a prize cow bound for sale at market.

She gave her grandmother a tender kiss on the cheek. 'I think that is very good advice, Grandmamma; thank you.'

Back in her bedroom, Clarice kicked off her slippers and lay back on her bed. All thoughts of convincing Lady Alice to return with her to London had evaporated upon Thaxter's arrival. Neither she nor her grandmother trusted him enough to leave him alone at Langham Hall. The only thing left for her to do was to avoid their house guest until either her father arrived from London, or David came to rescue her.

'If I'd had the good sense to realise I was in love with him, I could have made sure David had to whisk me off to Scotland,' she muttered.

She put a hand over her eyes. Robbing David of his wish for a proper wedding celebration would not have been the best way to begin their married life. No, Mr Fox and his calculated grin would have to be endured.

After a tour of the estate the following morning, accompanied by no fewer than three estate staff, Clarice took her leave of Thaxter and went in search of Lady Alice.

'How was your morning stroll?' her grandmother asked.

Clarice scowled. From the moment Thaxter Fox had arrived at dinner the previous evening, he had been the perfect gentleman. His manners were once more impeccable and he was warm and pleasant toward the estate staff. At one point during their inspection of the stables, he had even made a jest and laughed heartily.

Yet all the while, Clarice found herself continually comparing him to David. Where David's manners and amiable personality came naturally to him, she could see Thaxter Fox continually gauging and adjusting his behaviour according to the responses of others around him. He questioned at length the role of any senior members of the estate staff who were presented to him. She found it particularly disconcerting that he ignored any questions which were posed to him by the staff.

'It was fine, but I would not be surprised to hear he was keeping a detailed dossier on all of us. He continually wants to review the minutest of details. He asked the stable master no less than four times how much Papa would get if he sold the black mare at the market in King's Lynn. And that man of business of his is the oddest fellow I have ever met. He certainly doesn't dress or sound like someone who has worked for a gentleman before.'

'No?' Lady Alice replied.

Clarice clapped her hands and chuckled. 'The one good thing to come out of this morning is that Mr Fox has already begun to tire of the estate. He and his man are going to travel to Holt this afternoon and don't expect to be back until late. Which means I have the whole afternoon to roam the estate and not have to worry about dealing with him.'

The dowager gave a low hum in response. 'Don't stray too far from the main house, Clarice.'

'I shall stay on the estate; I will be perfectly safe,' she replied.

Lady Alice pursed her lips. 'I would like to think so, but I wish you to come to my side once Mr Fox returns from town. We may be on the family estate but with strangers in our midst, we should rely upon the protection that our trusted staff afford us.'

'I plan to take my paints and work on a new landscape down at the edge of the lake; I will only be a hundred or so yards from the main house,' Clarice replied.

Chapter Twenty-One

'Ah, so there you are,' the voice of their unwelcome house guest rang in Clarice's ears.

She cast a glance upwards at the sun and sighed. It had moved well past overhead and was now heading down the afternoon sky. The hour was later than she had realised.

Alone in this private, secure place, she had enjoyed Thaxter's absence from the estate and now he had found her.

'Quite a clever hiding place you have here; I have been scouring the estate for the past hour looking for you. I was on the verge of giving up and going back to the house when one of the servants mentioned you might be down by the lake.'

She gave him a disinterested glance and turned back to her easel. Running the brush over the canvas, she was putting the finishing touches to a scene she had painted many times before.

'How was your trip to Holt?' she replied.

He came and stood by her side and gave her painting a cursory look.

'Disappointing. I really do have little time or appetite for these provincial towns. Every shop in which I tried to purchase goods on credit initially refused me. Of course, once

I mentioned my connection to your father, they soon changed their minds.'

He opened the lapels of his jacket, revealing a deep crimson, mustard and burnt orange spotted vest.

'I told them that if they wished to secure my future custom, they had better convince me of the quality of their goods. What do you think of the cut of my new vest, Lady Clarice? I got it gratis.'

'It's very nice,' she lied. The colour palette was so hideous it hurt her eyes.

There were few places in Holt which supplied such goods, so it would not be an impossible task for her father's steward to discover which hapless tailor Mr Fox had pressured into giving him free goods. Her father valued his family's name and reputation in the local district. He would be furious to know his heir was trading on the Langham name for personal gain. The well-cut vest would be paid for, whether Mr Fox wished it or not.

He shrugged his shoulders at her curt response. She dipped her brush in first the blue and then the yellow paint, frowning when it didn't give her quite the shade of green she desired for the waterside reeds. She added a little more yellow before putting the brush to the linen canvas.

A cold shiver ran down her spine as he stepped closer. Endeavouring not to look at him, she continued to focus on getting the line and structure of the plants just right.

'Is this all you do down at the lake, Lady Clarice?' he asked. He was so close now, she could feel his hot breath on the side of her face. She stepped away and moved closer to the lake, praying that if she kept her eyes focused on the subject of her painting, he would soon get bored and go back to the house.

Go away. Please go away.

'Never been one for painting landscapes. Always thought it a pointless waste of time. Why bother painting a rustic scene of ducks swimming on the water when you could be shooting the blessed birds and serving them up on the table for supper?' he said, adding his usual self-satisfied laugh.

'Yes, well, it is more of a lady's afternoon pastime. I have a number of my pieces hanging in various rooms both here and in London. Papa says I have quite the eye for a landscape,' she replied.

He sniffed. 'My brother Avery had a gift for drawing when he was young. Not that it did him any good.'

She nodded, pleased at the change of subject. 'Papa mentioned you have a younger brother. Will we be meeting him?'

Thaxter harrumphed. 'Not likely. I haven't set eyes on him or the rest of my family for years. He joined the army the minute he realised there would never be enough money to send him to a reputable school. I understand he was injured at Waterloo. But enough about my wayward brother. What about you, Lady Clarice?'

He followed her to the water's edge.

When he reached out and brushed a hand down the side of her face, Clarice shuddered. She hurried away from him back to her easel, desperately trying to convince herself that he had not actually touched her.

'Don't be shy, Clarice. I know you enjoyed my attentions at the garden party; why should we pretend that you didn't? And now that we are here together in Norfolk, we should take the opportunity to strengthen our bond,' he murmured.

The garden party seemed like a lifetime ago. The afternoon spent with Thaxter had been for her father's benefit. By showing the other members of the *ton* that the Langham family had accepted him as one of their own, Thaxter's entry into London society would be made all that easier. He had been pleasant and gracious to a fault throughout the picnic and now she knew why. The gathered members of society's elite had seen them together, noted how well they were matched and drawn the obvious conclusion. Thaxter had carefully orchestrated the whole scene and Clarice had well and truly been played for a fool.

It all made perfect sense. The dashingly handsome heir to the Langham title takes the hand of the daughter of the house in marriage. He has someone to show him the ways of society and she continues the family bloodline. If she didn't know that Thaxter Fox was a manipulative rogue, it would be the perfect aristocratic fairy tale.

She straightened her back; her decision had been made, she was going to marry David Radley and Mr Fox would have to accept it.

Out of the corner of her eye, she saw him remove his coat and unbutton his waistcoat. The fragile hope that he was about to take a late afternoon dip in the lake died as soon as it entered her mind. He began to walk back to her.

Her breath caught in her throat and time slowed.

She heard the ducks on the lake and the wind whistling through the long grass. Slowly she scanned the horizon as an icy fear gripped her heart. Her carefully chosen hiding place was far away from the house. Far enough that no-one was likely to hear her cries for help.

She was alone with him.

She knew enough about life to know that no unmarried girl ever allowed herself to be alone with a man such as him. While David's letter had revealed much of the passion a man might feel for the woman he loved, the look of violent lust in Thaxter's eyes told her he had no plans for a tender wooing. Her situation was becoming more perilous by the second.

He reached her side and placed his hands on her shoulders. She froze. He bent his head and placed a kiss on the side of her neck.

'Don't you dare touch me!' she cried, and pushed him away.

He staggered back, laughing. Mocking her. 'My dear, dear

AN UNSUITABLE MATCH

Clarice, very soon I will be touching every inch of your flesh. I shall run my tongue over your naked breasts as I spread your legs wide and ride you like a young mare.'

She shook her head.

'No.'

'I see you need to have the facts of life explained to you, my girl. Once you and I are wed, I plan to have you on your back as often as I like. My heir should be growing within your belly well before Christmas. Which is why I think I should take you here and now. Seal the deal, as they say.'

'I think not. I shall never marry you, Mr Fox; we would never suit. Besides, I love another,' she replied, her voice wavering with fear.

He took a step closer. 'I couldn't give a damn what you want, LADY Clarice. Once I have had you, your tight-fisted papa will have to give you and your lovely dowry up to me. I can't wait to see the look on his face. Then when you are my wife, you will submit to my command. As your husband it will be within my rights to discipline you. Fight me and your pale, virginal skin will feel the lash of my riding crop. Don't be foolish enough to flatter yourself in thinking you will be the first filly I have broken in.'

His hand reached for the bodice of her gown and gripped tightly. She tried to pull away, but he viciously pulled her back and gave her a hard slap across the face. The paint palette flew out of her hand.

Shocked and dazed at this unprovoked violence, Clarice searched desperately for salvation. A few more blows to the face, and her strength would surely wane. Whether she was conscious or not when he took her, it would matter little. The outcome would remain the same.

She felt the paintbrush in her right hand and knew she had to take the chance. As Thaxter pulled her toward him, his thin hard lips opening in order to kiss her, Clarice struck.

'You bloody bitch!' he screamed as the sharp end of the

wooden paintbrush found its way into the soft flesh of his upper arm. He lashed out with his good arm and taking a handful of Clarice's gown, tore a large hole in the front of it, revealing her naked breasts.

The sight of the black onyx with the Strathmore stars on the bail hanging on its fine gold chain only served to enrage him further. He made a wild grab for the chain, but his grasping fingers found only bare breast. He lunged forward, and gave the delicate tissue a hard, cruel squeeze.

Clarice cried out in pain and slapped his arm away, then punched her fisted hand hard against his damaged arm.

'Think your duke's bastard will have you once I have finished with you? Think he will want you when you are a ruined whore?' he roared.

His good arm swung once more, but Clarice saw it coming and dodged. As she righted herself she saw the clear inevitability of the situation. It was now or never. Even with one damaged arm, Thaxter was too strong for her. She either fought back while she was still on her feet, or accept that he was going to force her to the ground and ruin her life. If she was going down it was not without a fight. He would have the scars to show for his evil brutality, she would make sure of it.

Pivoting on her right foot, she took hold of the leg of the easel, sending the canvas and her other brushes clattering to the ground. She swung it wildly at him. He ducked but was not quick enough. The top corner of the easel connected with the side of his face, just below the eye, with a sickening thwack.

He cried out in pain and dropped to his knees, clutching his face.

Clarice threw the easel to the ground and ran for her life. Scrambling up the small rise back to the gardens, she ran as fast as she could, not daring to turn and see if he had followed.

Clutching her torn dress to her breast, she reached the main house and slipped in through a side entrance. She locked the door behind her, knowing it would be in vain if he followed and demanded her hand.

Turning toward the stairs, tears streaming down her face, she encountered Lady Alice. Her grandmother looked at the torn dress and a strange look immediately passed over her face. Knowing no-one within the estate or village would dare lay a hand on Lord Langham's daughter, the answer as to who had attacked Clarice was obvious.

'Where is he now?' she demanded.

Clarice shook her head. 'I don't know; I fought him off at the lake and then ran here. He plans to ruin me so Papa will have to agree to our marriage.'

With Clarice's dowry at his disposal, Thaxter could go back to spending money like a madman. Lady Alice went to a nearby window and looked out on to the drive. It was empty.

'Are you ruined?' she asked calmly.

'No. Oh Grandmamma, I was so frightened!' Clarice cried. She took a step toward the dowager before her grandmother cut her off.

'Go upstairs this instant, cover yourself and wait for me. Make sure no-one sees you, not even your maid,' she ordered.

No hug, no words of comfort, just a direct command. Clarice stared at her in disbelief.

Lady Alice took hold of her arm and steered her toward the stairs. She gave her granddaughter a gentle push in the back and Clarice began to climb the stairs.

'Go, go! I cannot control this if you are here when he arrives back at the house. Lock your bedroom door and don't open it to anyone but me; I don't know if he has any of the servants in his pocket,' Lady Alice said.

Clarice heard fear in the old woman's voice.

She managed to climb the stairs and do as her grandmother bade. A gentle knock on the door half an hour later signalled the arrival of Lady Alice. Behind her a maid carried a bowl of warm water and clean towels. She dismissed the girl as soon as she had set the bowl down on a table. Following the maid to the door, she closed it and turned the key.

'Good, we shouldn't be disturbed this way. Much as I trust our household staff, we must bear in mind that if, God forbid, anything happens to your father, Mr Fox will be their new master. Considering the way he has been lording it over them since he got here, I expect they know what the years under his reign will be like.'

She came to Clarice and, pulling her into her arms, gave her a heartfelt hug.

'I am sorry I couldn't do that downstairs, but we need to keep this afternoon's events a secret. We need to play our cards close to our chest. If anyone knows you have been alone with him, a betrothal will be expected. If he suspects that I know anything, he will press his case.'

Clarice wiped away a tear and nodded. The threat of being married to Thaxter Fox still loomed large.

'Did you see him?'

Lady Alice nodded. 'Yes. Apparently Mr Fox had an accident this afternoon while out walking and fell, injuring his head. Cook is stitching up his cheek, and you should have heard the words he used the moment she set needle to skin. Evil man.'

She walked over to the bowl of water and dipped in a dry cloth.

'Now, let me have a look at you; those scratches were rather ugly.'

Clarice took off the warm woollen wrap she had put on to cover the torn dress and took a seat next to the table.

'You may wish to remove your necklace,' Lady Alice said, pointing to David's gift. Clarice shook her head.

'No. I have made my choice; the necklace stays,' she replied.

Her grandmother smiled and placed a tender kiss on Clarice's forehead. 'Good, that should make it easier for you to stick to my plan. Just remember, once false move or foolish comment and your dreams of marrying David will turn to ashes.'

Clarice nodded once more. She was fast learning to trust her grandmother's instinct for survival.

The Dowager Countess Langham was a woman of simple tastes, but one area in which she never pinched a penny was the food at her table. Later that evening as Thaxter joined the two women for dinner, he made several remarks as to the excellence of the roast lamb.

'Of course, nothing would be as good as the food I usually enjoy when I dine out in London, but one must make concessions for the country,' he remarked, hacking another large piece of meat off the roast and stuffing it in his mouth.

Ignoring the fact that Thaxter was eating directly from the serving platter, Clarice picked up her wine glass and took a sip. She pondered the fact that while he classed himself as a gentleman, Thaxter had not moved too far from his own rural roots.

'I do hope you have taken the estate steward to task over the state of the grounds, Lady Alice,' Thaxter said.

'I shall ensure the workmen make a thorough inspection of the stone wall near the lake, Mr Fox,' Lady Alice said. Her gaze locked for the briefest of moments on the large swelling which had appeared on the side of his face. A two-inch line of crooked stitches ran from the corner of his eye and down over his cheek. The dim candlelight could not hide the black bruising under his eye.

He nodded slowly.

'Yes, please do; the good Lord knows what might have befallen me if I had not been surer of foot,' he replied. The half-chewed piece of meat was still in his mouth, but he seemed no longer to care about his table manners where Clarice and Lady Alice were concerned.

Clarice studied the piece of roast chicken on her plate and silently rehearsed her line.

'Such a terrible accident to befall you, Mr Fox; a most unfortunate occurrence,' she said innocently.

He turned and fixed her with a look which could freeze the sun. Then in an instant, his demeanour changed.

'Thank you so much for your concern, Lady Clarice, it is truly touching to know you care for my welfare,' he replied.

She cut a small piece of meat from the chicken breast, but thought the better of eating it.

A sudden memory of the night David had saved her from choking crashed into her mind and she put down her fork. Under the table, she wiped her sweaty palms on her napkin. She turned to him and smiled.

'Of course, you are my father's heir and it would be terribly remiss of me not to be concerned when I heard of your misfortune.'

'Yes, and Cook did a wonderful job of stitching your wound,' Lady Alice added.

Clarice glanced at the battlefield-standard stitching. She dreaded to think what abuse the poor woman had suffered as Thaxter squirmed and swore under her hand. Odd, though, how Cook had made such an unholy mess of the stitches on his face. She was a woman who normally took great pride in repairing the wounds of those injured on the estate. Even Clarice's father had preferred to have her skilled hands stitch his riding injuries rather than send for the doctor from the local village.

She made a mental note to give the head of the kitchen an extra coin or two at Christmas. If any of the staff suspected there was more to Thaxter Fox's tale, they were keeping silent.

Thaxter stuffed another large piece of meat into his mouth and sat chewing it. All the while he continued to stare hard at

Clarice. She met his gaze and blinked slowly, hiding all trace of emotion. If he had thought to shame her with his display of injured pride, he could not be more wrong. Rather than weakening her, the ugly altercation at the lake had further strengthened her resolve.

Lady Alice cleared her throat and Clarice tore her gaze away. She silently berated herself. Her look had lingered too long.

The pretence of a pleasant evening meal must be maintained at all costs. Don't stir the dragon, Clarice; too much is at stake.

She leaned forward and stretched to pick up a tray of roasted carrots which were just out of reach. The necklace under her gown shifted between her breasts. She stopped and sat back in her seat, grateful for the reminder of David and all that she currently risked.

Thaxter rose from his seat and came around to where Clarice sat. As he leaned over the table she held her breath.

He picked up the tray and taking the serving spoon, placed a large pile of carrots on her plate.

'Lady Clarice.'

She gave him a polite smile. He put the spoon back on the tray and served her another two spoonfuls.

'One needs to keep up one's strength,' he said.

'Yes; thank you,' she replied.

His silent threat delivered, Thaxter returned to his seat.

Clarice looked down at the ridiculous number of carrots on her plate. If the stakes had not been not so high, the price of failure so absolute, she would have laughed.

'Did you make headway with your needlework, Grandmamma?' she said, looking up at Lady Alice. Earlier in her bedroom, the two women had agreed upon a short list of safe topics for discussion during the perilous evening ahead.

Lady Alice nodded, and then proceeded to give a long, and aptly boring, dissertation on the need for a lady of Clarice's rank to be better skilled with a needle.

Clarice, in turn, asked for guidance with her own piece of work. She accepted that the shop she had purchased her thread from was entirely unsuitable and Lady Alice gave a detailed description of the quality of thread she herself used in her sewing.

Thaxter sat silently eating and drinking, only giving the occasional snort as Lady Alice continued. Slowly the meal dragged on, all three players in the domestic theatre keeping close to their own scripts.

Finally, Lady Alice summoned a footman and the platters of food were cleared from the table. The dinner guests adjourned to a nearby sitting room and while Thaxter indulged in several glasses of port, Clarice and her grandmother continued with the dinner wine.

As she had been instructed earlier, Clarice went to her room, and brought down an old piece of her embroidery for her grandmother's inspection. The dowager slowly and methodically examined the stitching. Seated beside her, Clarice gave silent thanks she had not thrown out the long-neglected piece of needlework.

'Here you needed to have crossed back over the other stitch,' she pointed out to Clarice.

'Yes, Lady Alice,' she replied.

In the nearby olive-green armchair Thaxter yawned. Several minutes later he yawned again.

Lady Alice put down the needlework and, reaching over to a low table, picked up her Sunday Bible. Opening the book, she took hold of Clarice's hand and began to recite a long passage from the Old Testament.

Clarice had always found the stories of the old Bible rather interesting, but now the slow, painful way her grandmother spoke soon had her blinking hard to stay awake.

'Amen,' Lady Alice said as she finished the passage and put down the book.

She let go of Clarice's hand and rose from the chair.

Crossing the floor to where Thaxter now dozed in the armchair she stood, hands on hips, and examined him.

'Well-cut clothing, excellent boots. Not a bad-looking chap, but your grandfather always said that was not the measure of a good man. Something about never judging a book by its cover,' she noted, shaking her head. She picked up a small bell from the mantelpiece and rang it. Thaxter Fox stirred not an inch.

'Good.'

The door opened and three footmen came into the room. Being careful not to wake him, they gently pulled Thaxter out of the chair and carried him away. As the door closed behind them, Clarice stood and came to her grandmother's side.

'Are you certain the sleeping draught will keep him unconscious till morning?' she asked.

Lady Alice chuckled. 'Considering what was in the draught and how much I put in that bottle of port, he will be lucky if he wakes before next Wednesday. Have no fear, my girl; by the time Mr Fox comes to his senses, you and I shall be long gone from the Hall.'

'Now what?' Clarice replied.

Her grandmother took hold of her hand. 'Now we pack for parts unknown.'

Clarice scowled, and Lady Alice smiled.

'Well, Bedfordshire actually, but it won't be an easy journey and we shall have to travel as far as we can each day. I know your travel sickness will be a burden, but you will have to screw your courage to the sticking place and make do.

'Your father will no doubt discover soon enough that we are no longer in Norfolk, and will journey up from London. I sent an urgent message yesterday to the Duchess of Strathmore and it should have made the London-bound mail. Once Mr Radley receives it, he will no doubt make for here. Unfortunately he will discover that we have already left for Sharnbrook and be forced to make the journey to there. Where, of course, we shall be awaiting him.'

Instinctively touching the bodice of her gown, Clarice felt the hard shape of the orb under her clothes.

'I hope it won't take too much for him to realise that he has to put aside his foolish notions of insisting that we gain Papa's approval before we wed,' she replied.

Lady Alice gave Clarice's hand a squeeze. 'Honour is never foolish, my dear, but sometimes we have to be shown that there is more than one way to be honourable. Now, off you go and make sure your things are ready for us to leave at first light.'

Clarice nodded and turned to leave.

She stopped and turned back to her grandmother. 'Thank you. And if this does all end with a moonlight flit to Gretna Green and I am no longer received in polite society, I shall send a prayer of thanks to you every day.'

The dowager softly chuckled.

'My dear, if it comes to that, your Mr Radley may need to find a spare room or two for me.'

※

'I have the key,' Lady Alice said, as Clarice checked the door of Thaxter's room one more time. After having seen him safely locked away in his bedroom, she had twice made the journey to the end of the hall and tried the handle.

'Come away, girl; you and I have matters to discuss.'

She followed her grandmother to the upstairs drawing room which overlooked the grounds at the front of the house. A strong wind had sprung up in the past hour and the topmost branches of the giant oak trees on either side of the road leading up to the house were being whipped about.

'The summer is fading fast,' she said, standing and looking out of the windows.

'Yes, I hope you instructed your maid to pack your warm things. Something tells me you won't be needing any of your ball gowns where we are headed,' Lady Alice replied.

A flash of lightning lit the room, followed quickly by a loud boom of thunder. A late summer storm would soon be upon them.

And then it began to rain.

A huge torrent of water, tossed down to earth on a vicious swirling wind, fell. The dark, expectant clouds which had rolled in from over the North Sea in the late afternoon now hung over the valley and released their deluge.

'At least we don't have to flee into that tonight,' Clarice muttered. She shivered at the thought of being caught out on the dark road on such a foul night. As the wind whipped around, rain lashed against the window, shaking the panes in their frames.

'Come and have some hot chocolate, Clarice. Cook made some of your favourite oat biscuits this afternoon,' Lady Alice said from the small couch close to the warm fire.

Clarice closed her eyes and let her head droop forward. As her forehead kissed the chilly glass, she wondered how long it would be before next she stood in this room. Once her father discovered she had fled into the arms of David Radley, would he ever allow her to return to Langham Hall?

She sighed. All those thoughts were for the future. With her travel trunks packed and ready for a pre-dawn departure, she had cast aside all her fears and was resolute in her determination to dictate her own future. She bit on her lip as the thrill of the unknown beckoned.

Taking one edge of the curtain in her hand, she drew it closed. Then, stepping to the other side of the window, she took the opposite curtain in hand. With only a foot or two of window left uncovered, she stopped and stared out one last time.

A small light appeared at the other end of the driveway.

At first it was only a flicker, so small that she was uncertain it was really there. She pressed her face to the glass and squinted hard to focus on the light. Was it only a reflection from the moon as it peeked out from behind the clouds?

Looking up, she saw the moon was completely hidden by thick rain clouds.

She looked back at the road, hoping to catch a glimpse of the light once more.

Then she saw it. The light was moving.

'Grandmamma, someone is on the road!' she cried.

Who on God's good earth would be out travelling the roads in this sort of weather? Who would need to endanger themselves to visit the Hall at such an hour?

Lady Alice hurried to Clarice's side and peered out into the darkness. Clarice saw her lips move and caught the whisper of 'Heaven save us.' Only the bearer of momentous, life-changing news would be compelled to risk such a journey.

Hot tears sprang to Clarice's eyes as a chill of premonition seized her.

Not Papa; please let it not be news of him.

Her grandmother nodded her head and straightened her back. She turned to Clarice.

'We are Langham women, Clarice, and we shall deal with whatever news the rider bears with dignity and grace. Come, let us not wait here to discover our fate. We should go downstairs and greet our future.'

She reached out and went to take Clarice's hand but Clarice dropped her arm and squeezed her eyes shut. The prospect of losing her father only a few years after her mother was unbearable. For all her father's faults, he was her family and she still loved him.

Lady Alice put a comforting arm around her and pulled her close. 'It may simply be a traveller caught on the road in the storm who is seeking refuge here.'

Clarice wiped the tears from her eyes and nodded at the

lie. Langham Hall was miles from the nearest road to anywhere.

By the time she had dried her tears, the rider had arrived at the Hall. The thought of railing against Lady Alice's instructions was tempered by the knowledge that they would both be judged by how well they conducted themselves in the face of any grievous news. The messenger would no doubt make a full report to his masters.

Arm in arm, the two Langham women descended the grand staircase.

With dignity and grace.

She owed it to her mother not to repeat the hysterical scene of her death. The pressure of Lady Alice's grip on her arm firmed with every step.

Control; I must maintain control.

At the bottom of the stairs, she looked to the left and saw her father's steward holding an armful of wet towels. Facing him stood a cloaked figure, rubbing another towel through his hair. His thick black hair.

Her heart missed a beat.

The rider slipped the fastenings of his rain-sodden cloak and handed it to a nearby footman. Her father's steward motioned toward the stairs and as he turned the rider murmured, 'Thank you.'

In the blink of an eye, Clarice pulled free of her grandmother's hold, picked up her skirts and dashed down the stairs.

'David!' she cried and threw herself into his arms.

Dignity and grace be damned.

Chapter Twenty-Two

David closed his eyes and let the sheer relief of having found Clarice wash over him. Wet, cold and utterly exhausted, he held his prize tightly in his embrace.

The rest of the world did not exist.

Only her. Only Clarice.

'Mr Radley. I should have realised it would take a mad Scotsman to venture out on such a hellish night as this,' Lady Alice remarked as she reached the bottom of the stairs unaided.

A deep chuckle resonated through his chest. With Clarice still clinging tightly to his body, he bowed as best he could.

'Tis but a summer shower and a gentle breeze. Why, my mother and sisters would surely have had the servants pack them a picnic and be out enjoying such pleasant weather,' he replied.

Lady Alice clapped her hands together in appreciation. 'You forget, young man that I was born in Edinburgh, and even my father would have given a second thought to such folly as being out on the road tonight. Welcome to Langham Hall.'

She attempted to gently prise Clarice away from him.

'Now, my dear, that's enough; remember there are servants present.'

Clarice nodded, but her hand remained within David's grasp. He smiled. She could not have let go even if she wanted.

'Forgive me, Lady Alice, but I find myself unable to release your granddaughter,' he replied.

The dowager scowled, but the look in her eyes betrayed her.

'Yes, well; let us not dally in the front hallway; if you would come upstairs we can receive you properly.'

He followed them upstairs and into the warmth of the drawing room.

'Where is he?' David demanded as soon as the door was closed behind them. The absence of Thaxter Fox had not gone unnoticed.

'In his room, unconscious,' Lady Alice replied.

'She, I mean we drugged him,' Clarice said. As she turned toward the firelight, David saw the bruise and swelling on the side of her face.

A rage he had never thought possible flared through him and he released her hand. Fists clenched, he stood struggling to bring his anger under control. An overwhelming desire to smash his fist through Thaxter Fox's face coursed through his brain.

Clarice touched his arm and he flinched.

'It's all right, David, I managed to fight him off. Other than a few scratches and bruises I am intact,' she said.

His head felt light with relief. The fear that he would arrive too late to save her had kept him pushing his horses to the limit on the desperate race from London. With Clarice ruined, there would have been little choice but for her to agree to marry Thaxter Fox.

While he would still have been prepared to marry her, David knew that one word from Thaxter and her reputation would be in ruins. Her fall from grace would be immediate and irredeemable.

'How did you get here so fast; we only sent the letter to London yesterday?' Clarice said.

'I haven't seen any letter,' David replied.

'But how did you know he was here?' Clarice and Lady Alice replied in unison.

He stepped closer to the fireplace, seeking to warm his frozen bones. Lady Alice took a seat and pretended to ignore the fact that her granddaughter had once more wrapped her arms around David's waist.

'Actually, Lady Susan Kirk is the reason why I am here. From what my sister Lucy told me, she had a serious attack of guilt. It was Susan who warned us of Thaxter's plan to ruin Clarice.'

'Judas,' Clarice hissed at his side.

Lady Alice winced.

David shook his head. 'She didn't have a handful of silver in her possession when she revealed that blackguard's dirty plan. From my understanding, Mr Fox had made certain intimations to your friend which led her to believe he planned to make her an offer of marriage. Of course, as soon as she knew the real reason why he had left town and had followed you to Norfolk, she knew she had been taken for a fool.'

'He is after my dowry,' Clarice replied.

'Since there are now rumours that Susan's dowry may have disappeared, Mr Fox clearly decided you were the surer bet. If Susan hadn't swallowed her pride and revealed Fox's dastardly plan to Lucy, I wouldn't be standing here right now. When the dust from all this has settled, you may wish to find it in your heart to forgive her,' he replied.

Clarice squeezed him tighter.

'Let go, Clarice, we need to talk.'

She sighed but did as he asked.

He rubbed his hands together in front of the fire, relieved

when the pins and needles in his fingers signalled the return of sensation in his hands. Having spent much of his life in Scotland, he was well experienced in riding a horse through the peril of a winter's tempest. Tonight, however, his skills as a horseman had been tested to their limit.

After arriving in the village earlier, he had abandoned his driver and carriage, deciding to risk the journey in the fading light on horseback. The innkeeper had pleaded for him to wait out the storm, but as soon as David knew Thaxter Fox was in residence at Langham Hall, the hounds of hell could not have kept him from travelling on.

'You say Fox is unconscious, that you have drugged him?' he said turning to Lady Alice.

'Yes. I slipped a little something into his brandy before dinner and also into his port. He should sleep like a lamb until at least morning,' she replied.

David raised an eyebrow, silently grateful that she was on his side in the battle.

'And what did you plan to do with him once he wakes?'

Lady Alice smiled and jangled the ring of keys she pulled out from under the cushion beside her.

'The men who brought him up from London have not been paid. I offered them their outstanding wages, plus a little extra, to take him back to town tomorrow morning. They didn't seem to need much more of an excuse to leave the sunny climes of Norfolk,' she replied.

He nodded. 'Good.'

'Grandmother and I were going to leave here early tomorrow and travel to Sharnbrook,' Clarice added.

The hope which flared in his heart warmed him more than the heat of the well-stoked fire. Clarice had been coming to find him. He looked to her and the blush of red on her cheek confirmed his suspicions.

She reached into the top of her gown and, pulling on the chain around her neck, withdrew the pendant.

'Just so you know, I had made my decision before Mr Fox got here.'

She gave a brief glance toward Lady Alice. 'I'm not afraid any more. I will speak the truth to Papa and where that leaves us shall be his choice. All I know is that I have decided upon my future and it lies with David.'

He stood for a moment, silently savouring her words, all the while wishing they were alone so he could kiss her senseless.

David held a hand out to Lady Alice. 'I should like to check on your guest if you don't mind, your ladyship. I am dog-tired after my long journey, but I shall sleep more soundly if I am certain our friend is incapable of disturbing the peace before he is sent on his way tomorrow.'

Lady Alice stood and headed for the door. 'Follow me,' she said.

With Clarice's hand held firmly in his, David followed the dowager down the long hallway. Toward the end of the hallway was a door, similar in aspect to all the other doors which dotted the hallway, except that two large chairs had been placed in front of it. In each of the chairs, covered by a warm blanket, slumbered a solidly built estate worker.

'I thought you said the door was locked,' David remarked.

'It is, but I was taking no chances. I made the error of underestimating our Mr Fox when first I met him. I won't make that mistake again,' Lady Alice replied.

By his side, he heard Clarice stifle a laugh. Something had changed in her during their brief time apart. She had rediscovered her spirit. Her spark.

The men in the chairs stirred. One opened an eye, and seeing Lady Alice, shot to his feet. She waved a hand and bade him to sit down.

'Our guest has been quiet?' David asked.

The man gave a respectful bow. 'Yes, sir, silent as the grave.'

'Good man, get some sleep,' he replied.

He turned and was nearly at the top of the stairs when a sudden compulsion took hold of him.

'The keys please, Lady Alice,' he said and held out his hand.

Sleep would evade him if he didn't set eyes upon his nemesis.

He marched back down the hallway, leaving Clarice and her grandmother to wait for his return. Slipping the key into the lock, he opened the door. With both estate workers standing guard at the doorway, he entered the room.

The only light in the room was from the embers of the dying fire, but the shape of the fully dressed Thaxter Fox lying prone across the bed was unmistakable. Flat on his back, mouth open, he snored as he slept. The drool which had seeped from his mouth and on to the collar of his shirt would have been comical if it had been anyone else. If the circumstances had been different. Stepping closer, David loomed over his sleeping enemy. The ugly wound on his face was satisfactory evidence of Clarice's self-defence. She had fought off this rogue and won a future for them.

'She is mine, and the next time you so much as look at her I will thrash you to within an inch of your bloody life,' he said, his voice clear and even.

He marched from the room and locked the door behind him. He would deal with Thaxter Fox in the morning.

※

Lady Alice remained in the drawing room long enough to pour them all a small celebratory drink. She raised a glass to Clarice and David and quickly downed the wine.

'I just need to go and check on Cook, I shouldn't be too long,' she said as she slipped out of the room, closing the door behind her.

Clarice chuckled and turned to David. 'I would be surprised if she has ever set foot in the downstairs kitchen.'

Barely had the words left her mouth when David pulled her into his arms, bent his head and kissed her.

The first kiss they'd shared in the summerhouse had been tender and meant to woo, but this was an entirely different intimate encounter.

He didn't wait for her to soften to his enticing lips; rather, his tongue filled her mouth in a clear statement of claim. Her body responded with a surge of desire. She put a hand to his head and boldly grabbed hold of his hair, pulling him down to her.

He groaned and she exalted once more in the knowledge that she had this powerful effect on him. He began to trail kisses across her bruised cheek.

'I will kill any man who tries to touch you,' he breathed into her ear.

'Only you, there will only ever be you,' she whispered.

Seizing the initiative, she tilted her head and caught his mouth once more. She had only been kissed twice in her life, but she was a quick learner. Nipping at his bottom lip with her teeth, she challenged him to give himself up to her.

A deep sensual growl was her reward.

He pulled her hard against his body, and she felt the hardness of his arousal. Somewhere in the back of her mind, she prayed her grandmother would take a very long time before she returned.

They continued to meld their lips together, each giving and demanding more in return. When eventually they stepped back from one another, breathing hard as they sucked in air, Clarice held a hand to her swollen lips. Now she finally understood why Alex and Millie had fought so hard to be together. Looking at David, she knew without a doubt that he was her world.

'I love you and I want to marry you,' she said.

The memory of watching him realise and accept her words would remain long in her heart. He closed his eyes and slowly nodded.

'I will do everything within my power to make you happy,' he replied.

In the days since she had made her decision, Clarice had thought long and hard about how they could be together. With her father opposed to the union, the answer was simple.

'Come away with me to Scotland. We can be married as soon as we are across the border,' she said. There was always the chance that circumstances might have changed David's mind.

He took hold of her hand.

'The day I make you my wife will be the happiest day of my life, but we cannot elope.'

She scowled. Disappointed, but not surprised.

'If I steal you away to Scotland, then we begin our marriage with a scandal. Your father will no doubt attempt to have it annulled, and due to my lack of legitimacy he may very well succeed. So my answer is no. We shall marry in front of family and friends in London, and the Bishop of London shall give us his blessing.'

'Not wishing to start our first argument, but how exactly do you plan to get my father to agree to our marriage?' she replied.

He pulled her into his arms and kissed her on the top of her long, fair hair.

'I was already intending to leave London to come and fetch you before I got word of Fox's plans. The way to ensure that your father agrees to our union is the good old-fashioned way. I'm going to kidnap you,' he replied and laughed deeply.

After a nightcap, which Lady Alice assured him was not tainted by sleeping draught, David retired to the room which had been hurriedly made up for him. Sitting on the edge of the bed he found himself grinning like a fool.

The look on Clarice's face when he informed her she was about to be kidnapped was utterly priceless. When he explained it to Lady Alice only a few minutes later, she'd simply raised an eyebrow and then nodded in agreement. His intended had stood wide-eyed and stared at the both of them.

Now, as his head hit the soft pillow and the first wave of sleep washed over him, David smiled. Clarice had made her choice and she had chosen him.

'Foolish girl, how could you possibly think I was going to be that tractable? I won't rest until Langham gives me his full and happy approval to marry you,' he whispered into the darkness as he slipped beneath the ocean of sleep.

Chapter Twenty-Three

The room was filled with morning light when David woke from his deep slumber. He stretched his fingers out over his head and to his surprise, his hand did not touch the familiar wooden headboard of his bed.

Confused, he opened his eyes and looked around the room. Then he remembered where he was and softly chuckled. He was in a bedroom at Langham Hall, Norfolk. Home for the past three hundred years to the Langham family.

Clarice's home.

He rolled over and stared at the door, imagining for a moment how good it would feel to see her come walking through the door. She would be clad in a nightgown of such diaphanous fabric that his imagination would not be required. She would come to his bed and gladly give all that he demanded of her body.

Last night Clarice had declared her love for him. Once more he found himself grinning like a fool. 'She loves me,' he said and shook his head in disbelief.

A tap at the door stirred him from his pleasurable musing.

'A moment, if you will,' he called out. He quickly pushed

all thought of Clarice's naked form from his mind in an attempt to soften his now rock-hard body.

His valet entered the room a short time later carrying David's travel bag. Upon seeing him, a look of immense relief appeared on Bailey's face.

'Good to see you are awake, Mr Radley. I take it you had an uneventful ride here last night?'

A wry smile formed on David's lips.

Bailey had begged him not to ride out into the storm. He had pleaded the hardship he would endure when he was forced to tell the Duke of Strathmore that his eldest son had died alone on the road. Probably in a rain-swollen ditch, he had added for dramatic effect. His heartfelt pleas had all been for nought. As soon as David had been able to find a calm enough mount, one which would not turn skittish on the road, he leapt on its back and headed to Langham Hall.

'I hope you stayed close to the fire last night, but I trust not too close to the innkeeper's daughter,' David said.

Did the man just blush?

Bailey muttered a response, but seeing the look on David's face, he smiled. David climbed out of bed.

'A quick shave and wash this morning, I want us to be on the road shortly after breakfast,' he said.

'London, sir?' Bailey replied.

'Sharnbrook, Mr Bailey; I thought you would have had more faith in me than that,' he replied and gave his valet a slap on the back.

'Very good, sir,' Bailey replied.

Over breakfast David shared his plans with Clarice and Lady Alice. The dowager countess sat quietly listening and then added her agreement. A slow orderly journey westwards, stopping only at the best of the roadside establishments, was the order of the day. Nothing to draw attention to themselves.

Clarice sat silently at the table. Wiping her face with her

napkin, she rose from the table. David stood and bowed. He caught the look in her eye and his brow creased.

'You are not happy with the arrangements?' he asked.

She lay the napkin down on the table and shrugged her shoulders.

'I don't know; I just thought I would have more time. Excuse me, I have to check that my wardrobe is ready for our departure.'

In her bedroom Clarice stared at her travel trunk. How could she leave Langham Hall without telling David the truth of her past?

Lady Alice tapped on the door.

Clarice sighed and picked up her coat. She thrust one arm into a sleeve before Lady Alice took hold of her arm.

'Pouting and sighing will never get you anywhere, especially not with a man such as David Radley. Now, what is the matter?'

'I thought I would have more time than this to decide exactly what to tell him,' Clarice replied.

Her grandmother brushed a gentle hand against Clarice's cheek. 'You tell him the truth if you want your marriage to be one based on love and honesty. Men are not mind readers, they do not respond to wishes or subtle hints. My advice is that if you are not prepared to be completely honest with him, then the best thing for us to do is to return to London. You have to be able to trust your future husband.'

Clarice finished putting on her coat and wrapped a warm scarf around her neck. A moment of Lady Alice's counsel and the clarity she so badly sought came to her.

'I shall speak to David before we leave, but first things first: we need to be rid of Thaxter Fox.'

᎒

As soon as David reached the floor where Thaxter Fox had been sleeping, he knew their prisoner was awake.

The two estate workers who had spent the night keeping guard were sitting facing the door.

Bang! Bang!

The bedroom door rattled on its hinges and the two men exchanged an appreciative chuckle. 'You would think his fists would be bloodied and sore by now,' one of them remarked.

As David approached the door banged once again.

'I would say that was more like a hip and shoulder,' he remarked. He stopped outside the door, lay an ear to it and listened. At the next attack on the door, he lifted his head away and nodded.

'Yes, definitely hip and shoulder, with a string of foul words added for good measure.'

He went back downstairs and located the driver and his mate from Thaxter's carriage. After a brief discussion with them, David decided they were trustworthy enough to ensure that their client returned to London.

The third member of Fox's travel party, his supposed man of business, was a small weasel-like creature, whom David took an instant dislike to as soon as he opened his mouth.

'I ain't wiv them; and I don't work for that tosspot you've got locked up in his room. I'm here on me master's business,' he said with a sneer.

'And what exactly is your master's business? David replied.

'Money. Your Mr Fox owes a lot of people some serious blunt. He promised if I came to Norfolk wiv him he would get us our money. So far I ain't seen a blasted penny.'

Deciding Thaxter's cash problems were his own affair, David left the debt collector with the carriage. He assembled a number of able-bodied male servants who then accompanied David back into the house and upstairs.

Having thought long and hard as to how the feat was to be accomplished, David decided the direct approach was the best. He strode to the door and knocked loudly on it. 'Mr Fox, your carriage awaits.'

'Open this bloody door!' Thaxter bellowed from the other side.

David looked to the men and nodded. 'We are going to have to open the door if we are to be rid of Mr Fox.'

He turned back to the door. 'You may wish to take a step back, Mr Fox. The chap I have given my pistol to looks a mite nervous and I am afraid if you scare him, he may just put a bullet in you. If he does Cook will need to perform the surgery.'

The unarmed men looked at one another and grinned. Cook really had made a mess of the stitches on Thaxter Fox's face.

'All right,' came the reply from the bedroom.

Taking the key he had retrieved from Lady Alice, David stepped up to the door and unlocked it.

'Ready, gentlemen?' he said as he swung the door open.

Standing in the middle of the room, Thaxter looked quickly at David and then past him into the hall.

'There are five of us, Fox, and several more at the top of the stairs. I personally don't think even a man like you would chance it.'

'I wondered how long it would take for you to come in search of your little whore,' Thaxter spat back.

The staff muttered their disapproval at the daughter of the house being referred to in such a manner, but David held up his hand. They fell silent.

'Gentlemen, never allow an unworthy opponent to get up your ire. You are only playing into his hands.'

He stood to one side of the door and beckoned for Thaxter to exit the room.

'Shall we?'

'It would appear I have little choice in the matter. Have my man bring my bag down to the carriage,' Thaxter replied.

He walked from the room and with two men in front and two behind, descended the stairs. David lingered for a moment in the room and picked up the travel bag.

A very heavy travel bag.

He put the bag on the bed, opened it and shook his head in disgust as he removed a folded jacket to reveal several large pieces of silverware which Thaxter had intended to steal from the house. David tipped up the bag and emptied its contents on to the bed, then closed it and hurried from the room with the empty bag.

By the time he reached the bottom of the stairs, Clarice and Lady Alice had joined the party in the front entrance.

'I just want to make sure Mr Fox is sent safely on his way,' Lady Alice said.

David threw the empty travel bag at Thaxter. 'You certainly travel light,' he said.

The look he received in return put a spring in his step for the rest of the day.

It was only when they were out in front of the Hall and close to the travel coach that Thaxter finally made his displeasure at being forced to leave known.

David had taken his gaze from his prisoner for only a second when Thaxter made his move. Without warning he let out a roar and made a violent lunge toward Clarice, fists flying. Fortunately, she was further away then he realised and David was able to put his body between them before Thaxter could reach her.

He smashed a fist into Thaxter's face without restraint. Thaxter fell backwards, sprawled on the ground, his hands held to his bloodied face.

Clarice raced to a spot on the stones several feet away and

picked up a small object. Returning to David's side, she handed it to him.

'This was in his hand; what is it?' she said.

He looked down at the small sharp blade and knew exactly what it was. It matched the wound he had received at the boxing saloon.

The click of a pistol caught his attention.

Lady Alice stood pointing a pistol at Thaxter as he struggled to his knees.

'I shall put you out in the street the day I inherit the title, you old hag,' he said, and spat blood at her feet. Clutching one of the wheels of the travel coach, he dragged himself upright.

The dowager countess snorted. 'Perhaps I should just shoot you here and now and save us both a lot of trouble. I have lived at the Hall for over forty years and I doubt if the local magistrate could find a single man amongst these good people who would bear witness to my crime.'

David strode over to Lady Alice and held out his hand. She let down the cock of the pistol and handed it to him. She shrugged her shoulders.

'Well, it would have solved a lot of our problems. He does have a younger brother who is a war hero; I expect he would make a better heir.'

David shook his head. No-one would be committing murder on his watch.

'I think it is time for you to leave, Mr Fox,' he said.

'Oy! Where is my money?' the weasel man cried. He picked up Thaxter's empty travel bag and waved it in his face.

'I don't have it,' Thaxter bit back.

For a small man the debt collector packed a powerful punch. For the second time in a matter of minutes Thaxter found himself on his knees in the gravel of the driveway. When the man produced a horsewhip and made set to lash his hapless debtor, David stepped forward.

'Enough! Take your business with this gentleman elsewhere.'

'On yer feet Fox. You have until we get back to London to come up with the money you owe. After that…'

He brandished the horsewhip toward David and smiled tightly. Thaxter Fox was in for a very long and unpleasant journey back to London.

§⁂

They watched as the coach headed down the long driveway and disappeared over the hill. Lady Alice, having retrieved her pistol, went back inside to check on their travel arrangements. David turned to Clarice and took her hand.

'Are you ready to leave? You did seem out of sorts at breakfast.'

She shook her head. Once she got into the coach, there would be no time to talk privately with him. To tell him the truth.

'I need to talk to you,' she replied.

He nodded.

She led him across the drive and up the small path leading toward the dell. With her heart pounding as loud as a cannon in her ears, she struggled to hold back the tears.

'Where are we going?' he asked, glancing back from where they had come. 'Whatever you need to tell me, we are well and truly out of anyone's earshot.'

She continued walking. 'Only a little way further.' If things ended badly between them, then the familiar surroundings of the churchyard would at least give her some comfort.

When they arrived in front of the small stone chapel, Clarice released David's hand and walked over to her mother's grave.

Mama, I have to do this. I have to tell him. I cannot offer him only half my heart.

David came to her side and brushed a tender kiss on her cheek. He looked at the headstone and sighed.

'She was a lovely woman, your mother. She was always kind to me,' he said.

Clarice nodded and took a step back; she couldn't bear for him to be this near. The scent of his cologne enticing her to say nothing, to let things be. To claim him with a lie.

'If you decide that you no longer wish to marry me after what I say, I shall understand. It would be easy enough for me not to tell you the truth and go on with our plans, but I couldn't do that to you. You have bared your soul to me; now it is my turn. The only thing I ask is that you keep this secret between us, that you never speak of it to anyone. And I mean anyone.'

She watched him as he silently studied her.

'If you were unable to fight that rogue off, if he did force himself upon you, I shall still marry you,' he replied. In his eyes the truth of his conviction shone.

You don't deserve this pain.

She shook her head and with hands clasped together, turned to face the headstone.

'Elizabeth Langham was my mother, but as for my sire, he is *not* Henry Langham,' she said.

The wind rustled the grass and the nearby ash tree cracked as it moved in the breeze. A shadow passed over the grass as David came between her and the sun's light.

'Go on,' he murmured.

A warm, powerful hand lifted her chin and she looked into his eyes.

'I received a letter when I turned nineteen, informing me I had been left a substantial inheritance. The details it contained left me with no option but to confront my mother as to my true parentage. When I showed her the letter she became hysterical. Crying and tearing at her clothes like a woman possessed. It was truly the most awful thing I have ever seen.'

Tears rolled freely down her face. When David tried to wipe them away, she stopped him.

'We screamed at each other. I said the most horrible of things to her before I finally fled the room and ran to the stairs. And then she…'

Clarice buried her face in her hands. David pulled her firmly into his arms and wrapped them around her. The wind dropped and then stilled. Clarice was silent in David's arms for seemed an eternity.

'That's odd,' he finally remarked.

Clarice lifted her head. 'What is?'

'That bird. It's a Snow Bunting; they are native to the peaks of Scotland, and I've never seen one in England. Scottish folklore tells that they are soul of a departed one.'

She looked at the bird on a nearby branch. It was studying them both. Her breath caught in her throat.

Please, please.

'It appears to have taken up residence in the dell,' she replied. Now was not the time to tell him that she thought of the bird as her mother returned in spirit.

'David?' she said turning back to look at him. Other than to make mention of an ornithological aberration, he had said nothing of her secret.

'I love you,' he whispered.

His lips descended and met her mouth as his name escaped her lips. Softly, teasingly, he kissed her bottom lip over and over. Heat flared within her. Their tongues began their now-familiar dance. Hands cupped under her ears, David held Clarice's face as he deepened the kiss.

Locked deep in his embrace, she silently chided herself. His answer was not to be found in the long speech she had expected him to give, it was in his passionate claiming of her. She slipped a hand inside the opening of his coat and lay it over his heart. They had years ahead of them to talk about her past, to dissect the minutiae of events. He had given his response and that was all that mattered. He released her lips.

'Thank you,' he said.

She scowled. 'Why are you thanking me?'

'Because you trusted me with your secret.'

In the hands of others it could be used to destroy her. If the truth was ever known she would be ostracised from society, her father branded a liar.

'You don't think any less of me?'

David harrumphed. 'Why should I? Your mother's death was an accident; she slipped on the stairs. It was no-one's fault. And as for the status of your birth, you are Langham's daughter and always will be. No-one can prove otherwise. While I am humbled beyond words that you have shared this knowledge with me, it changes nothing.'

She nodded. 'I confided in Lady Alice not long after we arrived here, but I have never made mention of the letter to Papa.'

'Will you tell him now?'

'I'm not sure. As things stand between us at this moment, revealing it to him could shatter our relationship forever. He is the only father I have ever known; I couldn't bear to lose him.'

David brushed a wayward curl behind her ear and kissed her forehead. Considering everything that had happened, she would not have blamed him if he did tell her to throw the truth in her father's face.

'Of course he is still your father. He has raised you as his own, given you his name and with it legitimacy. Unless he brings it up himself, you should never make mention of it. Let the memories of your years as a family stay intact. He deserves your loyalty.'

Clarice rose up on her toes and kissed him.

'I love you.'

'About time,' he chuckled.

Clarice took David inside the small chapel and they sat for

a time, hand-in-hand in quiet reflection. After gathering some fresh flowers for Elizabeth's grave, they kissed once more. Now, with an unbreakable bond they would face their future together.

As they reached the top of the path leading back to the house, they heard the flutter of wings and saw the bird fly overhead.

'Yes, very odd,' David muttered.

Chapter Twenty-Four

It was late afternoon by the time their coach pulled into the yard at Sharnbrook. David could not have been more relieved to see his new home.

Three days travelling with Clarice and her grandmother had been pleasant enough, but although he tried to distract himself by reading, he could not stop worrying over Clarice.

All those years she had spent with the guilt of her mother's death and he had not been able to comfort her. He wanted to blame someone, and vacillated between Lady Elizabeth and Lord Langham. The countess for having left Clarice at such a vulnerable point in her life, the earl for having kept David at bay.

I should have been there to help her. I could have eased her pain.

Clarice herself sat quietly in the carriage, saying little, staring out the window. She refused any offers of food or drink. Doubt began to creep into his mind. Was she having second thoughts about them?

When they stopped at the next town, he took her to one side.

'You haven't said anything all morning, Clarice; have I done something wrong?'

She took hold of his hand and gave him a weak smile.

'You haven't done anything wrong. I suffer terribly from travel sickness and it takes all my strength not to be ill. We have to keep moving, but until we reach Sharnbrook it is unlikely you'll get much conversation from me.'

Relieved, he brushed a kiss on her cheek.

'My youngest sister suffers from it too. Have you tried ginger sweets? Emma sucks on them while we are travelling and then sips ginger tea at night. It doesn't cure her completely but at least she is not nauseous.'

'I will try them,' Clarice replied.

When they next stopped in a town, David quickly found a local shop which stocked all manner of sweets and purchased several large bags. For the rest of the trip, Clarice sat sucking on the ginger sweets, her face a little brighter. By the time they crossed into Bedfordshire, she was able to keep some food down and the spark had returned to her eyes.

As the coach slowed to a halt at Sharnbrook Grange, she sat forward in her seat and pressed her face excitedly to the glass. 'I shall remember this moment for the rest of my days. My very first glimpse of the Grange,' she said with a smile.

David smiled tightly back at her. There were several large mountains left to climb before Clarice became a permanent fixture at Sharnbrook.

'But not today; today is ours,' he muttered as he climbed down from the coach.

When Lady Alice took her customary afternoon nap, David and Clarice were able to spend some precious time together. They walked through the yard, where he introduced her to various members of the household. David said nothing when he noticed his steward Bannister had changed from his trusty old brown jacket into a slightly less tired blue one.

When Clarice made mention of how she liked the colour of his jacket, Bannister turned a deep crimson and bowed a second time. David strangled a snort. A wicked glint appeared in Clarice's eye before she mentioned that perhaps he should invest in such a fine piece of clothing. He raised an eyebrow. If his tailor in Bond Street saw him in such attire he would never be allowed to set foot in their premises again.

He took Clarice gently by the arm and steered her toward the path which led away from the house. 'Are you perhaps interested in livestock, Lady Clarice? I could show you my new flock,' he asked once they were away from the staff.

She giggled. 'Why, thank you, Mr Radley; I have a lively interest in all manner of animals. Especially the two-legged variety native to the parish of St James.'

A clump of trees now hid them from view of the house. David pulled her roughly to him and kissed her.

Hard.

As their lips met, he felt the heat begin to rise within him. Lust, pure and unadulterated, coursed through his veins. He wanted her, ached for her. Feared he would go blind with desire before he could have her in his bed.

He was too busy dominating her mouth with his lips to realise that she had flipped open the middle button of his shirt. The sensation of Clarice's bare fingers touching his chest caused him to gasp. She gave a wicked chuckle, before opening the next button.

He swallowed deeply and took hold of her wrist.

'We are not *that* far from the house,' he cautioned, before letting go.

She gave a mew of disappointment, but refused to remove her hand. Slowly he found himself backed up against a nearby tree. The arch seducer was being played at his own game. Her nimble fingers squeezed one of his nipples and he lay his head back against the bark of the tree.

'Clarice,' he ground out.

'Yes?' she replied as her other hand moved down toward a far more dangerous place on his body.

He looked up and saw the clouds swirling overhead. The

temptation to just stand there and let her have her way with him was deliciously enticing. He sighed as he reached down and took hold of one wandering hand.

'Not here, my love.'

She huffed and removed her other hand.

David buttoned his shirt and pushed away from the tree. His heart pounded in his chest as he tried to think of something that would calm the raging erection in his trousers.

'There was little point in bringing Lady Alice with you as chaperone if within an hour of our arrival you have lost your innocence. I will not ravish you out here in the wild,' he said.

She scowled. 'So when?'

He shook his head. 'Patience, my love. We have a whole lifetime ahead of us.'

She shrugged her shoulders and pointed to the nearby field, which was now stocked with a fine head of sheep. 'Come then, let me judge if your sheep are half as good as my father's,' she said, offering him her hand.

He took her hand. 'Actually, I am rather pleased with the Southdowns. They arrived while you were in Norfolk. The ram I am yet to see.'

He looked down, surprised to feel a tremble in her hand.

'Clarice?'

'Thank you for saving me,' she said, lowering her head.

The brave and sexy Clarice of a minute ago had disappeared. In her place stood a frightened, vulnerable young woman.

'You saved yourself, as I understand,' he replied, feeling an utter heel for having just rejected her advances. She needed reassurance of where she stood with him, not a lecture on morals.

He put a comforting arm around her.

'Not just from that evil man. I don't know if I could have done any of this if it hadn't been for your letter. I read it over and over so many times. When I think of how long you have loved me from afar, how you held on to those impossible dreams. You gave me the reasons and the strength to face my fears.'

He smiled at her, his heart swelling with pride.

'Do you have the slightest notion as to how wonderful you are?' he replied.

Lady Alice retired early that evening, leaving David and Clarice alone in the elegant drawing room. As the dowager countess left the room, David turned to Clarice.

'I am not certain of the protocol here, as we are now left without a chaperone. Should I ask your maid to come and sit with us?'

She shook her head before crossing to the door and closing it behind her.

'We need to talk,' she said. She ignored the questioning lift of his eyebrows when she took a seat next to him on the couch.

'Let me see if I have things straight in my mind. You won't elope with me to Scotland because you want a big London wedding?'

He nodded.

'But you won't ruin me. That part I do not understand, especially when it is the key to ensuring that we have to marry?'

He sighed. 'I won't ruin you unless there is no other choice.'

Clarice threw up her arms. 'So why did you bring me all the way to Bedford? I thought you said you were kidnapping me! If I understand it correctly, you should be ravishing me right now.' She nodded toward the door. 'Even my grandmother seems to have accepted the inevitability of us becoming lovers while we are here. Why can't you?'

Eyes closed, she immediately began to chastise herself. Surely the way to get a man to seduce you was not by behaving like a shrew.

He reached out and took her by the hand. Raising it to his lips, he kissed her fingertips. A warm heat pooled in her loins and her breathing became shallow. David placed a trail of kisses up her arm until he reached her shoulder, at which point he bit gently into the hollow of her neck.

She shivered, and prayed he would continue.

'Clarice, my darling, you must understand that being this close to you, knowing I could take you right here and now and you would let me, is the sweetest torture I have ever known. But until your father gives us his blessing, we should wait.'

He pulled away. When she looked at his face, his eyes were glazed and his breathing ragged. She heard him swallow deeply.

'I have brought you to Sharnbrook Grange to draw your father out. If I take you back to London, then negotiations have to be conducted on his terms. By making him come here, I have at least some chance of dealing with him on equal terms.'

Clarice rose from the couch and faced David.

'So how do you propose to get my father here?'

A knowing grin appeared on his lips. 'Because before we left Langham Hall I made sure he would know where we were going. At my reckoning, we have two, perhaps three days before he arrives here.'

She clamped her teeth together and nodded her head. She now knew how little time she had left to break David's resolve. The calm, controlled words he spoke said one thing, but when they were close his body screamed another.

'I might just go to bed, then. The ginger sweets certainly helped with my stomach, but travel does tend to tire me out,' she replied.

He stood and they shared a warm kiss. When David began to deepen the kiss, Clarice pulled away.

'Soon, very soon, my love,' she said with a smile.

'Do you have everything you need?' he replied.

'Yes, thank you. Good night, David.'

Once she was back in her room, Clarice allowed Bella to brush her hair and lay out a nightgown on the bed. She dismissed her maid for the rest of the night.

Crossing quickly to her travel trunk, she threw open the lid. At the very bottom of the trunk was a small parcel wrapped in paper. She retrieved it and unwrapped it. It was surprising how something so small had cost nearly the same price as a new gown.

Holding the cream nightgown up to the light, she gasped at how sheer it was. When she waved a hand on the other side of the gown, a giggle of wicked delight followed. She could see right through it!

Throwing off her sensible warm nightgown, she slipped the sheer muslin gown over her head. Scooting across the room to the mirror, she stood and admired the cream and lace perfection which now hugged the curves of her body.

Whoever had designed the gown knew exactly where to place the strategic pieces of lace which served as a whisper to modesty. The rest of the gown left nothing to the imagination. She put a finger to her lips and took a nervous breath. Could she really stand in front of David in this?

When Millie insisted she purchase the garment from the modiste's salon, Clarice had been horrified. What sort of lady would wear such a thing? Now as she looked at the fine lace and barely-there fabric she understood its purpose.

It was a weapon of seduction.

'You may have chosen the battlefield, Mr Radley, but I intend to fire the first shot. Besides, you only said we should wait, not that we must.'

She picked up her long travel coat and buttoned it up over the gown. Praying she would not encounter any members of the household, let alone Lady Alice, Clarice slipped out into the hallway.

David stretched out in his bedroom fireside chair. Clad only in his tight buckskin breeches and his white shirt, he had settled in for an hour or so of solitude before turning in for a well-earned night's rest.

A bottle of wine left over from dinner sat on a nearby table. He raised his glass and offered himself a silent toast.

Clarice now slept under his roof, under his protection. If Henry Langham wanted to resolve matters, he would now have to come to Sharnbrook.

He took a mouthful of the wine and picked up the book he had started on the final leg of their journey. After reading the same paragraph on the perils of travel in Northern Canada several times and absorbing none of it, he put the book down.

Clarice is asleep under my roof.

He groaned and rubbed the back of his neck. He was going to need another bottle of wine before he stood any chance of sleep tonight. He rose from his chair and headed to the door, ever grateful that Bannister was a man who knew his wine.

He pulled the door open.

On the threshold, with one hand raised ready to knock, stood Clarice. She quickly checked the hallway before side-stepping him and rushing into the room.

'You had better close that and lock it,' she said, pointing to the door.

'I didn't meet anyone on my way here, but I heard voices coming up from the kitchens a moment ago.'

David closed the door and turned to Clarice.

He blinked as he took in the sight before his eyes. Her hair had been let down and expertly brushed. Long blonde tresses kissed her shoulders and then continued to her waist.

She was clad in the travel coat she had worn for the journey from Langham Hall. He frowned, wondering where she could be headed for at this time of night.

His gaze drifted lower, taking in the bottom hem of the coat and the fine fabric of the gown she had on under it.

A scandalously sheer gown in his considered and knowledgeable opinion. The breath caught in his throat when he saw her bare ankles and feet.

'Clarice?'

She blinked and ran her tongue slowly over her lips.

'David,' she whispered and flicked open the topmost button of her coat.

He swallowed as the first spear of lust raced to his loins. Not even a monk living at the top of a mountain who had not set eyes on a woman for fifty years could mistake that look.

'I thought we had agreed to wait until I have secured your father's blessing,' he said. The puff of air he released from his cheeks belied his attempt at a cool exterior.

Clarice shook her head. 'As I recall, I didn't agree to anything.'

He wracked his brains for an answer, but his mind drew a blank.

She smiled and opened the second button.

'Do you remember what you wrote in your love letter?'

He shook his head. It had been many weeks ago and in that time the letter had been mostly in Clarice's possession.

'Not exactly,' he replied.

'Let me remind you,' she said and pulled her copy of the letter out of her coat pocket.

She opened the lowest button of her coat. Only the two middle buttons now remained closed. She unfolded the letter and he watched as her gaze ran over the paper, nodding when she found the passage.

'I would have you naked in my arms, loving you as a man should love his woman. In time you will reveal yourself to me and I shall know you completely.'

She folded up the paper and put it back in her coat pocket.

'I didn't understand what it meant when I first read it, but I think I do now,' she said.

She walked over to him, and undid the last remaining buttons. Shrugging her arms out of the coat, she allowed it to fall to the floor.

David was certain his heart had stopped when Clarice rose up on her tiptoes and placed her hand seductively at the back of his neck. She pulled him down to her and whispered before offering up her mouth to his, 'Know me tonight.'

David Radley, a man who prided himself on his strong self-discipline, knew he had reached the end of his tightly held tether.

Chapter Twenty-Five

As the heat of his bare hands burned through the flimsy fabric of her nightgown, Clarice sensed she was close to victory. While their lips were engaged in a sensual embrace, she pressed the advantage.

Sliding a hand up his chest, she made short, quick work of his shirt buttons, exalting when he swiftly pulled the shirt over his head and threw it across the room.

A gasp of surprised pleasure escaped her lips when he reached out and ran his fingers over her hardened nipples. He squeezed one and she whimpered.

'Good,' he muttered.

They pulled apart, briefly looking into each other's eyes. He brushed the hair away from her face and she nodded in reply to his silent question.

'Yes, I am sure.'

He stepped back and she smiled as he took in the diaphanous confection before his eyes.

'My compliments to the seamstress who designed that; she certainly knows how a man's mind works. I shall be certain to have an account arranged for future purchases by my wife, as something tells me one or two of these gossamer pieces may come to an untimely end.'

He smiled as he said *wife* and Clarice drew close to tears.

She lay a hand on his now-naked chest, running her fingers through the fine black hair. Taking her forefinger, she traced a line down his chest, over his toned, taut stomach, stopping only when the trail of hair reached the top of his breeches.

'What happened there?' she asked, pointing at the red scar on David's left side.

He shook his head. 'Nothing.'

She bit down on her bottom lip as she placed her shaking fingers on the button of his pants. The hard bulge of his erection gave her reason to pause momentarily.

'Would you like me to assist?' he offered.

She shook her head and steadied her hand. This was one gift she planned to unwrap all by herself.

She flicked open the placket of his breeches and slipped a hand inside. David's breathing became ragged and looking up she saw his eyes had closed. She gave his manhood a gentle squeeze and he reached out and laid his hand softly on her shoulder.

'Now run your hand up and down while still holding on to me,' he instructed.

He took her mouth once more and as she slowly stroked him, he worked his tongue against hers.

'Enough,' he finally murmured and taking Clarice by the wrist, removed her hand from his member.

'Was I not doing it right?' she asked.

A deep chuckle rose in his throat. 'You were doing it perfectly, but toying with my emotions in such a way will only get us so far.'

He stripped off his trousers and tossed them aside, allowing Clarice to see the fullness of his sexual arousal. Her eyes grew wide as saucers. He was large, long and…oh.

He took her hands in his and kissed her fingertips.

'This is the moment when I ask how much you know about the marital act. Having lost your mother at a particular age I don't expect you have been given *the talk*,' he said. The look of concern on his face was touching.

'No. But we do have livestock on Papa's estate and I have heard things,' she replied.

I knew I should have asked Lady Alice when I had the chance. Watching cows and horses probably doesn't count.

He pulled her into his arms and kissed her once more. Small, tender butterfly kisses on her face and lips.

'You took the first step and brought us this far, but I think from this point onward I should take the lead. Consider tonight as your first lesson in the art of pleasure and me your master,' he whispered hotly into her ear.

A shiver ran down her spine.

'Teach me how to please you, how to be your woman,' she replied.

With his mouth in possession of hers, he took hold of her breasts and gently kneaded. Their lips moved over each other in an ever-rising spiral of passion.

She realised the front of her gown was open when David pushed the two front panels apart and exposed her naked breasts to the cool night air. He had somehow managed to unlace the gown while locked in their fierce embrace. He slid the gown off the back of her shoulders and down her arms. He pushed it over her hips and with a swoosh it fell to the floor. Lifting her up, he spun her towards the fire.

'We cannot have you catch a chill so early in the proceedings,' he said as he put her down with her back facing the warmth of the fire.

Instinctively, Clarice attempted to cover her breasts and the thatch of hair at the juncture of her thighs. David gently pulled her hands away.

He took a step back and she heard the gasp of air as it escaped his lungs.

'You are so beautiful, my love. Perfect in every way. Never be ashamed of your natural form, Clarice, for I shall always worship it,' he said.

He came to her once more and kissed her mouth. Then slowly, the kisses moved down her neck and across her chest. He sank to his knees and taking hold of a breast, took a nipple into his mouth and sucked. A pool of heat formed low in her belly as her senses swirled.

When David rolled her nipple between his teeth, she sobbed.

'Oh David, oh god.'

She felt his hand begin to slowly slide up her leg, stopping when it reached the light brown thatch of hair between her legs. They were moving into unchartered territory. Needing to steady herself, she reached down and placed a hand on his head. He slipped a thumb inside her moist folds and began to rub gently around the tiny, nerve-filled nub.

'You want to learn to pleasure me, Clarice? Let me tell you, the first thing a man wants is to hear his woman scream as she reaches climax.'

Standing before him, Clarice frowned. She knew nothing of the pleasures between a man and woman. But whatever it took to make her his woman, she would do it.

'Just tell me how,' she said.

His fingers separated her wet, slick folds and kneeling further down, he set his lips to her heated entrance.

She put a hand to her mouth and bit down on the flesh as wave after wave of magnificent pleasure crashed through her body. His tongue circled and stroked her increasingly tight bud. She felt herself on the edge of madness when he began to thrust his tongue deep into her sex.

Her hands fell and took hold of his shoulders. The more deeply his rough tongue tortured her, the harder she gripped.

Her breathing became ragged as sob after sob escaped her lips. Finally, when she was on the brink of she knew not what, he released her. Sitting back on his haunches, he stared up at her. The fire of unbridled lust burned fiercely in his eyes.

He got to his feet and brushed a hand on her cheek. Whatever she had done, David seemed more than pleased with his pupil's progress.

'Come,' he commanded and carried her to the bed.

On the bed, he placed her on her back, and spread her thighs wide. He knelt between her legs, and inserted two fingers into her tight, wet sheath. Taking hold of her hand, he placed it over his manhood and she began to repeat the earlier stroking action.

'That's it. Grip me tighter and pull a little harder,' he said. When he closed his eyes and groaned, Clarice knew she had the rhythm right.

He grew harder in her hand. Each time her fingers reached down to brush over the soft head of his erection, he thrust his fingers deep into her. He leaned over her and took her mouth in a searing kiss. His tongue thrusting in time with his fingers. She felt the heat begin to build once more, the growing desperation to reach the end.

His fingers left her body and he whispered 'Let go.'

Rising up over her, his strong masculine body slid between her legs and he set the head of his erection to her swollen folds.

'Listen to your body, move to make it feel good. Don't stop until you reach the end,' he said.

Gazes locked together, he began to push slowly into her body. When she stiffened the first time, he took her breast into his mouth and sucked. She closed her eyes and let out a groan. This was pure ecstasy.

As he pushed further into her, the pressure began to build once more. She looked up at him, searching his face. Surely this could not be right? She was being stretched beyond her body's capacity; something had to give.

With his breathing ragged and his chest soaked with sweat, David thrust his tongue deep in her mouth. She rose up to greet his hungry lips as he thrust his hips forward and broke through her maidenhead.

A small sting, followed by the overwhelming release of pressure and the deed was done.

He stilled and she heard him say 'Thank god.'

'Was that it?' she said as her head cleared. He shook his head. 'No, but the hardest part is over. Now you shall know only ecstasy.' He pulled his hips back slightly and then thrust forward once more, seating himself fully within her.

'Did that hurt?' he asked.

She shook her head. 'No, it's fine.'

David began to slowly thrust in and out, grinding his hips against hers. With every deep penetration she sensed a rhythm taking form. Tentatively she thrust her hips up to meet his, emboldened when he groaned and begged her to do it again.

As the pace of their coupling increased, she gripped tightly to the sides of his chest. When he tilted his hips, allowing his manhood to rub hard against her clitoris, a bolt of pleasure tore through her and she cried out.

'David!'

He thrust once more, taking his cue from her increasing sobs and whimpers. Faster and harder he drove into her, until finally, with a soul-deep groan, she shattered.

Wave after wave of hot pleasure crashed over her as he continued to ride her. With every stroke, he would withdraw to the point of leaving her body, before thrusting deep and hard into her once more. She lay back in the bed, and watched with fascination at the passion which was etched on his face.

His movements now became frenzied, his hands holding

the bedclothes in a vice-like grip as he rode her ever faster. When Clarice tilted her hips a fraction more, he moaned.

'Lift your legs, wrap them around me. Take me deeper,' he commanded her.

She did and was immediately rewarded. As he sank into her a second time in this far more intense position, he let out a roar and stilled. He closed his eyes and bent his head.

Clarice reached up and placed a hand on David's chest, over his pounding heart. He opened his eyes and smiled down at her.

'I love you and now you are truly mine,' he said.

He slowly withdrew from her body, never taking his gaze from her. He sat back on his heels and Clarice sat up. She knelt in front of him and, taking his face in her hands, reverently kissed him.

'Thank you. I expect not every young lady has such a wonderful time when she is ruined by her captor. Nor does she fall in love with the rogue.'

He raised an eyebrow.

'I am a rogue? Remind me again who it was who came to my room and offered herself so willingly?'

He took hold of her hand and placed a kiss on the inside of her wrist. 'I would wish that our joining is always good for you. A man may find his release more easily than a woman. Promise me, my love, you will demand all I can give of you in the pursuit of your sexual pleasure.'

Clarice blushed, which, considering she had been engaged in a heated coupling with him only a moment ago, struck her as absurd. Staring into each other's eyes, they shared a soft chortle.

'Come, let me be your lady's maid,' he said.

David ushered Clarice to the small washroom which ran off his bedroom. A bowl of water had been placed there in preparation for David's nightly ablutions. She blushed more than once as he went about the task of removing the evidence of their lovemaking from her body.

Back in the bedroom, she picked up the nightgown and her coat. He frowned and shook his head. 'You won't be needing those until the morning,' he said and threw back the bedclothes.

With David on his back, Clarice lay her head on his chest and he wrapped his arms around her. The soft hairs on his chest tickled her cheek, but she did not mind. When he blew out the last candle, the bed became a warm, dark love nest.

'I shall have to return to my room before the servants are up and about,' she said.

'Don't worry, you will be safely tucked up in your bed before your maid arrives. Now sleep, my love; we cannot have you sitting with bags under your eyes at breakfast.'

Sleep took David first. In the dark, Clarice could hear his breathing slow and the thud of his heart settle into a sedate rhythm. The events of the evening had been far more than she had expected. The snippets of information she had garnered from overhead conversations in ladies' rooms had left her largely unprepared.

The memory of David setting his lips to her flesh had her stifling a nervous giggle. She was certain no-one had ever mentioned *that* aspect of matrimonial matters at a society ball.

And it had been good; wickedly so. She had heard enough stories of disappointed young brides to know that not every girl's first time was a pleasure.

David stirred in his sleep.

She snuggled up closer to him, surprised when a single tear found its way to her eye.

'I will never let you go. Whatever I have to do, my father must be made to see reason,' she whispered against his chest.

'He will; now go to sleep,' David murmured.

Chapter Twenty-Six

As Clarice sat at breakfast several mornings later, she pondered the meaning of the expression *cock's crow*. Whoever had coined it certainly knew what the dark and cold of an English country dawn looked like. Reluctantly leaving David and the warmth of his bed, she had stolen barefoot back to her room each morning. The chilly dash she made was the price she had to pay to keep their new status as lovers a secret from the servants.

Across the table, David sat reading a letter. Attired in the well-cut clothing of a gentleman, he showed no outward sign of the daring and passionate lover he had been during the night. And in the hour before dawn. Clarice picked up her napkin and tried to stifle a yawn.

'I am surprised to see you are tired this morning, Clarice,' Lady Alice noted from the other end of the table.

Clarice lifted her head and gave her a smile. A second yawn quickly followed the first.

'I did not sleep well last night. I am still unaccustomed to sleeping in a different bed,' she replied.

As soon as the words left her lips she felt her ears begin to burn. She stared hard at her plate, not daring to look at Lady Alice or David. Especially David.

David cleared his throat and folded up the letter.

'How odd that you say you didn't sleep well, my dear, as I failed to rouse you when I knocked on your door last night. I have finished the book you so kindly lent to me and thought to return it,' Lady Alice said.

'Oh,' she replied.

She looked up and caught Lady Alice smiling a secret smile. Clarice picked up a boiled egg and began to tap at the side of it with her spoon. After the exertions of the night and the early morning, she found herself hungry by breakfast.

Positively ravenous.

David Radley gave new meaning to the expression. An hour before the dawn he'd woken her with his wicked fingers and lips touching her in places that until a few days ago she barely knew she possessed. Places which still throbbed and tingled several hours later.

Clarice stole a glance at her lover, watching as he pursed his lips and blew cool air across the coffee at the top of his cup. Their early-morning lovemaking had been even more magical than the first time. And the second and the third. After their first night together, she had known a little of what was to come. Now, having been in David's arms every night since then, she also knew there was a great deal more.

She swallowed and curled her toes up in her slippers.

'How is your leg this morning, Lady Alice?' David asked.

Clarice let out the breath she had been unconsciously holding.

'It comes and goes,' Lady Alice replied.

To suit the occasion.

Clarice fixed a look of concern on her face that she knew would fool no-one.

'I was thinking of a walk in Temple Wood this morning,

but if you don't think your knee is quite up to a short hike, would you mind if Clarice accompanied me? It is on the edge of the estate, so she will perfectly safe,' David replied.

An image of a wolf in sheep's clothing suddenly popped into Clarice's head. He wouldn't, would he? Outside in the woods? She had seen enough couples stealing away into rooms at balls and parties to know private assignations took place. How naive had she been to think it was only for the purpose of sharing a kiss?

'If Clarice is not too tired, I see no harm in a ramble through the woods,' Lady Alice replied.

'Excellent. I shall make sure Cook gives us a basket; there is a blackberry patch a little way over the hill and with any luck we shall have fresh blackberries and cream for supper,' David said.

After breakfast, Clarice changed into a sensible pair of walking boots and a warm day gown before venturing out into the yard to find David.

Finding the yard empty, she buttoned up her coat against the chill of a late summer's morning and went for an exploratory walk. From inside the barn she could hear the voices of men. How very different the accents of the local men were from those of the workers from her father's estate in Norfolk. Then she heard David's clipped *ton* accent rise up and the men fell silent. He said something which she could not quite catch, but which brought forth a round of appreciative cheers from the other men.

She smiled. He certainly had a way with people.

And his lips.

A tug on her coat startled Clarice and she looked down to see the cause of the disturbance. Standing looking up at her with serious intent was a small girl.

'Hello, who are you?' Clarice asked.

The girl let go of Clarice's coat.

'I'm Lady Tunia,' she replied.

She studied Tunia for a moment. 'Lady Tunia, that's an interesting name. Is your father a lord?'

A patch of red appeared on Tunia's cheeks. 'No, my pa is the stable master. My real name is Petunia, but Mr Radley calls me Lady Tunia. '

'Does he now? That's very noble of him,' Clarice replied.

'Are you a real lady? Like one who lives in a palace?' Petunia asked, her brow furrowed deep with concern.

Clarice smiled.

'Well, yes, I am a real lady; my father is an earl, but I don't live in a palace.'

'Do you love Mr Radley?'

A gush of laughter escaped Clarice's lips. Petunia had come straight to the point of things. She nodded her head. 'Very much, very much indeed.'

It was thrilling to be able to finally voice her affection for David so openly to a complete stranger. She no longer doubted her path.

'So are you going to marry him and come and live here at Sharnbrook Grange? I think he would like that,' Tunia replied.

Clarice bent down and, taking hold of Petunia's hand, pulled her close. 'Well, that depends upon you Lady Tunia. Mr Radley has asked me to marry him and I would like to say yes, but it would mean you letting him become my special lord from now on.'

Petunia's face dropped in disappointment.

'I have to give him up?'

'Well, not entirely; you could still see him when he is in the stables and the yard. And since you are a lady, it would be all right for him to bow to you. But if you want him to be happy, you will have to let me marry him.'

Clarice felt tears coming to her eyes. After all she and David had endured to be together, it was heartbreaking to think of causing the stable master's small daughter pain.

Petunia stared down at the ground, before letting out a large sigh.

'Well, I suppose I shall just have to go back to Peter the butcher's boy.'

'Is he nice?' Clarice ventured.

Petunia, raised her head and nodded. She stepped in close and whispered. 'He gave me a kiss on the cheek last midsummer, but don't tell me ma, she'll skin me.'

'Thank you. You truly are a lady, to see your way to letting me marry Mr Radley,' Clarice replied. She reached into her coat pocket and withdrew a small cloth bag. 'Since you have been so generous, I think I should give you a gift in return.'

She handed the bag to Petunia, who reached inside and pulled out two long dark pink velvet ribbons.

'Oh!' Petunia gasped. 'They are so pretty'.

'They are yours, Lady Tunia,' Clarice said.

She stood and watched as Petunia scampered off with the ribbons held firmly in her hand. Trailing them behind her as she raced to her home, she quickly sidestepped David as he came out of the stables.

She gave him a wave of the hand as she dashed past. 'Mr Radley,' she said.

Clarice laughed at the look of disappointment on David's face as he approached.

'You didn't think she was going to stop and give you a curtsy did you? She is a true lady; clothes always come first,' she said.

'So you have met Lady Tunia, isn't she a charm? David murmured in her ear.

'She is, but it took my best pair of ribbons to convince her to give you up and let me marry you,' Clarice replied, turning to face him. 'Which is rather fortunate as I believe, after the events of the past few days, I have made it clear that my answer is yes.'

David took hold of her hand and placed a tender kiss on her palm.

'I shall never tire of hearing you say *yes* to me.'

She saw the wicked glint in his eye and gave him a playful tap on the arm.

'Beastly man.'

'Just remember that when I have you all to myself in the woods this morning,' he replied.

In his hand he held a wicker basket, in which was placed a folded blanket. Clarice looked down at the basket, then back to David and made up her mind. She held her hand out and took the basket from him.

'I was thinking of going into the walking-stick business,' David said, as they walked toward the gateway which led out of the yard.

Clarice looked at him quizzically. 'Why?'

He chuckled. 'I saw Lady Alice in the garden a few minutes ago; she was moving freely and at one point even bent down and smelled the flowers. She had left her walking stick leaning against the wall. I tell you, that stick of hers has magical powers. Depending on the social situation it either works so well that she does not require it, or she is suddenly an invalid. She is a canny woman, your grandmother; I think Mr Fox found that out to his detriment.'

Clarice nodded her head. 'Do you think she knows, I mean about us?'

David closed the gate to the yard behind them and pointed toward a large cluster of trees a half-mile or so in the distance.

'If she suspects anything, she is keeping mum, and I can understand why,' he replied.

Clarice swung the blackberry gathering basket gaily in her hand and took a deep breath. Being away from London and all its constraints was truly invigorating. In London, she and David would not have been able to go walking together without at least several servants or a suitable chaperone in tow.

'Yes, I suppose she is in a difficult position. If she is seen to have completely taken our side, then Papa will be angry with her,' Clarice replied.

'I think she is playing the game exactly as she wants. To all intents and purposes she is protecting you, but at the same time she is turning a considered blind eye to any developments between us.'

Clarice ceased swinging the basket and paused in her step. David stopped and came back to her side.

'What is the matter?' he asked.

'Can you promise my hair and attire will not be in disarray when we return to the house? I gave Petunia the ribbons I was going to put in my hair. And while matters have developed between us and I am delighted beyond words that they have, I think we need to tread carefully from this point onward. If I am to become lady of the manor, I would not like to think that the servants view me in a poor light.'

David frowned. He was clearly disappointed. She reached over and gave him a gentle thump on the arm. 'I thought we were going blackberry-picking!'

He rolled his eyes. 'Among other things.'

Out of sight of the main farm buildings, he grabbed her and pulled her to him, placing a hard kiss on her lips.

'I promise you will look immaculate upon our return, but I do intend to make you scream,' he murmured into her ear.

They crossed the fields and entered into the cool silence of the woods.

'Is this your land?' she asked.

He nodded. 'Yes, right to the other edge of the trees, about eight hundred yards and then the Great River Ouse marks a natural boundary between Sharnbrook and the adjoining estate,' he replied, pride evident in his voice.

David took her by the hand and led Clarice along a narrow

path which ran through the wood. The heady scent of the pine trees filled her senses. A few hundred yards further on, he stepped off the path and they made their way to a small sunlit clearing, where they stopped.

'May I have the basket?' he said.

She handed it over.

He took the basket and removed the blanket. He unfolded it and spread it out on the pine-needle-strewn ground.

Her heart began to pound in anticipation. Were they really going to make love here? He kissed her forehead and whispered. 'There is nothing to be afraid of, Clarice. No-one will disturb us.'

He put a hand into his coat pocket and took out a red silk ribbon. Her brow furrowed. What did he plan to do with the ribbon?

'Give me your right hand,' he said.

'Why?'

'Because until I can secure your father's blessing to our formal union, I want us to be hand-fasted. I know that may seem a little odd, considering how we have spent the past few nights, but it's important.'

She gave him her right hand.

'You do realise that we are in England and hand-fasting is really only practised in Scotland,' she replied, a wry smile upon her lips.

A lifting of one of his black eyebrows made her giggle.

'Aye, but you may recall that along with my father's English titles, he also holds several Scottish ones. And since he bought this land, I consider it part of his domain.'

David took hold of Clarice's hand and wound the ribbon around both their hands.

'Are we supposed to say something?' she asked.

'In olden times a hand-fasted couple agreed to live together for a year and a day. If after that time they decided they did not wish to marry then the hand-fast was over and they went their respective ways. Well, that is what I have been told. Usually the Church of Scotland got hold of them and they were made to wed,' he replied.

'So?'

He leaned down and placed a tender kiss on her lips.

'Say with me: forever and a day I pledge myself to you,' he said.

Clarice nodded. Any ceremony from this point on would be a mere formality. She was David's woman and that was all that mattered.

'Forever and a day I pledge myself to you,' they said in unison.

'I love you, David Radley.'

'I love you, Clarice soon-to-be Radley.'

David unwound the ribbon and placed it back in the basket. Clarice's mouth went dry when she saw him take off his coat and lay it on the blanket.

He came to her and together they slowly removed each other's clothes. When finally they stood naked, facing one another, she came to him.

His kisses began at her forehead. Each one hot and tender against her rapidly cooling skin. When he nibbled playfully on her earlobe she laughed.

'That tickles,' she said.

'Hmmm, I shall have to remember that,' he replied. His strong hands slid down her waist and over her hips. He knelt before her, leaving a trail of kisses down her stomach. When he reached the small thatch of hair at the apex of her thighs he stopped.

'Lie down on the blanket,' he said.

Desire thrummed throughout her body. She couldn't refuse him even if she wanted. As she lay back, she heard the crunch of the dry pine needles under the blanket. Looking up, she saw the bright blue sky above the green tree tops. The tall trees swaying overhead in the breeze disappeared as

David rose above her and once again took her mouth in a fiery kiss.

His hand slid up her leg and when he reached the opening of her sex, he slipped a finger inside. She pulled her lips from his and let out a deep groan of pleasure. David growled his satisfaction. It had only taken a matter of days for them to attain a deep understanding of each other's sexual needs.

A second finger slipped into her wet heat and Clarice lay back in David's arms as he brought her to the edge of madness.

'Now,' she whispered, pushing his hand away.

'Now what?' he teased.

'Take me. Fill me,' she begged. All pretence of ladylike behaviour had been abandoned the moment David slipped the first of Clarice's buttons open. Because of him and all that they had shared she could be unfettered in her sexual demands. He had made her wanton and she loved it.

He rolled over and sat up, giving her a wicked smile.

'Come here,' he commanded.

He positioned her, legs spread wide open over him, so they were facing each other. Slowly she lowered herself down and he guided her to him. She whimpered with pleasure as he impaled her on his manhood.

This was a new and untried lovemaking position for them, but she quickly understood the benefits. As David slowly lifted his hips up and down, she lay her hands on either side of his shoulders and gripped him. They quickly developed an intoxicating rhythm. David thrusting into her, Clarice pulling herself down as she rode him.

'I have dreamt of this for so long,' he said.

She threw her head back as the pace of their exchange increased.

Harder and faster David came to her, until finally every pleasure-heightened nerve in her body shattered and she screamed.

He whispered fiercely, 'Say it!'

She struggled to breathe, let alone say the words as his never-ending pounding of her body kept her orgasm rolling on and on. With his hands gripped tightly to her hips, he increased the rate of his deep, penetrating strokes.

'I pledge myself to you forever!' she cried. The roar of David's climax echoed throughout the woods.

He buried his face in her sweat-soaked breasts and wrapping his arms around her waist, held her to him. She closed her eyes.

If ever there was a moment that she could identify as being the definitive turning-point in her life, this was it. Gone was the Clarice of old, the girl who had hidden herself from the world. In her place was a young woman sure of her future and of the man she loved.

'I can't believe we just did that,' she said as she climbed off David's lap and leaned over to pick up her gown.

A large, heavy hand gave her backside a playful smack.

She whirled round, only to see a smiling David beckoning for her to come back to him. She crawled back to him and he pulled her on to his lap once more. Sitting facing one another, she took his face in her hands and kissed his still-heated lips.

'What was that for?' she said.

He kissed her deeply before replying. 'I hadn't given you permission to leave. As I recall, you have bound yourself to me now, and as your lord and master I will tell you when you may leave my bed.'

Clarice chuckled. 'You have no idea what you have let yourself in for, Mr Radley.'

She silenced him with her mouth.

It was early afternoon before they finally left the woods. The basket full of freshly picked berries had cost Clarice a pair of expensive leather gloves. She looked down at the ripped and stained gloves and shrugged her shoulders. She would need to buy gloves more suited to the demands of country life if she was to be a successful lady of the manor.

A quick check of the rest of her clothes revealed nothing of the other activities which had taken place that afternoon in Temple Wood. Beside her David strolled, a look of supreme satisfaction on his face. He had promised her he would make her scream in the woods, and he had kept his word.

Twice.

Chapter Twenty-Seven

'These will be wonderful in a pie. If I ask Cook, do you think she would make us one?' Clarice asked. She picked out several of the juicy blackberries and popped them into her mouth. When she licked the juice from her lips, David was tempted to take her back to the woods and continue to further her sexual education. The afternoon spent with Clarice in Temple Wood would forever remain in his memory.

He stopped and watched as she continued on for several paces. Eventually she realised that he was no longer walking beside her, and she stopped and turned round.

'David?' she said and walked back to his side.

He looked at her and forced a smile to his lips. Their happy afternoon was now at an end. He sent a silent prayer to the heavens that it would not be their last day together.

'He's here,' he replied. The calm in his voice belied his racing heart.

From the top of the hill he could see the yard at Sharnbrook Grange. Beyond the barn, in the middle of the yard, stood a black travel coach.

He did not need to see the Langham family crest emblazoned on the side of the coach to know Earl Langham had arrived; he felt it in his bones.

Clarice's bottom lip quivered and tears formed in her eyes.

He took her into his arms, watching over her head as the stable master unhitched the fine set of four horses from the front of the carriage.

'Don't be afraid,' he said. He bent his head to kiss her, but she pulled out of his arms and brandished the basket at him.

'Oh David, please let us run away to Scotland now! I can hide here until you find a horse to take us,' she begged.

He shook his head. Sharnbrook was his home and he would not run away like a coward. His days of living in the shadows were over. It was time to face Henry Langham and claim Clarice's hand.

The panic in her eyes tore at his heart.

'Clarice,' he said, reaching out to her once more.

'No, no, he will say no! But I know what to do. If I throw all those damn lies he and Mama told me in his face he will have no choice!'

She threw the basket on the ground, picked up her skirts and raced down the hill. David caught up with her after a few strides and grabbed her by the arm. As she swung back to face him, he saw the tears streaming down her face.

'Please, Clarice, you have to stop. You cannot do this; it will destroy us all.'

He quickly scanned the surroundings and his gaze fell on a tall, thin stone building set back from the rest of the farm buildings. He had barely noted the existence of the dovecote before.

He lessened his hold of her arm, but did not let go.

'We need to talk,' he said and led her toward the building.

While their sexual relationship had made significant progress, it had kept them from making a plan to deal with her father. David was angry with himself. He had allowed his lust to rule his head. Lying sated with her in his arms at night, he had felt ready to take on the world.

But if Clarice marched into the house and confronted her father with the truth of her birth, who knew what would follow?

They reached the dovecote, and with a hard push of his shoulder he forced the door open. They stepped inside.

'David?' Clarice whispered. Standing in semi-darkness, with only a shard of light from the half-open door, he found it difficult to read her face.

He thought for a moment, knowing he had to get the words right. She had to understand.

'Why did you swear me to secrecy in the dell at Langham Hall if you plan to use the truth of your birth as our first line of attack?' he finally replied.

She shrugged her shoulders. 'I don't know; I just can't bear the prospect of losing you.'

He frowned. 'You won't, but we need to plan how we deal with your father. Circumstances have changed. After the past few days and especially since this afternoon, you and I are now one.'

'You are going to tell him you have ruined me?' she replied.

He sighed. The moment she had got into the carriage and left for Sharnbrook Grange with him, she was as good as ruined in society's eyes. Her father would view it as such.

If Clarice confronted her father, he might reject her outright. A man cornered with his honour challenged was a dangerous beast.

'Do not throw away the greatest gift your father has given you: his name. The earl made sure he recognised you as his legitimate flesh and blood. There is no stain on your birth, Clarice. And after all the scorn and censure I have had to deal with in my life, I will do everything in my power to ensure you remain his rightful progeny.'

He stared at her; all the while, a silent fear that she would not understand his reasoning gripped his heart. Finally, she nodded her agreement. He let out a loud sigh of relief and headed for the door.

As soon as Clarice stepped outside into the light she pointed a finger sharply in his direction. 'But there is no negotiating on this point: if my father refuses to bless our union, we leave for Scotland tonight!'

'Yes,' he conceded. Having now taken Clarice to his bed, setting the date for a wedding was foremost in his mind. His children would not wear the stain of illegitimacy.

He retrieved the basket and they headed down the hill toward the house. Once inside the house, they sought out Clarice's father. Reaching the bottom of the staircase, David stopped and pulled her to him.

'I know this is *our* future, but Clarice, you must allow me to take the lead. I must deal with your father on my own terms.'

She nodded and took his hand. 'Yes.'

In the main upstairs drawing room, they found Lady Alice seated in a comfortable chair by the fire. Earl Langham stood with his back to the door, looking out over the estate. He turned as David and Clarice entered the room. His gaze fell on their entwined hands and he gave a barely perceptible nod of his head.

'Papa,' Clarice said. David let go of her hand and gave the earl a respectful bow.

'Are you wed, Radley?' Earl Langham asked.

A spark of hope lit in David's heart. The earl had directed the question to him.

'No, my lord, but we do intend to marry. Clarice has accepted my proposal. We ask for your blessing,' he replied.

A snort was the only response.

Clarice came to her father and stood, hands clasped, before

him. 'I am sorry I disobeyed you, Papa, but we had to leave Norfolk.'

The earl nodded. 'Yes, I must confess I was more than a little angry when I discovered you had left Langham Hall with Mr Radley, but I now understand the circumstances behind your flight. My steward gave me his version of events and they concur with Mr Radley's letter. Your grandmother apprised me of all the other pertinent details.'

'All of them?' Clarice asked Lady Alice.

'Yes,' she replied.

Lord Langham chuckled. David frowned. He had never seen the earl laugh before, and it unsettled him. Black-faced, raging anger he could counter, but humour? No.

'I would never make light of your ordeal, my dear girl,' the earl explained. He opened his arms and Clarice walked into his embrace. 'I was picturing how your grandmother looked with a cocked pistol in her hand. That blackguard Fox has no idea just how close he came to having a bullet in his head.'

Lady Alice rose to her feet and, leaning on her trusty walking stick, joined them.

'I didn't really plan to kill the man; I was aiming to wing him.'

David found himself simultaneously frowning and smiling.

'I have been travelling from London to Norfolk to Bedford without stopping for the past few days. My back is stiff and I need to stretch my legs. Ladies, would you please excuse us? Mr Radley, a turn about your estate, if you don't mind,' said the earl.

Clarice shot David a hopeful glance.

'After that I expect you to show me the best fare you have to offer and the finest wine from your cellar.'

David nodded. 'Yes, of course.'

The earl brushed a kiss on Clarice's forehead. 'Are you well? I have not slept because of worry for you.'

She took hold of her father's hand and kissed it. 'Yes, Papa, I am fine. The days spent at the Hall before Mr Fox's arrival were very beneficial to my state of mind. I spent some time with Mama and we talked.'

Her father gave her a quizzical look and David wondered just how much Clarice would tell her father when the time came. She had made peace with her mother, but more importantly, with herself. It showed in both her face and her manner. Lady Alice fumbled for a handkerchief. Having located it, the dowager countess dabbed it against the corner of her eye.

David was at a loss at the touching family scene as it unfolded before him. His own family was a loud, expressive group of people, but to see emotion such as this in another family was an unusual experience.

'We shall see you ladies at dinner. Now, Radley, if your man will be so good as to show me to my room, I should like to change out of my travel attire. I shall join you downstairs shortly. Rather keen to cast an eye over that flock of Southdowns I saw in your lower field,' the earl announced.

He bowed to the women before leaving David alone with Lady Alice and Clarice. David and Clarice exchanged looks, neither knowing what to say.

'Oh, go on with the pair of you. Give my granddaughter a kiss, young man and then go and fight for her,' Lady Alice said. She marched unaided from the room.

As the door closed behind her, Clarice came quickly to David and threw her arms around his waist, her uplifted face inviting his lips. He bent his head and gave her a tender yet chaste kiss. She harrumphed at his efforts and taking hold of the lapels of his jacket, pulled him in close.

'More effort, Mr Radley,' she whispered, mimicking her father's tone.

Her mouth opened and David swept his tongue inside. As the kiss deepened, he felt her hand slide to his backside and give it an unsubtle pinch. Her breasts, pressed hard against him, caused his mind to drift slowly to a different place. When she groaned in his arms, he felt himself begin to go hard.

Taking her hands, he removed them from his clothing and stepped back.

'I think you forget I am about to go and face your father. I cannot see how my arriving in an aroused state is going to further our cause,' he said.

She smiled. 'I just thought you might want a small reminder of what is at stake.'

He shot her a disapproving look, then gave her a kiss on the forehead.

'Let's hope this audience is more successful than the one you had with him in London.'

David raised his eyebrows. It couldn't possibly be any worse.

'He gave me short shrift then,' he replied, straightening his jacket lapels.

'Well, then you have achieved more than that already today. He invited you to walk with him; few men are accorded such an honour,' Clarice said. The look on her face showed she was not in jest.

He nodded, resolute. No matter the outcome of his meeting with Lord Langham, today would be the day he finally claimed Clarice.

'Just in case things do awry, you should ensure your travel trunk is fully packed and you have suitable travel clothes ready. We may need to leave for Scotland in a hurry if your father's answer is no. Strathmore Castle is a good day's ride from Edinburgh and we may need to hole up there for a few weeks until he comes to accept that we are wed. I want you to have all your things with you if we do have to make a dash for the border.'

'Good luck,' Clarice said as David stepped out of the drawing room and headed downstairs to meet her father.

'Luck I think I can muster; I just hope it won't require a bloody miracle,' David muttered as he raced down the stairs.

※

The men did not return before dinner.

'Three hours; how can you possibly look at sheep for three hours?' Clarice exclaimed. She was in the drawing room sharing a pre-dinner sherry with Lady Alice, but there was no sign of either her father or David.

Lady Alice smiled. 'But they *are* talking. If your father wanted you to leave, he would have marched in here long ago and demanded we pack. Remember that even after your father received David's letter, he travelled first to Norfolk to check with his steward rather than come directly to Sharnbrook. I think you give Mr Radley too little credit, my dear; your father obviously thought you were in safe hands.'

Clarice looked at her grandmother. Lady Alice had raised an important point. Earl Langham was not behaving like a man who thought his daughter was consorting with the devil. Could there really be hope for a future with David?

She fiddled with the black onyx pendant hanging on the gold chain around her neck, winding the chain around her fingers. She no longer made any pretence of hiding her allegiance to David.

'You will break that if you keep twisting it so,' Lady Alice said.

As the door of the drawing room opened, Clarice leapt to her feet. Her father strode into the room, followed by David, both elegantly attired in full evening dress. They were deep in conversation regarding the value of the flock and how best to maximise returns on David's investment.

Lord Langham crossed the room and greeted his mother with a kiss on the hand. As he did, Clarice shot an expectant look in David's direction. He lifted a hand and gave her a slight smile.

At least it isn't no.

'So how was your afternoon, Papa?' she asked.

The earl smiled. Clarice's eagerness to know how things were progressing with David was written all over her face, but her father was giving nothing away.

'Good. Quite a decent breeding flock Mr Radley is putting together, though as I have informed him *and* his steward he needs a second ram if he is to get his breeding program properly under way. That one he has unfortunately spent a good deal of money on looks a mite skittish. And not to put too fine a point on it, one cannot have a ram that is not up to the task.'

Lady Alice roared with laughter and clapped her hands. 'Absolutely!'

Clarice looked once more to David, but his social mask was firmly in place. His black evening suit was a study in perfection. The white linen shirt crisply pressed, its cravat immaculately tied and finished with a gold pin. He could easily be waiting to step into the ballroom of any London social event, rather than a small dining affair in a provincial home.

An overwhelming pride in the man she loved swelled in her heart. David was leaving nothing to chance.

'Shall we?' the earl said as he offered Lady Alice his arm.

Behind them Clarice smiled and took David's arm.

Dinner was a pleasant but subdued affair. Lady Alice engaged Clarice in a conversation about the availability of good French lace, while the two gentlemen continued their ongoing discussion about husbandry.

At one point Clarice shot her grandmother a questioning look. In London it would not be acceptable for gentlemen to shut the ladies out from their conversation in this manner. Lady Alice responded with a slight shake of her head and took a sip of her wine.

Eventually the meal ended and the gentlemen took their leave for cigars and port. Clarice and her grandmother repaired to the drawing room.

'That was an excellent meal, but my feet are killing me,' Lady Alice remarked. She slumped in a chair by the fireside, and kicked off the offending slippers.

Lady Alice waved a hand and motioned for Clarice to take a seat in the chair opposite.

'Don't worry, my dear, they won't be back any time soon. In fact I wouldn't expect to see either of them until tomorrow morning. Your father mentioned as we walked into dinner that he and David were going to have a formal discussion at some point this evening.'

Clarice blinked back sudden tears. 'Really?'

'Of course. Your father didn't spend a whole afternoon looking around the estate for nothing, Clarice. He has been methodically measuring the ability of this estate to produce a good income. I wouldn't be the least surprised if he asked David to produce the books of account.'

Clarice didn't hear much of what Lady Alice said after she uttered the words *Of course.* The fact that her father was seriously considering allowing his daughter to marry David Radley was all that mattered. She wrung her hands together. This was going to be the longest evening of her life.

'Clarice?'

'Hmm?'

'What did you mean when you said you had been speaking to your mother? Did you go back to Elizabeth's graveside after we spoke?'

She nodded, as Lady Alice took hold of her hand and gave it a gentle pat.

'You don't think talking to a gravestone is foolish?' she replied.

'Not if it helps you to find the answers you seek. Your grandfather and I have had many a long conversation at his grave. I knew something had changed within you, even before David arrived. The way you were able to conduct yourself that night with Mr Fox, even after he had attacked you, was something I don't think you could have done before you visited the dell. Have you forgiven your mother?'

'It was rather the other way round. I needed her to forgive me,' Clarice replied.

Lady Alice frowned. 'Your mother's death was an accident.'

'I know, but for so long I blamed myself. I was convinced that since I killed my mother I was not worthy of friends or love.'

Lady Alice closed her eyes. 'If only we could have helped you.'

'No. I had to do this myself. I had to overcome my fears.'

She returned to the fireside and Lady Alice embraced her. 'I wonder if that young man realises how fortunate he is to have you,' Lady Alice said.

Clarice smiled. 'I don't know, but I do wish he would hurry up and get Papa's blessing.'

Chapter Twenty-Eight

✦✦✦

Lady Alice turned in a little before midnight, leaving Clarice to ponder whether she should follow suit. Accepting that she would get little sleep while she waited for David, she kicked off her slippers and sat by the fireside, reading a book.

The clock on the mantelpiece ticked away and just before one o'clock, she closed the book and decided to try to get some sleep.

Walking the long hallway to her bedroom, she felt the silence in the house. Passing the room where her father and David still sat, she stopped and put an ear to the door. She could hear the low hum of male voices, but could not make out the words.

She wrinkled her nose in disappointment.

'Oh well, I shall know soon enough,' she muttered.

She lingered for a brief time in her own room, before deciding to allow her instincts to dictate her behaviour. She headed for David's room. No matter the outcome of tonight, she intended to sleep in his bed.

She sat on the edge of the bed and contemplated her future. Running her hand over the soft, luxurious red silk coverlet, she was reminded of how it felt against her naked skin when she lay in the bed at night. A bed she had secretly shared with David for nearly a week. Every morning and every night, she rejoiced in David's arms as he claimed her and brought her to release.

A smile came to her lips. She climbed off the bed and went to stand in front of the dressing mirror. The girl in the mirror was her, but so very different to the Clarice Langham who had refused to dance with David at the wedding ball only weeks earlier. Her clothes now fit to her curves. With her breasts no longer bound, she displayed a figure she found pleasing to the eye. There was no doubt that David approved of her new look; she had caught him staring at her breasts over the dinner table several times since they had arrived.

The smile on her face was an exact match with the one which Millie Radley wore every time Clarice had seen her since the wedding. The same bright happiness shone in her eyes. Another thing the Radley brothers had in common, she mused: the effect they had on their women.

She closed her eyes and made a silent prayer.

Lord, let there be a child already created within me. A child from our love.

She ran a hand over her flat belly. 'Do not fret, my little one, you shall be born into your father's name. You will never know the fear that someone may suddenly reveal your secret to the world. Your father shall always protect you.'

She lay back on the bed and with her eyes closed, sleep quickly took her.

Sometime in the night, she felt familiar hands removing her clothing and slipping the bedclothes over her naked body. David cuddled up to her, close against her back.

She rolled over and tried to see his face in the darkened room.

'David?'

'Yes,' he replied.

The smell of brandy from his mouth nearly overpowered her.

'Are you drunk?'

'Most certainly. Your father can half put it away. It took a lot to keep up with him.'

She pulled out of his embrace and sat up. Throwing back the coverlet, she started to climb out of bed, intent on lighting the candle on the bedside table.

He made a grab for her and she stopped.

'Don't go. I want to hold you,' he said, and clumsily wrapped his arms around her waist.

'All right, but you have to tell me what my father said,' she replied, and lay back in the bed. 'Are you and I still headed for the border at first light?'

He released his death-like grip and hiccoughed.

'No. You are not going anywhere. I, on the other hand, am going to Bedford in the morning to look for a new ram.'

Clarice sighed; it was worse than pulling teeth.

'David, are we getting married?'

'Yes.'

'Has my father given us his blessing?'

'Yes.'

'So are we getting married in London?'

Silence.

'David?' She shook him hard. The buzz of his drunken snoring filled the room.

She laughed. 'And to think I passed up on the chance of marrying your brother in order to get you.'

With considerable effort, she rolled David over on to his side and his snoring subsided immediately. Curled up against his back, arm draped over his hip, she lay in the dark and prayed for the dawn.

Much as she believed David, she wanted to hear the words from her father's lips.

'She has a wonderful knack of knowing exactly when to leave a room,' the earl said, as they sat at a late breakfast the following morning. Lady Alice had, without warning, found a pressing need to retrieve a book from her room, insisting that David be the one to accompany her.

Clarice smiled. Her relationship with Lady Alice had strengthened and deepened over the weeks since her grandmother had arrived in London. Her only regret was that she had held Lady Alice at arm's length for so long.

'She has been my champion,' Clarice replied.

They both rose from their seats and met each other at the breakfast room window. Her father took hold of her hands. Father and daughter stood and looked at one another.

'Happy that you are going to marry David?' he asked.

She nodded. 'Very. Though I am still at a loss as to why you changed your mind about him. I thought you were set forever against me marrying David. I know you have always thought him unworthy due to his lack of legitimate status.'

Lord Langham frowned.

'I was set against him, but not because he was born outside of marriage. I could never judge a man or woman because of the circumstances of their birth.'

Clarice's breath caught in her throat. Her father tightened his grip on her hands and she thought she saw tears in his eyes.

'You are *my* daughter. I held you in my arms within minutes of you drawing your first breath. I gave you my name and nothing can ever change that.'

He knew.

'But how?' she whispered.

'Your grandmother told me. I didn't know you were present when your mother had her accident.'

She stared down at the floor, ashamed to finally confess the truth of that awful day.

'I panicked when I saw Mama was dead. I ran and hid at the top of the landing until I heard you arrive. I didn't know what to do.'

Her father sighed. She wrapped her arms around him.

'Nothing changed three years ago and nothing changes now,' he said.

The earl looked down at her, the lines of worry still creasing his brow. 'And what of your new fiancé; have you told him any of this?'

She nodded. 'He knows as much of it as I do. After every slight he has had to endure during his life, I could not begin our marriage keeping such a thing from him. If I had lied to him when he asked me to marry him, our whole future would have been based on a falsehood. I also had to consider that someday, someone may confront us with the truth. It is better that he knows everything about me.'

'Then I have judged him right,' the earl replied.

'I still don't understand why you have finally accepted David,' Clarice replied.

A deep murmur of a laugh resounded through his chest. 'No, I don't expect you do. I never judged David because he was born outside of wedlock; I judged him and his brother because they were drunken, irresponsible rogues.'

Clarice winced, but she knew her father was right. Over the preceding years Alex and David had ruled the younger set of the *ton* like gods. Alex with his reputation as a breaker of hearts and David as the spark for all manner of heated mischief.

'I was set against either of them ever marrying you, truth be told. Only the very best of men would be good enough for you. If the Marquess of Brooke had formally asked for your hand, I was going to make his life hell until he showed he was worthy of you.'

'Is that why you had Alex beaten?' Clarice asked. She had wanted to broach the subject with her father many times, but only now did she feel strong enough to ask.

The earl shook his head. 'Alex humiliated you. He held you up to public ridicule. While I think perhaps the lads went a little too far with their fists, there are plenty of others who would say he had it coming for some time. No-one treats my daughter that way and walks away unscathed.

'Suffice to say, I decided that the man who would be good enough to marry you needed to prove it. I knew David had been given this estate by his father, and also that he appeared to have seen the error of his ways and tempered his behaviour. But that was no proof of how he truly felt about you. By disobeying my edict not to see you and then having the audacity to kidnap you from Norfolk, he made his position clear.'

The truth was now clear in her mind. Her father had not rejected David; he had been testing him. Only a man who was brave enough to stand up to Lord Langham would be good enough to marry his daughter. She stepped back and stared hard at her father.

'So you sent me away to see if he would come and rescue me?'

He smiled. 'Langham Hall was the closest thing I had to a high tower in which to put you. If he was your knight in shining armour then he had prove it to me. I just hadn't counted on you having to fight a real dragon yourself. But rest assured, Mr Fox is going to wish David *had* run him through with a sword when he had the chance. Or at least stood back and let your grandmother shoot the blackguard, because I intend to make life very unpleasant for him from now on. The next time Mr Fox is allowed to set foot in Langham Hall will be when I am cold in the ground.'

Clarice looked at her father, feeling she was seeing his true self for the very first time. No more lies or secrets lay between them. She reached up on her toes and gave him a warm, loving kiss on the cheek.

'Thank you Papa, thank you for everything.'

Her father put his arm around her shoulder and led her toward the door.

'Come on then, your young man will be waiting for us in the yard; he will think we have forgotten him. First rule of marriage, you shouldn't keep your husband waiting,' he said.

Clarice laughed; her mother had never been able to arrive anywhere on time.

Out in the yard, David was mounted on his horse, while Lady Alice, standing to one side was giving him an admiring look. Clarice noticed she didn't have a book in her hand.

'I must say I'm impressed. Considering how much port and brandy I forced down that young man's throat last night, I am surprised he can look at a horse, let alone actually mount one,' her father murmured as they stood at the gateway to the yard.

Clarice shook her head. No matter how much alcohol her father had consumed the previous night, he was clear-eyed and fit for duty. She could not honestly say the same for David. While her father, standing casually putting on his riding gloves, appeared no worse for wear from the previous night's drinking, she knew David was feeling every twitch in his horse's rump. He had acquitted himself in their bed that morning, but she had been the one making love to him and he had begged her to be gentle.

To his credit, her now officially betrothed future husband had managed to haul himself out of bed, eaten breakfast and been in the saddle at the prearranged time. She felt a flicker of disappointment, knowing there would be no chance of any afternoon frolic in Temple Wood today.

'He handles a steed well. Not reckless like his younger brother, but with a care for the beast. He definitely has an affinity with animals.'

Clarice looked at her father. She couldn't remember the last time he had said anything favourable about anyone. Something had changed.

She smiled.

The earl turned toward her and offered her his hand. She took it. He pulled her to his side and placed a fatherly arm around her shoulder, then went back to watching David as he marched the horse up and down the yard.

She sucked in a deep breath and blinked away hot tears.

'My girl.'

'Papa.'

No grand statement, no emotion-filled scene of reconciliation. Just a simple acknowledgement of how they saw one another and their relationship. The years they had spent as virtual strangers could never be changed. But it was if a book had been closed and a new one opened. One with a clean, blank page.

They would write their future relationship together.

'Did you agree on a place for the wedding?' she asked.

The earl chuckled. 'St Georges, Hanover Square. I sent a letter off this morning. Told the curate to speak to the Bishop of London. That should shock a few sanctimonious members of the *ton*. Then it will be on to Strathmore House for the wedding breakfast. The Duke of Strathmore can foot the bill for the huge number of guests I plan to invite. I'm interested to see how deep his pockets really are with two weddings in one season.'

David dismounted from his horse and Mitchell took the horse by the reins.

'Didn't want to tire him out too much this morning before we leave,' David said as he strode through the gate and greeted Clarice with a gentle kiss. Her father averted his eyes, but she could see he wore a sly grin.

Never again will I underestimate the power of a father's love.

She nodded her agreement. No-one was going to mention the tinge of green in David's face.

'Papa sent a letter to London this morning to book the church,' she replied.

A smile came to David's lips and he reached over and shook the earl's hand. 'Thank you, my lord; it will be an honour to have you as a guest as our wedding.'

The earl roared with laughter, and slapped David roughly on the arm.

'Guest! Who do think is giving the bride away, you cheeky bugger? Now come on Radley, I've had enough of watching you prance about on that pony, time for your first lesson in choosing good breeding stock. You can stare all moon-faced into my daughter's eyes later, it's your livestock bloodlines I want to improve. We need to make Bedford before early afternoon.'

Clarice and her grandmother stood and watched as Lord Langham and David mounted their horses and headed out of the yard. They rode slowly down the road which led out of Sharnbrook, stopping every so often while her father pointed out some matter of interest.

A warm breeze blew softly through her hair, carrying with it the scent of pine trees. She took a deep breath.

'I am going to love living here,' Clarice said.

'I'm sure you will,' Lady Alice replied.

As the men reached the end of the drive and out of sight, Clarice and her grandmother turned and headed back toward the house. Lady Alice was eager to get started on the wedding preparations. Lists were to be drawn up. And as soon as they returned to London, important appointments would need to be made.

Madame de Feuillide was at the very top of Clarice's first list, David having been proven right when it came to the flimsy nature of the muslin nightgown.

Clarice gave a little hop on the gravel driveway and laughed with joy.

She was about to become a bride.

Chapter Twenty-Nine

The absence of Mr Thaxter Fox from the wedding of Mr David Radley and Lady Clarice Langham was silently noted by the *ton*. He had made a number of enemies during the season, and only the most desperate of match-making mothers still had him in their sights.

Earl Langham's wedding breakfast speech set tongues wagging within London society. After welcoming his new son-in-law into *his* family, he announced David would be going into the livestock breeding business with him. Though it wasn't openly stated, others drew the obvious conclusion that by doing so, Lord Langham would ensure the value of the un-entailed property of his estate would eventually cede to his son-in-law.

Apart from the Langham title and its attached property, Thaxter Fox would get nothing.

When David queried him later, the earl simply replied. 'It's the best way to keep funds from that cur without having to change my will. I know he would waste a fortune in challenging it after I die if I did. Besides, I get the pleasure of being able to gloat over his disappointment while I am still alive. He came to see me as soon as we returned to London and he left

Langham House a very angry young man. He knows the first sign of a twinge in my knee and all maintenance on the properties linked to the title will cease.'

David nodded, relieved that the earl had a new enemy on which to focus his attention.

At the wedding ball later that week, David had other matters on his mind.

'Our waltz will be starting soon; are you ready to take to the floor, Mrs Radley?' David asked.

Clarice gave him the same secret smile she had been giving him all week. He raised an eyebrow in response.

'What?'

She drew in close and accepted the kiss he readily placed on her lips. 'Just be gentle with me when you take me through the turns. My constitution is not up to being spun around the room.' She chuckled as his expression turned slowly from that of polite interest to realisation.

'No!' he whispered.

She nodded. They had been married all of a week, but with the rush of late-season weddings, they had been forced to wait for an available booking at St Georges. David had steadfastly refused to be married anywhere else.

'By my count I am sixteen days late. Which, if I am correct, means our first child was more than likely conceived in Temple Wood,' she replied.

David chuckled. 'Remind me to keep that blanket ready for any future sojourns into the wilderness.'

He pulled her quickly into a nearby room, and closed the door, locking it behind him. 'We won't be disturbed here; no-one would dare enter my mother's sitting room without her permission.'

The noise of the hundreds of party guests dimmed to a low hum. Clarice put her arms around him and they shared a private hug.

'Of course, it will have to officially be a wedding-night baby, and then arrive a little early,' she said.

'As long as it has the Radley name, I don't care what anyone else thinks,' he replied.

She looked up at him, the look of pure, unbridled happiness on her face mirroring his own happy state. They had taken risks and defied the odds; their bravery was now truly rewarded.

Theirs was a most suitable match.

Epilogue

His evening dress was regulation black, his cravat simply tied. At first glance, he looked like any other gentleman present at the ball, but Lady Lucy Radley sensed something was different about him. Having spent all her life within the privileged world of the *haute ton*, she knew an outsider at an instant.

The uncomfortable way he held his shoulders back suggested that his jacket was too small for his broad shoulders. With one gloved hand held constantly behind his back, he looked thoroughly ill at ease.

Intrigued, she silently studied him. He was deep in conversation with Clarice's father, nodding his head every so often as his gaze roamed the room. The stiff, formal way he held himself suggested a military man, but perhaps not an officer?

Who was he?

When her curiosity finally got the better of her she sought out her new sister-in-law. If anyone would have a clue as to the identity of the stranger, it was Clarice. She found Clarice standing arm-in-arm with her new husband, chatting to some of their guests.

Lucy waited impatiently until the other guests took their leave and then gently seized Clarice by the arm. She waved David away.

'You can have her back shortly, I just need to borrow your wife for a moment,' she said.

She found a clear spot on the floor and stopped. Clarice furrowed her brow.

'What?'

'Who is that?' Lucy asked, failing to hide her interest. With a snap of her wrist, she pointed across the room to where the gentleman stood next to Earl Langham.

Clarice turned and gave Lucy a discouraging frown. 'That, dear sister, is Mr Avery Fox.'

Lucy winced. 'Don't tell me that dashingly handsome man is related to Thaxter Fox? Nature could not be so cruel.'

Clarice nodded. 'His younger brother. He spent many years abroad in the army and was wounded at Waterloo. He has only recently come to London and made himself known to us.'

'What a pity he is not the heir,' Lucy replied, her gaze still firmly fixed on the dashing Mr Fox.

'They are headed this way; I can make introductions if you like,' Clarice replied.

As the men strode toward them, Lucy only had eyes for the mysterious Mr Fox. When his gaze met hers, her mouth went dry.

'I expect he is the only Fox welcome at this gathering. Your father made his position regarding Thaxter very clear and I for one can't blame him. The nerve of that man in trying to steal the household silver from Langham Hall. I expect he is now trying to lie low from his creditors. It will, of course, make his wooing of any heiress rather difficult. One can hardly make doe eyes at a well-dowered prospective bride when you have the bailiff at your heels,' said Lucy.

She laughed, satisfied that Thaxter Fox was getting all that he deserved. Clarice took a firm hold of Lucy's arm.

'This is no matter for jest; Thaxter Fox has been missing for several weeks. Papa is beginning to suspect his evil ways might have finally caught up with him. Mr Avery Fox has been searching for his brother all over London. David wouldn't even name some of the places Avery has been in his efforts to find his brother, but he said they were vile dens of iniquity. Mr Fox thinks his brother has met with foul play,' said Clarice.

Which, if he has, now makes Mr Avery Fox Lord Langham's heir.

She gritted her teeth as a thrill of excitement raced down her spine. The London season was finally getting interesting.

'Ladies, may I introduce Mr Avery Fox, late of His Majesty's ninety-fifth rifles,' said Lord Langham.

Avery Fox looked deep into Lucy's eyes before dipping into a bow.

'Mr Fox, what a pleasure,' she replied.

Thank you for reading! I hope you loved Clarice and David's story.

The next book in the **Duke of Strathmore Series** is
THE DUKE'S DAUGHTER

Can Lady Lucy Radley, find her true love with the mysterious Avery Fox or has he left any chance for their happiness on the battlefield at Waterloo?

Turn the page to read the first chapter of
The Duke's Daughter

Sign up for my newsletter and receive your FREE BOOK.
A Wild English Rose

Regency London's wild child is about to meet her match…

The Duke's Daughter
CHAPTER ONE

By every measure of her own behavior, Lady Lucy Radley knew this was the worst.

'You reckless fool,' she muttered under her breath as she headed back inside and into the grand ballroom.

The room was a crush of London's social elite. Every few steps she had to stop and make small talk with friends or acquaintances. A comment here and there about someone's gown or promising a social call made for slow going.

Finally, she spied her cousin, Eve. She fixed a smile to her face as Eve approached.

'Where have you been Lucy? I've been searching everywhere for you.'

'I was just outside admiring the flowers on the terrace.'

Eve frowned, but the lie held.

Another night, another ball in one of London's high society homes. In one respect Lucy would be happy when the London social season ended in a few weeks; then she would be free to travel to her family home in Scotland and go tramping across the valleys and mountain paths, the chill wind ruffling her hair.

She puffed out her cheeks. With the impending close of the

season came an overwhelming sense of failure. Her two older brothers, David and Alex, had taken wives. Perfect, love-filled unions with delightful girls, both of whom Lucy was happy to now call sister.

Her newest sister-in-law, Earl Langham's daughter Clarice, was already in a delicate condition, and Lucy suspected it was only a matter of time before her brother Alex and his wife Millie shared some good news.

For herself, this season had been an unmitigated disaster on the husband-hunting front. The pickings were slim at best. Having refused both an earl and a viscount the previous season, she suspected other suitable gentlemen now viewed her as too fussy. No gentleman worth his boots wanted a difficult wife. Only the usual group of fortune-hunters, intent on getting their hands on her substantial dowry, were lining up at this stage of the season to ask her to dance. Maintaining her pride as the daughter of a duke, she refused them all.

Somewhere in the collective gentry of England there must be a man worthy of her love. She just had to find him.

What a mess.

'You are keeping something from me,' Eve said, poking a finger gently into Lucy's arm.

Lucy shook her head. 'It's nothing, I suspect I am suffering from a touch of ennui. These balls all begin to look the same after a while. All the same people, sharing the same gossip.'

'Oh dear, and I thought I was having a bad day,' Eve replied.

'Sorry, I was being selfish. You are the one who needs a friend to cheer her up,' Lucy replied. She kissed her cousin gently on the cheek.

Eve's brother William had left London earlier that day to return to his home in Paris, and she knew her cousin was taking his departure hard.

'Yes, well, I knew I could sit at home and cry, or I could put on a happy face and try to find something to smile about,' Eve replied.

Eve's father had tried without success to convince his son to return permanently to England. With the war now over and Napoleon toppled from power, everyone expected William Saunders to come home immediately, but it had taken two years for him to make the journey back to London.

'Perhaps once he gets back home and starts to miss us all again, he shall have a change of heart,' Lucy said.

'One can only hope. Now, let's go and find a nice quiet spot and you can tell me what you were really doing out in the garden. Charles Ashton came in the door not a minute before you and he had a face like thunder. As I happened to see the two of you head out into the garden at the same time a little while ago, I doubt Charles' foul temper was because he found the flowers not to his liking,' Eve replied.

※

It was late when Lucy and her parents finally returned home to Strathmore House. The Duke and Duchess of Strathmore's family home was one of the largest houses in the elegant West End of London. It was close to the peaceful greenery of Hyde Park, and Lucy couldn't imagine living anywhere else.

As they came through the grand entrance to Strathmore House she was greeted by the sight of her eldest brother David seated on a low couch outside their father's study. He was clad in a heavy black greatcoat and his hat was in his hand.

'Hello David; bit late for a visit this evening. I hope nothing is wrong,' said Lord Strathmore.

'Clarice?' asked Lady Caroline.

'She's fine, sleeping soundly at home,' he replied.

Lucy sensed the pride and love for his wife in her brother's voice. He had found his true soulmate in Lord Langham's daughter.

David stood and came over. When he reached them, he greeted his mother and sister with a kiss. His dark hair was a stark contrast to both Lady Caroline and Lucy's fair complexions.

He turned to his father. 'Lord Langham's missing heir has been found, and the news is grave. My father-in-law asked that I come and inform you before it becomes public knowledge. A rather horrid business, by all accounts.'

'I see. Ladies, would you please excuse us? This demands my immediate attention,' Lord Strathmore said.

As Lucy and Lady Caroline headed up the grand staircase, he and David retired to his study. As soon as the door was closed behind them, David shared the news.

'The remains of Thaxter Fox were retrieved from the River Fleet a few hours ago. His brother Avery, whom you met at my wedding ball a few weeks ago, has formally identified the body. Lord Langham is currently making funeral arrangements,' David said.

His father shook his head. It was a not unexpected outcome of the search for the missing Thaxter Fox.

He wandered over to a small table and poured two glasses of whisky. He handed one to David.

'Well, that makes for a new and interesting development. I don't expect Avery Fox had ever entertained the notion before today that he would one day be Earl Langham,' Lord Strathmore replied, before downing his drink.

'Perhaps, but he had to know the likelihood of finding his brother in one piece was slim at best. From our enquiries, it was obvious Thaxter had a great many enemies,' David replied.

'Including you,' said the duke.

David looked down at his gold wedding ring. It still bore the newly wed gleam which made him smile.

'He and I had come to a certain understanding. If he stayed away from Langham House and Clarice, I would not flay the skin off his back. No, someone else decided to make Thaxter pay for his evil ways.'

The Langham and Radley families held little affection for the recently deceased heir to the Langham title. After Thaxter had made an attempt to seize Clarice's dowry through a forced marriage, both families had severed all ties. Thaxter had disappeared not long after.

David would do everything in his power to protect Clarice. With a baby on the way, he was fully prepared to stare down the rest of the *ton* if it meant keeping his wife safe. As the illegitimate, but acknowledged, son of the duke, David had overcome many of society's prejudices in order to successfully woo and wed Lord Langham's only daughter.

'Unkind as it sounds, I doubt few at Langham House will be mourning the demise of the eldest Mr. Fox,' his father replied.

The Duke's Daughter
CHAPTER TWO

'You have a visitor, Mr. Fox,' the Langham House butler announced.

Avery quickly rose from his seat. As he took the small, cream-colored calling card from the silver tray, the butler scowled. He was clearly unused to his deliveries being met half-way.

'Thank you very much,' Avery said. The butler scowled once more.

The practice of never openly thanking staff sat uncomfortably with Avery. Was it any wonder the French had risen up and overthrown the ruling classes? While he couldn't see such a bloody and violent uprising happening in peaceful, verdant England, it still left him considering which side he would be on if it ever came to revolution.

He didn't feel he belonged among the *ton*. He doubted he ever would. While Lord Langham and his family had welcomed him cordially, Avery had a deep-seated suspicion that they were only showing their social faces to him. They certainly didn't trust him. At no point during any of his visits to Langham House had he ever been left alone.

Oh Thaxter, what did you do to these people?

He looked at the elegantly printed card and smiled.

'Send the major in, please.'

'Major?' Lord Langham asked.

'Yes. Major Ian Barrett. He was my commanding officer in the 2nd Battalion, 95th Regiment of Foot. His family were most generous to me after I was wounded at Waterloo,' Avery replied.

As soon as Ian Barrett entered the room, Avery stood stiffly to attention.

'At ease, Fox; neither of us is in the army any longer,' Ian said. He offered Avery his hand.

Ian turned to Lord Langham, and before Avery had a chance to make formal introductions, he reached out and gave the earl a hard slap on the shoulder.

'Frosty!' he laughed.

Lord Langham chuckled. 'I'm never going to live that down, am I? How are you?'

Ian nodded. 'Well. Though I hadn't realized you and Avery were related.'

'Only distantly; we were the last of the line when it came to suitable heirs,' Avery found himself replying.

He immediately regretted his words when he saw the disapproving look on Ian's face.

'How is your brother? Lord Langham asked.

Ian screwed up his face.

'Albert has his good days and his not-so-good ones. Unfortunately, the not-so-good ones appear to have become the norm.'

Avery recalled the odd occasion he had seen the Earl of Rokewood during the years he lived at Rokewood Park, the Barrett family estate in Northamptonshire. Usually it was just a glimpse of his back from another room, but he had once set eyes on the man properly. They had encountered one another late one night in the library at Rokewood Park.

The sunken, haunted eyes of the earl had drawn him in.

Avery's stammered apology for disturbing the house's owner was met with the merest of nods from a man who carried himself as if he were made of glass.

Lord Langham turned to Avery. 'I was at school with both Lord Rokewood and Ian. I spent a summer in my youth at Rokewood Park; marvelous place.'

Avery nodded. 'Yes.'

Rokewood Park had been Avery's salvation. He owed a lifelong debt to the Barrett family for taking a non-commissioned officer into their home. After the war, he had nowhere else to go. His own family home had long ceased to exist.

'So, what brings you to London, sir?' Avery asked.

'Oh, this and that. When I read the notice of your brother's death in this morning's papers, I thought I should come by and pay my respects. I assumed you would be in residence here. I am sorry for your loss, Avery,' Ian replied.

Silence hung in the room for a moment. Ian knew enough of Avery's traumatic childhood to know he would not be beside himself with grief. Lord Langham's response was consistent with the social veil which everyone seem to adopt when Thaxter's name was mentioned.

Once the funeral was over, Avery intended to get to the bottom of his late brother's life. To discover as many of his evil secrets as he could. Whatever damage Thaxter had done in the short time he had been Lord Langham's heir, Avery was determined to make restitution. To restore something of his family's name.

He stifled a snort. Why he should care for his father's good name was beyond reason. His father and brother had cared little for him. He had no memory of his mother. Yet despite all these years estranged from his family, it mattered to him.

'Thank you,' he replied.

'If you like, I will leave the two of you alone to catch up on old times. My son-in-law, David, will shortly be back from the city and he and I need to discuss business matters for an hour or so,' the earl offered.

Lord Langham shook hands with Ian and left the room. Of course, the earl would allow them time alone; Major Barrett would make certain nothing was stolen from the room while he was present.

'Well, you have had an eventful few weeks since you left us, Avery,' Ian said, taking a seat.

Eventful! More like a bloody nightmare.

'Yes, I had thought to start to look for employment, but it looks like I will have my hands full in dealing with Thaxter's legacy,' he replied.

Ian sighed. 'You always said he was a bad one. God rest his soul. Any idea as to what happened?'

Avery fiddled with the glove on his left hand. He wore it to hide the angry scars he had earned on the battlefield at Waterloo.

It had only been two days since the river police had dragged Thaxter's body out of the river, but already he was uncomfortable with the whole business of condolences. The sooner his brother was buried, the better.

'From what I understand, my brother made a lot of enemies over the past few months. He ran up a significant amount of debt, which he was unable to repay,' Avery replied.

The fact that Lord Langham had left his heir to the mercy of what appeared to be murderous debt collectors spoke volumes about how far Thaxter had become estranged from him. The Langham family had closed ranks against the outsider and left him to his fate.

Earl Langham's nephew Rupert, his original heir, had died the previous summer, and after a long search Thaxter Fox had been discovered as the next in line to inherit the title. With Thaxter now also dead, Avery stood in his brother's place as heir to the title and fortune. He dreaded the day someone bowed and called him Lord Langham.

'Nasty business, but it appears Fate has once more stepped in and given you a position with honour,' Ian said.

Avery shook his head.

As he saw things, there was no chance of him ever restoring his personal honour. He had killed another man and personally gained from it. From that place, no man could return.

Ian shifted in his chair. 'You cannot blame yourself for what happened. It was war. Many things happened on the battlefield that day; you should have no regrets. It was either you or that Frenchman. You served your king and country and that is all for which you need to account.'

Avery sighed; he and Ian Barrett had had the same argument countless times over the past two years, never once coming to agreement.

'Will you come to the funeral? It would be nice to have at least one familiar face at the church.' Avery asked.

Ian Barrett nodded. 'Of course.'

※

Avery looked around at the gathered mourners. Apart from Lord Langham, he knew only a handful of people.

Lord Langham's mother, the dowager Countess Langham, had cried off from the funeral, citing trouble with her leg and a terrible headache. During his visits to Langham House, Lady Alice had barely acknowledged him.

Standing on the front steps of St James church, Piccadilly, he could hear the whispers and murmurs of those assembled around him. There was not a tear to be seen among the mourners.

Fifteen years and it was clear that his brother had not developed the ability to cultivate close friends.

I should not think ill of the dead, but nothing changes, does it, Thaxter? You always were a nasty piece of work.

'Mr. Fox?'

He turned at the sound of his name and found himself staring at the fair-haired beauty he had briefly met at David and Clarice Radley's wedding ball several weeks earlier: David's sister, Lady Lucy Radley.

'Lady Lucy. How good of you to come,' he replied.

She offered him her hand and gave him a sad smile.

'I am truly sorry for the loss of your brother. A most distressing situation.'

He looked into her pale blue eyes, surprised that she appeared to be genuine in her concern for him. He found himself momentarily speechless.

On the way from his lodgings on the Black Prince Road to Langham House he had practiced his social face. The one where you were able to speak, but not show emotion. He had noted its widespread use at most social functions he had recently attended, and was beginning to understand its usefulness.

Lady Lucy was, however, a different story altogether. Her expression was one of fresh, open honesty. Her natural smile evoked an unexpected response: he longed to reach out and tenderly touch her face.

He couldn't remember the last time he had actually shared a genuine emotion or truthful conversation with another person. His years in the army had begun and ended on a lie.

The rest of the Duke of Strathmore's family paid their respects and they all slowly filed into the tall grey church. He noted with interest that Lucy Radley sat in the same pew as him, just to the left of Lord Langham.

Much as he had detested his brother throughout the long years of their alienation, he was surprised to find this act of solidarity to be a source of comfort. Lord Langham clearly felt duty-bound to show his support to his new heir, but Lady Lucy wasn't bound by such social strictures. She was simply being kind.

The Radleys were only recently linked to him, by the marriage of the duke's illegitimate son David to Lady Clarice Langham. Of all the members of London society to whom he had been introduced, he found himself inexplicably drawn to the Radley family.

He cast a quick glance over his shoulder. The first three of the dark oak pews of the church were full, but the rest of St James was empty. Across the aisle, he could see that a number of Lord Langham's household staff were present.

Making up the numbers.

The final family members to arrive were the recently wed David and Clarice Radley. Lady Clarice wore a dark blue gown with a black rose pinned to the front. Her husband, also clad in blue, wore a matching black armband.

Avery frowned. Had things changed so much in England that no-one wore black to a funeral, especially the members of the deceased's family?

Clarice smiled at him as she took a seat in the front pew next to Lucy. David reached over and shook Avery's hand.

'Thank you for coming,' Avery said.

As the priest began the funeral service, Avery kept his mind diverted by staring at the stained-glass window high above the altar. The image of St James in his layered crimson robes, holding a staff, stared down benevolently at him. It was odd that he felt at home in this place, as he couldn't remember the last time he had been inside a church.

※

From where she sat in the front pew, Lucy stole the occasional glance at Avery Fox. His hair, which she decided was on the light side of sable, had been flattened by his hat. The offending hat sat next to him on the seat. Inwardly she smiled. The men of her social class all knew to give their hair a ruffle after removing their hats, but Mr. Fox, it would appear, was not used to the custom. It was an awkwardness which she found charming.

She also noted the pair of black leather gloves Avery wore. Casting her mind back to their first meeting at her brother's wedding ball, she recalled that Avery had worn only one glove that night, on his left hand. She had made discreet enquiries with Clarice as to this odd habit.

'He was injured during the final onslaught at Waterloo. I haven't seen his hand, but I expect he keeps it covered so as not to show the scars. Papa tells me they are quite unsightly,' Clarice said.

She looked up and saw Avery's gaze was fixed upon her. For a moment, she was captivated by his emerald-green eyes. He blinked. It was a simple action, but it had an immediate effect on her. A flush of red heat filled her cheeks and she quickly moved back in her seat, her heart racing.

She sat and pondered her unexpected response to a simple blink. Had she lowered herself to the level of flirting at a funeral?

I can't be that desperate to capture a man's attention, can I?

Ashamed of herself, she made certain for the rest of the service that she sat so as to keep Avery blocked from her view. Lord Langham, seated between them, fortunately did not appear to have noticed anything was amiss.

※

After the service Thaxter Fox was buried in the small church graveyard. The bells tolled out the number of years of Thaxter's life: thirty-one. Silence finally descended on the graveyard as the death knell came to an end.

Standing beside the grave, along with the other male mourners, Avery pondered his rapidly changing circumstances.

After visiting the undertakers to formally identify Thaxter's body, the earl had taken Avery back to Langham House. Thereafter followed a long evening of whisky and toasts to dearly departed friends. Sipping the finest Scottish malt whisky, Avery had forced himself to show the outward signs of grief for his brother.

If he were honest, there were a dozen men he had grieved over more than Thaxter. Old pains and injustices could not be overcome through the simple act of dying. He, for one, could never forgive his brother.

Lord Langham cleared his throat at the graveside.

'I trust you will understand why my family will not be going into full mourning with you, Avery. We buried my wife some three years past and while I came out of mourning a year or so ago, Clarice has only recently begun to wear colors again. I will not ask it of her to wear blacks again so soon. David has agreed that the men of the family shall wear black armbands for a month, and Clarice shall wear a black rose pinned to her dress. I trust that meets with your approval,' Lord Langham said.

Avery looked down at his own set of mourning clothes. David had kindly lent him a black suit and it fitted him surprisingly well. He stifled a wry grin: black was his favourite color; he could wear it every day and not be concerned. He certainly didn't miss the rough wool of his old green regimental uniform and its very uncomfortable high hat.

'Social appearances must be kept,' he muttered under his breath.

It began to rain and the priest hurried through the graveside service.

'Ashes to ashes, dust to dust.'

The rest of the mourners, though few in number, each picked up a handful of the soft graveside soil and tossed it on to the lowered coffin. They walked away, some giving Avery a final offer of condolence, while others departed silently.

Finally, he was left standing alone beside his brother's grave.

He picked up a handful of dirt and for a moment stood looking at it, sorely tempted to spit on it. He looked toward the churchyard gate, and saw Lord Langham and Ian Barrett sheltering under a tree, waiting. He gave them a nod.

In the long years since he had fled his home, he had made every effort to be a better man than his father and brother. Until that fateful day on the battlefield at Waterloo, he'd thought he had succeeded.

He threw the dirt on to the coffin. He would not embarrass either gentleman by showing what he truly thought of his brother.

'Goodbye Thaxter; sleep well,' he said, and turned from the grave.

A small wake was held at Langham House, attended almost exclusively by the Radley and Langham families. Ian Barrett stayed for just one drink. As he had other business matters to attend to whilst he was in London, Avery accepted his apologies with good grace.

'It was kind of you to come all this way, sir; I know you don't make it up to London that often, so I appreciate your coming today,' he said, shaking the major's hand.

'Yes, well, considering the delightful young lady I have met today, perhaps I should change that habit for a new one,' Ian replied. He nodded in the direction of Lady Lucy.

'Yes, she is rather pretty and she has been kind to me,' Avery replied.

He had caught her looking at his hands during the funeral service and wondered how much her brother David had told her of him. It didn't take much for a casual observer to note that Avery favored his right hand over his left.

He turned away from Lucy.

Ian raised an eyebrow.

'So how long do you intend to mourn your brother?' he asked.

Ian knew the full story of Avery and Thaxter's relationship and why Avery had falsified his age in order to join the army a full two years before he was eligible. Avery shrugged his shoulders. The idea of a month with a black armband didn't appeal to him greatly, but he suspected with his elevation to earl-in-waiting, his every move would be scrutinized by London's elite.

'It's a pity I couldn't come back to Rokewood Park with you,' Avery replied.

He knew it was impossible. He had a new role to fulfil. New responsibilities which he could not in all good conscience avoid by hiding away in the countryside.

'Well, perhaps next time you are over Northampton way, you could call in and see us. Best of luck, Avery. Lord Langham is a good man; I think you will do well. And don't be too hasty in dismissing those who might be the kind of friend you need in the *haute ton*. Lady Lucy Radley is very well connected. Not to mention unwed.'

※

Lucy had caught Ian Barrett and Avery Fox looking in her direction and knew instinctively they were talking about her. She was in two minds as to whether she should go and talk to Avery once she saw Ian Barrett making his farewells.

The effect Avery had had on her during the funeral left her unsettled. She couldn't remember having ever felt that awkward, nay, vulnerable when she looked at a man. To her mind men were usually overstuffed peacocks or boring as house mice. Descriptions which matched closely to the two suitors whose proposals of marriage she had rejected the previous season.

The perfect man with the right mixture of intrigue and

social grace was yet to cross her path. Or so she had thought until the night she met Mr. Avery Fox. He was an entirely different and more alluring prospect from the norm.

There was a something in the way he carried himself, compared to other men. At times, a stiffness appeared in his gait which at first, she had thought to be a sign of uncertainty. Now, as she observed him from a distance, she was not so sure. Was he perhaps possessed of a sharp mind and therefore constantly reassessing the situation and how he should approach others?

'We should go and pay our final respects before we leave,' Lady Caroline said. Roused from her musings, Lucy did as her mother bade and followed the duchess over to where Avery stood.

'Mr. Fox, once again may I offer my and my family's condolences for your loss,' the duchess said.

'Your Grace,' he said.

Lucy swallowed back a tear as a wave of pity washed over her. She saw pain in the depth of his eyes and her heart went out to him.

Avery's strong Yorkshire accent was clipped with something else which she could not put her finger on. Was it perhaps Spanish? Whatever it was, she liked it. The flutter in her stomach when he spoke was strangely enticing.

The poor man had lost his brother and had been thrust totally unprepared into the world of London's elite. His voice, while alluring, also stamped him as an outsider. Her empathic heart sensed he might be struggling with the changes in his life.

'Mr. Fox, if there is anything I can do to help, you only have to ask. We are close enough for you to consider us family,' Lucy said.

The instant Avery took her hand and awkwardly bowed, Lucy made up her mind. There was something she could do for him, something she was uniquely skilled to manage. She would become his champion and help him find his way in the world of the *ton*. Her search for a husband had come to naught this season, but here was a new and worthy charitable cause. Or at least something to keep her mind occupied until the family left for their estate in Scotland later in the month.

She ignored the odd look of suspicion which appeared on Lady Caroline's face at that very moment. Let her mother make what she wanted of Lucy's words, her cause was a true and just one.

In the short carriage ride home to Strathmore House, she began to formulate a plan.

Continue reading The Duke's Daughter.

Also by Sasha Cottman

SERIES

The Kembal Family
The Duke of Strathmore
The Noble Lords
Rogues of the Road
London Lords

The Kembal Family

Tempted by the English Marquis
The Vagabond Viscount
The Duke of Spice

The Duke of Strathmore

Letter from a Rake
An Unsuitable Match
The Duke's Daughter
A Scottish Duke for Christmas
My Gentleman Spy
Lord of Mischief
The Ice Queen
Two of a Kind
A Lady's Heart Deceived
All is Fair in Love

Duke of Strathmore Novellas

Mistletoe and Kisses
Christmas with the Duke
A Wild English Rose

The Noble Lords

Love Lessons for the Viscount
A Lord with Wicked Intentions
A Scandalous Rogue for Lady Eliza
Unexpected Duke
The Noble Lords Boxed Set

Rogues of the Road

Rogue for Hire
Stolen by the Rogue
When a Rogue Falls
The Rogue and the Jewel
King of Rogues
The Rogues of the Road Boxed Set

London Lords

Devoted to the Spanish Duke
Promised to the Swedish Prince
Seduced by the Italian Count
Wedded to the Welsh Baron
Bound to the Belgian Count

USA Today bestselling author Sasha Cottman's novels are set around the Regency period in England, Scotland, and Europe. Her books are centred on the themes of love, honor, and family.

www.sashacottman.com

Facebook
Instagram
TikTok
Join my VIP readers and claim your FREE BOOK
A Wild English Rose

Writing as Jessica Gregory

Jessica Gregory
SASSY STEAMY ROMANCE

Jessica Gregory writes sassy steamy rom coms. She loves strong heroines and making her heroes grovel.

Royal Resorts

Room for Improvement

A Suite Temptation

The Last Resort

Sign up for Planet Billionaire and receive your FREE BOOK.

An Italian Villa Escape

Printed in Great Britain
by Amazon